Scorpion Wind

Joseph E. Mosca

Advance Praise for *Scorpion Wind*

"*Scorpion Wind* captured my attention from the beginning. Mosca's book is the real deal about law enforcement agencies working together to develop and investigate large scale complex international narcotics trafficking cases. The time period in this book takes place in the exciting, dangerous and deadly early 1990s known as the Miami cocaine wars. The riveting descriptions of Colombia, Miami, characters and events in this book make it a must read."

—Floy Turner, Special Agent Florida Department of Law Enforcement (Retired) and Best-Selling Author

"*Scorpion Wind* is an intriguing read! The book does a great job of showing the local side of law enforcement, as well as a broader scope of multiple agencies coming together to fight the war on drugs. It's very interesting to have a glimpse into the drug cartels' side of the story!"

—M. Nooyen, daughter of a Law Enforcement Officer (Retired)

"*Scorpion Wind* is an intriguing story with real, authentic characters. A good read."

—Edward S. Scott, Author of *Dark Daze and Foggy Nights*

"*Scorpion Wind* started out interesting and didn't let up. Mosca's take on the escalating drug war in the 90s and law enforcement's constant struggles to keep up with the cartel's changing technical methods has vivid descriptions of individuals on both sides of the drug war and give us a peek into a world of danger and duty."

—Brian Oppermann, Former United States Marine, Computer Systems Engineer

Scorpion Wind

Joseph E. Mosca

Green Bay, WI 54311

Publishing Editor: Brittiany Koren
Copy-editor: A.L. Mundt
Cover Art Designers: ENC Graphic Services, Christopher Wait and Deirdre Wait
Print Interior Layout Designer: Katy Brunette
Ebook Interior Layout Designer: Maria Connor

Category: Mystery
Description: *Trooper John Stella, his K-9 dog Spec, and his partner Florey Baker enter the venomous den of Cali drug trafficking.*
Hard Cover ISBN: 978-1-951375-25-6
Paperback ISBN: 978-1-951375-26-3
Ebook ISBN: 978-1-951375-27-0
LOC Catalogue Data: Applied for.

First Edition published by Written Dreams Publishing in September, 2020.

Green Bay, WI 54311

For Joey

"It is a valley I've known all too well. Void of light and shadow, for only darkness resides there. If any were to tell you otherwise, they would speak a great untruth revealing their treachery—ultimately dodging their personal commitment to their fellow man and diminishing the valor of those who persevere."

—Joseph E. Mosca

Prologue

Miami, 1993

After the captain announced a flying altitude of thirty-six thousand feet, Peter Haus noticed the muffled drone of the 747's jet engines began lulling other passengers to sleep, adults and kids alike, for the long evening flight to Colombia. Even as most of the overhead lights clicked off, Peter was still unable to close his eyes. He'd never get used to flying. Just the occasional jolts and changes in altitude alone kept him in a state of perpetual nausea. This flight was proving no different.

When Peter had told his family the news about this summer's trip, his wife hadn't asked why he'd picked the South American country. Hans Mueller's wife hadn't questioned the destination, either. Globetrotting was part of the two colleagues' professional lives, and both wives were used to it by now. That was because, as senior fellows of Leibniz Institute for Polymer Research in Dresden, Germany, the two were recognized experts in molecular chemistry, and that led to traveling the world and consulting with all kinds of industries and scientific societies.

Their teaching and research schedules offered limited time for public speaking, but the two of them got around that policy by scheduling speaking engagements in August, along with their vacations.

Peter smiled to himself. Hans called it "killing two birds with one stone."

After years of working side by side, he and Hans had built a solid friendship, and bringing their families along had turned their trips into real vacations. Their two traveling families had already been to India, Italy, Russia, Hong Kong, Cuba, and twice to the United States. So, this time, when Peter and Hans had described their latest trip as a fully-paid "working vacation," nothing seemed out of the ordinary. That was the goal. Making this look like every other trip was how they could keep their secret.

This was an unsanctioned trip, outside the auspices of their institute. That was one reason Peter stayed wide awake while most other passengers nodded off.

"Hans… Hans…" Leaning forward, Peter spoke in a strained whisper so he wouldn't disturb the other passengers.

Hans turned his head to the space between the seats. "Yeah, Peter?"

"Are you sure this will only take a few weeks?" Peter asked.

"Like I told you, we've done seminars that took less time," Hans said, his tone reassuring. "They say they have all the equipment ready. This should be easy."

"Then why do they have us under escort?" Peter periscoped his head up and eyed the young man sitting in an aisle seat a few rows ahead.

"They've given us everything we asked for, yes? Have they done anything but be generous?" Hans asked, keeping his voice low.

"No, I suppose you're right. But doesn't it seem odd to you?" Peter asked, still uneasy.

"Well, I don't suppose many people speak German there. If I were paying a million dollars to learn what we're going to teach them, I'd make sure my investment got to me safely, too. Wouldn't you?" Even speaking in a hushed tone, Hans' voice grew coarser with each word.

"I… I suppose," Peter admitted, feeling his partner's impatience.

"Besides, it's August," Hans said, tucking his pillow between the seats, which effectively blocked more questions. "The boy just wants to go home with his family. Now, get some sleep. There's much to do, or we *will* be there forever!"

Peter sat back and shifted slightly to the left so he could peek down the aisle to the seats ahead. His gaze became fixed on his student from Colombia. He and Hans were just doctors, and Hans was right about how long it should take to do what had been asked of them: no more than a few weeks. Then the rest of August would be theirs to spend with their families. The pay was more than generous and the risk was slight. Besides, the young man had been an excellent student, despite struggling to master German. Peter gave him credit for trying.

Still, no matter how Peter tried to rationalize it, this trip was more than just a seminar. Should the Colombian or American authorities discover what they were about to do, the consequences would be severe.

As Peter stared ahead, he reassured himself that all would go as anticipated.

"Papa?" The gentle voice of Nikki, his eight-year-old daughter, startled Peter and drew his attention to her in the seat next to him.

"Hey, Nikki, why aren't you asleep?" he whispered, concerned that his wife and two teenage daughters might also wake up. Peter leaned over and tucked Nikki's blanket around her little body.

"Papa, do they have swimming pools in Colombia?"

"Yes, my love. They have big, beautiful swimming pools."

Yawning and pulling her blanket tighter, Nikki closed her eyes again.

Peter watched her drift back to sleep. Then, satisfied his youngest was settled, he couldn't help but look down the aisle once again at his student before turning and resting his head against his pillow, squirming just a bit to find a comfortable spot. Slowly, his eyes grew heavy and he let them close. He rested a gentle hand on Nikki's blanket, feeling the subtle rise and fall of her back as she breathed shallowly in sleep. Able to give in to his body's demands, he felt himself finally relax.

***

The end of the school semester had led into the summer break Rigoberto Morejón had been looking forward to. Full of energy, he reclined his seat back as far as it would go, his earphones blaring Latin music dialed in from the armrest control panel. Restless, he longed for home, for Colombia, where he would be free from the rigor of molecular studies, the tortuous lessons in what he considered a confounding language. Even the food kept him permanently homesick for his mother's kitchen. His file of memories of home had been with him all the time he'd been away: family celebrations, his friends, endless hours of playing soccer in the park his great uncle had donated to the city—a park named after Rigoberto's late father. That had been part of keeping the man's name known in perpetuity.

The loss, however, had been branded upon Rigoberto's soul. He needed no reminder.

Thinking back to that day, vivid images of the events replayed before his eyes, although he'd learned to stifle their effects. No longer did he break out in a rage and cry from helplessness. Those years had long ago passed. The images had become more blurred, as if finally being relinquished to history, releasing their grip from his throat.

But now, as he longed for home, the images in his memory came back with a vengeance, as if moving beyond his mind's eye and coming to life on a video screen. Long ago, dedication and loyalty to family had replaced the rage, but flying home, the memories fluttered back.

His father, Wilfredo Morejón, rushing to not be late, had parked in front of the Liceo Francés Paul Valéry School to drop off Rigoberto. Later, it was clear to everybody he had let down his guard and failed to notice the two motorbikes, each with a driver and armed passenger, weaving rapidly through the hazy, smog-ridden street.

Rigoberto remembered his father getting out of the Chevy Suburban and rushing to the rear door to let him out just as the motorbikes arrived. His father had reached for the door handle when the first burst of nine-millimeter bullets had been fired into the air. It had been a well-planned distraction.

Wilfredo had pivoted just fast enough to watch the first motorbike speed by, but he had also exposed his torso to the oncoming traffic. With no time to react, Wilfredo had been instantly struck in the chest by a second burst from the trailing motorbike. The assassins had sped away and disappeared into the congested city traffic.

Young as he had been, Rigoberto had lifted the interior latch of the door and slid feet-first to the street. Sitting in the growing pool of blood, he'd held his father's head cradled in his lap only to hear him faintly whisper, "Rigo. Te amo." Wilfredo had closed his eyes and died on the dirty, bloody pavement.

Rigoberto remembered the tears streaming down his own face. The street had grown eerily quiet. No moving traffic. No voices. All he'd heard was the anguish of a child's voice yelling, "Papá! Papá!" At some point, he had become aware that he was that child. Rigo had continued crying as police covered his dad's body.

By the time the funeral came, the tears had long passed. Rigo had watched stoically as his father's coffin was lowered into its crypt. Uncle Justo had stepped up, behaving like a father, helping to channel Rigo's anger and transform it into focused determination. Justo had showed him how to prioritize family and education first, vengeance second. Justo's tutelage had proved invaluable to Rigo as a boy and later in the family business.

As the painful memory slowly released its grip on his psyche, the rhythmic sounds of a Latin beat returned. Rigo lowered the volume of his headphones and wondered if he would do well as a manager. As his eyes became heavy, he grew certain that Europe was not for him.

He hoped his time in Germany had culminated in this single endeavor, and when the summer was over, he could stay in Cali and coordinate the business alongside his uncle.

In the meantime, Rigo's instructions had been clear. After finals, he was to travel with the two families and stay with them until they deplaned in Cali. At age twenty, Rigo was well-versed in the family business and knew not to ask too many questions. His uncle's refrain echoed in his head: "Better not to know until you need to know."

He shifted slightly in his seat, thinking of real Colombian food and salsa dancing with his girlfriend in the Juanchito neighborhood clubs.

As his eyes closed, he smiled at the thought of how a country as large as Germany did not have as much as one bottle of Aguardiente. *Barbaric*. Thank God, he was going home.

Chapter One

"Miami to 968… Miami, 968…" The voice of the Florida Highway Patrol dispatch came over Trooper John Stella's radio but, as usual, he was not in a position to respond. "Miami *9…6…8.*" The dispatcher's voice rose in frustration.

Ignoring the radio, John yelled, "Hey, asshole! I'm only going to say this once. Keep struggling with me and I'm gonna end up breaking your arm."

John noted his suspect's frantic look and bulging eyes. Here was a guy who wasn't sure what had just happened to him. But John knew. He'd just made Rally James' world take a turn for the worse. A simple traffic stop for speeding that had gone horribly wrong as the driver exited the vehicle and rushed the trooper. Now Rally was on the ground with a trooper's knee firmly planted in his back.

"No sir! I ain't gonna do nothin," Rally replied between breaths.

John shifted his knee off Rally's back, holstered his Colt .357 Magnum revolver, cuffed his suspect, and unholstered his hand-held radio to answer the dispatcher. "Nine-sixty-eight, go ahead, Miami." He kept his voice calm and steady, as usual.

The radio dispatcher quickly responded as if inconvenienced by the delay, "What is your location, 968? The captain wants to know."

"Miami. I'm on top of I-95 just south of State Road-112 on a traffic stop," he said, trying to mask his growing frustration. As if it wasn't enough to defend himself against a raging motorist, he was also looking at a busted bag of crack cocaine that had fallen out of Rally's pants, all while trying not to get run over doing his job on the busy interstate. Plus, now he also had an impatient dispatcher to deal with.

The interstate and expressway systems in Miami weren't the safest locations for a trooper to be, let alone work in. Like all troopers, John knew that if something bad was going to happen, it would probably be on one of these many twisted and chaotic roadways.

John scoffed. He wasn't a fan of working alone, but this was where all the bad guys eventually showed up.

In his rational moments, John figured it was an even trade. He hated working on expressways, but he loved finding dopers. Besides, if having an accident or being run down by one of Miami's "finest drivers" were reasons to give up this career, he'd have left law enforcement years ago.

"The captain wants you to come by the station. Reference to your 10-47s," the dispatch replied.

"Paperwork? *Really?*" John blurted. He stared at the antique communications device in his hand and considered his next move. This piece of late 1970s technology couldn't have been *that* expensive. He took a deep breath and gave his prisoner a smile. Rally sat quietly watching the six-foot-tall trooper as he threw his radio off the three-story-high overpass into the parking lot below, directly into one of Miami's many inner-city project communities and watched it turn end over end on its effortless descent.

John smiled in satisfaction when it exploded into pieces on the pavement below. If only he could do that to the dispatcher.

Scowling, he turned his attention back to Rally, who had likely had more than his share of experiences with the police. The guy began to stammer, "Hey, man… Um, look, um, I ain't wantin' no more trouble, Troop."

John instantly changed his game-face to his trademark crooked grin. "Come on, Rally. Get up. We get to go meet the captain!"

As John helped his prisoner to his feet, he carefully brushed the dirt off Rally's shirt before walking him to his patrol car.

"Hey man. You ain't from around here, are you?" Rally asked.

"Born and raised," John said, his confident smile framed perfectly by his chiseled jawline.

Rally felt the pressure and tug from John's hand, his grip just strong enough to remind the prisoner who was in control. "Well, you ain't acting like no cop I ever known. Most of them cops," Rally motioned with his head towards the heart of downtown Miami, "they would've kept on with the beating."

John noticed the skyline, the heart of his hometown. He took a breath. "Well, I ain't no cop, Mr. James. I'm a trooper."

John was a rarity among his fellow Miamians because he'd been born and raised there. Growing up in the Westchester suburb, he'd had a fairly average upbringing, except for his mother's push to get everybody involved in Charismatic Christianity. As much as he'd tried to fit in, if only out of respect for his parents, he had never quite made sense of it. Too intolerant all around. He'd finally had enough of the gay-bashing, fire-and-brimstone types who demanded rigid obedience and submission to the church before family or even country.

After a stint with the Marines, John had gotten a degree in criminal justice at Miami-Dade Community College. No matter what other careers he'd considered, from accounting to real estate, somehow, that first class in criminal justice had showed him law enforcement was a perfect fit. Even dealing with the Rallys of the world hadn't changed his mind. And Miami was in his blood.

John shook off the memories and put Rally, now cooperating, into the car. He made sure to shield his head from bumping the doorjamb and got Rally seat-belted in. He got behind the wheel and used his car's mounted radio to advise the dispatcher he was on his way.

He drove west on State Road 836, passing the Miami International Airport, turned off the exit ramp, and entered the parking lot of the Florida Highway Patrol, Troop E Headquarters. The drab and nondescript building was typical of state government offices, with its only distinction being the brown and tan exterior walls meant to imitate the colors of a Florida Highway Patrol cruiser.

That was the outside.

Unfortunately, inside, a stifling odor of mold and mildew was constantly fed by a leaky roof and an aging air conditioning system that was either broken down or "under repair" for more days than it worked. The odor was so pungent that on those rare but dreaded days John was assigned to the desk he usually found some lame excuse to leave early.

Pulling up to the back of the station, John parked in one of the many "administrator only" spots and got out of the car. Opening the rear door, he gave Rally James a stern look.

"Hey, I don't want to have to tell you twice, so listen up… No screwing up my patrol car. Just sit and relax. This won't take but a few minutes. You okay with that?" John asked.

"Hey, man, I ain't fixin' to mess with nothin'. I'll be right here waiting for ya, Troop," Rally said, smiling.

That's right. Turn on the charm.

"You want something to drink while I'm in there?" John asked.

"I mean, you okay with water? I wouldn't want anything sugary to damage that fine dental work of yours," he remarked, noticing Rally's gold-capped teeth.

"Yeah man, water be just fine."

John figured Rally was used to that kind of comment, mostly made by guys like him who didn't know a thing first-hand about life in the hood. But John understood enough from his years in the military and working the streets to get how important it was to sport a *grill*. Rally was not a man to be taken lightly, at least not in his neighborhood. Nonetheless, John could almost read his mind as Rally scrutinized him. The guy probably wondered if maybe there was something different about John.

Not surprising. John had seen that kind of intuition before. No doubt Rally had refined his over years of surviving on the streets. That intuition was how a guy like Rally stayed alive in the most violent urban area in the country.

Rally now reclined back in his seat, trying to get comfortable by moving his cuffed wrists to one side of his lower back, taking the pinch and pressure off his hands. His head rested against the top of the back seat, his eyes fixed on the felt-lined ceiling.

John noticed the scaring on Rally's face and knew he wasn't exaggerating about his previous experience with police. He'd probably needed medical attention a time or two.

Before he left, John made sure the air conditioning was blowing cool air and the vents were directed towards the back seat.

"I wished we had air conditioning growin' up," Rally said, closing his eyes.

Entering the station and taking the elevator to the second floor, John came to the door of Captain Juanes DeLeón, one of the few FHP administrators John considered worthy of his respect. Captain DeLeón had spent ten years as a trooper before moving up the ranks. Having had his share of close calls earned him the respect of the rank and file troopers.

Knocking on DeLeón's door, John was met by a loud voice, "Stella, if that's you, get in here!"

John entered the office to find the captain glaring at him. His athletic build and short frame only made him look more antagonizing. A gentleman in a pricey suit stood next to DeLeón. The captain motioned to two empty chairs. "Have a seat."

John sat in one of the worn-out wooden chairs, circa 1972, the year the last captain had bought it new. It hadn't been replaced since. Just like their radio system. Meanwhile, the guy in the suit stood silent.

John managed a quick wink at the well-dressed visitor. His gesture was received with a barely perceptible smile. DeLeón hadn't noticed.

"I know you stay busy, and you keep this office knee-deep in felony arrests," the captain explained, "but something has come up I think you'll be interested in."

Perplexed, John said, "Ah, Captain… I was told this was about my paperwork or something…"

"Forget the paperwork. We have another assignment for you, John." The captain's expression softened as he motioned to the man in the suit. "John, we want to team you up with Florey Baker, and we'll assign both of you to the Feds." He paused, apparently waiting for John to respond.

John turned to the man in the suit and flashed a polite smile. "Sir, with all due respect, who the fuck are you?"

DeLeón's jaw dropped, but the guy in the suit returned John's sarcastic grin as he took a step forward and introduced himself, his muscular frame becoming more prominent as he leaned towards John. "I'm Agent Rick Lotz with the Drug Enforcement Administration. Currently, I'm assigned to South Florida's HIDTA. Do you know what that is, Trooper?" Lotz grinned wider.

John stood, sensing the familiar challenge in Lotz's tone. The two were now less than a foot apart. With a lopsided smile, he said, "High Intensity Drug Trafficking Area. Do I pass?"

Lotz nodded. "That's right. Have you ever worked with the DEA before?"

John tensed, moved in closer and glared at Lotz, who glared back. "Yeah, you guys usually work the cases I start when I find the drugs you can't. But what does this have to do with me?"

"Trooper!" Captain DeLeón shouted. "You'll treat a guest of the Florida Highway Patrol with respect."

Lotz and John began laughing.

The captain looked back and forth at them both and slowly realized the ruse. "Are you saying you know each other?"

John answered, still staring at Rick, "Yeah. I did his sister in high school."

"Jesus Christ. And I thought you guys were going to end up in a fight," DeLeón said. His shoulders drooped in exaggerated relief.

"What's the matter, Captain? You afraid someone might mess up your beautiful furniture in here?" John blurted.

Rick slapped John's shoulder, laughing. "No appreciation for antiques, John?"

"You guys are hilarious," the captain replied with only a hint of sarcasm. "But there isn't time to waste here. Rick has an opportunity for us to help them, and it involves some serious stuff." He headed for the office door. "Rick, fill John in and I'll see where Trooper Baker is. If he insults you again, you have my permission to *kick his ass*!"

Rick smiled to acknowledge the captain's remark, but John noted it was short-lived, and the mood quickly changed as John noticed his friend's expression become more serious. Rick began to explain the details, but John interrupted him. "Hey man, you could never pretend with me. I get whatever this is must be important. Let's wait till Florey gets here."

Of course, John knew Florey Baker, already a 20-year veteran of the FHP. The two had a history. At almost six feet tall, she was an attractive blonde, who kept her hair just below the regulation collar-line length for female troopers. That restriction was a little too masculine for her taste. So far, no administrator ever attempted to make an issue of it. But Florey Baker wasn't a woman to be taken lightly.

After working a few drug cases with Florey, John had nicknamed her "The Iron Maiden," based on her courage and perseverance. She was confident enough that she didn't think she had to compete with her male counterparts' trash talk or body-building. John thought of her as someone who could do her job at a high level, but still be what his old-fashioned mother would have called a "lady." Yet if there was a worthy fight, Florey would be in the middle of it.

John had seen first-hand how iron-willed Florey Baker truly was when they had first met. On a routine traffic stop, John hadn't noticed another car stop behind him.

Florey had been traveling on the opposite side of the expressway, saw the driver from the second car exit and attempt to ambush John from behind. She had quickly pulled her car into the inside emergency lane, jumped the median wall, dodged traffic, and flung herself at the attacker just as he had lunged towards John's gun.

When John heard the thud, he had turned to see Florey wrestling the nearly-unconscious subject onto his stomach. John handcuffed his guy to the guard rail as Florey had cinched her cuffs on her subject's wrists. That's when John had given her the nickname. And it had stuck.

Both John and Florey had developed a disdain for the drug trade, and an absolute hatred for what it had done to communities in South Florida. Florey, more civic-minded than he was, had dragged him to community groups, homeless shelters, and fundraisers for inner city kids.

At first, John had hated it, referring to it as "civic nonsense." It wasn't until Florey had taken him to Liberty City and Overtown—Miami's worst impoverished areas—that John had made a real connection between the effects of drugs on people and the community. John had always credited Florey for opening his eyes to those things he was unaware of and making him a better trooper. Of course, Florey was married and had a couple school-age kids of her own. What Florey cared about professionally matched what she cared about at home.

Slightly older than John, Florey watched out for him, too. It hadn't taken her long to spot his potential to become an excellent drug officer. When they were working the same shifts, they were partners on the road. As a team, they put in long hours and eventually were responsible for most of the drug and other felony arrests in the troop.

That sparked the ire of more than a few administrators. Most were jealous of their success, while a few others were mean-spirited types who thought a trooper's job was only to write traffic tickets. Captain DeLeón was that one exception. John and DeLeón went back a ways, too.

When John looked back on it, Miami herself, already knee-deep in a drug war and rampant drug use, seemed to lure him into the battle. Seldom would a day go by without a drug murder, drive-by shooting, or any number of bizarre crimes. John was eager to roll up his sleeves and put some criminals in jail. If he put in the hard work, he could take advantage of the opportunities to do just that, too—at least, that was what he thought.

But when John joined the Florida Highway Patrol, he had quickly caught on. The department had one goal: speeding tickets. The Highway Patrol headquarters in Tallahassee wasn't impressed with felony arrests or drug confiscations. The whole state could've been covered in cocaine, and the administration was only interested in how many tickets a trooper wrote. The more drug arrests he made, the more his supervisors complained about his lack of traffic tickets. None of it made sense to the troopers, and John wasn't inclined to wreck some kid's driving record for doing the same stupid stuff that he'd done as a teenager.

Instead, John had set out to make even more drug arrests. He even became a canine handler for two years before the Patrol had discontinued the program. Nothing had broken John's heart like having to turn over his dog to a kennel. But, as a consolation, he had enrolled for all the tactical training he could find.

Soon, more arrests piled up. As far as John was concerned, if that upset the brass, all the better.

When it came to DeLeón, John knew him to be a hardnosed trooper with three decades of service under his belt. He had the distinction of being the first Hispanic to make the rank of captain on the Patrol. DeLeón shared John and Florey's distaste for the drug trade.

Long before John had joined the patrol, DeLeón's nephew Ramon had been killed in a shooting at Club Mystiques out near the airport. It had happened in the early 1980s. The kid had been gunned down on the dance floor with his fiancé. An armed assassin had tried to eliminate his rival in a turf war, but instead, five young people ended up dead, and a suspected drug smuggler was wounded and on the run. The county police would eventually find the shooter—a Colombian national who'd arrived in Miami two days before the shooting.

DeLeón had become something of a legend in the department—and even beyond. The way John had heard it when he'd first joined the force, DeLeón took a leave of absence after the shooting and gone to the courtroom to watch the trial every day. Ramon had been like a son to him ever since the boy's father had died some years before. When he had been killed, Ramon, only a month away from getting married, was headed for the Marine Corps. Throughout the trial, as the story went, Captain DeLeón had clutched the wedding announcement, while the defendant's three high-profile defense attorneys worked over the state's case.

One by one, witnesses either had sudden amnesia, or just didn't show up for trial. Every attempt had been made by the prosecutors to locate them, but it was as if they had fallen off the face of the earth. To make matters worse, the prosecutor had watched as most jury members nodded off during the testimony.

When the jury had come back with its "not guilty" verdict, Manuel Cepedes had triumphantly walked out of the courthouse flanked by his three lawyers clad in their thousand-dollar suits, each wearing diamond-encrusted Presidential Rolex watches.

DeLeón walked out of the courthouse and wasn't there to see it.

From what John had heard, as the back-slapping gaggle had turned the corner of the courthouse, a man in a tattered, stained coat had lunged forward towards Cepedes and landed a solid right cross at his chin that sent him crashing onto the sidewalk.

The attorneys had stood motionless, apoplectic and unable to physically defend their client as the dark figure leaned over his prey, eyes fixed and determined, conveying their intent like a soldier's thousand-yard stare. "When you think of Miami, you sick fuck, remember there is one Cuban who will be waiting for you if you ever come back!" A defiant Juanes DeLeón had turned and walked away. He had given the soiled coat to the homeless bum sleeping in the bushes under the sign that read "Metro Justice Center."

The subsequent complaints of police brutality had fallen on deaf ears. However, the FHP sent DeLeón to anger management classes. Begrudgingly, the captain went, but not before telling the appointed counselor, "I did *manage* my anger, Doc. After all, I only *hit* the prick!" Nothing else was ever said about it.

John was lost in his thoughts when Florey came into the office, the captain close behind. He introduced Florey to Rick.

John could instantly see Rick was taken with Florey's pleasant smile as the two shook hands. "It's nice to meet you, Trooper."

"Likewise," Florey replied.

"Agent Lotz has a detail for us," John said. "Captain says it's important."

"And here I thought this was about my paperwork," Florey said.

"Ah, yeah. About that…" The captain closed the door. "I've briefed the major and we've decided that this detail is best kept, well, shall we say, secret."

"Secret from who?" John asked.

"Everyone." DeLeón sat behind his desk and tilted his chair back until it creaked under his thick, muscular frame. "Agent Lotz, go ahead and explain."

"We've developed information that suggests the Cali cartel is importing drugs that are combined with plastic," Rick said, leaning against a storage cabinet near the desk.

"That's not new," Florey said. "Haven't they been doing that for some time?"

Rick nodded. "Yeah, but this time they're combining the cocaine with plastic on a molecular level."

John frowned. "Sounds complicated."

"So complicated, in fact, that they kidnapped two German chemists and took them to Colombia." Rick shook his head. "One of them ended up here in Miami. The technique allows them to combine the cocaine in Colombia and mold it into industrial parts and stuff before shipping it out."

"What kind of stuff?" John asked.

Rick sat down in the chair alongside the captain's desk. "The kind of things you'd use in large manufacturing. You know, plastic gears, industrial components, cabinets." He shrugged. "Anything, really. When it gets to Miami, they plan to take it where they've set up the other chemist and break it back down into powder."

"Awesome. How much coke can they get through?" John spit out the words in disgust.

Rick shrugged. "Well, in its plastic form, it's not detectable by any machine or canine. We've tried everything. It has to be put through a chemical process and reduced back to cocaine, so, I guess the answer is, as much as they want."

Florey extended her hands palms up. "So, how do we fit in?"

"We know what they're up to, but we don't know how far this new network reaches. It's most likely separate from their other drug cells, but we can't say—yet. You guys will come in to handle some traffic stops as we develop information on suspects," Rick said. "You know, busy work, rustle-the-bushes, so to speak. See what shakes loose."

"So, what about the chemist? Why not just follow him around?" Florey asked.

Rick lowered his eyes. "That's kinda the problem."

"What problem, buddy?" asked John. "We're all ears."

"Um…we lost the chemist," Rick admitted. "We have no idea where they took him."

"Nice." John couldn't stop the sarcasm from slipping into his voice.

"Hey, John, there's more. Let Rick finish," Captain DeLeón interjected.

Rick shot him a grateful look. "The cartel is holding both chemists' families in a remote location in Colombia. We're monitoring every communication we can in that area, hoping to figure out their code words and get an exact fix on where they're held. We know there's a total of six children, plus both wives. We believe strongly that once the Colombians figure out what the chemists know and how to work this plastic process on their own, they'll kill the whole lot of them once they're confident they no longer need them. It seems their usual radio traffic has dropped off for now, and that's got us concerned."

"Dropped off?" DeLeón asked.

"Cartels in Colombia have been communicating by short wave radio for years. They know we constantly monitor their conversations," Rick said. "Normally, they talk in code, you know, calling cocaine by different names, referring to themselves with code words. Even their rendezvous points are a scramble of gibberish. We've had to guess at most of it. The recent lull in the transmissions has only made pin-pointing the locations that much harder."

"I bet they've had you guys running around like crazy, huh," John remarked.

Rick smiled in a self-deprecating sort of way. "I can tell you it's made for an interesting game of cat and mouse. Our agents with South American Operations have been pulling their hair out trying to zero in on these guys."

"You think they went quiet on purpose?" Florey asked.

Rick nodded. "No doubt, but we do have some leads here to follow up on in the meantime. We'd like you guys to be the faces of the local enforcement effort. Hopefully, by poking around a bit, we can develop some more leads. If we're lucky, we may even be able to intercept some of their cocaine. If our efforts prove to be enough of a pain in their ass, the thinking is, they may start broadcasting again. We need them to get back on their radios so we can hone in on their signals."

"Why these two?" DeLeón asked, gesturing to John and Florey. Once again, he leaned back in his office chair, wincing against the creak of the worn wood and metal frame.

"No disrespect, Captain, but I've known John for a long time, and I've heard great things about Trooper Baker," Rick said. "It could get rough. Dealing with some of these characters is going to require some nerve." Rick turned to John and Florey. "And, there's one more thing. We can't let *anyone* know of the Fed's involvement. The cartel will shut their whole operation down, and what they'll do to those kids is anyone's guess."

John was curious about something else. "What other agencies are involved?"

"You name it. In fact, there isn't a federal law enforcement agency that's *not* involved," Rick said. "And, I should add, it's by Executive Order of the President, acting in his role of the Commander in Chief."

John laughed. "So much for secrecy!"

Florey shook her head. John knew she was envisioning how confusing an assignment could get when it involved a proliferation of agencies.

"Calm down, guys," Rick said. "It was officially declared an 'Item of National Security' because everyone in D.C. is in a bit of a panic about just how much cocaine might flood into the U.S. You guys understand that there will be no stopping this unless we stop it first."

John looked at the others. "I see. So, when do you want us to start?"

"There's a briefing at the FBI headquarters in North Miami tomorrow at 3 P.M.," Rick said. "You guys think you can make it?"

John shot a glance at Florey before answering his friend. "No, that doesn't quite work for me. How about another day?"

Rick laughed. "Yeah, I'll call the president and let him know you're *inconvenienced*."

DeLeón rolled his eyes and got to his feet. The chair groaned as it swiveled on its pedestal. "Okay, you guys, keep me posted on what's going on. I want an update every day. If you need anything, contact me directly. Remember, not a single member in this department aside from the major and the colonel is to know of this detail."

When DeLeón moved to the door, John knew they were being escorted out. The meeting was officially over. "I have a conference call with the major and the colonel now," said the captain as he passed the group and walked down the narrow hallway to the major's office.

"Hey, you two," Rick said. "Have you had anything to eat? I know a killer Cuban restaurant down the street."

John thought about it but realized he had forgotten about Rally James. "Shit! I got a prisoner to take to the jail."

Florey chuckled as John prepared to take off in a sprint. "Relax, John. I took it upon myself to have a rookie take him for you. That's why I was late to the meeting."

John smiled, then shook his head. "Thanks, partner."

"Don't thank me too much. Your perp kept saying he liked you and wanted to work as an informant. So, I gave him your cell number," Florey joked, handing John a scrap of paper on which she had written Rally's telephone number. "I think he wants to be your new friend."

John rolled his eyes. Most case information was developed by prisoners looking for leniency: the more desperate the character, the faster they wanted to snitch on other criminals. The sudden cooperation of a perp was motivated also by their desire to eliminate the competition. Rally James would have to wait his turn.

"Great! We get assigned as partners and the first thing you do is stab me in the back. Remind me to repay you one day," John teased as the three stepped into the elevator.

"Well, since it looks like we're all free to go get some Cuban food, how about La Carreta? John is paying." Florey looked pleased as the elevator doors slid open on the ground floor.

"I think your new partner just stabbed you in the back. *Twice.*" Rick laughed as they ambled to the parking lot.

Suddenly, John stopped. He had to do one more thing. "Hey, give me a minute. I gotta get something out of supply."

"It's on your driver's seat," Florey said.

Doing his best to feign an innocent tone, John said, "What are you talking about, Florey?"

"Rally. He told me an interesting story and suggested I get you another radio." Florey cast a broad grin at John. "Something about how you lost yours and may need another?"

Sure enough, as he approached his car, he glanced through the driver's window. There, on the seat, sat another handheld radio.

John grinned. "You're amazing, Florey Baker."

As they got in their cars, John placed the note containing Rally's contact information under a heavy metal clip attached to his sun visor, then slid his newly-acquired handheld radio onto his duty belt. John couldn't help but laugh at himself all the way to La Carreta.

Chapter Two

Cali, Colombia

Justo Dellacruz Morejón's driver guided the Toyota Land Cruiser through the dark streets and turned past the Comune Uno barrio along Cuarta Avenida. Endless rows of connected shacks fabricated from discarded pieces of corrugated metal and cinder blocks dominated the many barrios the poor called home. Few had running water or sanitation, making their neighborhoods plagued by poverty and crime. There were places where murder was a daily occurrence.

Justo knew the slums also provided a haven—of sorts—from the federal police. Since local gangs controlling these areas out-manned and out-gunned law enforcement, the police had given up on nightly patrols long ago. Mostly, the cops were inclined to let the poor fend for themselves. On this night, Justo ordered his driver to be extra alert. Even after adding extra bulletproofing to his vehicle, he wasn't taking any chances.

Entering the elite Normandia section of Cali along Quinta Avenida was like crossing into another world—the world of the wealthy, of manicured lawns, sidewalks, parks, restaurants, theaters, and clubs. Not much of a middle class in Cali. Families that might have made up that group wanted a decent life away from crime and drugs, as well as the violence linked with the cartels and paramilitary factions constantly at odds with the government. These were the people who fled to the States if they could, and they often found the comfortable life they sought in cities like New York and Miami.

Making a final turn onto Calle 50, the Land Cruiser arrived at its destination. Cameras mounted outside the twelve-foot stone walls trained their view on the Land Cruiser as Rivero, Justo's driver, rolled down his window for the entrance camera above the driveway keypad to get a closer look at him.

As the camera pivoted and focused on Rivero, the arched iron gates bearing the crest of the Orejulla family opened. Just inside, two men carrying Mac 10s with silencers emerged from the darkness onto the drive and moved to either side of the Land Cruiser.

Even as often as Rivero had made this drive, Justo knew he was wary of antagonizing these guys, whose only order was to shoot anyone thought to be suspicious, even those considered friends. Mass shootings, assassination attempts, and bombings had become commonplace. Kidnapping had also skyrocketed. Under the right circumstances, even a known associate could enter the compound in the company of assassins or carrying explosives. Between the Medellin Cartel and FARC guerillas, the Cali cartel was always on high alert.

Rivero drove through the entrance and stopped to wait. Eventually, the gates moaned as the two sides swung shut with a loud *clank* as the metal locking pins engaged. The two armed figures carefully scanned the inside of the Toyota and its occupants, not easy in the shadows of the tree-canopied entrance. Apparently satisfied, they motioned with their weapons to move ahead and disappeared into the dark tree growth as quickly as they'd emerged.

With his headlights turned off, Rivero drove down the winding, heavily-landscaped driveway, which obscured the multitude of motion sensors and thermal imaging cameras. Finally, the drive gave way to a sprawling Italian-style villa enveloped in the glare of high-intensity security lights. The meticulously manicured lawns stretched toward the main house, reached by the gravel drive that crunched under the Toyota's oversized tires. They passed the eight-bay garage filled with exotic, antique cars.

Just part of the landscape. Justo suspected Rivero barely noticed them anymore.

Once in front of the villa, Rivero stopped and got out, while Justo waited. Two more men walked down the front entrance steps, their machine pistols bulging from their jackets. Rivero waved to acknowledge them before opening the rear passenger door.

"We are here, Heffe," Rivero said in a low tone as he moved aside.

Justo stepped out of the SUV, and not knowing how long he'd be, told Rivero to park and wait. He put on his jacket and brushed it off, preparing to go inside and meet the men who'd arrived in the other cars that filled the gravel drive. They were waiting for him.

He went up the stairs to the pórtico that led to two large oak doors, each displaying exactly one half of the Orejulla family crest: a large black scorpion with open pincers and a menacing barbed tail. It fulfilled its purpose, which was to suggest power and fear.

With a loud crack, the right door opened and split the menacing arachnid in half as Justo was greeted by the butler.

Justo smiled to himself as he glanced around the flashy main foyer, walls, and floor gilded in polished Italian marble, each stone married seamlessly to the next. It was like a crypt, Justo thought, complete with an eerie circular chandelier, ten-foot in diameter and suspended by a hand-made iron chain retrieved from a sunken galleon.

The butler led the way to the meeting in the library across the foyer, also marked by another set of oak doors. By any standards, it was an ornate room with high ceilings and tall, seemingly-endless dark wooden racks filled with rare books and art. A wooden companionway attached to a catwalk ascended to a second level of narrowly-lined shelves. Justo had long ago concluded that many of the pieces were likely stolen outright or purchased through the elusive underground black market.

Justo had always thought the art ranged from the Renaissance to the ridiculous as he had never understood the fuss over these paintings, especially the ones that looked like someone had flung paint onto canvas. As he continued into the room, he groaned inside, hoping he had missed the dreaded lecture on each newly-acquired piece. It happened every time he came to the villa. The first thirty minutes of his visit were eaten up by his boss rambling on about each new acquisition. Another reason he was cautiously late to the meeting. He'd rather risk annoying the boss than enduring yet another lesson on so-called culture. Justo's interest in this home, this library, was strictly related to business.

Moving to the center of the room, he passed the large fireplace, another showpiece reconstructed stone by stone from a Tuscan castle. The other guests watched as he made his entrance. Justo liked knowing these people envied him.

"It's about time you got here, Justo," said Juan Miguel Orejulla, the son of the Orejulla family's patriarch, greeting his latest guest. "We were about to start the meeting."

Good, he'd timed it right to miss the art lecture. Men from the other four Cali families sat around the rectangular oak table. Juan Miguel gestured to one of the oversized chairs, where he wanted Justo to sit.

Juan Miguel Orejulla's father, Don Pedro, had been the mastermind of the Cali cartel, but after announcing his retirement some years earlier, Juan Miguel had taken control of the multimillion-dollar-a-month empire. The family business had begun after Juan's grandfather had emigrated from Spain to Colombia many years ago. The family had become pioneers in the coffee and tobacco business. To the outside world, those were still the only businesses the family conducted. But the Federales, and the American government, too, knew differently. It was a standing joke that every poor person living in the Cali slums also knew.

But as long as Juan Miguel, or as he was known among the poor, *El Padrón,* was funding sporting events, schools, churches, transportation, and the popular twenty-four hour food centers, many of the locals gave more of their loyalty to the cartel than to their country. Justo had seen it all his life. El Padrón taking up for a victim of some horrific crime. He even provided justice and compensation to them, as long as the media touted it and the Orejulla name was mentioned in a positive way. It was of no consequence that most of those tragedies had been brought about—even ordered—by the same cartel.

It was a smart tactic in public relations—anything to keep prying eyes from the ever-expanding drug operations. Thanks, in part, to the insatiable appetite for cocaine and marijuana in the United States. When Juan's father began producing drugs, it was easy to use the existing coffee and tobacco distribution network that they had until the Medellin Cartel began competing in earnest. Eventually overtaking Cali production.

That was what had driven him to streamline the Cali group into a business model based on maximizing production and delivery of cocaine, while minimizing interference from authorities. Unlike Medellin, Juan's father would put safeguards in place to ensure for the growth and returns they projected—like expanding into a new technology like molecular science.

So far, so good, Justo thought as he headed to his chair. He kept his eyes on Juan Miguel, whose hair, long and prematurely gray, reflected the amber hue of the large chandelier above, framing his head in an almost angelic light.

***

Juan Miguel paused and waited for Justo to find his seat, trying to move the thirty-pound chair without calling attention to himself. That night, everything his father had taught him about business weighed heavily on his mind, but at the same time, he was excited about this new business venture.

Finally, after Justo sat, Juan Miguel said, "Today we're entering a new area of business. A journey that will give us total control of the U.S. and European markets. We've acquired new technology, and with the help of our new *friends* from Germany…" Juan Miguel paused to let the group laugh with him, "we can move cocaine anywhere we choose with no need to worry about the American police. These, my friends, are exciting times, but we need to take every precaution."

Juan Miguel paused and scanned the group around the table. The co-conspirators nodded their approval, looking around at each other with oozing confidence. "Our test shipment to Miami ran into no difficulties," he said, "and once we begin major shipments, we'll all need to work together to find new ways to bring back all the extra money!" He laughed as he held out his arms in a mock embrace of an imaginary pile of cash.

The others at the table laughed along with him, but he quickly warned them they'd have to make sure their cell networks, each controlled by a *cellero*—a manger—were insulated from the others. Completely, one hundred percent. That way, if the police broke up one cell, those arrested could never lead the authorities to another. The genius of the Cali cartel model was created and perfected by Juan Miguel—and he was proud of it, too. It kept the Cali cartel growing even as the Medellin traffickers suffered under the interference from law enforcement. But if the Colombian Federales or the Americans discovered drugs or money in one Cali cell, nothing would expose the others.

Juan Miguel stood and rested his hands on the table. "For this operation, we'll use our companies in New York and Miami. We'll transfer funds to our banks in Europe and then loan back to our companies in Colombia, or put it out of sight in our banks in the Caymans. We will add to our money network in Miami and New York to handle the extra cash. It's imperative the dollars we get are cleaned through our system of offshore accounts and businesses."

Once again, he cast a stern look at his guests around the table. "We'll operate where the Americans aren't looking. Besides, with all the chaos in Miami right now, the DEA or FBI will be looking at our friends further north, I'm sure of it." Sitting back down, Juan Miguel smiled to himself. Everyone in the room knew he was referring to Medellin. Their strategy counted on diverting attention to them.

One of the cartel members said, "Please, Heffe, if I may?"

Juan Miguel nodded to the junior partner. "Go ahead, Julio."

Julio Cortés Mendoza was the cartel's new point man for distribution and part-time Miami resident. A capable man by cartel standards—a complete disregard for life when threatened and a unique focus on expanding profits. "What happens if they *do* start to poke around our new venture?"

Juan Miguel answered with a laugh. "Then you hand them one of the Medellin lieutenants and let them work backwards for a while."

And why not? Juan Miguel thought. It was a tactic successfully used by both cartels—plant drugs on one of the known mules working for the competition, something big enough to get local attention, but not so big as to involve the federal authorities. A kilo brick of marijuana would do just fine. Then, they could leak the info to one of the undercover cops conveniently kept on the payroll, and make sure papers or notes in the mule's home led police back to a cartel member in Miami.

With a warrant in hand, the police could search the mule's home and conveniently find evidence pointing to Medellin cartel members. Sometimes, it only took a phone number scribbled on a piece of paper for American cops to run with it.

Juan Miguel had seen this happen many times. By the time the local cops worked backwards to try to find the source of the drugs, the lawyers had bailed out the mule, who seldom had any kind of record. Then he was on his way back to Colombia. They'd always make bail on something as common as a kilo brick of marijuana, especially in Miami or New York. Mules knew to keep their mouths shut until the lawyer came to get them. The cartels banked on the Americans' greed for quick arrests with the least amount of effort. He knew there was always the risk of one of their own mules getting caught with drug notes or phone numbers, but the risk would only expose that one cell.

"So, the cops get a cheap drug arrest, and should they nose around our business, the cartel restructures its cells so the organization doesn't skip a beat," Juan Miguel said, a point not lost on the co-conspirators, each having a Master's in Business and Finance—a requirement of the Cali cartel. "And we know the American authorities are *so good* at sharing information among themselves," he added sarcastically. "That's why our ruse usually works flawlessly."

He was done. The men had their marching orders and pushed back their throne-like chairs. They began heading into the formal dining area, where Juan Miguel's small army of waiters and cooks were ready with dinner. Juan Miguel pulled Justo aside and asked him into his office, taking care not to be overheard.

He led Justo down a hallway next to the grand staircase and to the rear of the house, to the smallest room in his villa. It was 200 square feet, and not intended as a place to socialize. It had a simple utilitarian oak desk, file cabinets, and tables with banks of radio and communication devices.

Yet, Juan Miguel mused, despite not being much bigger than a closet, it was a critical space, filled with a series of military radios a local general in the Colombian Army had given him. The cartels couldn't just pick up a phone and talk—not with every line under surveillance. The Cali cartel used short wave radio communications and they spoke in euphemisms. For as long as Juan Miguel could remember, he knew the current code words, almost like learning a second language, changed in an instant. Right now, they called kilos "the kids." "Stork" or "pigeon" was a boat or a plane transporting drugs. But Juan Miguel was prepared to change these quickly, because the Feds always figured out the lingo. The trick was to change it first.

And it almost always worked. Only rarely would someone catch on and intercept a shipment. When it did happen, the cartel had to shrug it off as the inconvenient cost of doing business.

Juan Miguel closed the door behind them. "I need you to make sure the doctor in Miami stays busy with his job, Justo. I don't trust the Americans to sit quietly if they get *even a suggestion* of what we have. I need you to make sure the doctor's babysitters are taking every precaution. Your oversight is essential, should we have any problems."

"Okay, how do you want me to do this?" Justo asked.

"Our resources can be in Miami quickly—and quietly—should something happen. But nothing comes back to us. You understand?"

"Yes, Heffe," Justo said. "What would you have us do with the doctor that's here?"

"Once we know the process, we won't need them anymore. Do whatever you need to do, but remember... *Nothing leads back to us.*"

"Understood."

"Until we know this is going to work," Juan Miguel said, "use the utmost caution with this operation. This is between us. Not even Julio is to know. Understand?" He put his hand on Justo's shoulder.

"Absolutely, Heffe."

"And your nephew? Does Rigo understand?"

"Completely," Justo said.

"Excellent. You've taught him well. We need good leaders like that. You tell him I am very proud of him. His handling of the doctors was superb. If he continues to work this well, he has a bright future ahead of him," Juan Miguel added.

Justo nodded. "I will. And thank you."

"Good!" Juan Miguel opened the office door. "Now, let's eat!" He draped his arm across Justo's shoulder as they walked to the formal dining room.

Justo had been the obvious choice to turn to and he'd been right, Juan Miguel thought. The cartel had taken care to keep Justo away from controversy. Besides having an MBA, the cartel used his military background and explosives specialty when they needed it. Justo managed to stay a few steps ahead of the authorities and far removed from the possibility of failure or capture. With the help of the scientists, nothing would stand in the way of controlling all the cocaine traffic around the world.

And just as important, Juan Miguel was confident Justo Dellacruz Morejón knew that if anything went wrong, he'd pay dearly. There would be no more dinners at Villa Orejulles.

Chapter Three

The Redlands

John awakened to the explosive combustion of the eight-cylinder diesel irrigation pumps. Their open exhaust screamed of the arrival of another morning. Ever since John had moved his singlewide trailer to the property of the Sunrise School for the Handicapped, he'd had no use for an alarm clock. The ten-acre property the school occupied was itself surrounded by the Palma Nursery with its endless acres of greenhouses and packing facilities all fed by strategically placed irrigation pumps.

He rose from the bed, wiping the sleep from his eyes as the pumps settled back into their daily labor of pushing endless mists of water over the rows of carefully tended ornamentals.

John opened the rear sliding glass door and walked onto his back deck, taking a long look at the pre-dawn sky. His morning ritual. His view of the heavens was unimpeded by the white noise of city lights. The morning stars still shone bright as John raised his arms in a long stretch, breathing the morning air deep into his lungs.

Only thirty minutes from the chaos of the city, the Redlands seemed like he lived half a continent away. John had grown to love the serenity, especially after his career had started with a series of successive moves from one apartment complex to another. Invariably woken from a sleep, he'd find himself pulled into someone's domestic unrest or loud music complaint. It had become more than just an inconvenience. He'd moved out of his last apartment within a day of taking the offer from the school realizing it'd be the closest thing to a *real* home for some time—given the paltry wages paid to Florida's troopers.

John returned inside to start his morning coffee, closing the sliding glass door behind him.

"Hey, you gonna get up?" John shouted from the kitchen. "Hey!"

"Yeah, man… I'm up, I'm up!" his cousin Joey called back. "What time is it?"

"It's the same time I woke you up yesterday, cuz," he said, tapping the un-tanned strap mark on his wrist where his watch usually was. "Now, get up and get ready."

"Alright!"

Joey was glum, but John didn't care. Joey would be crabby and out of sorts until he got off the couch. John had taken in his cousin, offering the spare room, while the kid was in town working as a painter for a construction company. Joey had no need to spend his money on an apartment, since John offered the nineteen-year-old the other bedroom for free.

"Hey, Joey. Last night was a late one, huh?" John looked over at Joey, trying to shake off the morning slumber as he stretched his sprinter's physique and stood.

"Yeah, man. I didn't get in till around two." Joey bent over and grabbed his blanket off the couch.

John smiled, remembering what it was like to be Joey's age. "Ah… You can't keep that shit up, little cuz. It's gunna bite you in the ass."

Joey sauntered down the hall to the guest bathroom. "Yeah, but the girls were everywhere last night!" Joey closed the bathroom door behind him, and John soon heard the sound of the shower.

"You're shittin' me!" John yelled, shaking his head. They were ten years apart but John had always watched out for his cousin. Ever since the kids' parents had separated, John had been more like a big brother to Joey. When John had offered him a room until the construction job closed, Joey's mom had been relieved her boy wouldn't be alone in Miami. John's aunt had never liked Miami much. Its big city feel in a small-town state had always made her uneasy.

Not Joey, though. He loved the city. Latin girls weren't in stock back home in Micanopy where his mom lived. But Miami was easy pickings, especially for a boy with a southern accent. The Latin girls loved their little "gringo." Joey had also learned that affection wasn't shared by the girls' Latin fathers. But Joey, like John, wasn't planning to get married any time soon.

With his roommate dealt with, John siphoned off a cup of coffee as it dripped into the pot and walked out on the deck. As the sky brightened in the advancing morning sun, he found his favorite deck chair and sat. Just as he closed his eyes to take in the morning sounds, John heard his pager go off.

He put down his coffee and got up to find it. Pulling his gun belt from the hall closet hanger he kept it on, John pushed the button on the pager and stared at the flashing narrow screen.

Ah, that was Florey's number with a message behind it. *Meeting at FBI. 7:30. Where is breakfast?*

John smiled and picked up his cell phone. Flipping it open, he called Florey's pager then pushed in the text message using the number keys. *Tony's Donut Shop.*

Two hours later, John and Florey had wolfed down their egg and grits platters at Tony's and pulled up to the austere regional FBI headquarters in North Miami in their separate cars. They parked, then made their way through a labyrinth of security doors and secure access rooms. John hated the idea of needing an escort to enter the building. It always made him uneasy that he couldn't move around without an FBI agent in tow. This morning was no different. An agent escorted them to the fourth floor conference room.

John recognized some of the people already there, including Rick Lotz and Captain DeLeón. John and Florey's major, Randy Carris, was also in the room. He and Florey were still in the doorway when a distinguished man beckoned them inside.

"Troopers, please come in. You're early. I'm Brent McKenna, the Special Agent in Charge for the Miami Office of DEA."

As they moved into the room, they also met Tom Ridgeway, the SAC of the FBI Miami Field Office.

"And you know Agent Lotz, I believe," McKenna said.

Chief McKenna took a seat next to the head of the table, while four other agents came into the room, the last two still wearing their sunglasses.

"Okay, it looks like everyone is here." McKenna asked Rick to close the door, and once the room was secured, he did a run-through of the agencies represented in the meeting, starting with his colleagues from the FBI. He continued with the introductions of his DEA agents, the Florida Highway Patrol, the U.S. Attorney General's office, U.S. Customs, the U.S. Army, the IRS, the National Security Agency, and the State Department.

John flashed a pointed look at Florey when he noted the two guys in the sunglasses were introduced as State Department representatives.

Seeing his glance, she leaned over and whispered, "What?"

John leaned in closer but held back his caustic remark. Not the time or the place to explain his reaction. "I'll tell you later," he whispered.

"We're here to bring some of you up to speed on a case that has been directed by the President of the United States as an item of National Security," McKenna said. "Naturally, this case is highly sensitive and depends on the cartel never finding out about any Federal involvement. Not until we at least know where their assets are in Cali and where they are here.

"We have reason to believe that the cartel has found a new way to smuggle cocaine into this country. If they're successful, they will be able to do it without detection anywhere in the world," McKenna explained, pausing to look down over his notes. "It involves the molecular binding of cocaine with polymers and forming them into anything they can mold it in to."

He nodded to Rick Lotz. "Agent Lotz, please tell us how this all came to be known."

Rick stood up from his chair and pulled a brown, flat box towards him. "About three weeks ago, we received a tip from the U.S. Customs hotline. It was somewhat cryptic. The man on the phone left a message that indicated only that he was kidnapped somewhere in downtown Miami. His voice told me he was in a panic, but he also said he was there to *help* Colombians smuggle drugs. I wanted details, but he said he'd have to call later. That was it. He ended the call." Rick put his hands on the box as he said he'd had a hunch the guy was for real, and monitored the phone line for the next several days to catch the next call.

"He said his name was Peter Haus," Rick said, "and was a chemist from Dresden, Germany with apparently only a few minutes to speak. The guy said he'd gained the confidence of his captors to leave his motel room and walk across the street to buy some groceries. He didn't know where he was, but saw a banner in the airport that read, REPORT DRUGS. CALL 1-800 CUSTOMS. So, he did."

Rick explained how he'd volunteered to work the phones at the Customs Hotline for a friend who was getting married, so he'd talked to the Doc on the second call. "I'm glad I didn't write him off as some kind of crank."

During that conversation, the Doc told Rick they were holding him in a blue and white motel somewhere north of downtown, but the grocery store didn't have a name on it. The pay phone was in the back of the store and out of sight of the motel room window and the prying eyes of his captives. "That's how he was able to call the hotline."

By the reactions in the room, John knew he and Florey and the others from the FHP personnel were not the only ones hearing this for the first time. The agents and detectives from the various agencies were looking around at each other in disbelief, everyone except the State Department employees. They remained expressionless behind their dark sunglasses.

"A trace of the number came back to an unlisted business, so after a day of driving the area, I found the Wanderer motel," Rick explained. "It matched the Doc's description, and sure enough, a grocery with no name was across the boulevard. I gave it a look and found the pay phone in the back. It matched the number."

Rick gambled the guy was for real and spent two days waiting to see if he would show up and use that phone again.

"Let me guess," John chimed in, "a big guy with no tan walked in."

Rick nodded. "Exactly. In two more meetings, Dr. Haus filled in the details. He and another doctor, Hans Mueller, plus their wives and a total of six children, had been asked to go to Colombia. Once in Cali, Doctor Haus was immediately redirected to a plane and escorted by a young Colombian student named Rigoberto Morejón and three other men. Rigoberto left them, because the doctor was then forced to board the plane for Miami with the three goons. He was told that if he did as they said, nothing would happen to his family, or to the other doctor. If he didn't comply, then the Doc would never see them again."

Rick paused to take a breath and refer to his notes.

"How exactly do these doctors fit in?" Captain DeLeón asked.

"Doctors Mueller and Haus are both senior fellows at Leibniz Institute for Polymer Research and have developed a way to synthesize plastic and cocaine on a molecular level," Rick said. "It seems there were some meetings set up between their student, Rigoberto Morejón, and some unsavory types from Slovakia. We think the eastern Europeans were probably hired muscle. Nonetheless, the doctor admitted that the money was too tempting to say no to the scheme."

"How much?" asked an agent from the IRS.

"One million each to teach the techniques to a group of Cali technicians." Rick's answer caused the agents to mutter to themselves, even causing a few at the table to whistle in disbelief.

"So, they knew what they were getting into?" Florey asked.

"Yes and no," Rick said. "Doctor Haus claimed he had no idea he was going to be threatened, kidnapped, and taken to the States. However, he now feels certain that the Colombians will kill all of them once they know how this binding process works."

The room went silent.

John kept writing notes, and Florey leaned in to get a better view of his notepad. Out of the corner of his eye, he saw her frown when he kept tracing over one word he had written: sunglasses.

"Last week, we intercepted this because of Doctor Haus' information." Rick lifted the thin cardboard box and pulled open the flaps to remove a black plastic gear. To John it looked to be about ten inches in diameter with a very rough finish.

"Here, pass this around." Rick handed the gear to one of the agents. "The shipment contained a bill-of-lading for a thousand of those pieces," he said, pointing to the gear as it was handed off from one person to another. "Our friends at Customs put the shipment to the back of the bonded cargo area to give us time to steal a sample."

When the sample made it to him, John closely scrutinized the large cogwheel. It was thick and heavy. "What would this be used for? Supposedly, I mean?"

"Industrial parts," one of the representatives from the U.S. Customs service said. "They're very common. We see quite a few passing through. Nothing that would raise any suspicions."

"That's right," Rick confirmed. "But what you're holding there is a three-pound plastic gear that is thirty percent pure cocaine. Totally undetectable unless you use some serious industrial equipment. You can run a dog by that all day long and there would be no alert."

John stared at Rick. They both understood this plastic cocaine was a game changer. And judging by the faces of the agents and officers in the room, they knew it, too. Cocaine like this could be shipped to the U.S. or anywhere in the world without detection.

Letting that sink in, John went back to analyzing the gear. Thirty percent pure cocaine was a lot of product. The more he thought about the thirty percent, the more he wondered about the other seventy percent.

"Hey, Rick. What happens to the plastic when they're done extracting the cocaine? That's going to be a problem, isn't it?" John passed the gear to Florey. He caught the two men in sunglasses as they turned their heads and focused their attention on him.

"You got ahead of me, John," Rick said.

Others were staring at him now. *Maybe I shouldn't ask so many questions.*

"The doctor was frantic when he told me he's here to receive the plastic," Rick said, talking faster now. "The other guy, Dr. Mueller, combines the plastic with coke in Cali. Once the product is sent here, the Colombians supposedly have a lab where Haus will break down the plastic and extract the coke. From there, it is supposed to be bagged and transported like any other kilo bundle."

Rick gestured to John. "Like John…uh…Trooper Stella noted, there'll be a large amount of plastic refuse left over. We don't know if they plan to discard it or set up a shell company and actually manufacture other things with it." Rick nodded to his boss, McKenna.

SAC McKenna stood and addressed Major Carris. "As I explained over the phone, your troopers are here to assist with any traffic stops we may need. It's essential that we find out who these players are without letting the bad guys know the Feds are involved."

Carris looked up from his notebook. "Fine. Just as long as it's understood my troopers can only stop a car if they have probable cause. Otherwise, it is grounds for a pretextual stop and a rights violation. I need to be clear that we *aren't* in the business of violating anyone's rights."

Always looking to cover his backside, John thought. Not that he could blame him. Of course, Major Carris learned long ago not to leave the little details out of any scenario when reporting to the head of his own agency. With his colonel's support or not, if anything went horribly wrong, as the man in charge of the FHP's effort in this case, it would be Carris' career on the line. At his level, the politics of police administration were a constant concern.

"Understood," McKenna said, "and during this operation we'll get DEA radios to your troopers so we can have a way to communicate. We're putting safety first." He made eye contact with everyone in the room. "The cartel will do their damn best to keep their secret. There's no telling how far they're willing to go to keep it hidden."

"One more thing," Rick interjected. "We've lost the doctor and his three zookeepers. Sometime during the night after I last talked to him, they vacated the motel and disappeared. We know they must be in Miami somewhere, but until FHP makes a few stops, we may not know a whole lot for a while. As we get anything new, we'll keep everyone up to date. That's all I've got for now."

After Rick ended the meeting, McKenna asked them to fill out the contact sheets left on the table, adding that they had to be ready to move quickly. "Remember, the lives of two families somewhere in Cali hang in the balance, too."

John noted the men in sunglasses were the first to get out the door. As agents made their way to write down their contact info on the list, the room filled with idle chatter. John couldn't wait to get the hell out of there to tell Florey what was bugging him.

"Hey, you guys, if you don't mind," a DEA agent said, "can you drive your cars around back to have the radios installed? It will only take about an hour."

John looked at his watch. 11:30 AM. *Great!* In a less than enthusiastic tone he said, "Yeah, sure. Come on, Florey. Looks like it's a late lunch."

Rick crossed the room holding the black plastic cocaine gear in his hands. "Hey, not so fast. You picked up the tab yesterday. Let me take you guys to lunch today."

John grinned and noticed the gear-like cog in Rick's hand. "Sounds like a deal, but what about that?"

Rick looked curiously at John.

"You sure about a dog not being able to detect the drugs in it?" John asked.

"We're positive," Rick replied.

"Sure I can't try?"

"Sorry, buddy. This has to get back to Customs. We got word that Cali already knows the shipment made it to the States. The importer is just waiting for the clearance to pick up his shipment. Besides, I need you to drop off your cars out back and leave the keys with our radio techs," Rick said. "I'll be there in a few to pick you up." Rick handed the plastic cog to one of the U.S. Customs agents.

John and Florey walked out of the building and headed towards their cars. John took Florey's arm and began to walk faster to get ahead of the others.

"Hey, what's the big secret?" Florey asked, her tone not particularly friendly.

"When was the last time we worked a detail with the CIA?" John asked.

Florey began scanning the area.

He glanced at her. "Looking for the guys in sunglasses? Don't bother, Florey. They got out of there before anyone else, and didn't put their numbers on the list, either."

"How do you know they're CIA?"

"First of all, when does the U.S. State Department do any work in the field in a drug investigation?" John asked, a laugh in his voice. "Besides, I've seen those types before—sunglasses and all."

"Where have you seen them before?" she asked.

"I can recall exactly where. October 24, 1983. Beirut. The day after the bombing of the Marine barracks. We ran into those secret-squirrel types all the time." John ran his hand down the back of his head and grabbed his neck. He hated thinking about that day. "They were always up to something 'classified.'"

"I understand," Florey said. "Beirut has been a sore subject for you for a long time." She paused a moment, then feigned a serious face. "Hey, John. Should we tell the captain? This sounds like *serious stuff.*"

John let out a chuckle. Florey knew just how to get him to lighten up. His answer was a short, "*Hell,* no!"

Both of them knew how skittish Headquarters in Tallahassee could be. Any complications might scare the bosses and give them a reason to pull the troopers off the investigation. John always thought "no" was their preferred response. In this case, John was sure Florey would agree it was better the brass knew as little as possible.

Besides, Florey understood and accepted the dangers of this case. He knew she was worried about what could happen to those families in Colombia. The last thing they wanted was to give the brass any reason to pull them off the case. The mystery men would be their little secret.

"Come on, let's get the cars back there. And John?"

"Yeah, kiddo?" he said, nearly stumbling over a broken concrete curb.

"Make sure they use extra-long screws to mount your radio." She was struggling not to snicker out loud.

"Why's that?" John asked, puzzled.

"So it doesn't end up in a parking lot," she replied, her eyes squinting to emphasize her sarcasm.

John thought about responding with a single-finger-salute, but instead grinned and drove to the back lot to the waiting technicians. For John, though, it wasn't easy to shake off the mention of Beruit for long.

On the way to lunch, the memory of the Beruit bombing became entangled with what being in the Marine Corps had done for him, first in providing a path to creating his own future. He took advantage of any training he could get, and it turned out he was good with guns. A gunny sergeant had taken notice of his proficiency with firearms, even though John had been raised in a home where guns weren't allowed. Ironically, shooting had come naturally to him. Thanks to the gunny sergeant, John had signed up for the next sniper school and graduated first in his class.

His next stop had been the American peacekeeping mission in Beirut, Lebanon. Only a few weeks after he arrived there, his squad was rushed back to base from a patrol to face the rubble that had formerly been the

American and French barracks. He spent the remaining weeks pulling bodies—many who were his friends—from the ruins.

The days dragged on endlessly as they waited for the opportunity to hit back against the criminals that murdered their friends. The word from command never came. Instead, the entire military contingent was ordered home. The whole affair left John feeling dissatisfied and angry—and guilty for not being with his friends on that October morning. He'd never gotten past that feeling. He had never forgot how he felt watching the men in sunglasses staying behind while he boarded that flight back to the States. When his tour was done, he left the Corps and came home.

Now, he was fighting a different kind of war.

Chapter Four

Returning from lunch, John and Florey trekked through security at the FBI building to their parked cars in the rear garage, where a DEA technician was ready to give them a quick but tedious lesson on how to use their newly-installed radios.

With Florey right behind him, John headed out of the parking lot, toying with the knobs and turning up the volume on the new device. Mostly, though, the idea of another radio to deal with annoyed him.

Unlike other departments, the Feds didn't use dispatchers. Instead, everyone talked to each other directly. The radio was monitored, but the dispatchers would only respond to calls requesting their help.

The first thing John observed was how quiet radio traffic could be when people weren't hustling around and doing things like running tags and driver license numbers.

Florey pulled up alongside John's car, her passenger window rolled down. "Hey!"

"Yes, ma'am?" John asked.

"It's 1:30. I'm headed to the house. What time you wanna meet up tomorrow?"

Looking at his watch, John realized he'd have just enough time to make it home before risking a tongue lashing from the administrative sergeant for going over his hours. The administration in Tallahassee never budgeted for overtime. *God forbid the rank and file actually get paid for working beyond their shift.* John muttered the sentiment to himself more frequently than he liked. But on the patrol, troopers earned comp time—hours over the regular shift would be subtracted from the next duty day. For John, that meant staying home when he'd prefer to be out on the street working.

"How about we come out at 10 AM?" John suggested. "That way, we can work between both shifts." The few times John had worked with other task forces, he had seldom managed to get home by the end of his shift. These special details could drag on for hours.

"Sounds good, kid. See you at Tony's in the morning." Florey smiled as she rolled up her window, then made a left onto NW 186th Street.

John put away the new DEA radio and immediately got caught in afternoon traffic. As the signal changed to green, he eased into the southbound lanes of I-95, keeping his fingers crossed for no crashes on the way home. Driving a marked highway patrol car meant pulling over for car accidents or stranded motorists. No passing by an incident, pretending not to see it. That never sat well with him.

He cringed at hearing stories about troopers driving past a crash at the end of a shift, calling it into the dispatcher and heading home instead of stopping and trying to help. John at least tried to put himself in the other people's shoes. How would he feel if someone in his family needed help and an officer drove by without so much as a quick check to see if they were hurt? Like he told rookie troopers, that was no way to represent the department—or the whole state of Florida, for that matter.

John exhaled a groan as the endless rows of cars undulated like the bellows of an accordion along the five lanes of concrete highway, inching along and then speeding up again. At this rate, he was in for a long commute.

As he moved across the interstate to the far-left lane, he heard Florey's familiar voice over his radio, "644 to 968." She was calling him on the talk-to-talk channel, the frequency the troopers used to speak directly to each other without the hassle of a dispatcher.

"This is 968. Go ahead," John replied using his radio ID number.

"Turn on your inner-city scanner and listen to what's coming up behind you!"

Reacting to Florey's frantic warning, John instinctively snapped his attention to his rearview mirror while still trying to gauge the traffic ahead. He reached down and pushed the scanner button on his FHP mounted radio.

Behind the backdrop of a siren, John heard an officer transmitting, "2368... He's now southbound, Broward...I-95...entering Dade County."

John recognized the unit number as a Broward sheriff's deputy.

The deputy was pursuing a vehicle approaching from behind as John drove south. The FBI office was only two miles south of the Broward county line. He was close.

John waited to hear more radio traffic as he continued to scan his mirrors.

His voice in a heightened pitch, the officer transmitted, "…2368, he's across all lanes of traffic—now southbound in the emergency lane next to the median wall… Speed is in excess of 110. Notify FHP!"

John slowed again, scanning his rearview mirror, his heart already pounding. Adrenaline pumped through him. Hailing Florey on his radio, he called, "968 to 644… Where are you?"

"I exited at 125th Street. Getting gas, almost done. Keep monitoring your scanner and switch to transmit on the dispatch channel. I'll do my best to catch up."

Since neither of them were ones to back down from a pursuit, it made no sense to stay on the 'chit-chat' channel when they needed to be talking to dispatch. John smiled to himself as he quickly switched over to the main radio frequency while still monitoring the inner city scanner. Florey would have to hustle if she was going to keep up with him.

"2368… We are passing 135th Street… Speed still over 100… Silver Honda Accord." The deputy's radio was barely decipherable over the blare of his siren.

"One mile behind me. Damn it!" John exclaimed, his hands sweating now.

He grabbed his mic and was about to notify dispatch of the chase when he heard some trooper in Hialeah running a series of tags. It sounded like the Stolen Vehicle Recovery Squad. Man, he hated them with a vengeance, but so did every other trooper. When that squad was out working, they always managed to tie up the radio just when everybody else needed it most. Today was no different. "Damn it!"

John pressed down on his mic, trying to interrupt the other trooper's transmission, "Miami… 968 to Miami." No luck.

He checked his rearview mirror. Suddenly, a glint. Then another and the faint shimmer of headlights, followed by police lights, approached from behind. Both cars were in the inside emergency lane and moving quickly. From a look at his speedometer, John gauged traffic was going back and forth between 10 and 40 miles per hour. He hoped whoever was fleeing would pass him without noticing his marked FHP cruiser.

Looking in his rearview mirror, John gritted his teeth. The idiot was doing over double the speed limit in a lane reserved for emergency vehicles and broken-down motorists. It was the last bit of pavement before contacting the eight-foot concrete barrier wall that separated the roadway in half. Adding to the hazard, since the emergency lane was seldom cleaned or maintained, the force of passing traffic whisked highway debris into rolling piles like dunes on a beach, each festooned with metal debris just waiting to blow out a tire.

"2368… We're approaching 125th Street… Still southbound." The deputy's voice was high-pitched from the strain.

"968 to Miami…" Still no luck getting through.

"Fuck!" John yelled as the dispatcher started broadcasting back a series of tag information. It was hopeless. He had no way to break into their transmissions. He would have to give chase and notify them as he went.

John steadied himself.

The fleeing vehicle, with its spray of metallic road debris and dirt behind it, barreled along in the emergency lane. John was ready, though. He'd get behind the deputy and follow as his backup. Easy. He'd done it countless times. But for now, he could only watch as the shock of the reckless offender's driving caused most of the traffic to swerve in panic, each driver trying to avoid a collision. John winced at the near misses. All he could do now was wait.

"2368…TC! TC! Patrol car, TC! On top of the 125th Street overpass… Subject still southbound. I think he is passing an FHP car."

Familiar with deputy lingo, John clenched his jaw when the deputy advised he had a TC—a traffic crash. *Poor SOB.*

But John had no time to worry about the deputy's bad luck. The vehicle approached and passed John as a wave of rocks, sand, and other junk peppered his patrol car. The car went by in a flash but John managed to get a mental snapshot of the driver—white, Latin male, somewhere in his forties.

As he pulled out of his lane, the Impala's engine howled, the overdrive gear kicking in as John entered the emergency lane and quickly caught up to the fleeing car. He was so quick, he backed off just a bit, the cloud of dust and debris making it nearly impossible to see. John turned on his overhead blue lights and blaring siren to warn traffic of the approaching chaos.

"968 to Miami."

"Go ahead, 968," the dispatcher answered, as if it were his first attempt.

"Miami, BSO, just chased a car into Dade… We're southbound on I-95 coming up on 119th Street." John paused to let the dispatcher absorb the fact that a pursuit was happening and wasn't a request to run a tag. "Miami, Broward Sheriff's Office. Make sure BSO know their deputy crashed on top of 125th Street… And get me a reference to this chase!"

"10-4, 968… Go ahead with the tag number."

"What the fuck?" he yelled. John didn't know who he was pissed off at more—the deputy for crashing or the dispatcher for thinking John could actually see the tag number. He chose to ignore her.

The Honda's speed was exceeding 100 miles per hour and kicking up more flying debris.

"Miami, we are at 103rd Street… Still southbound… Speed now 105 miles per hour… Silver Honda four-door… I can't see a tag." John raised his voice on every word as the thud and ping of sand and rocks pelting his car grew louder than the howl of his engine.

"10-4, 968, BSO advises the reference is carjacking and grand theft… Subject is armed with a black pistol… Unknown type… Stand by… All units stand by."

Instinctively, John pushed harder on the gas. The dispatcher's update was all he needed to justify going after this guy. His heart pounding in his chest, he had no time to panic. The slightest mistake could prove disastrous, even fatal.

His movements precise and sharp, John swerved side to side to avoid the larger chunks of flying debris—rubber tires, wood pieces, and even the metal top of a garbage can whirled in the air behind the Honda. Their speed increased to 105…110…120…

"Miami, advise 644's location," John demanded.

"644…crossing 119th Street." Florey's response came without waiting for the dispatcher to ask.

Good. She wasn't that far behind.

Ahead, the Honda's brake lights suddenly flashed on and off, on and off, sending the car rocking forward and back. The Honda driver could be trying to stop. He'd bail out of the car and run away on foot. Or, maybe he was looking for a break in traffic to dart into while making his escape.

The car's brake lights glowed red and the back end of the vehicle rose quickly as its speed plummeted. Blue-gray smoke billowed out from behind as it skidded and slid to the right.

John slammed on his brakes, his body pressing against the seat back, preparing for an inevitable collision.

Within seconds, the Honda turned, squeezing miraculously between two cars, then continued cramming its way through traffic towards the other side of the highway.

"Goddamn it! Where's this fucker think he's going?" John checked traffic to his right and left so he wouldn't crash into nearby cars as he followed the Honda, leading now by a few cars. Smaller than his full-size Chevy, the Honda did a better job in tight spaces.

John sounded his overhead air horn to grab attention as he squeezed through the gaps—200 watts of pure obnoxious. But no other emergency equipment was better at getting Miami drivers to move. Even the most cooperative drivers treated police sirens more like requests than orders to get the hell out of the way. Not so much for the air horn. The next best thing to a bulldozer.

"Miami… He's moving across all lanes of traffic… We are approaching NW 62nd Street exit ramp." John hoped this guy wouldn't get off the interstate. Chases in neighborhoods were way too risky. Between the cars and pedestrians, the odds of hurting a bystander went way up.

The Honda moved into the outer emergency lane, and with no cars impeding its movement, the driver picked up speed. John tried to get a guy driving a yellow Porsche 911 to pull up so he could get in behind him. But the driver was snapping his fingers and bouncing his head.

You gotta be kiddin' me.

Leaning on the air horn button, John inched closer.

No response.

John edged even closer still, checking the Honda's progress as it pulled away, dust and debris indicating its path. *Shit! I'm gonna lose this asshole over some douche in a Porsche pretending to be a Mambo King.*

John gritted his teeth and pushed forward. He hit the Porsche's rear bumper and then applied the gas. No match for the patrol car, the light sports car jerked forward as the driver began to frantically stand on his brakes, panicked, checking through each window, his head pivoting wildly. John knew the guy was straining to figure out what was going on.

Satisfied with the space created, John backed his patrol car off the Porsche's bumper, skidding backwards, then slamming his gear into drive. The cruiser lunged forward as John negotiated ahead into the newly-created gap in traffic, his lights and siren still blaring.

Finally, John entered the emergency lane. The Honda had quite a jump on him as it fled south, and that meant pushing down on the gas, the force causing his thigh muscles to ache as they bypassed the NW 62nd Street exit. It was the last exit before the highway forced traffic to veer off, to the airport, Miami Beach, or downtown.

"968 to Miami," John yelled through the mic.

"Miami to 968… Go ahead," the dispatcher replied.

"Subject is currently approaching State Road 112. I'll advise which direction he goes… Stand by." John kept his eyes on the suspect to catch any indication of a direction change.

On the radio, several senior troopers acknowledged they were in the area. He knew every damn one of them would be breaking their backs to try to catch this guy. But he sure wasn't going to let some other trooper get to him first.

The Honda raced up the exit ramp to State Road 112. It nearly hit an orange sign warning of construction ahead, placed just off the travel lane, as the ramp gradually pulled away from the main southbound lanes of I-95. Behind it, the large black and white REDUCE SPEED AHEAD sign blew over as the Honda flew past it.

John entered the ramp, and the Honda suddenly jerked left. "*East bound, Miami*," John yelled. "Towards the beaches… Notify Miami Beach PD." John's voice strained as he pushed the patrol car into the sharp left curve of the interstate. Its rear wheels squealed as the tires strained to grip the road's surface and keep the car from flailing out of control. The G forces pushed back on John's body and pressed him towards his passenger door. His knuckles turned white from the strain of his death-grip on the wheel.

Dispatch announced, "All units! Be advised… 968 is in pursuit of a silver Honda four-door currently eastbound on State Road 112, headed towards Miami Beach… Subject is considered armed… Any unit in the area, advise."

John heard no response to the dispatcher's request. Troopers understood instinctively: *Better to just go than to tell the station. Less paperwork that way*. The lack of response didn't faze him. He knew better than to think nobody was coming.

The Honda screamed across the overpasses as it raced along the causeway. Serene Biscayne Bay appeared on either side of the narrow causeway. The surrounding islands and large mansions dotting the shores were like a backdrop for a movie. John quickly caught up to the suspect, but the Honda made a few rapid lane changes—to the center, back to the left, and then all the way to the right.

He closed in and waited. Inches off the suspect's bumper, he saw the driver clearly. Medium length brown hair, yellow collared shirt. The glint of the blue-white ring on his left hand suggested a large stone. Despite the chaotic driving, John imprinted that information in case the driver fled on foot and he had to provide a description of the suspect.

The Honda raced up the last of the bridges connecting the causeway to Miami Beach. John readied himself to report any change of direction and played out the various scenarios of what could happen next and how he'd react. What to do in a bail out. Watch the subject's hands. Note streets and direction on a foot pursuit. Training and experience on the job and in the military played back in a flurry of thoughts.

"Miami, stand by," John warned dispatch as he and the Honda approached the end of the causeway. "Alton Road… Southbound Alton Road," he called out, his tone calmer now.

John entered the ramp to southbound Alton Road at nearly 100 miles per hour, its curve tighter and more harrowing at high speed than any other ramp on the expressways. With a steely grip on the wheel, he negotiated the sharp right banking turn as the car drifted, its tires squealing in protest.

He saw the Honda nearly driving off the pavement, finally losing control. It crossed the center divider curb and was sent airborne before landing with a thud on the opposite lanes of traffic, nearly striking other cars as it fishtailed from side to side before accelerating again. The car then sped south in the northbound Alton Road lanes, navigating wildly through the oncoming traffic.

John snaked his patrol car between the traffic in the two southbound lanes. He accelerated and braked over and over, negotiating whatever space he could find to force his patrol car south. He scoffed. It was like trying to pass a camel through the eye of a needle.

John gave the side streets his attention as he fought off the growing tunnel vision. His heart racing, sweat breaking out on his brow, he drove up on the sidewalk as he passed the last of the pack of cars between him and the Honda.

He pressed down on his air horn and held it. Finding a break in the trees that grew along the shoulder between the sidewalk and the street, John cut hard to the left towards the street, the patrol car lunging towards the pavement.

"Miami, we are passing West 21st Street, coming up on Michigan Ave." John's car descended back onto the street with a loud thud, gouging the paved surface beneath it and sending the car fishtailing.

He mashed the gas, regained control, and sped forward. The Honda was two car lengths ahead. A good space, just in case he needed to take evasive action.

The Honda braked again as it approached Michigan Avenue, its wheels locking up. The car turned slightly sideways as it yawed through the red light at the intersection. Its tires began billowing smoke behind it as it returned to the southbound lanes.

"Miami, he's through Michigan, still southbound."

"968… Advise a tag number."

"Miami… its D: delta, X: x-ray, G: golf, 546… Florida tag." John was about to repeat the information when he looked in his rearview mirror and saw the FHP car.

"644… I'm with him, Miami," Florey said to dispatch.

"Yes!" John exclaimed. He didn't know how she'd managed to catch up, but he was glad she was there.

"Miami, stand by… Subject is breaking heavily again." John waited, and suddenly the car made a sharp turn left, nearly striking a car that had been stopped at the light facing the opposite direction.

"Eastbound, Miami… Eastbound on 17th Street." This guy wasn't going to last long on the beach. John had chased a lot of people on the long narrow island and none of them had managed to get back to the mainland without capture.

"Florey, I see Miami Beach units waiting up ahead by the convention center," John advised as he scanned the roadway beyond the subject's car. A response from Florey wasn't needed. He knew she was listening.

As the Honda crossed over Meridian Drive, John noticed the driver leaning over to the front passenger seat. He was looking for something. The car slowed to 90, then 70.

John's senses were pushed to their limits, but he kept his focus on the driver and prepared himself for anything. Almost. A quiet, well-mannered surrender wasn't one of them.

The Honda kept slowing down as it passed the stationary Miami Beach cruisers. The driver leaned back into his seat as he approached the waiting police cars. Holding a large black pistol in his right hand, the driver moved his arm across his body as the officers came into range. Before John could react, three distinct blasts came from the gun. John's grip on the microphone tightened.

"Shots fired, Miami… Shots fired!" John mashed the gas and forced his cruiser to regain its speed. Just as he began to close in, the Honda accelerated, quickly moving forward and barely escaping an imminent collision with John's car, Florey still following close behind.

The city police cars nearly crashed into one another as the Miami Beach officers jockeyed to get into the chase.

John updated the dispatcher. "Miami, we are still eastbound

approaching Collins Ave… Stand by."

John looked ahead to the rapidly approaching Art Deco district packed with tourists. Hordes of white-skinned visitors taking pictures of pastel-colored, aging hotels would be oblivious to the approaching chaos. The chase would have to end. As much as John hated the thought, it wasn't worth the risk of killing an innocent bystander. However, an armed subject firing at cop cars could not be overlooked either.

Ahead, the Honda skidded sideways, nearly sideswiping a city bus at Washington Avenue. The bus came to a rapid stop, blocking the Honda's path and preventing it from continuing into the masses of visitors.

Now facing south, the Honda sprung forward, taking off again, weaving its way rapidly down the avenue. John—and Florey—turned to follow.

"968 to Miami, we're now southbound on Washington from 17th… Beach units and 644 are behind me," John advised.

"Miami to 968… Shift commander says to fall back and let the Beach units take over," the FHP dispatcher advised.

No way. John ignored the transmission.

"968 to Miami… We're still southbound on Washington approaching 11th Street." The weaving Honda avoided colliding with traffic and merging police cars.

"Miami to 968… We're now being advised the vehicle tag comes back to a silver Honda four-door. It's Signal 10, carjacked after the subject committed a home invasion."

John feared this guy was capable of anything. He was not going to care what he destroyed with a stolen car, especially after committing a violent and heinous crime.

As the caravan of cruisers led by the silver Honda worked its way south on Washington Avenue, John looked at Florey in his rearview mirror. She was flashing her high beams at him to get his attention.

He looked again. She bumped her fists together in between negotiating her car behind John's. He understood.

John took another breath and updated the dispatcher. "Miami, be advised we are crossing 5th Street… Stand by."

John backed off one car length from the Honda, giving himself just enough room. He checked his rearview and saw Florey giving him a thumbs-up. Ahead on the right was an empty lot across the street from the Big Pink restaurant. That was as good a place as any.

John mashed the accelerator again, held on to the wheel with both hands, and leaned back in his seat, resting his head on the headrest, preparing himself for the impact.

Metal on metal crashed loudly as skidding tires resounded over the howl of John's revving motor. With both bumpers contacted, the Impala pushed into the trunk of the Honda, sending it spinning to the right against a curb and then airborne into the vacant lot.

John pressed hard on his brakes as the Honda landed in the center of the lot and flipped over twice before resting on its passenger side. The windshield had flown off and landed in a condominium pool as the car slammed into the ground.

The subject managed to crawl through the opening where the windshield had been and took off on foot.

John zeroed in on the black pistol in the subject's right hand as he ran from the stolen car. And the subject's white leather shoes.

John forced the gear into park and jumped out, running after the subject before his Impala came to a stop.

He grabbed for his handheld radio, bobbing up and down in its holster. His 170-pound frame offered no cushion for the heavy duty belt as it dug into his hips. "Miami, foot pursuit… The alley between 5th and 6th…southbound…subject wearing a yellow collared shirt, blue jeans, and white shoes."

Unholstering his Colt Python .357, John slowed to check on Florey.

"Coming up behind you," Florey cried.

Assured she was okay, John broke into a sprint. The radio was blaring, but John couldn't make out the transmissions. He heard the sounds of accelerating cars echoing between the buildings and figured the Beach cops were boxing the area into a perimeter—and it was a safe bet the suspect knew that, too.

John watched the suspect unsuccessfully grab at a door in the alley. Locked. He grabbed at another door and another, checking behind him, keeping an eye on the officers and noticing their rapid advance. Every door was locked. Apparently spying a break between buildings, he turned right and took off in a full sprint, disappearing from John's line of sight.

John held up his hand to keep Florey from calling to him. Any noise could give away their position.

Florey broke from her sprint and stopped.

John stepped to the left, away from the building corner, to sneak a quick look in the direction the subject ran. It was another alley, but this one was shorter, maybe 20 yards long, closed-in by a barbed wire fence about 12 feet high. No noise, no doors. The only windows were two stories above the street. Two green dumpsters stood at the far end.

John took another peek. Still nothing. But he knew the guy had to be there. Two Miami Beach officers ran up, their equipment still jingling as they slowed to a trot. John held his left index finger to his lips, demanding silence. He pointed to the short alley and made a fist signaling not to enter. Then John, Florey, and the two Beach officers heard a sound that brought grins to all their faces. Barking.

A Miami Beach Canine Unit drove up and parked on the next street.

John made eye contact with the dog handler and pointed to the alley. The K-9 officer acknowledged John and removed the dog's leash from behind his seat, opened his rear door, and hooked it to a large, pure black German shepherd. John recognized the handler from the time he had had his own dog.

"Hey, John, sorry I'm late," the canine handler whispered as he walked up.

"Glad to see you, Phil. Our suspect is down that alley," John said. "Doesn't look like there's any way out. You've got two dumpsters and a tall fence. Subject is armed with a black pistol."

"I know about the pistol." Phil looked in the direction of the alley. "It was me at Convention Center Drive. Fucker shot a hole in the center of my windshield. I'm pretty sure even Thunder took a crap," he whispered.

"Okay, brother, it's all you," John said. "I'll be right behind ya." He turned to Florey and the other Beach officers and whispered, "Cover." They spread out to cover the opening of the small alley in case the suspect managed to get by.

Phil moved towards the corner of the building. His dog was already fanning his nose on a scent. Phil's wave got John's attention, and he nodded when Phil pointed toward the alley, understanding the alert of the dog. Phil then cleared his throat.

"Suspect, come out! Give up, or I will send in my dog!" Phil shouted loud and clear.

In training, John had played a bad guy, and every time he'd heard the handler's warning, his heart had raced. A dog's jaws snapping shut on a forearm at 1900 psi hurt—even while wearing a protective bite sleeve.

Phil listened. Thunder's ears were forward, every muscle tensed. He was ready to do his job.

Phil yelled out another set of commands. No response. He reached over and unhooked Thunder from the leash. Phil paused, but only for a few seconds, before giving the command. "Get him."

Thunder tore off down the concrete drive, his nails relentlessly scratching its surface as he gained traction. Phil immediately followed his furry partner, his gun drawn. John followed to provide cover for Phil. Thunder ran at full sprint, the sunlight shimmering off his black coat.

Suddenly, Thunder's head went down as his shoulders slumped, tail whipping sideways, allowing him to change direction. His nose caught it well before he even saw his prey—the scent of fear. The one thing a man on the run could never cover up, the smell excreted from the pores as his body reacted in panic. An odor that permeates and lingers, tempting and drawing in a canine's hypersensitive olfactory sense. Thunder redirected his energy and broke into a full gallop towards the dumpsters.

The sound of a one-hundred-pound canine impacting human flesh and bone was like no other. John had always winced when his dog would apprehend a suspect. He couldn't help but feel a little bit sorry for the poor fools that thought they could get away from a dog's nose. This time was no different.

Approaching, John saw Thunder had the Latin male squarely by the testicles. A full mouth bite. The pain and fear were so great that the suspect had immediately dropped his gun. His screams were muted as the dog pulled and dragged him hard to the ground, knocking the air out of the suspect's lungs.

Phil grabbed the guy's arms, spun him around with the dog still attached to his nether regions, and handcuffed him. Only then did Phil yell, "OUT!"

Thunder released his bite and sat at his handler's side. Phil moved in and patted the subject down.

Grinning, John holstered his gun and notified dispatch. "Miami, be advised… Beach K-9 has the subject in custody… Cancel all units."

Florey and the other Miami Beach officers came around the corner, guns still drawn, but holstered them when they saw everything was under control. The Beach officers grabbed the suspect and sat him down when Phil took the dog back to his car.

"I suppose you want me to follow you to the hospital before we book this perp?" Florey asked.

Picking up the suspect's gun, John said, "Ah, yeah. And you should be thankful, by the way."

"For what? Another six hours of paperwork?"

John leaned towards his partner. "No. For all the fun shit that I get you into."

Before she could answer, Madison, a senior trooper in his fifties, ran up from the spot where the suspect's car had crashed. He looked serious.

"Hey Madison, figures you'd get here before the other troopers," John said.

Seeing the action was over, Madison slowed to a walk with his breathing labored. He planted his hands on his hips. "Hey, guys. Sorry, I got here as soon as I could."

"I figured the senior guys had my back," John said, concerned at how long it was taking Madison to breathe normally. "You sure you're gonna be okay?"

"Yeah, just a little too much rice and beans, buddy." He rubbed his hand over his belly. "You probably want to get back to this guy's car and take a look at what's inside. Oh, yeah, and another thing. The captain pulled up right behind me."

"Great," John said, and he and Florey trotted back to the Honda. John hoped they wouldn't find a dead body, or worse. *Bodies.* It happened.

Captain DeLeón met them at the car, holding up his hands. "Easy, you guys. Slow down." He looked stressed out.

"Hey, Captain," Florey said. "Madison said it was serious."

"Stella, you didn't waste no time, did ya?" DeLeón said, pointing to the car. The bent and twisted stolen car had been pushed back onto what was left of its wheels and the trunk was open.

"It's amazing that stuff didn't fly all over the place. Lord knows the beach is already knee deep in powder as it is," the captain said as he surveyed the crash scene.

John and Florey leaned towards the trunk and peered into the compartment. John let out a low whistle. Two large duffel bags. The kind you *could* put a body into. One was unzipped and open. John couldn't count exactly how many kilos there were, but he didn't have to. Nothing unusual, either. It wasn't uncommon for dopers to rip each other off, especially since the victim wouldn't report the crime. Unless, of course, the victim had no idea what was in the car to begin with.

"That answers the question of why that prick committed a home invasion and stole a car." John cocked his head into the twisted wreck, trying to see more contraband, and still wondering to himself if the victim was truly innocent.

Florey, beaming ear to ear, nudged DeLeón with her elbow. "I guess we should notify Rick."

"Yeah, Stella… Why don't you call him on that expensive DEA radio you have in that fucking *wrecked* patrol car." DeLeón glared at John. "Damn it, son, you just had them installed."

John knew it was a righteous pursuit but was still troubled by the man's scowl. Something else must be bugging the captain. "We can get that fixed, Cap. It's a bumper. Couple of hours at most. Besides, the car still drives. Although, I'll admit, it kinda looks like hell."

"Listen, I've been trying to get you back your dog. I almost had the major convinced. His only concern was you."

"Me?" John was shocked. "And when did they decide to reinstate the K-9 program?"

"Yes, *you*. You're a *fucking* cowboy sometimes, Stella, and the decision came down from HQ last month," said DeLeón.

John looked down at his feet, knowing he shouldn't argue with the captain. After all, he was one of the few people above the rank of lieutenant who consistently proved he knew the job. This wasn't the time to ask how the major had reacted to the idea of giving him back his dog.

John looked up. "Cap… There was no avoiding what happened. I had to end it where I did. At the end of this street, there's a boys' camp, a private school, a home for the elderly, and a dead end. There was no way I was letting this creep get that far and take out a kid or granny."

The captain seemed about to respond, but loud screaming diverted their attention. The suspect was being wheeled away on a stretcher by the city fire rescue squad. Both medics pushed the contraption with one hand while attempting to hold bandages to the affected area with the others. Their patient writhed in pain as each bump made the screaming louder.

The fire commander walked up and spoke directly to John. "Hey, you in charge here?"

John pointed toward his supervisor. "No, that would be Captain DeLeón."

"Oh, hey." Appearing embarrassed at not recognizing the polished bars on DeLeón's epilates, the fire commander continued. "This guy has to go to Ward D. He may lose a testicle or something. Dog did a pretty good number on his sack."

John groaned inside. Troopers dreaded the infamous Ward D, the infirmary ward at Jackson Memorial Hospital. It was usually manned by doctors with the bedside manner of a feral cat. And not much patience for the troopers, either. But if the suspect was injured, they were the only ones authorized to give a medical clearance. The jail wouldn't touch an injured prisoner without one.

"I'll have Trooper Baker meet you at Ward D, Commander," DeLeón said. He turned to Florey and asked her to follow them in.

"Cap, I can go," John interjected. "Florey doesn't have to."

Captain DeLeón gave him a lopsided smile. "No, John, you need to stay and count kilos. Besides, this is our arrest. We take the body and the dope. Contact Broward Sheriff's Office and the Beach. They're going to want to charge this idiot, too." He managed one final order as he walked to his patrol car. He pointed to the Honda. "Stella, you're on it!"

John glanced at Florey, who wouldn't get home to her family at anything close to a decent hour. It was going to be a long night for them both.

"Hey, Florey. I'm sorry, hon," John said.

"Sorry for what, John? This is what we're best at. I wouldn't have anyone else with me than you. You have nothing to apologize for." She shot him a warm smile and put her hand on his shoulder. "Besides, this douchebag needed to get taken off the streets. Who better to do it than us?" She paused and let out a heavy exhale. "So, when we clear the hospital and get to the jail, I'll see what he has to say. Just do me a favor and call Rick. They may want to interrogate him since he was carrying all that powder."

Proud of his partner, John said, "You got it. And thanks."

"You're welcome, *hon*!"

Knowing she hadn't taken offense to him calling her that, he also knew she was letting him know it hadn't gone past her, either. If it had been anyone other than him, Florey would have been quick to show her disdain. Her prerogative. It came with being the senior female trooper in the state. Smiling at him over her shoulder, Florey left to follow the ambulance while John got to work on the kilos.

Chapter Five

John's eyes slowly opened the next morning, adjusting to the dim bedroom light. For a moment, he remained motionless as he toyed with the idea of taking the day off—if only he could convince Florey to do the same. Deep down, he knew he couldn't convince himself, either. They had already planned to meet at noon at the station to drop off his car for repairs. Begrudgingly, he got out of bed and yawned, as he attempted to negotiate the tight spaces in the room on the way to the coffeemaker.

The marketing plan may have labeled his bedroom a master suite, but to John, it was just slightly larger of the trailer's rooms. His bed, dresser, and nightstand were all that fit in the confining space, forcing him to sidestep within the short and narrow hallways. He was used to it, though. It was even a source of levity whenever he shared his bed with a lovely overnight guest. He got a kick out of listening to the muffled curses as the woman bumped into the walls and furniture as she negotiated her way to the bathroom.

While waiting for the coffee to brew, John sat at the round kitchen table and opened the manila folder lying next to his duty bag. *What a night*. He rubbed the sleep from his eyes, and then glanced over at the couch. His cousin was no longer where John had found him when he had come home at 2:30 that morning. That meant Joey must have managed to get to work on his own.

Once he had a full mug of coffee on the table next to him, John separated the arrest affidavit from the rest of the reports. That affidavit served as the state's charging document with the courts, and this one ran to eight pages of narrative and a lengthy list of charges. Every detail of the pursuit and canine apprehension was carefully documented. After hours of photographing, transporting, and locking up the evidence, he and Florey had met at the station to finish their reports. Each form required its own synopsis of the events—a duplicative exercise that no trooper ever enjoyed. He sighed. The work was necessary to get the case accepted by the state attorney's office. All it took sometimes was one mistake in documenting or processing the evidence, and the case was lost. Florey and John had trudged through the maze of forms, trying to be extra attentive to detail. That's why they'd worked well into the early morning hours and fought back the urge to sleep.

John went over them again line by line just to make sure they hadn't missed anything.

Name: Julio Mendoza Cortés.

No known local address

Driver License: Colombian

Age: 35

Occupation: Import/Export

John's gaze traveled down the list of felony charges, ending with: **Armed Trafficking and Possession of 325 kilos of Cocaine.**

He put aside the copies of the suspect's medical clearance and looked through the paperwork of the Honda's registration before he got up to pour another cup of coffee. He noted the stolen car was registered to a black female from Hollywood, Florida. She had reported her car stolen the previous day to the Fort Lauderdale Police Department after she'd been struck in the head by a blunt object from behind. When she came to, she noticed the vehicle was missing from the parking lot where she lived, the Casa D'Amour, an adults-only boutique on Las Olas Boulevard. She rented the upstairs apartment. The teletype from the Broward County Sheriff's office showed she had no criminal history on record. Well, one incident of driving with a suspended license, but that was an offense so commonplace in South Florida, John didn't consider it worthy of being called a real crime. At least, not one to raise an eyebrow over.

He thumbed through the rest of the papers and checked his memory to make sure he'd faxed all the reports Rick had asked for. It'd been such a long night, he couldn't remember. When they'd all met up at the jail, they were nowhere near done with the paperwork. Rick opted to leave with a handful of notes and some photocopied forms. Even John and Florey's interrogation of Mr. Cortés had proved worthless. As soon as they'd advised him of his constitutional rights, he'd lawyered-up. From that point on, he'd refused to answer any questions.

Florey had joked that it was probably better that way, since their prisoner was on copious amounts of painkillers. Any defense attorney would've had a field day obtaining a statement while the prisoner didn't have his normal faculties.

When they'd told Rick about the lawyer, he immediately made a few phone calls. John saw the check in the box next to "Miranda Rights Read," and another in the box indicating the prisoner's refusal to give a statement. Florey had drawn a diagonal line across the paper with a large "N/A" in its center.

Glancing at the clock, John saw it was 9 AM. Time to get ready.

Just as he stood, he heard the door to the back bedroom open and Joey shuffled down the hallway in his boxers.

"Hey, man," Joey mumbled, rubbing his eyes.

"Good morning, kid." John chuckled. "What? No work today?"

"I've already been there and back. We got rained out. Foreman sent us home for the day. Hey, is the coffee done yet?" Joey squinted as he tried to focus on the grumbling coffee maker.

"Help yourself."

Joey grabbed a mug from the shelf above the sink and filled it from the pot, watching silently as John organized the reports back in the folder.

Leaning over to look out the sliding glass doors, John noticed an ominous wall of dark clouds spanning the northern horizon. Meanwhile, the sky above was tropical blue. Not a cloud to be seen. It was shaping up to be a typical South Florida day. Dark and rainy as hell one moment, eye-squinting bright the next. He hoped it would blow over by the time he left for work. There were no rain day passes for cops.

"Hey cuz, what the hell happened to your patrol car?" Joey said as he shoveled a tablespoon of sugar in his cup.

"Had a little meeting with a doper…the doper lost."

"Anyone get hurt?"

Joey's fascination with police work always led to endless questions, but they never annoyed John. In fact, he hoped Joey would take on the profession himself one day. He might've gone into a long description of yesterday's events, but had to cut the conversation short. He'd promised the captain to have his car in the station by noon to be fixed.

"Nah, I think the doctors saved his testicle," John said. He put his coffee cup in the sink. "Hey, I gotta get going. Another long day."

"What? His *testicle*?" Joey's mouth was agape.

"Yeah. Dog bite. Long story." Knowing he offered only a teaser, he changed the subject and asked Joey what he planned to do with his day off.

Joey responded with a quick shrug, apparently caught off guard. "I don't know. Maybe watch some TV or something."

"Is that before or after you cut the lawn?" John purposely furrowed his brow. He didn't take too kindly to Joey's idea of a laid back, on-the-couch day.

"Ah… After, I suppose," he said in a sheepish tone.

"You suppose right." John smiled.

"But I want to hear the rest of the story."

"I promise to tell you the rest tomorrow." Knowing his cousin would pester him until he heard every detail of the chase, John retreated to take a shower. The story could wait, and he had too much to do and no time to get caught up in incessant questions.

As he was about to step into the shower, his cell phone rang.

"Leave a message," he yelled.

John pulled the plastic curtain closed, cranked on the hot water, and lathered a dab of shampoo into his hair. The phone stopped ringing—for a couple of seconds. Then it rang again.

"Damn it." He threw back the curtain and slid across the wet shower floor. Righting himself, he grabbed a towel from the rack. Dripping water and soap onto the floor, he retrieved his phone from the clip of his gun belt. Finally. He flipped it open and answered with a terse, "Yeah?"

"Get dressed, if you aren't already, and head up to the station now." Florey sounded excited, in a good way. "Rick's going to meet us there."

"I'm jumping in the shower. I'll be on my way in twenty minutes."

"Make it ten, John. He said it's important."

The call ended.

"Hey, John! Your phone is ringing…"

John turned as Joey entered the open door to the bedroom and paused at the sight of him—naked, soaking wet with a head of shampoo suds, phone in one hand and a towel in the other.

"John, ahh… You're supposed to wash off the soap *before* you get out of the shower." Joey was unable to contain his nervous laugh.

Not amused, John gritted his teeth. "Go *cut* the lawn."

Fifteen minutes later—ten was impossible—John drove to the FHP Headquarters sandwiched between the 836 Expressway and the Florida Turnpike.

After maneuvering to the rear parking lot of the building, he backed his cruiser into an open space among other wrecked vehicles. The property lieutenant, a guy named Freech, walked towards John holding a clipboard.

Before climbing out of the car, John took a deep breath. He'd always been annoyed at Lieutenant Freech's demeanor. Out of respect for the rank, though, John managed to ignore all the little things the lieutenant had said over the years.

"Damn it, Stella, you guys keep wrecking these cars," the lieutenant ranted. "All I do is inventory the cars troopers can't drive. What the hell did you do to this one?" Freech fumbled through the papers on his clipboard until he came up with the one he was looking for.

"Excuse me, Lieutenant?" John was taken aback. Even the prickly lieutenant didn't usually sound this bad.

"You heard me. This lot is packed with wrecks. Now I gotta inventory all the equipment and document the damage." Freech stared at the clipboard and continued fingering through the forms. "Shit! Like I got nothing better to do!"

John stared at his least favorite supervisor, doing his best not to smart off at the senior officer. Meanwhile, his mind played a game of see-saw. Which was better, fight or flight? He bit down on his pride and chose flight, striding towards the station.

Freech looked up, his expression disbelieving. "Stella, I'm not done with you."

John stopped, his body tense. Blood pulsed harder in his chest causing the veins in his neck and forearms to bulge. That internal see-saw pitched the other way. He spun around. "Did you have something else for me, LT?"

"Yeah. You need to read me all the serial numbers off your equipment so I can document it," Freech said snidely.

John's jaw strained and his lips drew tight as he walked directly towards the lieutenant.

Freech took a step back.

"Listen," John blurted, "troopers who wreck their cars do it in the line of duty. Have you forgotten, Lieutenant?" John leaned in a bit closer and pointed to the charred and crushed remains of a patrol car. "That car over there was Robbie's. Or have you forgotten him already? Or maybe you think the drunk should have killed him on *someone else's* shift so you wouldn't have to be *hassled* with the inventory."

Anger drove John beyond where he could stop himself. "And those other cars? You forget them as well?" John could see Freech had become apoplectic, but he didn't wait for a response. Instead, he pointed down the row of damaged patrol cars. "Those two got hit by drunks and Morsey's was used to take out an armed bank robber."

Freech's eyes grew wide as John came nearly nose-to-nose with the supervisor.

"Furthermore, *Lieutenant*…if you'd spent more than one year as a working trooper *before* you worked your way up the chain, you'd know crashing cars comes with the territory. *And* if I ever hear you talk shit about guys like Robbie, I will personally kick your lame ass right into the major's office. Trust me. That's one reprimand I would gladly sign."

John cleared his throat before lowering his voice to say, "You have a nice day with your *serial numbers*." When he pivoted away, he kept walking this time. He was willing to take a reprimand for his outburst. He'd call it letting off steam after the incident that damaged the car in the first place. But that's as far as it went. He wouldn't pay for a physical altercation, tempting as it may have been. Deep down, he was satisfied with his response, if for no other reason than it made up for all the times he'd bit his tongue and put up with the petulant lieutenant.

As John crossed the parking lot, he noticed Captain DeLeón standing at the back door of the station. He cleared his throat. "How are you, Captain?" John purposefully kept his tone humble.

"I'm fine, Stella. I should be asking how *you're* doing." DeLeón stared past John towards the row of damaged cars.

John looked back and watched Freech walk around his car and fumble through the stack of inventory sheets on his clipboard. He wondered why the butter-bar hadn't already bee-lined it to the major's office and filed a personnel complaint against John for the outburst.

"What is he doing, Captain?" John asked.

"Hell if I know. You think he might be looking for this?" Captain DeLeón held up John's vehicle inventory sheet.

John cocked his head sideways and looked puzzled.

"He was told not to mess with your car, Stella. I guess he couldn't help himself when he heard *you* crashed it."

John and the captain continued to watch the lieutenant scratch his head and stare at John's car, as if dumbfounded.

"Yeah, I kinda cussed him out a bit," John confessed.

DeLeón cast a stern look John's way. "You figured it was worth the counseling letter?"

John snickered. "Yeah, I did."

The captain put his hand on John's shoulder. "What'd ya expect from a guy who would do anything to get out of working back when he was a trooper." DeLeón smiled and shook his head. He opened his mouth as if to speak, but apparently caught himself and kept quiet.

Hell, John knew it wasn't DeLeón's policy to speak poorly of staff within the lower ranks, so he got it.

"Go on upstairs," DeLeón said. "I'll be up there in a few minutes. Rick and Florey are in my office."

John acknowledged the order with a nod and went inside, but he couldn't help but glance back to watch the captain walk towards the other end of the parking lot.

John found Florey and Rick in DeLeón's office having a conversation with Major Carris. The major thrust his hand out to shake John's. "Outstanding job yesterday! The colonel was briefed and wants to commend each of you for a job well done."

John took the major's hand and gave it a robust shake. "Thanks, Major." The glad-handed gesture reminded John of the way politicians shook hands while mugging for the cameras—a bit over the top.

"You guys hit the jackpot with that arrest yesterday," Carris remarked. "I've been on the phone with Tallahassee all morning. Seems your suspect is no ordinary doper."

"Yeah, it was quite the haul of kilos," John said.

"Not just that," Rick said, enthusiasm in his voice. "You guys captured Julio Mendoza Cortés. He's the nephew of one Juan Miguel Orejulla. The head of the Cali cartel. Our friends at the State Department had Julio transferred to the Federal Corrections lock-up downtown."

"He lawyered up with John and me last night. He wouldn't say anything," Florey said.

Rick shrugged. "Maybe, but those guys at State have a different protocol when it comes to interrogating suspects on the FBI Most Wanted List. And part of the Cali cartel."

"Damn. I didn't see that come across the teletype. What's the big secret?" John asked.

"Seems your boy decided to cooperate after he was told he would never leave the inside of a Federal prison," Rick said. "He's been wanted by the Feds for several years but hasn't been seen in the States for over five years. He owns a house on Star Island, but his cousins live there. Those boys at State were able to get the FBI to document him as a Cooperating Individual."

John couldn't believe it. "They got the nephew of the head of the Cali cartel to be a CI?”

“Evidently, it didn’t take much. Seems his wife and son are with the cousins at the Star Island home right now,” Rick said. “Both are here on overdue visas, so Cortés was faced with the threat of having all his assets frozen and seized by Uncle Sam. When we told him his family would be sent to immigration and locked up at Krome Detention Center, he suddenly decided to work with the FBI as a paid CI.”

“Paid?” Major Carris asked.

“Yeah. Unfortunately, it’s one of the best ways to get to the bigger fish. With the way the Cali group has its cells networked, this guy is proving to be a treasure trove of information. He’s singing like the nutless wonder he is.” Rick smiled at his own words.

“At least I know what to tell Joey when he asks about the testicles,” John muttered under his breath.

Florey cast him a sidelong look and chuckled.

“Oh, about that,” Rick said. “I got a call this morning from the marshal’s office. Seems the surgery didn’t take. So, Cortés is walking around on crutches wearing an adult diaper to keep the one he has left from falling out.”

John glanced at Florey, and the two began to laugh. John noticed even Major Carris allowed himself a smile at the mental image of Cortés reduced to diapers and crutches.

“So, where does this big arrest leave my troopers, Agent Lotz?” Major Carris frowned as he asked the question. “I want to be ready for questions from Tallahassee.”

“Well, Major, based on what Cortés is saying, we think we need to move pretty quickly on these dopers,” Rick explained. “Cortés tells us the cartel is setting up our doctor in a warehouse near Hialeah out on U.S. 27. Cortés also ‘fessed up that they are doubling down on their powder, cash, and plastic ventures. Cortés knows most of the cell organizers in South Florida. That’s significant, because we think he’s got the ability to convince anyone else we catch to do the right thing and cooperate.”

Rick’s frown deepened. “Seems Cortés has fallen in love with all things American and will do anything to keep his family safe and in the States.”

“Wow, this is a development, alright,” Florey said.

“And there’s more,” Rick said. “After we told him we knew of their secret plastic scam and intended to hunt them all down, it didn’t take long for him to figure out that anything he faces with the American justice system is still a better deal than what his uncle plans to do to him should he fail.”

"Outstanding," John exclaimed.

"Washington seems to be impressed, too," Rick added. "They want us to move and take these guys down. ASAP."

"So, what's *our* next move?" Major Carris asked.

The office door swung open and Captain DeLeón came inside, quickly closing the door behind him. "Major, have you told him yet?" DeLeón asked.

"Oh, yeah, I nearly forgot. John, these are for you." Major Carris reached in his pocket and pulled out a set of new car keys with a yellow inventory tag attached to them.

John was puzzled.

DeLeón smiled and patted John's shoulder. "Congratulations, kid, you're back in K-9."

"*What?* You're giving me back my dog?" John was elated by the surprise, but because he distrusted all things bureaucratic, he kept a lid on his emotions. Suspicious and still a bit confused, he didn't know what was behind this sudden change in policy. One minute they terminate the canine program, the next he's reinstated to a *newly* constituted canine program.

"For efficiency's sake, it seems Washington thought it would be best if a dog was assigned to the unit," Rick acknowledged. "They expect this to blow up fast should Cali get word that Cortés was arrested."

Major Carris pointed to the keys in John's hand. "Tallahassee was on a conference call this morning. Everyone agreed the quickest way to get it done is for you to go to the kennel and pick up your old canine. Those are the keys to one of the new K-9 vehicles that came in year before last. They've been parked in Broward County collecting dust, so we had one brought down this morning. You may as well have it."

John stared at the keys in his hand, unsure if he should allow himself to feel exhilarated at the news or remain suspect of Tallahassee's sudden acquiescence in reestablishing a K-9 team. The memory of giving up his four-legged partner was a wound not quite healed.

Florey leaned towards her partner and whispered in his ear. "It's kinda what you always wanted, isn't it?"

"Yeah, I just didn't think it would ever happen," John said. "I need to be honest here, Major. How do I know GHQ isn't going to make me give up the dog after I put my heart and soul into this again? I mean, I'm going to need some time to get up to speed—me and the dog."

Major Carris's expression told John he understood. "I can assure you that won't happen again, John. The colonel mentioned that he was considering a reinstatement of the entire program and making it permanent. Between you and me—and this stays in this room—I hear it's a done deal."

John couldn't have heard better news. Glancing at Florey, he allowed himself to let down a little and let her see in his face just how pleased he was.

"So, Rick, how much time do we have for John to prepare himself with the dog?" Major Carris asked.

"Not too long," Rick said. "The task force is already following a suspect that is supposed to meet up with a different cell member in a few days. We expect they'll exchange kilos for cash to the tune of half a million dollars." He gestured to include John and Florey. "We need you guys to make that stop. We can't let the dope hit the streets. And we *are not* letting that money disappear."

John wasn't surprised. Once a law enforcement agency knew about a large cache of drugs, they were obligated to at least try to keep it from working its way to the streets and eventually into the hands of kids. The money was icing on the cake. Nobody wanted the bad guys to walk off with the cash. Money was the lifeblood of the cartels. Taking their money was more crippling than taking their cocaine. And John had no problem delivering a crippling blow to dopers. When it came to their work and interfering with the drug trade, he and Florey were on the same page.

"Can you get your dog back in shape in a few days?" the major asked.

John waved off the major's concern. "Yes, sir. I'm sure the dog will pick it back up quickly. But what about the Feds' radios?"

"Look out the window," DeLeón said.

John went to the window behind the captain's desk. There in the parking lot below, parked next to John's old car, was a white van. Two FBI technicians were pulling out radios and installing them in John's new K-9 car. John laughed.

"What's so funny, Stella?" the major asked.

John shook his head and kept laughing. Lieutenant Freech stood by the van gesturing and pointing to his clipboard, as if the installation work was going on without his official okay. John laughed as the technicians ignored Freech's antics. It was as if Freech wasn't even there.

"You might as well write me that counseling letter now," John said.

The major looked confused, but DeLeón corralled Rick and his troopers towards the office door. "Yes, well… I think you all had better get going before something changes. Right now, we have some time for you guys to get your affairs in order." He stopped his fast talking long enough to clear his throat. "Go get that dog of yours, John, and anything else you need. And be sure Lieutenant Freech gets the purchase orders. For this operation, don't worry about authorization, but keep track of everything." As if he'd just thought of it, the captain added, "That also goes for overtime."

With so much to think about, John hadn't said a word as he, Florey, and Rick walked down the hall to the elevator. They were all quiet.

Rick broke the silence when the doors closed inside the elevator. "What are you guys worried about?"

"I've never seen any of these guys or this department so damn happy to work with other agencies," Florey mused. "Kinda makes me wonder if something is going to go wrong. GHQ in Tallahassee doesn't do bad news very well."

"Yeah, no shit," John said. "And to put a canine back into service and tell me *not* to worry about charging supplies or overtime? That's just weird."

"You can thank your governor," Rick said as the elevator doors opened. "He found out that the Patrol terminated their canine program but kept taking the budgeted funds for it. They kept quiet about it, too."

"How the hell did the governor find out?" John asked.

"Seems our director made inquiries to the governor at a luncheon," Rick explained. "When the governor was told that FHP had been using the funds to pay lieutenants instead of using it to find drugs, he was furious. Or, so I heard."

"*Lieutenants*?" Florey asked, incredulous. "They used that money to pay *lieutenants*?"

John squeezed his eyes nearly shut, feeling the familiar pounding in his chest. He picked up his pace as he headed towards the rear exit, his eyes transfixed through the glass door on the far end of the parking lot.

"Hey, John, slow down. I'm sure they're not done yet." Florey had broken into a near jog to catch up to him.

Through gritted teeth, he said, "I'm not worried about the car. I'm fixing to get my second counseling letter. Paying lieutenants? Guys like Freech. Are you kidding me?"

"I know, John. Believe me, I understand."

***

By late the next afternoon, John had been at Trebuchet Kennels training with his dog for ten hours. The session had started when Tomás Lopez, the kennel owner, had John's dog, Spec, brought up to the front and got her ready for training. For the last year and a half, Canine Spec had been in limbo, all because FHP had cancelled the Drug Interdiction Program.

Tomás kept up Spec's training and had even taken her to the Southeast United States Canine Trials for patrol apprehension and drug detection. Spec, one of the few female dog participants and the only female dog on the Patrol, took home the top trophy. Tomás had been quick to display her title in any publication willing to print it.

Allowing him to compete with the dogs was a concession the Patrol made when they asked Tomás to warehouse their animals. John—and everyone else—knew Tomás was a serious trainer. He'd won nearly every civilian title in working dog competitions throughout the nation. His dogs were regarded as some of the best, and Spec was in top shape.

John had a lot of respect for the trainer, who had come from Cuba as a boy and started his dog business with what Tomás called "a hope and a prayer." But now, it was one of the most respected, even revered kennels in the States. Tomás had started small on a stamp-size parcel of land in the Redland District, but now he ran a sprawling twenty-acre complex that included fifty kennels, mock houses, warehouses, cars, and a full array of training apparatuses.

Early on, John learned not to doubt Tomás' talent as a breeder and trainer. Despite his 5'6" frame, Tomás could—and would—handle the biggest and strongest breeds. His favorite was the Malinois. John had to repeat *Mal-in-wha* over and over until he got it right.

Tomás also liked the cousin to the Malinois, the Dutch Shepherd. Every trainer John knew boasted about having the best dogs, but John believed in Tomás. The guy would travel to Europe to hand pick dogs to meet specific requirements. He knew the dog's temperaments and capabilities, plus he had an uncanny knack at pairing the right dog with the right handler.

Tomás had handpicked Spec for John. A black and brown brindle-colored Dutch Shepherd, she was a maniac when it came to searching for people and drugs. Her ability to apprehend a suspect was like no other. For a medium-sized dog, she had no problem knocking down a full-grown man—a real crowd pleaser, too, when she'd launch like a missile from a full run and crash the decoy like a wrecking ball. Tomás enjoyed taking her to compete—and why not? She took home the trophy more often than not.

Spec was as happy to see John as he had been to see her. They got right to work, and the whole 10-hour day had been one training exercise in finding hidden drugs after another. She performed brilliantly. And so had John.

"Okay, Gringo," Tomás said, approaching John. "You take Spec and try to find the hides in the six cars I have lined up. I will tell you now, there's only one drug."

Tomás' challenges pushed John to the top of his game. That's the way it had to be. In the real world, cops had to trust their dogs. John was sure of Spec's abilities. If there were drugs somewhere, Spec would find them.

John called Spec to a heel as they walked back to the patrol car. She obediently paced along his side, leaning against his left leg, looking up, and waiting for John's next command.

"Hey, Gringo. You gonna put that bitch on a leash, or what?" Tomás yelled.

John grinned. Tomás had been calling him "gringo" for as long as they had known each other. To Tomás, it was a term of endearment, so John never took offense. In fact, he was used to responding to the moniker.

"Quit being such a rafter," John quipped, using his nickname for Tomás. "I think she can handle it."

He stopped at the front of the first car and commanded Spec to sit. He leaned to his left as she tensed, muscles trembling in anticipation, and waited for the command. John spoke softly. "Easy, girl… Ready? Dope-Seek!"

With the command to seek out the odor of drugs, Spec bolted towards the car, then slowed on her own as she worked her nose low, then high, scanning the air around the vehicle for any number of imprinted scents she was trained to find.

John followed behind to watch for the dog's alert.

As she finished sniffing around the first car, John pointed to the next. Again, she slowed and detailed the exterior of the vehicles with her nose. The process repeated with the third car. Spec began sniffing at the front bumper and continued towards the driver's door. It was just behind that door that Spec stopped. Her head canted sideways as she inhaled deeply and took in the familiar odor of drugs. She immediately faced the car door and began scratching at the seam between the bottom of the door and the car's frame. She'd found it.

John grabbed her collar and pulled back as she fought with him to keep scratching. She was fixated on the odor, her whole body tensed and focused.

John reached with his other hand and opened the door, releasing his hold on her.

Spec leapt into the training vehicle.

John quickly closed the door and watched as Spec now scanned the air in the car. She moved from one side of the vehicle to the other, finally identifying the source of the odor. It was coming from the bottom cushion of the back seat. She pounced, then furiously scratched at the vinyl padded cushion.

John reached behind his back where he kept her favorite reward. He had wedged the heavy rubber pipe in his waistband under his belt. He drew the toy forward and tossed it into the car.

Spec snapped her head to the side and caught it before it landed on the seat. She jumped out of the car towards John, who caught the end of the toy and began playing a furious game of tug-of-war with her. Spec pulled and twisted as she tried to wrench the pipe from John's grasp. John did everything he could to not let go or get pulled to the ground.

Occasionally, he would purposely let her have the pipe, but she would always return, rushing up to his side and bear-hugging him while thrusting her snout up, demanding he not quit the game.

"That's a girl, Spec. Good girl!" John couldn't have been happier. She had passed every test they threw at her. Under the seat, Tomás revealed a small one-gram bag of cocaine.

"What you think, Tomás? She ready? Did she pass?" asked John sarcastically, his confidence now boiling over.

"Damn, Gringo, I already knew the dog was ready. What did you think? This was for her?" Tomás began laughing. "Hell, John, this day of training was for *you*. I already know the dog works, you Gringo shithead!"

They laughed as they put Spec up in the cage in John's new K-9 patrol car.

"Let her rest. She's had quite a day," Tomás said. "You remembered a lot of handling, John."

"Yeah, man, it's been a while." John sighed. "But there is nothing I love more than working a dog. I'm happy as hell to get her back. Hopefully, you didn't give her any bad habits."

Tomás flashed a shocked look. "Bad habits? Like what?"

John couldn't hold back a grin. "Like, she still eats dog food, doesn't she? Or have you been feeding her rice and beans?"

Tomás chuckled. "No, dumbass! She is healthy and eats regular dog food. Okay, maybe every now and then I throw her a fried plantain."

John knew his friend liked to tease. To Tomás, canine training was even more than a way of life—it was a belief system. He had unflinching respect for Tomás' work ethic. The only thing that mattered was the performance of the animal and the handler. Too much was at stake to provide a dog with any defects, and it wasn't only cops who wanted these highly skilled animals. Tomás had built his reputation in the civilian market for providing top grade dogs for personal protection, industry guard dogs, and even a few bomb detection dogs for the military.

But the dopers wanted them, too. Drug traffickers would use them to see if their new ways to conceal drugs would make their shipments "police dog proof."

To most kennels, it would be all too easy to sell to anyone with no questions asked. After all, fully trained dogs would carry a hefty ten-thousand dollar price tag. Easy money for a kennel.

But not for Tomás. For him, it was personal—dopers gave Hispanics a bad name. He considered the *marimberos* to be nothing but a scourge in the Latin community. So, it was a moral obligation to provide the best trained animals to the police.

John looked at his watch and realized the time. "Hey, man, it's getting late. I got one hell of a week coming up."

Tomás nodded. "By the way, a guy came out here last month looking for a dog. He said he wanted a drug dog for his business to check his employees. I thought it was kinda strange, but I still let him come out and take a look at a few dogs."

"Was that a problem, *hombre*?" John asked.

"Well, it wouldn't have been a problem, except this guy drives up in a Ford F350 with the doper rims and chrome pipes and the works. He gets out wearing a Presidential Rolex and gold chains two inches thick around his neck! Plus, he didn't look like he'd ever worked a real day in his life. He says he's got a warehouse by the airport and exports clothes to South America."

John laughed. "You didn't believe him, did you?"

"Hell, no," Tomás said. "This guy opens a brief case with bundles of twenties. All rubber banded together. He said he didn't care how much. All he wanted to know was when he could have the dog."

John frowned, knowing banks didn't wrap bills in rubber bands. "So, did you tell him to leave?"

"Yeah, but he called me again and wants to come back. Says he'll pay double, and now he wants two dogs," Tomás said. "So, I'm wondering… do you think you could find out if he's mixed up in something?"

"Yeah, I can do that. You got a plate number or name?"

"Yeah, man, what you think? That Cubans are stupid or something?" Smiling, Tomás put his arm around John's shoulder, and they headed to the office. "I had Louisa put his information in a file. I pretended to need it if I was going to consider his offer. I also got the tag off his truck when he wasn't looking."

As he went into the office behind Tomás, John saw the plaques and trophies covering the walls. The last time he'd been here, the competition awards had only taken up one wall and a small shelf. Many had been added.

"Damn, Tomás." John gestured around the room, taking in the clutter of trophies and awards. "You're going to need a new office if you keep winning competitions."

Tomás grinned widely. "Look over there." He pointed to the far corner of the office as he grabbed a folder off his desk. "That whole corner is *your* dog."

John stepped closer. He scanned the awards hanging one above another, eight in all. Two top awards for apprehension and six awards for drug detection. Five of the drug awards were for Top Dog, a designation reserved for animals exceeding the minimum benchmarks for first place. John's gaze stopped on the last plaque, one for second place. "Hey, what's the second place one all about?"

"That was my screw up. I lost my concentration on the pattern and she missed one of the finds," Tomás mumbled. "Trust me, it wasn't her fault."

John smirked. "So, the rafter can actually make a mistake?"

"Yeah, Gringo. I'm still friends with you. Isn't that proof enough?" Tomás chuckled, and handed John the file. "Here is everything I got on this guy. Maybe you can check him out. If he is a doper, then you do what you got to do. If he is legitimate, then let me know. I can make twenty grand on this buffoon."

"I'll look into it," John said. He opened the door and walked out into the ninety-degree Florida heat. "When are we going fishing, Rafter?"

"Fishing? We've never been fishing. You got a spot to go to?" Tomás asked, following him.

"I sure do. I think you'll love it." John climbed into his car.

Tomás flashed him a squinting look, as if he suspected he was taking the bait. "Okay, where would that be, you Gringo shit?"

John savored the moment. "Oh, a nice little island about ninety miles south of here."

"Fuck you, Stella." Tomás chuckled, and raised both his hands in mock surrender. Turning away, he shook his head and headed toward his office.

Chapter Six

Off the coast of Miami, south of Key Biscayne National Park, the freighter moved sluggishly towards the first markers indicating the shipping lane to Miami's Government Cut, the main channel into the Port of Miami and the Miami River. The captain had made this trip so many times he seldom thought twice about running close to the reef line. He had learned just how close he could get without triggering any suspicion from a nosy U.S. Customs radar operator or the Coast Guard. This moonless night was no different. He quickly reduced his speed by half. The rusted hulk, scarred with chipped and peeling paint, crawled along, slowly bobbing up and down with the rise and fall of the seas.

"Macho…macho!" the ship's VHS radio blared.

Arriving now at the pre-selected location, the captain had expected the call. "Dígame, dígame," the captain responded.

"En tres minutos, no más," answered the unknown voice.

The captain looked towards the west. Even from his elevated vantage point high above the waterline in the ship's wheelhouse, he could barely make out the breaking water shimmering against the bows of boats approaching in the darkness—seven offshore speedboats coming in fast.

The captain turned to his first mate and crew, and directed them to open the portside door. The order sent the crew scrambling towards the ship's stern, reaching what had been painstakingly designed to look like a piece of metal welded onto the backside of the freighter along its portside but below its stern deck. Like many of the old freighters bringing in rice and wood from Haiti and South America, this tub had its share of patches and fixes to the hull. But this one was faked. Moving aside the two support beams exposed two handles and latching pins on each side of the four-by-four foot plate. The crew rushed along the metal gangway, funneling in through the watertight door to the storage locker under the rear deck. They quickly dismantled the false metal supports holding the door in place, each constructed to look like the ship's support structure. They carefully pushed the plate to the side, exposing a large, makeshift portal.

As the first speedboat came alongside the freighter, a buoy attached to a rope was thrown overboard. Attached to each rope were twenty-five nylon sacks, each filled with fifty kilos of pure cocaine. Each sack trailed its buoy as the go-fast crews gaffed the lines and hoisted in the rope.

After the first boat had collected their chain of bags, the next boat immediately pulled up, and the process was repeated. The whole operation took no more than 15 minutes. As soon as the last of the bags was overboard, the freighter crew replaced the fake door and put back the pins and support beams.

The captain didn't need to issue any further orders. The crew knew what to do. The first mate grabbed a bucket of sea water mixed with liquid iron and soaked the entire door. By the time they reached the Miami River, the liquid iron would work its magic and the newly formed rust would more than hide any sign of their handiwork.

The captain waited for the first mate to signal him with a flashlight, delivering the message the job was done. The captain powered up the lumbering freighter back to speed and continued towards the docks on the Miami River. He turned to watch as the armada of speedboats headed inland back into the vast darkness and disappearing into the bay.

***

John loaded Spec into the car, having arranged to meet Florey for breakfast at Tony's Donut Shop known for serving up a great all-American breakfast and home-cooked meals. It was also a local gathering spot for Homestead's local business leaders and farmers. It seemed every time they met there for breakfast, some comic genius would make a wisecrack about cops and donuts. Florey seemed able to brush off that talk, but John had no patience for these jokers and hated the crude association. That was why he never ate what most cops jokingly called "energy rings."

"Hey," Florey said.

Hearing her voice, John lifted his head. He'd been holding his head in both hands.

"You okay?" she asked.

John sat upright. "Yeah, I'm fine. Just a little tired."

Peering into his face, she said, "Well, you look like crap."

"Thanks. It was a long day at training with Spec. When we got home, I had forgotten all about an off-duty job I had watching the power company replace light poles." He rubbed his eyes. "It was one of those hurry-up-and-wait jobs. I hardly got any sleep."

"You can't keep running at full speed, John. Take some time for yourself every now and then." Florey finished her sentence and winced.

Probably because she sounded like someone's mom. He stretched in the booth seat and exhaled. "I'd love to, but the salary doesn't pay the bills, not when I'm trying to stash money away to buy a house someday. I'll never do it on FHP's salary alone."

"I know. How far along are you?" she asked.

He diverted his attention to scan the menu. "About twelve thousand. I figure I'll be in good shape when I got fifty."

"Well, you don't have to do it all in one year. Pace yourself," Florey said, moving her coffee cup towards the end of the table so the waitress passing by with the pot could fill it.

She was right. John knew that. But after the training and working a midnight off-duty shift, he was too tired to care. A quick breakfast and some more coffee usually did the trick. He and Florey had learned to find their second wind after long hours and endless workdays.

"Did Rick call yet?" John asked.

"Yeah. At 5:30 this morning. We're meeting the DEA guys at the Museum of Science in Miami," she said. "They have word of a load of coke coming in out of Key Biscayne."

That news perked him up. He slid his menu aside when the waitress returned with his order: scrambled eggs, bacon, and a side of grits with extra butter.

Florey looked at him expectantly.

"You going to order anything, sweetie?" the waitress asked Florey.

Florey smiled. "No, thanks, not this morning."

"Well, if you change your mind, you let me know." The waitress headed to the booth across the way.

"You not eating?" John asked as he mixed his eggs with a healthy dose of ketchup. He laughed at the face Florey made watching what she'd often called his culinary science project. As southern as eggs and ketchup were, John didn't understand why Florey couldn't stomach the two together.

"I ate. Toast and jam with my coffee earlier."

John swallowed down a heaping forkful of the yellow and red mixture. "No wonder you stay so trim, kiddo. You eat like a mouse."

She snickered. "Yeah, well, I don't know why you haven't ballooned your waistline eating as much as you do."

John began stirring butter into his grits. "God, I hope I don't ever become like some of those guys whose stomachs rub up against their steering wheels." He shook his head and smiled at the sight of his fork loaded with buttery grits.

It didn't take long to polish off his plate of food and order two coffees to go. John followed Florey along Bayshore Drive toward the City of Miami and the Museum of Science. They were meeting there, John knew, because aside from the occasional school field trip, Miami's oldest museum was seldom used. It was the perfect place for law enforcement meetings, since it was tucked away in an untouched hardwood hammock preserve. Entering through the narrow winding drive, John followed Florey's car into a mostly-deserted parking lot.

After checking on Spec, he and Florey joined the DEA agents who were already grouped together under a stand of gumbo-limbo trees, with their peeling reddish-brown trunks and limbs reaching high above like giant outstretched arms. Besides the thick canopy they provided, the trees also gave the area an almost haunting aura.

"Hey, guys," Rick said, lifting his hand in greeting. "Damn, John. You look like shit."

"So I've been told," John muttered.

"I've been on his case all morning," Florey said, her motherly tone returning.

Let 'em talk, John thought. He was too tired to care.

Rick grinned and pulled out his notebook and operational plan. "Okay, last night we got word from our informant from the Miami Beach chase that a shipment of coke came into Key Biscayne last night by go-fast. Probably a dope-on-a-rope type off-load. We checked with Customs and the Coast Guard, and the only vessel in the area was the Managua, some ragged tub of a ship registered out of Haiti."

He looked up from his notes and remarked about the ship's long reputation as a dirty freighter. "So, our informant tells us the coke will be moved off the Key and delivered to a warehouse in Hialeah, supposedly in a yellow or tan colored van." Rick handed copies of the plan to the troopers. "That's all we know."

"How confident are we about the source?" John asked.

"Really confident," Rick said. "That ball-less wonder from the beach is still singing like a bird. Our friends from the State Department have been passing along the info."

Florey spoke up. "Is there any more information about this van they're using?"

Rick shook his head. "Unfortunately, the source only knows that it should be driven by a Latino male, and it was either yellow or tan."

"No problem," John scoffed. "I mean, how many yellow or tan vans driven by a Latino male heading to Hialeah can there be?" Only hundreds.

"I know, I know," Rick said, amused, "but it's all we got and we have to try. The source was adamant about the shipment leaving the Key at 9 AM. They're planning to catch the peak of rush hour traffic and avoid police. They hope. I guess they figure they'll blend into the masses and sneak by."

Scanning the documents Rick had handed out, John said, "Alright. I guess me and Florey should wait on the Key and see what drives by."

"Exactly. You'll have us in the area," Rick said. "I'm going to put a few agents at the end of the Key and see what comes out of the neighborhoods. The rest of us will try to blend into beach traffic. We'll be on DEA frequency 15," he reminded the agents. "Make sure everyone is on the right channel."

"I guess we better head out," John said. "It's almost 8:25. I don't want to miss these guys."

Taking John's cue, the agents shook hands all around and headed to their vehicles.

"So, John, where do you want to set up?" Florey asked when they got to their patrol cars.

"There's a vacant parking lot exit from the beach on Crandon Boulevard. We can park there and watch everything that passes by. It has good cover in case the bad guys have anyone looking for cops. It'll be perfect." John remembered the location from his high school days, when he'd used the spot to hide from truant officers.

"Okay, I'll follow you."

They got in their cars and joined the caravan leaving the museum parking lot.

John drove past Brickell Drive onto the Rickenbacker Causeway, which was flanked on its north side by some of the most modern and pricey condos in the state—and built with drug dollars laundered in the many start-up banks that had polluted the Miami landscape over the last dozen years. That fact was never lost on John. He'd spent his youth on the water and watched the downtown landscape explode into a multitude of skyscrapers, each one exceeding the architectural benchmarks of the last. Many buildings sat vacant, too. But filling them with tenants wasn't the objective. Laundering the drug money through shell investment corporations while having them built was the goal. To him, these drug-financed buildings had always seemed like tall, dark monoliths eerily standing watch over the bay.

John and Florey entered the first bridge connecting the thin strip of islands together that made up Crandon Park Beach, the Village of Key Biscayne, and Cape Florida Park.

As they crossed the second bridge onto the island of Key Biscayne, John noted the Crandon Marina where he'd scraped barnacles and algae off of boat bottoms as a kid for a few dollars each. He'd ridden his bike to the marina or caught a ride with one of his older cousins. The old timers had long since moved on. Now, every slip seemed to be occupied with large, brand-new yachts or speedboats. The go-fast boats, usually modified Cigarette boats whose engines had been tweaked for higher performance, had become common among the "newly rich" in Miami.

John found the unused exit from the Crandon Park Beach onto the boulevard and parked behind a hedge of sea grape bushes.

Florey pulled in next to him, so they both had a bird's eye view of the passing traffic leaving the Key.

"Hey, how did you know about this exit ramp?" Florey asked, rolling down her window. "As many years as I've been out here, I've never noticed it."

"When I was in high school, I used to come out here at night with dates. That entrance gate has a broken latch. You just pull the pin and it opens up." John kept his eyes on the passing traffic as he spoke.

"I bet you were one popular dude in school, weren't ya?" she teased.

"Yeah, real popular. Just ask Rick."

John momentarily took his gaze off the boulevard and glanced at Florey. "His dad found me and his sister out on the beach. Not the best memory I've had out here."

Florey snorted a laugh. "Geez, John. You mean you haven't changed since high school?"

"Change? Why *should* I change?"

The crackle of the DEA radio grabbed his attention.

"Okay. Stand by, FHP. I just had a bunch of traffic go by—including three vans," the agent announced. "One is cream colored and two are tan. I'm trying to catch up. Give me a second."

John sat up in his seat, checking Spec to make sure she was awake. With the sudden attention, she got to all fours and licked his ear through the bars of the dog cage.

John refocused on cars and vans passing him by while Spec continued to lick his ear.

"Hey, Florey," he called out. "When the traffic goes by, pull out and take one of the vans. Try to get a violation on it and pull it over." John scanned every approaching vehicle coming out of the Village of Key Biscayne.

"Will do," Florey said, rolling up her window.

"Okay, FHP…we're passing Crandon Park now," the radio blared.

John put both hands on the wheel. He could see the cluster of traffic the DEA was observing as it approached. The first few cars went by as John's radar clocked them at 62 miles per hour.

Perfect, John thought. The road had a forty-five mile per hour limit, and if the rest of traffic would follow behind at the same speed, then finding probable cause to pull someone over would be that much easier.

The next several cars went by just as fast. They were followed by a tan Chevrolet van. John caught a glimpse of the driver, a black woman. He quickly looked at Florey and shook his head. Not that one.

The next van that passed was the cream colored one. A beat-up Chrysler Town and Country. The driver was a gray-haired Hispanic male.

John motioned to Florey to pull out as another van drove past. That van was driven by a fair-skinned elderly woman. John wasn't taking any chances.

John picked up his DEA radio and called Florey. "Take the last van, Florey. She was traveling 58 miles per hour. I'll get that Chrysler rust bucket."

"Ten-four," Florey responded.

John guided his squad car seamlessly into traffic and accelerated. Spec had immediately picked up on the tension in John's voice and sudden increase in speed. She'd learned by trial and error to brace her body in the corner of the cage and counter each of the car's sudden movements, much like a surfer's body undulating to the rise and fall of the ocean while maintaining position on the board. John maneuvered through the spaces between the speeding cars.

As he approached the Chrysler, he noticed that the backdoor windows had been crudely painted over with white brush strokes crisscrossing the glass panels. He moved into the next lane and drove alongside the van to get a glimpse of the driver through the side window. He confirmed his earlier impression of an older male driver, probably in his early to mid-fifties. He appeared to be alone in the vehicle, but a homemade partition behind the driver's seat blocked any view to the rear of the van. John held his speed and clocked the van traveling 55 mph in a 45 zone. The van's driver had locked his gaze straight ahead, telling John the guy was pretending not to notice the marked patrol car alongside him.

"Good enough," he said aloud.

John reduced his speed and maneuvered behind the van, activating his blue overhead lights and sounding his siren.

He waited, but there was no change in the van's speed or direction. He decided to give the old guy just a few more seconds to do something. The last thing he wanted was another chase.

John picked up the mic. "Florey, I think I got the van. He's not stopping. We are northbound approaching the second bridge."

Florey said that she would pass up her van and move ahead through traffic to come alongside him. "I'll get in front of him once we clear this bridge."

Boxing in a car was against FHP Policy, but John knew a chase wasn't worth it, either. John's emergency equipment continued its rapid-fire light show and piercing two-tone serenade.

Florey came up on the passenger side of the van. "The driver is glancing at his mirrors now, John, like he just got it that he's the one being followed. He's clutching the wheel in a death grip. I opened my window. I'm waving at him now, and he's looking frantic. He won't make a break for it now."

Sure enough, John eased his speed to match the van slowing down and pulling onto the grassy median. Florey soon pulled behind John.

John opened his door and used his public-address system to call the driver back to him. He knew not to approach unless he had to. He never knew when suspects might unexpectedly go on the offensive and fight, or even use their vehicle as a weapon. Hyper-attentive now, he worked from his training and experience, watching every movement and listening to every word, always anticipating the need to take defensive moves.

The driver's door opened slowly, creaking most of the way and stopping only after a loud pop.

John tried not to flinch at the sharp noise.

Slowly, the gray-haired driver got out and stepped away from the door. John noted the guy's worn painter's pants, white T-shirt, and cap.

"Come on back here, sir. How are you today?" John acted as casual as possible, doing his best to treat this as just another traffic stop for a simple speed violation.

"Con permiso, mi Heffe. I peekie poco inglish," the driver said.

In his best Spanish, John asked for the driver's registration, insurance, and license.

The driver carefully pulled his wallet from his front pocket. Despite his age, the old guy was in good shape. John noticed two tattoos on the driver's hands. In the web of each hand, between the thumb and index finger, he had a makeshift cross on one hand and two dots on the other. The dark black color and crisp lines had long ago faded and blurred into a dull, greenish-blue hue.

John looked at Florey. She nodded, letting him know she also recognized the primitive tattoos common among inmates held in Castro's prisons.

John told the driver he'd been stopped for speeding, and the man said he understood. Florey walked the man to the rear of John's car, where she began to issue the citation.

John looked on, noticing that the driver kept turning back to look at the van, worry in his eyes. Based on the body language, John saw a solid indicator of a guilty conscience.

John grabbed his leash and cracked open the rear door of his car.

Spec bounded towards her handler.

"Easy girl," said John. "You're getting the leash for this one. There's way too much traffic."

Spec calmed down when she heard John's voice. He clipped on her leash and grabbed the rubber hose used to reward her. John breathed deeply to calm himself. It had been a while since he'd worked with a dog on the street.

John walked the dog to the front of the van and paused to check for traffic. While standing at the bumper, John saw two unmarked cars parked on top of the bridge behind them. DEA was staying far enough away to not let their presence be known.

The driver was staring hard at John's dog. The look on the driver's was face quickly went from stressed to panicked. Florey picked up on the body language as well, sensing the man's heightened fear. She managed to divert his attention to her ticket book and away from John as she explained the citation and stalled for time.

"Come on, girl. Let's do this by the numbers." John got Spec to sit at the front of the van and wait for a command. John looked down and whispered, "Dope-Seek."

Spec bolted forward, then slowed into a methodical sniff of the front bumper. By the time she reached the driver's door, she was in full alert. Her scratching pulled off a chunk of flaked paint on the van's door.

John moved her to the rear doors, and she took one sniff at the door seam and quickly stood on her rear legs and began scratching furiously. John threw down the rubber hose and Spec immediately retrieved it. As John played tug-of-war with his furry partner, he couldn't help but smile as the adrenaline rush made him laugh out loud.

As he put Spec back in the rear of the patrol car, he winked at Florey and gave her a thumbs-up sign.

John went back to the van and opened the rear door. The chemical odor emanating from the illicit cargo was thick and pungent, nearly making him short of breath. He closed the door and turned to give Florey a second thumbs-up sign. Then he quietly walked up behind the driver.

Florey calmly put her ticket book away.

He knew the old guy never saw it coming. John grabbed him by his shoulder and pinned him against Florey's car in an arm lock. Within seconds, Florey had him handcuffed and sat him on the ground.

"So, how much?" asked Florey.

"It's loaded. Stem to stern. More than I've ever seen during a traffic stop. Let's put him in your car so we can process this. Oh, and make sure you turn off your radios." John pointed to his ear to indicate to his partner that he didn't want the old guy hearing any DEA broadcasts while in her car.

Florey opened the rear door of her car, patted the guy down, and sat him behind the police cage and seat belted him in. John also noticed she turned up her air conditioning after turning off her radios. Of course, Florey would want the old man to be comfortable. He could be sitting there for a good while.

Before joining John at his patrol car, she turned and double-checked on her prisoner. He was sitting, slumped in his seat, tears running down his cheeks.

John went back to his car and notified DEA that the van was loaded and they would go through the motions of a routine drug bust.

When John's cell phone rang, he wasn't surprised it was Rick.

"Hey man! How much is there?" Excitement had raised Rick's voice an octave.

"Brother, it's loaded from top to bottom, front to back. Hundreds of kilos. I'm sure this wreck must have air shocks to keep it from scraping the pavement!"

"You need us to do anything?" Rick asked.

"Yeah, you're damn right. Someone's gotta help us load up this evidence. I can't fit it all in my patrol car. Spec will go nuts!" John said, laughing.

Rick offered a plan.

John got off the phone and told Florey to take the driver to the FHP station for processing. She soon got the prisoner out of the area.

Rick arrived before the other agents he'd arranged to load the cocaine into their vehicles. He took charge of counting the bricks, as one by one, agents pulled up and opened their trunks and loaded the bricks, all of which were stamped with the figure of a black scorpion.

"Total count, twelve hundred and fifty kilos," Rick said.

Simple math told John the street value of the haul was twenty-five million dollars. Speechless, he stared at Rick, who also knew what it was worth. No words needed. It was a good haul, more than expected. John was pleased for Rick. As the case agent in charge, Rick had to be satisfied. No injuries, plus they were confirming the information they got was accurate and paying off.

"How you figure it got out here on the island?" John asked.

"Probably a night run from the Bahamas or a freighter," Rick answered. "That's about twenty-five bags, if they had been tied together on a rope."

"Seems like a lot," John said.

"One day, I'll have to show you some of the surveillance tapes we have at DEA. Twenty-five is about right. Sometimes a little more. Sometimes a little less," Rick said, giving John a friendly punch in the arm. "Come on. Let's get going."

John called in another trooper to sit with the van and wait for the tow truck; he would follow Rick and the agents with their cocaine-laden cars to the DEA evidence locker at their office in North Dade.

Once there, John managed to get a head start on his paperwork. After the kilos were safely locked up and Rick had signed John's evidence form marked CONFIDENTIAL, John headed to the FHP station to interview the driver, with Rick following in his own car.

John found Florey doing her report in the squad room.

"Hey, Florey, where's the old man?" John asked.

"In the interrogation room. Figured I'd leave him alone with his thoughts before we hit him with reality," she explained.

John got her point. Letting a suspect ruminate in the interrogation room usually had one of three effects. Sometimes, they made up a completely implausible story, or they realized they had better cooperate and cut themselves a break. But the smart ones just said nothing and called a lawyer.

"I've got a hunch that with the amount of dope in the van, and the guy being older, he's likelier than not to spill the beans and tell everything he knows," Florey said. "But you never know."

When Rick came into the room, John opened the uniform locker and took out an FHP raid jacket. "You want to have a swing at the interrogation, Rick?" John handed him the jacket. "Here, you're now an FHP detective."

"You guys don't have detectives." Rick took the jacket and put in on.

"We know that, but do you really think the old guy does?" John teased.

Rick pulled the jacket tight and took off his DEA badge and ID card, leaving them in a desk drawer.

John followed Rick through the interrogation room door, where the old man was holding his head in his hands. Tears had made a small pool on the tabletop. John caught Rick's eye, knowing Florey's hunch was right.

John stayed quiet and left the interview to Rick, who began interviewing the suspect in perfect Spanish. Language was one of Rick's strong points, and it also got him special assignments in South America. More than he cared for, as John recalled. Rick spoke Spanish so well, most people refused to believe he wasn't Latino.

After thirty minutes, it was clear the old man was just a mule paid five thousand dollars to drive the van from a parking lot in Cape Florida Park to a warehouse in Hialeah. If he encountered the police, he had a number to call and the lawyer would do the rest. The number and an address were on a piece of paper wadded up in his pants pocket.

When Rick asked why he didn't want to make the call, the aging mule shrugged and said he knew they would kill him. He was from Cuba and that's what they did with mules that got caught.

Rick wrote down the address and the number the driver could have called.

The old man buried his head in his hands again and sobbed.

John had seen plenty, and figured the guy was hoping someone would show some mercy. He left the room with Rick to give the man a break from the questions.

"Listen. Part of me says this guy should go down for the crime," Rick said. "The other part says we should call the FBI and see if they want to do anything with him. What do you guys think?"

Looking at Florey, John shrugged. "I have to charge him with the state trafficking offenses. If the FBI wants to adopt the case later, that's fine with me. He's going to pay for his stupidity one way or the other. What about you, Florey? You care either way?"

"That's not a problem for me," she answered. "We'll need to file in state court or someone down south will definitely know something is up with the case. First thing they'll figure is that the Feds are involved."

"So, let me make a phone call," Rick said. "Here, John, take this jacket. For a minute, I actually felt like I was an underpaid public servant." Grinning, he grabbed his gun and credentials and walked outside to use his cell phone.

John and Florey went on with their paperwork, and by the time they were finished, Rick had made his calls and had answers about handling the case. SAC McKenna would adopt the case eventually, but the old man should be charged through the state. They'd wait till just before the 90-day speedy trial date expired and take over the case, filing the charges federally before the state was compelled by law to begin their trial. That gave Rick and his people more time to work the case.

So far, no one had any idea where the German chemist was. They also didn't know to what extent the Colombians had organized their efforts to swamp America with plastic cocaine. As for the Federal authorities, everyone knew the president wanted this issue rooted out from beginning to end. That meant confiscating the cartel's cocaine and finding where their money was. Taking away their finances hurt the cartels the most. But locating that chemist needed immediate attention.

By the time John and Florey were updated, Major Carris and Captain DeLeón had come down from their offices to congratulate their troopers.

"Agent Lotz, what do you think? Should these two be put in for the Narcotic Officer of the Year award?" the major asked with a beaming smile.

John shifted his weight from one foot to the other and glanced at Florey, who didn't look enthusiastic, either. Like John, she didn't care for all this recognition.

"Absolutely, Major," Rick said. "That's the best idea I've heard in a while."

John rolled his eyes. Didn't anyone care that he and Florey were self-conscious and didn't like them all staring at them? But no one was interested in his input.

Florey's rib jab compelled him to plaster on a smile. "We'd be honored,

Major," she said, wearing her best political grin. She shook the major's hand, and John followed suit. Florey was so much better at these things than he could ever be.

The major repeated his congratulations and left the room for the elevator to his office. Captain DeLeón stayed behind, crossing his arms and shaking his head.

"Okay, enough of the ass-kissing," DeLeón said. "Let's get back to business. Rick, is there anything else our guys need to be doing?"

"I think we're doing all we can on this end," Rick said. "We have countless agents and analysts working on the informant and the logistics." He paused, and the room went quiet. "Again, our main concern is the whereabouts of our chemist. We know he's here in Miami somewhere. We hope today's arrest might bring up some leads. Our counterparts in Colombia and the State Department boys are working on tracking him down. And both of the chemists' families. All we can do is keep doing what we have been."

"Very well. You guys have heard enough bullshit for one day, so finish up here and get out of my hair." DeLeón took long strides to the door and was almost out of the room before turning and giving them a distinct wink.

As the door closed, John turned to Florey and Rick and thrust his arms out from his sides. "Narcotics Officer of the Year award? Really?"

"You guys deserve it," Rick said with a shrug. "Besides, it's exactly what we need to mask the Feds' involvement. It's like icing on the cake. The longer we can keep the Feds out of the picture, the cartel will be inclined to keep doing what they do. As soon as we show up, those families are at a much higher risk."

"Alright. I get it. I'm in for the dog and pony show. May as well get a plaque, 'cause we ain't getting paid for shit!" John laughed loudly at his own joke.

"Listen, in the meantime," Rick said, "I think we'll need to follow up on that address the old man had and see what's up with that warehouse."

Suddenly, John remembered the favor Tomás had asked. "Damn. That reminds me, Rick. I got a file in the car from a friend of mine. Says he met this guy that has doper written all over him. That's all I know. When you get a chance, do you think you can run his ID and vehicle through your computer system and see what comes up?"

"Sure," Rick said, "not a problem. I'll give it to the analysts when I go by the office on the way home."

John left with Rick, stopping to get the file out of his car. He filled Rick in on the details of what Tomás had told him. Rick seemed interested in the fact that the man wanted two dogs to sniff drugs and was willing to pay double for them.

Rick gave the file a quick shake and left for the DEA office.

When John and Florey had finished booking the old man into the county jail, John's cell phone went off. "It's Rick," John told Florey before answering. "Hey, man. Miss me already?"

"Very funny. I just dropped your file off at the analyst's office. Did you happen to run that tag on the F-350 through your system?" Rick asked.

"No. I just gave you what I had. Why? Is there a problem?"

"Only that the tag comes back to the same address that the old man had in his pocket."

John began running scenarios through his head, each one playing in quick succession.

"John? You still there?" Rick asked.

"Yeah, but I was just thinking we better take a look at that address ASAP. Just to make sure we aren't missing more dope."

"Agreed. But we should put it under surveillance first and see what goes in and out of that place," Rick said. "I have a call into the SAC's office. Give me a few to work on that. Why don't you and Florey come up to the DEA office? I should know something by the time you get here."

John agreed and hung up the phone.

A few minutes later, they were in their patrol cars for the short ride to the DEA office. It occurred to John he should call Tomás and tell him to forget about any deal with his suspicious-looking customer, but then he decided it was better to wait to see what developed first.

Rick was waiting in the parking lot with SAC McKenna.

"We got here as fast as we could," John said, getting out of the car.

McKenna stepped forward to shake hands with both of them as they stood in a cluster away from other people. "Rick filled me in on the development concerning the F-350 and the address in your mule's pocket," McKenna said. "Great work. I just got off the phone with the FBI. We're setting up surveillance on the place. Let's see what we can find out by snooping. If we can develop anything into a warrant, I think we should take the place down." McKenna paused and gestured toward them. "I'm hoping both of you would join in on the surveillance. Rick will have one of the undercover electric company vans so you can take the dog with you."

As if on cue, Rick immediately turned away and headed to the motor pool.

"Sir, we have to let the captain know what's up," John said. "I'm not sure the FHP wants us on a surveillance."

"You leave that to me, John," the SAC said. "It's important to have the canine there just in case we need to run a sniff on the building or cars. Anything could be going on there and it'd be nice to have the dog around."

"We understand, sir," Florey said.

"John, tell me about your trainer, Thomas. Is he someone you trust?"

"Absolutely, sir. He's the best at what he does," John said.

McKenna paused for a moment. "You think he would help us?"

"Well, that's just it, sir. Tomás is waiting for me to get back to him. He's not inclined to sell any dogs to a doper. He wants nothing to do with those people."

McKenna stared at the ground and frowned. "Does Tomás train the dogs, or does he have help?"

John looked McKenna in the eyes. "He does the bulk of the training himself, but when he works with cops, he's training the officer, too. Why?"

"Let's say, just for argument's sake," McKenna said, "you help Tomás train the dogs. Maybe our doper even meets you, and you offer to do some on-site training to acclimate the dogs to the area where they will be placed. Does that sound doable?"

John thought for a moment before it hit him. "You mean put *me* undercover?"

McKenna smiled. "Exactly."

John looked at his partner for some feedback. "Florey?"

"Hey, don't look at me!" Florey feigned indifference, albeit unconvincingly. "If they can get FHP to go with it, then why not, John? When do you think you'll ever be able to do any *real* undercover work with the Patrol?"

John didn't answer. But what would happen if he made a mess of things? What if he screwed up an undercover detail?

"I'll tell you what. Leave your dog here. Both of you head out with Rick and get a peek at that warehouse," McKenna said. "I'll make a few calls. From what I understand, your governor can be very convincing with your brass. I'll let you guys know what they decide."

"Okay, I guess. I just hope I don't screw anything up, Chief." John heard in his voice both his reluctance and sense of gloom. Not an impression he intended to leave.

Agent McKenna grinned politely. "Don't forget. We still need to find that chemist and DEA doesn't have a canine section. I don't even have an agent that used to be a dog handler. And, if you can get on the property to get a firsthand look around, then that makes you a perfect fit. Besides, I've never met a cop who couldn't act like a bad guy."

Florey started to laugh.

"What's so funny?" John asked, annoyed.

Florey put her hand on his shoulder and turned to McKenna. "Sir, take it from me. He'll do just fine."

John shook his head. "Thanks a lot, Florey."

Chapter Seven

Once Rick started the van, the ride to Hialeah took only a few minutes. The worn-out van had faded paint, dents, and a bogus phone company logo on its sides, but its interior was jam-packed with the latest high-tech surveillance gear. The warehouse was just east of the Florida East Coast Rail line along NW 103rd Street. Hialeah, the largest municipality within the county, had its own unique street system that made finding any address nearly impossible. Even worse, most of the signs had long been vandalized and removed. Finally, though, with the help of a map, they located the Las Palmas Commerce Park entrance.

Talking out loud, Florey double-checked the addresses as they drove down an endless line of connected loading docks and office entranceways. They'd reached the end of the main drive when Rick pointed out a stand-alone building on the far end of the complex. It was painted the same drab, off-white color as the rest of the commerce park buildings, but this one was surrounded by a ten-foot fence topped with barbed wire. Its only entrance was an electric gate facing the main parking lot. Rick pointed out the surveillance cameras mounted on all four corners of the building, including one at the entrance door.

"You think this is it?" Florey asked.

As he turned the van around in the neighboring parking lot, Rick told John to get his binoculars out of his black bag in the back.

John leaned forward from his seat in the cargo area and fumbled through the bag until he got his hands on the binoculars. He pulled off the lens covers as Rick maneuvered the van into a spot under a utility pole. John got the building into view and adjusted the focus.

"Do you see any writing on the doors?" Rick asked.

John struggled to see through the van's dark window tints. "I can just make out what's on the door…Fleitas Import and Export."

"That's it. Let me get back there. I need my camera." Rick squeezed between the van's front seats and made his way to a small storage drawer in the back, where he found his 35 mm camera. After loading it with film, he positioned himself next to John.

Whispering, Rick asked him to get the telephoto lens. "There's some movement at the warehouse door—it just opened."

Reflexively, Florey sank down in her seat, still able to keep a watchful eye forward on the outside chance a nosy tenant, or perhaps, a suspicious doper came snooping around.

Rick snapped on the large lens. A few seconds later, he mumbled, "Shit. How many people are in there?"

John watched Rick steady his focus and heard the camera clicking off photos in rapid-fire succession. "How many can you make out?" John asked.

"Six, no, seven…wait…eight. Eight people. By the looks of it, they're workers, more like laborers." Rick snapped more shots of the group. "They're not dressed as if they work in an office."

Suddenly, a loud horn blared outside the van. John's body jerked in reaction to its undulating high to low tones.

Rick nearly dropped the camera.

A maroon lunch truck drove past them, directly towards the security fence. Its familiar two-tone melody announced its arrival.

"That explains it," John said. "It's their break time."

Rick quickly regained his composure and snapped more pictures, while John watched the movements of the warehouse occupants. The lunch truck entered the compound and pulled up next to the loading dock alongside the entrance doorway.

The driver got out and lifted the truck's metal canopy doors to expose a buffet of food and drinks. The employees became ants swarming the truck, taking pastelitos and pastries and pouring themselves café cubano from a thermos, while the lunch truck operator collected bills and coins. John watched every move through the binoculars.

"Hey. Hold on…some big fucker just came out of the door," Rick said, looking through the camera lens. "It may be our guy. He's waving his hands around like he's telling them to hurry up.

"Okay, now they're all going back in and the truck driver is closing up shop. Stand by." Rick clicked off a dozen or so pictures as the employees re-entered the building. Then the lunch truck went out the same way it had come in.

Once it passed, Florey sat back up in her seat.

"From the looks of it," Rick said, "we're going to need some time to figure out what the hell is going on in this place." He looked through the side window of the van. "I don't think we'll do any good here during the day. Besides, we should put up some remote cameras so we can keep an eye on this place. We don't want to get burned in this van by some snoopy citizen. What do you guys think?"

"Sounds right," John said, glancing at Florey, who nodded.

Rick got behind the wheel, and after confirming the coast was clear of nosy onlookers, he started the engine and drove out of the commerce center.

"Now I know why this guy wants drug dogs *and* guard dogs," John remarked. "Looks like he wants them for outside security."

"If he buys the dogs, do you think you'd be able to talk Tomás into letting you deliver them in person?" Rick asked.

"I'm pretty sure he normally does that," John said. "You think McKenna was serious about the dogs?"

"He wouldn't have said it if he didn't mean it," Rick said. "I've never known him to beat around the bush. If he says it, he's seriously considering it."

John sat back in the rear jump seat as the van turned down Executive Drive and headed for the DEA office. Could he pull off working undercover? Not being Hispanic, he knew it was going to be a tough sell. Ever-vigilant for undercover cops, gringos always made the cartels nervous. Despite his confidence in handling dogs, John had his doubts. He was deep in thought as the van entered the DEA parking lot.

"Don't worry, John, I know you can do this," Florey said, as if reading the apprehension in his thoughts.

Inside the DEA office, McKenna asked John and Florey to join in the FBI meeting, since both federal agencies had been talking about setting up the warehouse for surveillance. John called DeLeón and gave him a heads-up on the undercover request. But he soon learned McKenna had already made the call and sent the information up the chain of command to the colonel. DeLeón promised he'd let John know as soon as he heard back from GHQ, but he repeated what John already understood—the colonel didn't like the idea.

During the meeting with McKenna, the FBI agreed to set up several remote cameras, and the DEA would monitor them from the undercover van. After John vouched for Tomás' character, they all agreed to go ahead with the scheme if the kennel operator was willing to cooperate.

It was John's job to convince his friend. The plan details began to take shape so quickly that John had forgotten to tell them he was still waiting on approval from his chain of command. He raised his hand to say as much when his phone rang.

"Hi Captain, it's Stella. Did they get back to you?" John asked, walking to the rear of the room as agents continued analyzing maps and formalizing their plans.

"You got the approval," DeLeón replied. "But GHQ made it clear there'd better not be any problems. The major has put his ass on the line here, John."

"I know, Captain. I appreciate the trust. I won't let you down, sir."

"You let me know if you need anything. And keep us briefed daily so we can keep the brass at ease," DeLeón said.

"Absolutely, sir. And thanks again." As John ended the call, it was becoming even clearer the DEA's calls to the governor's office must be influencing FHP's ability to deny assistance in any case that went beyond mere traffic enforcement. Just as he began relishing the mental image of the colonel getting called on the carpet by the governor, he remembered he had a call to make. He quietly stepped into the hallway, out of earshot of the conferring agents.

"Hey Tomás, it's John Stella."

"Gringo, how you been?"

Bypassing the small talk, John plunged in. "I got some information on your *marimbero* friend with the F-350."

"*Oye, mi amigo*! He's no friend of mine. What you got?" Tomás asked eagerly.

"Good thing he's no friend. He's as dirty as they come," John explained.

"Shit! There goes that deal."

"Not necessarily, buddy. What if I told you that the Feds want you to sell this guy the dogs?"

"Why the hell would they want me to do that?" Tomás asked.

John ran down the details of the operation, and without hesitating, Tomás agreed to work with the Feds. Probably driven more by his desire to see a doper arrested rather than making a sale. But John read his friend's excitement, too, evidenced by Tomás' habit of speaking English nearly as fast as his native tongue. John had to slow him down, keeping him calm more than once while they made a plan to meet the following day to go over the details.

After the call, John went back inside the briefing room, where the sound of the heavy door latching shut drew attention to him.

"The kennel operator is in," he reported. "I'll go there tomorrow and be there when he calls Fleitas about the dogs."

"Excellent, Trooper!" one of the senior FBI agents exclaimed. "We'll need to record that call. Does your man understand what he is getting into?"

"I don't see a problem. Tomás is all in." John pulled out a page from his notebook and wrote down the kennel's address, and then handed it to the agent. "I'm going to be there at seven in the morning to fill him in on the details. I'll let him know to expect your guys there, too. Have the techs call me so we can set up the call."

"FHP will work with the dog trainer and develop a way onto the Fleitas property from that angle," McKenna said. "We all know our respective roles with surveillance, but again, I just want to be clear. We need as much intel on this as possible. Remember, we still have a missing German out there."

The meeting over, John and Florey left and drove the four miles to the FHP station to brief the captain and major. After he and Florey offered many assurances, Major Carris called Tallahassee and updated the brass on the operation. John was beat after the day's events. He wasn't the only one. Florey looked pretty exhausted, too.

Daylight was fast fading, but they weren't done yet. Headquarters was giving the major a hard time about the detail, but Carris kept at it and gave him his best sales pitch. Not that it mattered. John knew about the governor's involvement, and that meant GHQ had no choice but to give their permission. Still, making subordinates squirm was the way of the patrol. It was an insurance policy if something went wrong. Then the blame would rest squarely on Major Carris and Captain DeLeón. Even knowing his immediate supervisors trusted him, he hated the politics all the same. So did Florey.

John watched as Major Carris began rubbing his temples as if fighting back a headache. There was an uneasy silence in the room. John looked at Florey for some guidance.

"We'll see to it that everything is taken care of on our end," she said. "John and I will make sure the captain is updated regularly."

Silence again filled the room as the major took a deep breath.

"Major. Speaking on behalf of Florey and John, I just want to thank you for putting your trust in us. We won't let you down," DeLeón said.

"Thanks, Juanes, but I want to be notified immediately if anything happens."

"Yes, Sir."

The captain looked at his troopers and motioned with a look towards the office door. John quietly opened the door and let his partner and the captain out first, before exiting himself. As he closed the door, he noticed the major move to rest his elbows on the desktop and cradle his head in his hands.

"Listen, you two. Especially you," DeLeón whispered, pointing his finger at John. "Watch your back. I can see this investigation is building up speed. If you think you are in too deep at any point, or if you need *anything*, call me."

John glanced at Florey, who nodded along with him.

"Try to update me daily," DeLeón said. "GHQ isn't happy about the whole undercover thing, and that makes it more important to communicate often. I don't care how small the detail, I expect a call. That way I can update the major. You understand?"

John nodded again.

"It's the only way he can keep those pencil pushers in Tallahassee off our case. Got it?"

"Absolutely, sir," Florey said.

"That man is taking a big risk with Tallahassee. You guys understand that, right?" "Absolutely," Florey answered again.

"Alright, now get out of here." DeLeón pointed towards the door. "You've both had a long day."

As John walked through the parking lot with Florey, his mind raced with the details of what he'd just taken on, and his preoccupation wasn't lost on his partner.

"Hey, John, why the frown? You still worried about working undercover?"

"Nah. I was just wondering why it always takes an act of Congress to get this department to do real police work."

"Hey, partner, we *do* real police work," Florey insisted. "The Patrol has a niche to fill. That's traffic. Look at all the stuff we got over the years just from issuing tickets. What other department gives their officers the freedom to drive around all day doing traffic stops and search for dope?"

"True. But Tallahassee is always so damn reluctant to take those cases to the next level." John heard the complaining tone in his own voice. "It doesn't feel like they have my back, especially now with a case this important."

"The captain and the major won't let you down. And I'll always have your back." Florey squeezed his shoulder. "Don't worry about the brass. You and I will never make sense of what administrators think.

Besides, I'm in your corner. I have total faith in ya—what else you need?" Laughing, Florey gave his shoulder a playful shove.

John smiled. She was right. He gave her a wave before getting in his car. When he started the engine, he picked up his phone and called his house. Joey answered. "Hey, put that six pack of beer in the freezer. I'll be home in thirty minutes."

Chapter Eight

Seven AM came way too early. Leaving Spec at the house, John drove out to Tomás' kennel on Krome Avenue in his personal car. No surprise. Tomás was half an hour late.

"Hey, Gringo! You are early," Tomás said, exiting his car.

"No, my friend. *I'm* on time. You're on *Cuban time.*" Miami's version of being "fashionably" late. But John had lived with that custom for a long time.

"Yeah, so? That makes me *on time*," Tomás said, snickering. "Haven't you learned anything, Gringo?"

They walked to the back of the property towards two rows of kennels. A couple of recently-added pens offered a generous amount of space. John was impressed. The pens were big enough for a grown man to stand in, making them easy to clean and sanitize. Tomás had personally overseen their construction. John had seen that for himself when he'd once found Tomás standing on a milk crate, barking out orders to the construction workers. He directed all his employees like a drill sergeant, moving them from one task to the next, driving them as hard as he drove officers during canine training.

When John closed the kennel gate behind him, the sound triggered the dogs into a barking frenzy, a response habituated by a rigorous schedule of training, exercise, and feeding. Tomás took the noise in stride, but John found it almost deafening.

Tomás stepped up to one of the pens and yelled, "These are the two I think we should start with."

"Do they have any training in them?" John carefully eyed the two tan Malinois dogs inside. Both animals stopped barking and sat in front of the pen door with their tails wagging.

"Well, the kennel I bought them from did some basic stuff, but nothing too elaborate."

"All we need them to do is some basic obedience and bite work. Nothing crazy," John explained. "Oh, yeah. One more thing."

"What's that?"

"They are going to need to respond to me over any other commands they get."

"You mean, you want the dogs to see you as the alpha?" Tomás asked using the term for the pack leader.

"Exactly."

"Okay, I get it. Come on." Tomás grabbed a leash hanging on a post. "Let's go get some cafecito to fire up the engine, and then we get started, my friend."

"I took the liberty and got us a colada from the corner market."

"Just one?" Tomás asked.

"Jesus, Bubba! How much you need?" John didn't wait for an answer. "I got two. One for me and one for my friend the rafter!"

"Ha-ha. You see. You are learning. Soon, I will be calling you *Juanito*!"

John took off to get the coffee from the car and left Tomás to leash one of the dogs and put the animal in a pen by the training area.

The dog could wait, John thought, as he and Tomás shot back the dark coffee from Styrofoam cups and poured another. Ah, the morning had officially begun.

Coffee consumed, they headed into the office to wait for the DEA technicians to arrive and set up the recorder for the Fleitas phone call.

"One more time," John asked Tomás, "reassure me that you know what you're getting into, the risk that we can't deny. Are you still willing to do this?"

"Fuck these guys," Tomás blurted. "They come to this country and cause misery for everyone. Everyone should be lining up to do what they can to run these bastards out of here."

Direct and to the point, John thought. Plus, Tomás was right. John knew exactly how he felt. After immigrating to the States from Italy, his own family had put up with local mob bosses in Brooklyn where they first settled. Those bosses had seemed to run every neighborhood. His grandmother told stories of people assuming if you were from Italy, you must've been connected to the mob. Every time a mobster was arrested with an Italian surname, the hardworking Italians considered it a cultural black-eye.

A white sedan pulling into the lot drew him out of his thoughts. John recognized the techs and opened the door to greet them coming in. Tomás, showing he was all in, didn't waste a minute with small talk. He showed the techs his office phone, and the guys took only a minute to install the mic and plug in the recorder. The lead technician did a few final equipment tests and gave John a thumbs-up.

"You ready for the call, buddy?" John asked.

Tomás took a deep breath and exhaled. With a determined game face, he picked up the phone's handset. "Let's do this." He pushed in the phone number.

One second, two seconds…ticked by. But Fleitas finally answered, and Tomás morphed from trainer to salesman, talking up the deal and adding a few extras—leashes, collars, and a bag of dog food.

Impressive, John thought.

By the time the call ended, the subject had agreed to buy both dogs, which would be ready in a few weeks. Tomás made sure to add that he'd throw in some on-site familiarization for the animals. Fleitas eagerly agreed to the deal.

After the call, the techs let out a collective sigh.

Tomás was quick to notice the relief. "What you guys think? I couldn't do this? Come on! This guy is a doper—a real bullshitter. And he is not going to out bullshit me!"

The technicians laughed as they carefully unplugged the device and packed up their equipment.

"No time to waste, my friend," Tomás said, "not if these dogs have to be ready in two weeks."

John understood. Training would begin immediately.

The unrelenting South Florida heat and humidity of June made the next few days seem endless. Every day, John and Tomás ran the dogs through the paces of obedience training and bite work. The dogs responded even better than John anticipated.

Tomás's training was equally relentless, making for ten to twelve-hour days, made worse when John had to wear the heavy padded bitesuit. The heavy layers of burlap stuffed with a dense foam filling were worn over street clothes, so the contraption was almost unbearably hot. The bulky pants and coat were designed to protect against a penetrating dog bite, but trainers still had to be super alert to avoid the crushing pressures of a dog's clenched jaws. Not to mention guarding against dehydration just from wearing the gear. When the long days ended, John barely had the energy to eat dinner before passing out.

On the fourth day of training, John and Tomás took a break and put the dogs in the front pen to let them cool down and slurp water. John pulled himself out of the bitesuit and was about to hold his head under a spigot when his pager buzzed. Sitting on the wooden picnic table, its vibrations pushed the little black box to the edge of the tabletop, but he grabbed it before it fell to the ground.

Call me now flashed across the digital display. He pushed the button again. Florey.

He jogged over to his car and grabbed his phone from the center console, calling her on speed dial.

"What's going on?" he asked, wiping away sweat running down his face as he tried to catch his breath.

"I hate to do this to ya, John, but I'm with Rick on surveillance in Redland, just south of you," Florey said. "Some guy is supposed to move a load of cash to a house in Broward County. Rick really needs you and Spec when we stop this car."

"Shit!" John groaned. "Okay, no problem. I gotta haul ass home and grab Spec and throw on a uniform. Where are you set up?"

"At the Redland Tavern on Krome Avenue. Call us on DEA 15 when you head this way."

"I'm on my way."

He ended the call and checked the time. He had to hustle. Tomás had been through this before. It was not unusual for an officer to rush away in the midst of a training session. One of Tomás' men would don the bitesuit and finish the day's training.

"Don't worry about nothing, John," Tomás said. "You be safe, and I see you tomorrow."

"I'll be here at seven," John replied as he cranked up the Mustang and headed down the gravel drive.

John pulled out onto the roadway, punching the gas and causing the modified engine to come alive, spinning its rear tires before grabbing at the road and catapulting forward as he sped south to his house. In less than ten minutes, he was sliding to a stop in his driveway. He ran inside, stripping off his clothes as he went.

Watching as he scrambled to get into a uniform, Spec instinctively knew to be ready. By the time he left the house, Spec was waiting at the gate, her body twisting side to side and her tail wagging in anticipation.

John opened the rear door of the cruiser. "Come on, girl. Time for you to earn some money today," he said.

Spec jumped inside her compartment and let out an excited bark.

On his way, he turned on his DEA radio to channel 15 and called ahead. "We're less than five minutes out," John said.

"I'm still here at the Redland Tavern. Take your time and watch out for speeding Mustangs. I just saw one go by here at warp speed!" said Florey, amused.

John smiled as he turned west on SW 232nd Street and headed for the tavern. For generations, Redland Tavern had been a local redneck drinking spot and not a place the average money launderer was likely to frequent. Its rear parking lot was surrounded by a heavy growth of trees and bushes.

Without doubt, Florey chose the location because it provided the cover needed to hide her patrol car. But he knew where to look and found her backed into a spot at the end of the lot.

John pulled straight in so that his driver's door would be next to hers and rolled down his window. Just as he was about to greet Florey, the DEA agents on surveillance began broadcasting over the radio.

"Okay. Units stand by. I got a Latin male walking out of the house with a box." The agent paused. "He's opening up the rear door of a white Ford van. He just put the box in the back of the van. From the way he was holding the box, it could be heavy. Stand by."

"You want to make the traffic stop, and I'll come up a few minutes after and run the dog?" John asked.

Before she could answer, another broadcast started. "I got an older Latin male carrying another heavy box. Looks like they're loading up with a bunch of boxes."

"Yeah, that will work," Florey said, responding to John's question.

Again, the radio blared, "Stand by. We've got ten boxes that went into the back of the van. The Latin male is driving and the younger one is getting into the passenger seat. Stand by."

Florey sat up in her seat. "I almost forgot. Rick said that the older man is an informant. He'll be wearing a white-collared shirt."

"Gotcha! Hopefully this goes smooth and quick. Spec doesn't like how I smell right now."

Florey scrunched her nose. "Is that what I smell? I thought you ran over a dead animal or something."

"Very funny, kiddo," John snapped as the DEA radio started another update.

"The van is pulling out of the driveway. The gate is opening… Stand by. They are eastbound on 232nd Street. Troopers, it's all yours."

Florey acknowledged with "Ten-four," and drove through the lot, moving as close to the roadway as possible without being seen. John strained to see through the bushes and spotted the van approaching a green signal at the intersection of Krome Avenue and continuing east. To his well-trained eye, it looked as if the van was already speeding.

John looked on as Florey waited to allow for a few cars to file in behind the subject before she made her turn. Those vehicles gave them additional cover until they needed to make their move.

"Okay, I'm three cars behind the van and we're still eastbound on 232nd Street," she broadcasted.

It only took a minute for her to match her pace with that of the van. As she continued following, John knew she would quickly get the probable cause needed for a stop.

"I got the van at fifty-three in a forty zone. We're still eastbound, coming up on SW 162nd Avenue… Stand by," she advised. "Okay, the van is through the intersection. We're still going east on 232nd Street."

John moved out of the tavern's parking lot and turned onto 232nd Street, keeping pace with Florey ahead and following the line of cars.

"Okay, we're coming up to 157th Avenue," Florey said. "Stand by. He's through the intersection, still eastbound."

Sensing Florey would make her move soon, John sped up a little. Already his heart rate had increased.

"We're coming up to 147th Avenue. Stand by," she said.

Ahead of him, Florey passed the last of the few farmhouses on the street as they approached a stretch of fields and avocado groves. "Looks like he's turning… He's going left," she advised. "I'm going to stop him right here."

John pulled into a parking lot that left a half a mile between him and Florey, part of making the stop look as routine as possible. It wouldn't be unusual if another patrol car drove up a few minutes after the initial stop. He mentally saw Florey going through the paces: license, registration and insurance, and, "Sir, I stopped you for speeding."

Of course, she'd have to listen to the driver's lame excuses. Any minute now, she'd call for him to come and have Spec sniff the van.

As he waited, he watched the surveillance units pass him on their way to keep an eye on Florey. But there was nowhere to park without being noticed. John watched them drive by her location, figuring they'd drive to the next intersection before turning back around. Otherwise, they ran the risk of being detected.

"I had to pass her. She's out of the cruiser, talking to the driver," the agent said on the radio. "Stand by… Damn it! Who can get the eye?"

Another surveillance unit immediately rounded the corner. "I'm coming up on her. I'll advise," another agent said. "I had to pass, but it looks like the passenger is getting out. Rick, are you somewhere you can drive by?"

"I'm almost at the corner. Hold on…" Rick advised. "Okay, she's still talking to the passenger. I'm going to have to pass her. Hold on… I got her in my rearview. Looks like she's handcuffing the passenger. Shit!" he yelled over the radio. "He just hit her! Subject is running west across the road. I'm turning around."

John slammed down his gear lever and mashed the gas pedal, sending his unit yawing sideways out of the lot. Racing towards his partner, he grabbed his FHP radio mic. "Florey!" he hailed. "You there?"

No response. He increased his speed—eighty, ninety, one hundred miles per hour. "Florey!" he shouted again.

Still nothing.

John slammed hard on the brakes as he approached the spot where Florey had stopped. Out of the corner of his eye, he saw a Hispanic man walking in the other direction. He looked to be in his forties and wore a white-collared shirt. With his head lowered, he quickly shuffled along the grass shoulder.

John slid the car sideways through the intersection and spotted Florey ahead of him. She was holding her head with one hand and had her gun in the other as she moved towards her car. John screeched to a halt. He bolted out of the car and broke into a full sprint.

"Hey, you okay?" he yelled, noticing the wound on her forehead. Blood streamed down the side of Florey's face even as she pressed down on the wound with her left hand.

"That son-of-a-bitch hit me with my own cuffs!" Florey pointed with her gun to the opposite side of the road. "He ran that way."

"Let me see your head."

Florey moved her hand exposing a deep, two-inch gash to her forehead.

"He got combative. When I went to cuff him, he spun around and slashed me with my cuffs!"

John saw the embarrassment in her face. A young guy had gotten the jump on her and that always stung. But mostly, she was mad as hell.

"I'll call in the perimeter. Let me get my first aid kit," John said. "You go sit in your car."

"Fuck, no. I'll call fire rescue. I'll be okay," she shot back. "*You* need to get that asshole. The older guy went towards 232nd Street." She waved in the direction.

John ran back to his patrol car.

"John," Florey shouted, "remember he's an informant."

John turned and saw her wince in pain. "Sorry, kid. All bets are off. Everyone is going down."

He slid behind the wheel and glanced over at Spec. She was already balling herself up in the corner of the cage. "Good girl," he muttered as he grabbed the wheel. "Now hold on."

He spun the cruiser around, turned the corner, and scanned the road ahead. He spotted the man up ahead, his white shirt a contrast with the scenery. He'd made it farther than John would have guessed he could.

John punched the gas and tightly gripped the wheel. The guy turned his head, saw the car, and broke out into an awkward sprint.

John pulled his patrol car onto the grass shoulder and slammed it into park, forcing the vehicle to shudder and skid to an abrupt stop. He pushed open his door and hit the ground running.

He quickly caught up to the fleeing driver, dropping his shoulder as he hurled his body forward. The force of the collision sent both men crashing to the ground in a heap, but John wrestled the man into an arm lock.

That triggered Spec to bolt from the car and take off in a full sprint. John noticed her coming as he cinched the last cuff on his prisoner's wrist before turning back and yelling, "Down!"

Spec immediately broke her stride and slid on the grass, paws extended, stopping inches from the prisoner's face. Her eyes glared; her body tensed. Limbs quivering, she was ready to pounce. Slowly she raised both lips to expose her ivory teeth and barked, spraying the almost-catatonic prisoner with splashes of her saliva.

John ordered her to stay as he helped the man to his feet.

Spec sat up and stopped her barking and growled.

Nearly out of breath, eyes wide, the man stared at the dog. The prisoner began to tremble. John wasn't sure if the guy was just scared or going into shock.

"Don't worry about her, buddy. Unless you try to pull a fast one like your friend back there, you'll be fine." John purposely spun the driver around so he wouldn't be able to see Spec, a tactic that could keep the biggest badass at bay. The inability to see a police dog sitting an arm's reach behind them invariably kept a person motionless. John patted the driver down, removing his wallet, keys, and coins from his pocket.

Rick drove up and screeched his car to a stop in the roadway at the same time John finished the pat down.

"Goddamn it! You were supposed to stay with the van," Rick yelled at the driver. "You were told to stay put, regardless of what happened! You dumb shit! A trooper got hurt, for cryin' out loud! And you just ran away?" The veins in Rick's neck bulged as he tore into the driver.

The man stood still, silent.

John got Rick's anger. As the case agent, he was responsible for everyone. Nobody had gotten shot or seriously hurt, but any injury on the detail meant lengthy debriefings back at the DEA. John didn't envy his friend, but had no time to think about it, either. He had bigger fish to fry.

"Rick, I gotta make sure we have a solid perimeter around this area. I need your guys to fill in until I can get some uniforms here."

"No problem," Rick said. "I'll get right on it. I have a map of the area in my trunk."

"Let's go get it." John pivoted to check on Spec, still sitting on her haunches, staring at the driver.

John called her name and she looked up, waiting for the next command. "Protect!" he ordered.

Spec bounded up and ran up to the driver's backside, resting her chin on his buttocks as she stood straddling his right leg.

"Good girl." John glanced at the prisoner, who was taking air deep into his lungs. "Hey, Paco, I wouldn't move if I were you. Unless you want to have only half an ass." Satisfied, he said, "Come on, Rick, show me that map."

"Is she going to stay there?" Rick fixed his gaze on Spec.

"Yup. Until I tell her not to."

Rick was dumbfounded. "I've never seen that."

"Well, son, you've seen it now." Taking Rick's arm, John grinned and steered him to the car. "Let's get that map."

Minutes later, map in hand, Rick coordinated a tight perimeter around a square mile of farm fields, woods, and avocado groves by using the available DEA agents. John radioed the FHP dispatch to coordinate the arrival of responding troopers and Metro-Dade police officers, each sent to fill in for Rick's agents.

John and Rick made notes on the map to make sure every position was filled with an officer. John gave the map a final go-over and was about to call Florey when the first of the troopers arrived and parked his cruiser on the side of the road behind Rick's car.

"Hey, John. Where do you need me?" The trooper got out of the car and put on his hat.

"Good to see you, Tom. I need to put a subject in your car. After that, you can stay here and watch this area of the perimeter."

"Sure. Not a problem. Where is he?" Tom asked.

John gestured to his patrol car. "He's right there in front of my car."

Tom looked ahead over the roofs of the cars. "You left him alone?"

"Nah. Here, wait a minute…" John leaned to the side to face his car and yelled out, "Lout!"

Without moving from her position, Spec immediately began to bark.

John yelled, "*No*," and Spec stopped.

"There, follow that noise. That would be our guy." John again turned his attention to Rick.

"Stella, you are one messed up unit, you know that?" Tom said.

Tom had been a former canine handler and was the polar opposite of him, John thought. Quiet and reserved when around people, Tom had impressed John as the quintessential state trooper. In his off time, he was the pastor of the Liberty City Missionary Baptist Church, which provided a source of plenty of good-natured joking between the two.

Tom laughed. "Call your dog before this guy has a heart attack."

John smiled. "Spec…*car!*"

Spec bolted from her position behind her captive suspect and ran to the patrol car, jumping onto the driver's seat, bounding over the center partition and into her cage.

"There. Happy?" John asked in mock sarcasm.

Tom shook his head. "You ain't right, man." He walked away to take custody of the prisoner.

Along with Rick, John double-checked the assignments on the perimeter, making sure the police units along the streets and avenues had effectively boxed in the area where the subject had run. That tactic usually worked well. The tighter the box, the less real estate the subject had to run around in. The only problem with doing a perimeter in the Redlands was the sheer size of the properties. Using the closest intersecting streets and avenues still left almost a square mile area to search. Not that one dog couldn't do it. But they didn't have time to spend searching and run the risk of their assailant getting away.

John called the Metro-Dade police K-9 squad to assist, and was pleased to hear they were sending five dog teams. Plus, they'd all flown out of the office when they'd heard the call go out that a trooper was hurt and the assailant had escaped.

The assignments done, John and Rick returned to Florey's traffic stop location and found her sitting on the rear step bumper of a fire rescue truck being bandaged up by a paramedic.

"She's lucky as hell. Another inch over and she'd have lost the eye," the first responder remarked as he put the finishing touches on the thick wrap of gauze that held the bandage against her head wound.

"Florey? You okay?" John asked softly.

"Yeah. I'm gonna need some stitches. But I want to see this guy get caught first."

"No way, partner. You need to take care of *that* first." John eyed her bandage while gently moving a lock of her blonde hair to the side. "I don't need you trudging through the woods getting that slash infected. We'll take care of this. Besides, Rick is relieving his guys from the perimeter to come babysit the van, so there's no need for you to stay here."

Florey reached up and ran her fingers over the wad of gauze taped to her head. She grimaced and shut her eyes.

"That bad, huh?"

"Yeah, just touching it almost blinds me. It's throbbing hard."

"Then you know I'm right."

Florey nodded. "I won't argue, but do me a favor, will ya?"

"Of course, kiddo. Anything."

"Be careful with this guy. He made a move that was something out of a Kung-Fu movie."

"Don't worry, hon. He's as good as caught," John said, squeezing her shoulder. "Now go get yourself to the hospital and I'll catch up to you later."

Florey nodded. "Oh, before I forget," she added, "I called the captain. He's on his way, too. And John?"

He'd taken a step away but turned back to her. "Yeah, kiddo?"

Florey reached into the rescue truck, grabbed an antiseptic wipe, and began carefully cleaning the dried blood off her face. "The bad guy will be wearing my cuffs on his left wrist." She folded the blood-stained wipe and tossed it in a biohazard bag. "I want them back."

Relieved all over again that his partner wasn't seriously hurt, John said, "Consider it done."

As the fire rescue truck drove off with Florey, John heard the approach of sirens from the side street.

Rick was already in the middle of the intersection, his arms motioning like a traffic cop as he directed the metro K-9 units to park on the side of the road and indicated where they were to meet by his car.

John wasted no time as he quickly greeted the teams and began assigning each to a geographic area. He planned to have the teams begin their searches from the fringes and move inward, converging at the center of the massive perimeter. He kept for himself the area where the suspect was last seen—an area he was somewhat familiar with. Most of the land in the area belonged to one of his elder neighbors, Ronnie Winslip. The two former marines would talk for hours about the corps. Usually, while sipping beers on old man Ronnie's porch.

John dismissed the teams to their respective assignments and asked Rick to be his backup officer.

Rick ran to his trunk and put on his tactical vest and holster, strapping on each over his street clothes. The ad-hoc getup made him appear a bit out of place among the uniformed canine teams. Not that it mattered.

Rick double-checked his gear while John made the final adjustments to Spec's leather tracking harness, making sure each of the straps crossing over her neck and torso weren't so tight she'd be uncomfortable while she concentrated on the suspect's scent.

"Hey, man, I'm ready when you are," Rick said.

John gave his new getup a once-over. "You look like an accountant going into battle," he joked.

Rick glared at him. "Very funny, buddy, very funny."

John called to a deputy and asked him to check in with the other teams to see if they were set up and ready. The officer nodded and got on the radio.

"Listen, Rick," John whispered, "these Metro-Dade guys are probably searching already."

Rick looked perplexed. "But you told them to wait, didn't you?"

John chuckled. "We all want to be the one to find this creep. Besides, if it were me, I'd do the same thing. If you ain't cheating on canine, you ain't trying."

"Hey, trooper!" the deputy yelled, his radio still next to his ear. "The dogs are on the ground."

John glanced at Rick with a mock sinister smile. "Told ya. Come on. Let's not waste any more time."

He walked Spec to the last place the assailant had been seen before entering the brush. He reached down and switched his leash from her collar to the back loop on the harness to let her forge ahead on point.

"Find him, girl," John directed.

He repeated the command until he watched the dog's snout scan the surface of the grass shoulder as she moved back and forth, taking small steps, searching for the subject's scent trail. Irresistible to a trained canine, the odor of crushed plant material where a subject had walked, decomposing skin cells, pheromones, sweat, and any other less desirable excretion a person gives off when fleeing capture draws a dog like a magnet to iron. Every time John started a search, he couldn't help to remember the first lesson in searching from Tomás. John had asked if they needed to present the dog an example of the odor from an article of clothing that had been worn by the person.

"You're an idiot!" Tomás shouted. "That is for the movies and for bloodhounds. Not for these dogs!" The embarrassment had caused John to research all he could about scent and working a modern police canine.

"I'm going to let her out about six feet on the leash so we don't get tangled up in that brush," John said. "Stay behind me as we walk, and use hand signals."

Rick nodded.

The trio made their way to the grass shoulder. John continued watching Spec as she slowly moved forward, sniffing the side of the road. She suddenly paused, putting her nose down into the grass, and then lunged forward.

She found the trail and quickly pushed herself into the wooded overgrowth. She pulled hard, passing broken twigs and stems. John was certain Spec was on the right track. She followed her nose and pulled John around trees, bushes, and clumps of razor grass—a barbaric plant. If he ran across it, its leaves would easily slice through his flesh. Each of the elongated blades was packed with thousands of tiny, razor-sharp teeth.

Spec charged around one clump of the stuff after another, but John knew to stay wide. He'd had his share of cuts over the years.

Rick wasn't so lucky.

Before John had a chance to warn him, Rick's blood trickled crimson down both arms from the second clump. John glanced back, little stabs of guilt going through him over failing to warn Rick about the merciless plant. Thankfully, Rick was smart enough to make sure that only happened once.

Spec slowed her pursuit and moved back and forth, sniffing hard at the ground as they approached a clearing.

John held up his left hand, signaling Rick to stop.

Waiting for Spec to work out the scent, John moved forward a few feet to slacken the leash and give her more room. She inhaled the ambient air and exhaled as she moved to her right, her ears slowly perking up and pointing forward. Anticipating his dog's movements, John motioned for Rick to move right.

Suddenly, Spec galloped, pulling hard on her harness and leash as each paw dug hard into the dirt. It took everything John had to keep the leash from slipping off his hand.

In the distance, he heard other teams getting close. So far, his plan was working. The sound of barking police dogs came from every direction, except from Spec. Her training kept her focused on the trail and didn't allow for barking, something Tomás had insisted on. Stealth beat broadcasting your position to a bad guy.

With Spec still pulling, John noted they were headed directly towards the clearing. He added some resistance to the leash to slow her down.

As she came to a stop, John held up his hand to Rick to stay still. Then, John knelt next to his dog.

Rick came up behind them slowly, arms still bleeding from numerous collisions with the razor grass.

"You sure he went this way?" Rick whispered.

"No doubt. She's on this guy's track." John pointed to the middle of the clearing where a single-story wooden barn sat isolated. The far end of the clearing was hemmed in by a large stand of avocado trees. Its dark green canopy cast an almost impenetrable shadow below that, contrasted with the glare of reflecting sunlight bouncing off the barn's metal panel roof. A plowed field was to the right of it, a large grass field to its left.

"I don't see any furrows disturbed in that plowed field," John whispered. "He either is in that barn, or he went across the grass into those groves on the far end."

John pointed to the barn to draw Rick's attention to it. "I'm willing to bet our boy is in there."

"Ready?" Rick whispered.

"For sure. Let's do this before those Metro-Dade cowboys get here," John said. "But listen, if Spec heads for the barn, I'll need you to cover the back. If we head towards the grass, just stay behind me and watch the other side where the avocado groves start."

"Got it."

John made a hissing sound to draw his dog's attention, and then whispered her name.

She cocked her head to her side as if to ask him what he wanted.

John said softly, "Find him."

Hearing the command, Spec rose on all four legs and picked up her sniffing where she'd left off. Her heavy pulling started again, and with each step, her intensity grew.

At one point, she started lunging, nearly pulling John off his feet.

He stumbled, regained his footing, and she forged on. Her nose no longer siphoned scent from the ground but lifted up, scanning back and forth, sniffing as she used her muscular frame to pull herself forward. John knew she no longer needed to smell for footprints. She'd found airborne scent floating from the subject's body delivered by a cooperating breeze. Her path was a bee-line, heading directly to the barn.

John didn't slow her down. He struggled to keep up and let her work out exactly where the odor was coming from. Spec answered that question when she stuck her head into the double door of the wooden structure.

John motioned for Rick to cover the rear of the barn, leaving him free to move to the side of the structure and wait for him to get set up. Spec's ears stayed forward, her head canted sideways, trying to listen for any noise coming from inside the barn.

Rick took a safe position behind a stack of wooden crates behind the barn, then peeked around the side.

John raised his hand and extended his five fingers. Then four. Then three.

Rick gave him a thumbs-up and brought up his firearm. He covered the rear as John stepped to the front entrance and knelt next to Spec. After removing her leash from the harness, John slowly pulled open one of the double doors just wide enough for him to enter. He whispered in Spec's ear, "Find 'em."

Spec leapt forward through the opening, immediately scanning the air with her nose.

John side-stepped to his right, closed the barn door behind him, and scanned the immediate area as best he could while his eyes acclimated to the dim environment. He positioned himself next to a push lawn mower.

In the middle of the barn sat an antique tractor with an old, rusted tiller attached behind it. When Spec began sniffing high, John looked up into the rafters where he saw several loosely wrapped rolls of canvas sagging between the wooden rafters. John didn't think they'd been disturbed in a while, so the odor likely came from somewhere else.

When Spec ran to the opposite side of the barn, John squatted to see under the tractor as she detailed her sniff along the opposite barn wall. Suddenly, she stopped sniffing and stood still.

John went motionless, too, his heart pounding.

The sounds of the approaching dog teams became distant, as if they'd been pulled away. But that didn't matter. His vision zoomed in on Spec. He waited for her next move, and from her reactions, this guy was close.

John braced himself while keeping an eye on his dog as she again started to slowly sniff and walk frontward with her ears perked as forward as he had ever seen. The dog's movements were stealth-like, the creep of a lioness going in for the kill.

With an explosion of movement, Spec bolted to her right, forcing her body under a large tarp on the floor. Pushing forward, she made her way deeper under the large gray canvas.

As John moved to her side of the barn, he heard her muffled growls. A familiar sound, unique to her and made when she clenched her jaws around a subject's arm or leg. Strange, though. No screams.

Spec arched her back, and with all her force, lunged backwards. With each explosive move, she worked her way from under the tarp exposing more of her catch. First, his bloodied arm, twisted in resistance to her bite, all 2,300 pounds per square inch of it. Then his shoulder.

As a precaution, John backed up to give her room. In doing so, he almost hit his head on the tractor's rigging and the large wooden axe handle resting on its rear fender. Taking no chances, he grabbed hold of it—there was no telling what this guy could have armed himself with while inside the barn. John wasn't about to let Spec get hurt.

Spec bolted backwards again. Now she had the suspect sliding on the concrete floor, his body still half-covered by the heavy canvas. She began to bite down harder as he tried to twist his arm away and free himself from her vice-like grip.

Moving back again, Spec pulled the assailant further out from under the concealment of the tarp. The subject began to scream. The pain threshold had been reached. Spec's teeth remained firmly sunk into his arm.

The subject let out a blood-curdling yell and flung aside the rest of the canvas, exposing himself and the machete firmly grasped in his free hand. He raised the rusted blade higher.

Seeing Florey's handcuffs dangling from the guy's wrist, John moved in. The assailant's gaze remained squarely on Spec, so John took advantage of the lapse in attention.

The man didn't see it coming—the axe handle descending on his head.

The man fell to the ground, and John called Spec to release the now unconscious criminal. She bounded back to his side, tail wagging.

He grabbed the weapon and walking out of the barn, John and Spec were met by Rick. He'd come running when the screaming started, and three Metro-Dade K-9 teams quickly approached from the clearing.

With one hand, John motioned for them to slow down. Then he grabbed a towel from the cargo pocket of his pants and used it to wipe down Spec's mouth. Blood and saliva froth mixed deep in her fur. Gently wiping her snout, he murmured, "Damn, girl. You're a mess." In his other hand, John still held the machete and axe.

"Stella, you get the guy or what?" one of the county police officers shouted as he walked up.

"Yeah. Our guy is a little unconscious right now," John said, grinning and gesturing to the barn, "but aside from Spec nearly tearing off his forearm and the knot on his head, I think he'll be fine."

The other handlers knew, just as John did, that for canine handlers, the competition of finding a suspect transcended everything. Bad weather, darkness, or even a hurt partner. Once canine teams hit the ground, their number one objective was to be the first dog to locate and arrest the subject. Didn't matter what department the canine handlers worked for. It wasn't personal; it was competition. And today, John could go back and tell Florey that it was Spec who had found her assailant.

Seeing Rick on the phone, John knew he had other concerns. But that didn't stop the cops from backslapping and congratulating themselves on a successful perimeter and team effort. But from what he could see, Rick's conversation wasn't as happy, not like the banter among the K-9 guys.

An ambulance made its way onto the property, jostling side to side on the uneven, narrow dirt service road connecting the barn to the outside street.

John directed some of the troopers that had gathered to help load the prisoner onto the stretcher and retrieve Florey's handcuffs. John swung open both doors to allow more light in, and the troopers went inside the barn with the ambulance attendants in tow.

"Over to the right. On the floor," John said.

"Hey, man. What's that?" one of the deputies asked.

John held out the machete in front of him as the paramedics began to wheel the unconscious assailant out of the barn. "This, gentlemen," John explained, "is the weapon he armed himself with when he tried to kill my dog." Despite its rusty finish, its long menacing blade revealed a finely-honed edge.

"Damn, Stella! You didn't shoot him?" one of the deputies asked, his tone incredulous.

John paused before answering, "Yeah, wouldn't ya know it? Son-of-a-bitch slipped and fell. Hit his head. Knocked out cold."

"What's that behind you?" asked one of the troopers walking out of the barn. John looked over his shoulder.

"Axe handle," he curtly replied as he quickly walked away. Damn, he'd forgotten all about that handle. "I'll see you back on the road." John pulled on the leash signaling Spec to walk by his side. He'd meet up with Rick and head back to the patrol cars before he had to answer questions about clubbing a bad guy. Besides, it would all go in his report.

"Bubba. You don't look too happy," John said when he'd reached Rick.

"Was there any way this guy could have seen you?" Rick asked.

"I seriously doubt it. And besides, I don't think he is going to remember a whole lot, anyway."

Rick squinted, as if thinking hard. "The SAC needs to make sure. You're about to go undercover, and our driver said he was supposed to deliver this to another Hialeah warehouse owned by Fleitas."

Walking back to the street, John reassured Rick, "There's no chance he got a look at me. He had a dead stare on the dog as he tried to hack her with that machete. Besides, this guy is going nowhere fast, he's a no-bonder for sure. After attacking an officer, no way a judge sets bail."

Rick nodded. "Okay. I just don't want to take any chances."

John poked at Rick's shoulder in jest. "You're worried about me, aren't ya, buddy?"

"I've always worried about you," Rick replied, feigning a serious expression.

"Hey, man. I ain't the one that goes down to South America and jumps out of helicopters and shit," John teased.

"No. You just go running after violent felons in closed buildings."

"Yeah, but I'm not jumping out of a completely good aircraft." John gave his friend an energetic punch in the shoulder.

John got a kick out of Rick laughing along with him as they approached the patrol cars, where the scene buzzed with activity. Crime scene investigators had arrived to print the van and were about to open the doors, but Rick ran ahead, shouting, "Open that van before the dog sniffs it for drugs and I will personally shoot every one of you!"

The gaggle of uniformed and plainclothes cops gathering around the van froze in place. All eyes were on Rick. Not sure if he was serious or not, both crime scene techs backed off.

One tech offered a defensive, "Hey, man. The FDLE agent told us to print it."

Rick gritted his teeth and escorted the technicians away from the van. "Yeah, well FDLE isn't running the show here, pal. I don't think there's a question about who was in the van, and this is still an active investigation. If the patrol wants your services, I'm sure they'll ask for them. Not FDLE."

Rick glanced at John, his eyes widening.

John caught the cue as a silent request for help and said, "Hey, guys. This is my scene, but I'll tell you what. Let me run the dog, and if we find anything that we need printed, we'll go from there. Fair enough?" John liked his diplomatic tone much better than Rick's needling one.

The technicians agreed, although John saw the fuss was confusing them. He walked to his car to take off Spec's harness and grab her toy. He looked around and noticed a Florida Department of Law Enforcement agent talking to Captain DeLeón and FHP's public information officer.

Patting Spec on the head, he also noticed the first of the TV news vans arriving. John rolled his eyes. He had seen this too many times before. A trooper would make a great newsworthy case and suddenly, the FDLE shows up as the *premier* state agency to make all the public statements. Only this time, he was sure the captain would handle their antics. But he figured it was best for him to stay out of that fray. He watched Corporal Smith, the FHP's public information officer, take notes while the captain spoke. The FDLE agents, however, didn't look especially happy.

"Okay, Corporal, just so we're clear," the captain explained. "FHP stopped the van for speeding and Trooper Florey Baker was attacked by the passenger, who is now in custody after an FHP canine handler found the subject hiding in a barn. You with me so far?"

"Yes, Captain." Smith wrote feverishly, never taking his eyes off his pad.

"With the assistance of the Metro-Dade police department, FHP officers were able to contain the perimeter, which led to our canine's successful apprehension of the violent felon. Our trooper is in stable condition and having her wounds tended to at a local hospital. That *is it* for now," the captain said as he glanced towards John.

"Let's give Stella a chance to run the dog. There is no telling what is inside this van." DeLeón motioned for everyone to move away from the van, giving John and Spec a wide berth.

Some of the FDLE agents stubbornly remained close by the van, acting as if it was beneath them for a traffic cop, despite the brass bars on his shoulder, to tell them what to do. John could almost read the captain's mind, and he didn't like the disrespect. On the other hand, none of them wanted a scene in front of the press.

John asked the FDLE agents to step aside so he could work Spec, speaking as professionally as possible. The agents looked unhappy, but they moved aside.

He fumed at the slow response and open disrespect for his captain. It was time for a different way to get the agents the hell out of the way. John looked down at Spec and whispered, "Lout."

Immediately the dog began a tirade of barking.

That did it. The saliva-spewing, pissed-off, and blood-stained police dog reared up on her hind legs, appearing to be in attack mode, sent both agents running towards their cars.

John gave the leash a tug and Spec went quiet.

Then he turned Spec around and focused on the van, but he managed first to glimpse his captain.

DeLeón's face was glowing red. Angry over his stunt? John wondered. He looked again and the captain's face beamed in a wide smile as he collected himself and cleared his throat.

"Stella, get to work. Let's not be here all day!" he barked.

"Yes, Sir."

Doing it by the numbers, he directed Spec's actions, starting at the front bumper. After a few steps, she dragged John directly to the rear doors and began scratching. John grabbed hold of her collar, opened one of the rear doors, and allowed Spec to thrust her head forward, sniffing the stack of brown cardboard boxes. She immediately began scratching at them.

John threw her toy in front of her and she snapped it up, turning to play tug-of-war with him. After a few pulls, John patted her head before moving her to the shade under an avocado tree.

At that point, Rick stepped up and entered the rear of the van. He carefully opened the box Spec had alerted him to.

"Jesus Christmas!" He reached in and held up a bundle of one-hundred dollar bills wrapped in a rubber band and raised it to show John.

"Nice, but uh, news cameras, buddy." John pointed to the news teams now descending on the captain.

Rick quickly stashed the bundle back in the box and checked the rest of the cargo. Each box was packed with U.S. currency. Rick backed out of the van, closed the door, and went to his car.

A few minutes later, John was putting evidence tape over every box and door on the van, and then called for a tow truck from nearby Homestead. Uneasy sitting idle in a vehicle packed with so much cash, he was glad to see it show up only a few minutes later. John wasted no time directing the driver to hook up to the van, an operation that took only a few minutes.

John asked the captain to assign two other troopers to escort the truck and Rick's guys directly to the DEA office. Security was critical, and that meant making no stops along the way.

Watching the motorcade depart, he saw Captain DeLeón and Corporal Smith finishing their last media interview. When DeLeón was free, John told him he was heading to the hospital to check on Florey. "You need me to do anything before I leave?"

The Captain gave John's arm a light whack and led him away from prying eyes and ears. "That was one of the funniest things I think I have ever seen, kid. You should have seen the look on those idiots' faces when your dog scared them off." He tried to suppress his laugh. "Make sure I get the canine bite report by tomorrow. I'll take care of the teletype for Florey's injury and the dog bite with Tallahassee. If you're going to be at the kennel, have a trooper meet you to bring the reports in. And, Stella…thanks."

"For what, sir?"

"Thanks for not getting us in to a shooting," DeLeón said. "Otherwise FDLE *would* be handling this investigation."

"They don't handle slips and falls, Captain?" John asked with a hint of sarcasm.

Still chuckling, the captain shook his head as he walked to his car.

John was finally free to go. Not home, though.

A few minutes later, he arrived at James Archer Smith Hospital in Homestead, where Florey was being treated.

"There ya go, hon. Three stitches and you'll be as good as new," John heard the nurse say as he came around the corner to the treatment cubicle.

"Thanks for taking me so quickly, Linda," Florey said.

"Are you kidding me, sweetie? What are friends for if they can't help each other?" Linda said.

John had known Florey's friend for a long time. She'd been a nurse at the hospital for as long as Florey had been a trooper, and they'd been best friends since Florey's first year on the job. John snuck up behind Linda, wrapped his arms around her waist, and whispered in her ear, "Peek-a-boo."

Linda spun around, surprise showing in her beaming smile. "John Stella! Where the hell have you been? You never come by anymore. I was starting to think that both of you left town together."

John hated it when his face got hot. For sure, he was turning red. He shot Florey a glance. He was used to that kind of remark. Having a female partner on any police force meant someone couldn't resist suggesting that the working relationship was more than just professional. Sure, he knew she was only joking, but there he was, blushing all the same.

"Yeah, well anyway, how's she doing?" he asked.

"Oh, she'll be just fine," Linda said. "You're the one who looks like he's been run over by the Miami Dolphins' defensive line. What happened to you?" She put her hand on his forehead as if checking for fever.

"Oh, nothing. I went running through the woods with my dog to catch the guy that did that." He pointed to Florey's forehead.

"You got him?" Florey asked as she sat up from the examination bed.

John noticed the dried blood on her uniform had turned from a vivid red to a crusty dark brown. "Yeah, kiddo. No worries. Spec took a piece of his forearm, but he's on his way to jail," he explained, reaching into his cargo pocket and taking out Florey's cuffs. "Here, these are yours."

Florey took them from John's hand and put them on the exam bed next to her.

"That's good news," Linda said.

John didn't provide any details on the arrest. He'd wait until they were alone to tell her more about what had happened to their subject.

"What did you find in the van?" Florey asked.

"Spec alerted, and Rick found boxes of money," he answered, doing his best to be nonchalant in front of their friend.

"Money?" Linda exclaimed. She was washing her hands on the other side of the room, but had chimed right in. "How much money?"

John might have known she'd ask. Linda was inquisitive mostly because she liked a good story, and Florey and John could provide them. But John wasn't in the mood for more storytelling, even retelling his own. He guessed Florey wasn't up for it, either.

"I have no idea, Linda, but there were a bunch of boxes," he said, and turned back to his partner. "Right now, Rick is on his way to the DEA. I came straight here to check on my favorite partner. Next to Spec, of course." John flashed a smile at Florey, which she returned. "So, is there anything I can get you?"

"No." She stared at the floor. "I'm sorry, John."

"Sorry for what?"

She looked up at him with sad eyes. "I just didn't see it coming. I should've known better."

"That could have happened to anyone, Florey. Don't forget the time you saved my ass. Shit happens. Don't apologize. We have each other's backs. You know that."

Briefly closing her eyes, Florey nodded. "Thanks."

"See?" Linda said, winking at John. "I told you he would say that."

Linda said a quick good-bye and they were alone.

When Florey stood up and grabbed her gun belt, John figured he would answer before she asked. "I had to hit the shithead with an axe handle I found in old man Ronnie's barn. Your boy tried to take a swing at Spec with a machete."

Florey stared at John, but then abruptly looked away.

Not fast enough. John saw her eyes grow watery and knew she struggled not to cry.

He put his arms around her. "Hey, it's okay. I promise I won't let anyone know the Iron Maiden has feelings." Secure in his embrace, she let her tears flow. That was fine with him. Physical attacks on the job were traumatic, and everybody had a way to unwind its grip. It was private, though. This was one of those moments that would remain between partners. "Come on. Let's get out of here and take you home."

Chapter Nine

It was nearly noon by the time John managed to drag himself out of bed and start out for the kennel. When he got there, he found Tomás already waiting for him under the training area overhang. John couldn't help his cynicism about anyone, even Tomás, anxiously awaiting the details of the story that had broken on Channel 7 and led the broadcast the previous night. On the other hand, John was glad to see Tomás had left his house early enough to pick up cups of Cuban coffee and a bag of pastelitos to share.

"My friend." Tomás greeted John with an ear to ear grin and briskly shook his hand. "I understand your partner is okay?" Tomás handed John one of the cups of coffee.

"Yeah. She'll be fine." John downed it as if it was a shot of tequila. He noticed Tomás doing the same.

"Good to hear," Tomás said. "Now, tell me how your dog did her job."

John gave Tomás a step-by-step account of the prior day's events, answering his questions as he went. As usual, the master trainer was keen on the technical aspects of a search and wouldn't hesitate to ask about wind direction, humidity, and temperature—all the little things that went into a successful deployment of a police dog.

"So, how come the news showed this guy out cold in the ambulance? Spec scare him unconscious?" Tomás asked with undisguised sarcasm.

That final question caught John off guard. "He slipped and fell. Hit his head."

"Bullshit, Stella." Tomás could barely suppress his laughter.

Being evasive was John's way of toying with Tomás. But John also knew he'd end up telling his observant friend the entire story before the day was over. Not surprisingly, Tomás played along as he walked away to pick up a bite sleeve.

"Okay. Maybe you tell me later," said Tomás, still smiling. "Go get the first dog. We have a long day ahead of us."

***

Cali, Colombia

Five miles outside the Pacific resort town of Buenaventura, the Land Cruiser turned north onto a narrow dirt roadway. Justo sat back as Rivero negotiated the ruts and potholes created by the constant seasonal rains. Even so, with each turn, the truck, laden with its additional bulletproofing, swayed violently from side to side as it fought for traction in the deep, mud-filled trenches. Justo knew Rivero did his best to keep him from bouncing off his seat in this bucking bronco ride. Finally, they passed the grass airstrip and Rivero stopped at the first building he came to.

He pulled the Land Cruiser under a small canopy extending out from the structure, hoping it would provide cover from the sheets of rain coming down.

From the front, the metal building looked like any other in the area. Designed as a plane hangar to house the various aircrafts transporting marijuana in the 70s, it was now mostly used as a garage where local farmers could fix their tractors and other equipment. Occasionally, the Colombian Federal Police would pass by to search, but mostly, put on a good show for whatever American law enforcement official happened to be touring the area.

The gusting wind and heavy rain was making any idea of staying dry hopeless. Before bolting from the vehicle, Justo instructed Rivero to stay in the truck and keep the engine running.

Justo winced from the sharp sting of rain hitting his face as he ran the short distance to the front door. Turning the handle, a gust of wind forced it from his hand and the door violently crashed into a file cabinet inside. Justo fought the howling wind as he shouldered the door closed and secured the large deadbolt.

As he brushed himself off and used his hand to squeegee the water from his face, he noticed a few mechanics standing quickly, apparently surprised by the appearance of one of the cartel's captains. Justo could see they'd been watching a fútbol match on a small television propped up on cases of brown packing tape. He waved to the men as he passed through, indicating they should go back to their game.

Entering the garage area, he made his way around several tractors and broken down trucks, each in various stages of repair. They emitted the migraine-inducing odors of gear lube and gasoline, which permeated the space.

Justo quickly went up the wooden stairs at the back wall and then made his way down a dark, narrow hallway. He passed several vacant supply rooms and offices until he came to the last door. He fished his key out of his wet pants pocket. The lock clunked loudly when he twisted it and pushed open the door.

He took off his raincoat and tossed it onto a desk chair. On the opposite side of the office, he pushed gently on a chair rail along the wall, and a large panel opened to reveal a hidden room. Illuminated by a single light dangling from the ceiling, the cramped space was filled with short wave radios and electronics used to scan government and military frequencies, a setup like the one at Villa Orejulla.

Justo turned on the equipment and sat behind a small desk. The sounds of the storm outside were quickly interrupted by the static of radios coming to life as he dialed in the shortwave radio frequency. He checked his watch, knowing the weather had him running a few minutes late.

"Macho. Macho." The radio began to blare. "Are you standing?" a voice asked between the crackling of static.

Continuing in the cryptic dialogue, Justo answered, "I'm standing. How is El Gordo?"

"El Gordo is doing well," the voice answered.

The poor reception and the constant din of the downpour hitting the metal roof above made it difficult to hear. Justo rolled his chair to the desk and leaned forward, putting his ear as close to the speaker as possible.

"Is the family okay in Miami?" Justo asked in a raised voice while making slow, deliberate adjustments to the radio frequency knob, being careful not to lose the reception.

"The family is having some problems, Macho. You may need to send a doctor, maybe a surgeon."

Justo understood. When he had been summoned that morning by Juan Orejulla to talk about the new business, Juan had been very upset by a series of reports coming out of Miami. He'd instructed Justo to personally take care of the issues. Permanently, if need be. Checking in with Miami via the shortwave radio was his chance to get a firsthand idea of what was really going wrong.

"I will send a doctor to see if they can find what ails the baby," Justo said.

"*Bueno, Macho.* He needs to get here quick," the voice said.

"*Entiendo, chico. Adios.*" Justo turned off the radio before any meddlesome American DEA agent could triangulate his location. He pushed his chair to the other side of the desk and placed the telephone receiver in the cradle. Then, he turned on the computer and waited for the signal to register before typing: **Call me. I need some legal advice. Use the office phone.**

Impatient, Justo checked his watch again as the metal walls of the building shuddered with passing thunder. It was just after noon in Miami. He sat back in his chair and closed his eyes, listening to the wind and rain and thinking how strangely peaceful it was. He put his feet up on the desk, but the ringing telephone interrupted his respite.

He swung his feet off the desk and picked up the receiver, pushing the encryption button on the handset.

"Justo, Jack Costello here. I got your message."

Jack Costello was well-known around Miami law enforcement as a drug attorney. It was an open secret who among the lawyers in town had taken the cartel on as a client. Most lawyers avoided the association since payment with any type of drug proceed was illegal and ran the risk of having the Feds confiscate their bank accounts. For Jack, morals and legal ethics always played second fiddle to making a quick buck.

"Were you able to check into that problem I mentioned to you?" Justo asked.

"Yes, indeed," Jack answered. "Seems there have been several issues with the police. Strangely, it's the same two officers."

Justo frowned. "What do we know about these *officers*?"

"Nothing special. They're state troopers."

"Troopers? Why are they handling drug enforcement?" Justo understood the roles of the various Florida law enforcement agencies and this only added to his suspicions.

"I have no idea. But we're going to see if we can find out. I have a few lawyer friends that can help out. Of course, they won't want to be forgotten," Costello said.

"Yes, yes. I will take care of them," Justo said. "Just let me know what you find out. El Heffe is not very happy about this interruption to business."

"Give me three or four days and I'll get back with you," Jack advised.

"*You will get back with me?*" Justo shot back, indignant. "You have 'til tomorrow, five in the afternoon, your time. Call me back at this number." Justo returned the handset to the phone base and pushed back in the desk chair.

As much as Justo hated dealing with American lawyers, they were an absolute necessity. The American police were a completely different issue. Unlike Colombia, where paying off the police and politicians was commonplace, U.S. cops were not quite so pliable. Although there were a few on the payroll, they were not as easy to come by. In the States, the cartels depended on the lawyers—they were the real tools you paid for to keep you out of trouble.

When the drone of rain hitting the roof finally stopped, Justo checked his watch again and left the hidden room, closing the secret entranceway behind him. As he got back into the Land Cruiser, he found Rivero sitting behind the wheel with the air conditioner blasting. The returning sunlight had already baked the surrounding landscape back to an uncomfortable ninety-four degrees.

"Everything okay, Heffe?" Rivero asked hesitantly.

Rivero probably wondered what was troubling him, but Justo said he was fine. He pointed towards the hillside. "Let's go up to the ranch."

Rivero pulled out from under the overhang and continued driving up the winding mud road, passing a series of buildings used to package flowers for transport to the United States. One of the many legitimate businesses used by the Cali cartel, but had the police ever looked in the back of either of those buildings, they'd have discovered an elaborate cocaine processing lab. The fact that the cartel's bribes and community work kept most of the Colombian police away, or simply blind, served as yet another reminder to Justo of the potential problems with doing business in the States. He couldn't afford for anything to go wrong.

The heads of the syndicate, especially Juan Miguel Orejulla, wouldn't look favorably on anyone that compromised the success of the operation. Justo wasn't willing to become yet another statistic in the increasing violence now typical of cartel management. He knew to always keep his options open.

But for now, his focus was making sure everything was going as planned. Especially at the ranch, where his other concern was Don Chepe.

Rancho Chepe was named after one of the founding cartel families. The vast spread was nestled atop a secluded mountain plateau overlooking the town of Buenaventura. The owner, Don Chepe, was known as a cold and calculating man. Giving up a career in engineering, he had quickly risen up the ranks of marijuana smugglers before consolidating his ventures with Juan Miguel Orejulla. He had since become more reclusive, his cautious behavior turning paranoid, considering the ongoing conflict with Medellin. It was Don Chepe who was the most critical of security and had been making the greatest demands for a quick resolution to the problems in Miami.

Once at the ranch, Rivera drove the Land Rover past the houses to a large metal building at the far end of the compound's airstrip. A black stovepipe chimney rose ominously above the roof line. The billowing black smoke kept the area bathed in an acrid cloud of chemicals that not even the heavy rains seemed to be able to neutralize.

Rivero stopped at the side entrance, and Justo got out and glanced up at the chimney as he walked past the armed guards. He wrinkled his nose to hold back a sneeze before ducking into the building.

The brightly lit space inside had rows of tables alongside open vats of various chemicals. Vials and tubes coiled around Bunsen burners gave the whole operation the appearance of a chemistry classroom rather than a coke lab. Each of the tables was tended by workers in smocks who carefully monitored the equipment. They were learning the German process of molecularly combining raw nylon with pure cocaine. The noxious mixture was eventually poured into forming molds.

Justo observed what was happening. The molds were set up in stations, each one creating a different plastic item. One made industrial gears, while others manufactured plastic chairs or statuary. One even made a plastic case functioning as an art kit for children's crayons and paints. Newly created products were being sorted and boxed at the packaging and loading dock at the far end of the building. All the merchandise would then be loaded onto trucks and taken to the Gerardo Tobar Lopez Airport at Buenaventura. From there, the planes would enter the United States at Miami and eventually, as the plan expanded, at Houston and New York.

Justo scrutinized the workers until his eyes finally landed on a tall, white-skinned man standing next to a long lab table, hovering over a series of vials and papers.

"Doctor Mueller," Justo said, approaching.

Mueller nervously looked up, startled at the unexpected interruption.

"How is everything going, Doctor?"

"Everything is on schedule," the doctor said. "It's a little difficult to understand some of your workers, but we're managing."

"Good. Is there anything I can get you or your family?" Justo asked.

"Yes. I was hoping…maybe…if some of the children could call their father, Doctor Haus? Do you think that is possible?"

"I think that can be arranged," Justo answered.

The doctor's grin widened as his body loosened from its rigid stance. "Other than that, we're looking forward to finishing up so we can get back home."

Justo scanned the warehouse and the workers in their white lab smocks. Glancing up at the doctor, who towered over him by almost a foot, Justo noticed that his eyes were bloodshot, most likely from working in the heavy chemical fumes. For a moment, Justo felt sorry for the good doctor. Quickly, though, the feeling passed.

"As long as the helpers we have provided you are clear on the process and can do this on their own, we will get you and your family back home," Justo said, knowing the doctors were wary about this job and wanted their families kept safe. The cartel had done everything to make their stay seem like a vacation for the two families.

"Tell me how you're progressing," Justo said.

"Yes, well, we are able to process our mixture with more ease. I think you should be able to run this on your own very shortly," Doctor Mueller explained. "Please, if you don't mind my asking a question?"

"What is it?" Justo asked.

"Is all going well with Dr. Haus? I mean, the operation. Are they able to do the separation?"

Justo stared up at the doctor, never changing the stoic expression on his face. "Yes. All is going well. We are very pleased with your progress."

The doctor smiled nervously and returned to his work as Justo walked away.

Justo's eyes were already watery and burning from the pungent chemical fumes. He went outside quickly to get away from the toxic air.

He found a spigot and cranked open the valve so he could splash water onto his face to relieve the stinging in his eyes. He cupped his hands and took in a few gulps, swishing the water around in his mouth to get rid of the metallic taste the fumes had left behind, before spitting the water, now toxic itself, onto the ground.

"Uncle?" The voice came from the shadows.

Justo turned quickly, not expecting to see Rigo coming up from the guest houses.

"Rigoberto!" Surprised to see his nephew, he stepped forward to give him a hug. "What are you doing here?"

"Don Miguel asked me to keep an eye out for our guests. I've been acting as the translator and camp director for the families," Rigo explained.

Justo grinned. He knew this wasn't exactly the job his nephew had expected when he'd asked to come back and work the family business. "Have you noticed any problems?"

"No, Uncle. Everything seems to be going well."

"Has anyone called Miami or made any calls to the other doctor?" Justo asked.

Rigo frowned. "No. Why?"

"We may have a problem in Miami. The bosses are pissed off," Justo mused. "The lawyer down there will call me tomorrow. Perhaps we may know more then."

"What kind of problem?" Apparently mindful of the security guards standing nearby at the doorway, the young protégé spoke in a slightly lowered voice.

Following his nephew's gaze, Justo lowered his voice as well. "Seems the same cops keep finding our product, and now they're finding our money. Don Orejulla and Chepe seem to think there is a leak."

Rigo stood silent, but Justo was sure he understood. Since the cartel had put Justo in charge of overseeing the overall operation, any blame would also fall on his shoulders.

"You can count on me to help with anything. You know that," Rigo assured him.

Justo looked deeply into his nephew's eyes. He had watched a scared and lonely child grow up into a young man he loved like a son. Secretly, Justo was concerned for him. Perhaps the boy would be of better service away from the ranch. Far away, he thought.

He paused and took a deep breath to conceal his emotions before responding. "We will know more tomorrow. For now, Rigo, let's just keep them happy and working. Oh, and no phone calls to Miami."

Rigo nodded, and the two men started out for the main house.

***

Beatrice left her cubicle in the Crash Report and Records Department and walked to the lobby of the Miami FHP station to unlock the front doors. They were open for business. Struggling to push open the heavy double doors, she noticed an attractive young man in a suit climb out of a white Mercedes sedan and walk towards her. He arrived just as Beatrice managed to force the doors open. She asked if she could help him, noting the quality of his suit and the glint from his gold Rolex watch.

"Yes. Actually, I need to find out how to get some reports from two of your troopers." The stranger smiled politely.

Beatrice wasn't fooled by the superficial manners. He couldn't keep his eyes off of her tight jeans and spiked heels. She'd accentuated her curvaceous Latin figure with her choice of clothes, and she wouldn't apologize for a touch of vanity.

"Okay. Hold on. Let me get back to my office." Feeling her face heat up, Beatrice walked to the records area and opened the service window to the lobby. "I just need you to fill out this form." Beatrice handed the gentleman a Public Records Request form.

She watched the stranger scan the form and begin to fill in the information, all the while surreptitiously taking in the cut of his jacket and pants. By the looks of it, the morning was off to a good start—a quick public records request and some harmless flirting.

"Here you go, Miss. It is *Miss*, isn't it?" the stranger asked coyly.

Her cheeks on fire, Beatrice took the paper from under the service window and replied, "Why, yes, it is." She quickly turned away as she read the records request. She had to read it twice before she understood it. Her skin cooled and she assumed her pink cheeks had faded.

"Do you want *all* copies of tickets, warnings, and crash reports for these two troopers from the last *two* years?" She stared at the young man.

The stranger nodded with a wide grin, exposing his flawless teeth.

She scratched her head and examined the form again. Letting out a sigh, she put the form on the desk and coyly placed her hand on her hip as she dug one of her stiletto heels into the carpet. "Okay. But you know this may take some time, right?" she said, now secretly hoping he would go away.

"I'll be right here, Miss."

"Yeah, I hope so. You also know it's five cents a copy, right?" she blurted, wondering if that may change his request to get slightly less information.

"Sure do. Says it right there on your little form. It won't be a problem," the stranger assured her.

Beatrice put both of her hands on her hips and turned to face what now seemed like an endless wall of file cabinets. "Tickets," she murmured to herself. "Might as well start there." This was going to take a while.

The handsome stranger still stood at the window.

She laughed nervously. She read his name on the request form. "Mr. Costello?"

When the man nodded, she reached for the phone and said she was going to bring in some help from the secretarial staff to process his request. Actually, the day was off to a pretty bad start.

Chapter Ten

For John, the next week and a half seemed to go by in a flash. Tomás had postponed any training with his regular police department clients to make sure they wouldn't be interrupted from their work to get the dogs ready in time. John still had to pull double-duty.

During the training with Tomás, Florey and Rick had called him away on three different occasions to sniff out cars for contraband. Each time, he'd had to race home to grab Spec and the patrol car. Those traffic stops had produced over two and a half million dollars in cash and another fifteen hundred kilos of cocaine.

Julio Mendoza Cortés, despite having one less testicle, was proving to be quite an asset in helping to turn each new suspect into cooperating informants, all of them opting to play along rather than face stiff prison sentences. The DEA and the FBI's interrogation of those suspects had begun to paint a clearer picture of the players and the cell network operating in South Florida. Even though there was the risk of exposing Federal involvement, it was, nonetheless, a calculated risk that had to be taken. Washington had made it clear to its agencies: the president wanted arrests and the cartel dismantled before new supplies of cocaine hit the streets.

Rick had kept Florey and John up-to-date on the overall progress of the case as they increased their understanding of the cells distributing drugs and money. Still, the missing piece of the puzzle was the whereabouts of Doctor Haus.

Rick thought Javier Fleitas was their strongest lead so far and provided the best opportunity at finding Haus. John and Florey agreed. Getting onto the Hialeah warehouse property was becoming more urgent, especially since the positive developments by the FBI surveillance teams.

Video of the warehouse had turned up some promising images, including a blurry screen shot of a suspect taken from a distant rooftop surveillance camera. It was grainy, but Rick was convinced it was the doctor.

At a task force intelligence meeting, Rick produced the picture and video. The FBI had brought in their forensic specialists and compared the image to known images of the doctor. It was a tough call to make, despite the FBI crime lab's use of the latest photo enhancement techniques on the images.

Not all the experts agreed with Rick. But still, the ghost-like image sent a sense of urgency charging through the task force. It was decided to move ahead with the delivery of the dogs as soon as possible. John would see if he could confirm in person if it was the doctor.

Doing his best to calm his nerves, John got into his Mustang and headed to Tomás' kennel. This was the day Fleitas would come see the dogs. The FBI and the State Department were concerned about involving Tomás, but Rick and John both insisted that he was essential to the ruse.

John considered Tomás' safety his personal responsibility. As he entered the kennel property, he noticed the F-350 parked next to the office. Extra cautious, he parked his car by backing it as close to the training building as he could, to conceal its tag. He immediately went to work cleaning kennels.

As he scrubbed down one of the front holding pens, John heard the voices of the two men as they left the office and walked towards him. He felt his heart rate pick up a beat as he suddenly became self-conscious about his regulation haircut and his choice of wristwatch, a G-Shock—the durable timepiece commonly used among police officers. He had thought about taking it off, but the bright tan line had only made it look more obvious that he regularly wore a watch. He had decided to just leave it on and keep his finger's crossed.

"I will have my man get the dogs for you to see. I think you'll be happy with them," Tomás said, approaching the kennels.

John pretended not to notice and continued to briskly scrub the cage floor.

"John, go get the two dogs for Mr. Fleitas," Tomás ordered.

Feigning surprise, John looked up from his scrubbing. "No problem, Tomás." He put down the broom and left.

"John, hold on a minute." Tomás pointed to his client. "This is Javier

Fleitas, the gentleman we have been training dogs for."

John stepped up, wiped his wet hands on his pant leg, then firmly grasped Fleitas' hand.

"Good to meet you, sir. I think you'll be pleased with the dogs."

Fleitas smiled politely.

"So, you help train the dogs?" Javier asked.

John nodded, noticing suspicion written on Javier's features.

"He's helped me train quite a few," Tomás said. "He's one of the best. He wouldn't be here if he wasn't." Tomás beamed and flashed his best salesman's grin.

John remained impassive, although he still read concern on Javier's face.

"Is there a problem?" Tomás asked.

Javier grinned cynically. "Has anyone ever told you, John, you look like a cop?"

"Cop?" Tomás laughed, and John joined him. "He's a friend of my wife's brother. John turned out to be one of my finest trainers." He shrugged. "That's because I taught him everything he knows."

Impressive, John thought. Tomás didn't even bat an eye at the sudden need to lie. But they'd discussed cover stories. John had expected Fleitas to be wary.

Without making a comment, John went off to get the dogs. When he returned, he introduced the suspect to his new purchases. "This is Schmutz," he said, pointing to the darker of the two dogs. "And this is Tasche."

"They are incredible-looking!" Fleitas was clearly impressed. "Are they friendly?"

"Absolutely." Tomás gestured toward the dogs. "Go ahead, pet them."

Fleitas gingerly patted each of them on the head.

In a chastising tone, Tomás said, "Come on! Walk with them."

John stepped forward and handed over the leashes, and Fleitas slowly walked his dogs in a circle around the training field.

Tomás pointed towards the far end of the field. "Take them around again and pick up your pace a bit."

This time around both dogs relaxed and acted more like house pets than attack dogs.

"You see?" Tomás called out. "They like you!"

"Yes, they are amazing!" Fleitas shouted from the far end of the field.

"You think this guy is buying it, Tomás?" John whispered.

"Of course. This guy is an idiot. Now, quiet. He's coming back."

Fleitas returned to the shelter, his huge grin an indicator of his satisfaction. Clearly comfortable now, he included John in a conversation about what to feed the dogs. Seamless. John could see Javier's stress ease, a good sign he didn't suspect a ruse.

"John, tie Schmutz up to the fence and hold on to Tasche," Tomás instructed, as he began putting on the heavy bitesuit.

"Okay, my friend," he told Fleitas, "we'll show you the bite work and obedience first. Then, we will show you how they find drugs."

Tomás zipped up the heavy coat and crammed his legs into the padded pants. He began the labored walk to the middle of the training field. "Okay, John! Send him!"

John patted Tasche on the head, and as if flipping a switch, the dog's demeanor completely changed. Tasche focused his full attention on Tomás and began his excited barking as he anticipated the order to pounce on his prey at the end of the field. John unleashed the dog, who remained at his side, still barking, foam building around its jowls.

"Get him!" John yelled.

The animal took off in a full sprint, taking just a few seconds to cover over fifty feet. He leapt forward, tucking back his legs and rocketing with an open mouth directly at its target. Tomás anticipated the attack and turned to the side to absorb the impact of the seventy-five pound Malinois. He held up his right arm, allowing for the dog to bite down on the padded sleeve as the rest of his body slammed against Tomás' shoulder in a loud thud.

Tomás spun around, absorbing the momentum of the collision, and immediately began the theatrics of fighting the dog. His movements were quick and well-calculated—partly for show and partly to avoid getting bit or hurting the animal unintentionally.

Even for John, the display was impressive. He looked at Fleitas and saw him grinning, his saucer-sized eyes focused on the exhibition.

John ran out to calm Tasche and yelled for him to stop while he leashed him. Instantly, the dog released his vice-like grip and returned to John's side.

Walking back to the start position, John tied Tasche to the fence and repeated the process with Schmutz. The results were the same. Fleitas drank in every moment. The dogs performed exactly as they had been trained, and the drug detection exhibition was no different.

By the time they were done, Fleitas was all smiles. So was Tomás. And John had a new respect for his trainer friend. His fast-talking and showmanship had clearly won over the once-skeptical Javier Fleitas.

"Okay. So, what you think?" Tomás asked.

"They are incredible. I couldn't be happier!" the suspect exclaimed.

"That's good. So, when do you want us to deliver the dogs?"

Fleitas paused, appearing surprised, as if he hadn't expected the question. "I can take them today."

"No. You don't want to do that." Tomás seamlessly shifted from a theatric performer back into a salesman. "These animals have been here since they came from Germany. You're going to want us to acclimate them to their new home. In case issues come up, we can train them on site. You know, we'll see how they adjust. It's all part of the service."

Javier Fleitas thought for a moment before he gave his answer. "I see. Well… Ah, how about tomorrow. Say around noon?"

"Excellent," said Tomás. "Come. Let's go in the office and sign some papers, and we'll get you on your way." Tomás put his hand on Fleitas' shoulder and guided him to the office. "Later, John will have Carlos give them a bath. We know you don't want to get dirty animals."

John nodded. "Of course."

Tomás exuded great confidence when he said, "Come, my friend. I will even throw in a few bags of dog food and some leashes and collars."

Javier paid Tomás in cash he pulled from a zippered bag in two stacks, ten thousand dollars each. The two piles of bills were wrapped in bank bands stamped: *Ocean Bank of Miami.*

After Javier jotted down the delivery address in Hialeah on one of the bands, John watched Tomás escort him back to his vehicle and shake his hand before Fleitas got in his truck and drove off the property.

"So. How do you think it went?" John asked when Tomás came back.

"This guy doesn't have a clue." Tomás laughed. "I thought he wouldn't be happy about us delivering the dogs, but as soon as I told him I would throw in the food, leashes, and collars, he wasn't going to turn it down." He shrugged. "You offer us Cubans free stuff and we lose our minds."

John smiled but offered no comment.

"So, Stella, I've never seen you speechless. What're you worried about, my friend?"

"We still have to get through tomorrow." He didn't feel as carefree as Tomás.

"Relax. You did excellent. This guy thinks you are the best trainer in the world." Tomás gave John a reassuring smile. "We just won't tell him that *I* am the best trainer in the world. Let him think that an Italian can actually train dogs." Tomás laughed at his own remark.

But Tomás' reassuring tone grated on John. "Well, that will be two things now that he has in common with you, Tomás," he snapped.

Tomás squinted, his expression turning suspicious. "Yeah, Gringo? What would that be?"

"One, he now has dogs like you. Two, you're both fucking rafters," John said.

Tomás threw his head back, laughing even harder. "You are fucked up, Stella. Come on. Let's go to Redland Grill. I'll buy you dinner."

"Hey man, I should be buying you dinner. After everything you've done for us? You know we couldn't have done this without you. We can't ever repay you," said John.

Still shaking his head, Tomás smiled. "We take it out of what the Feds say I can keep from this deal. Besides, look at it this way. Fleitas is buying us dinner. After tomorrow, I will throw a party. He will be paying for that, too." Tomás gave John's shoulder a friendly bump.

In spite of himself, John smiled.

"Besides, Stella. You look like you can use a beer."

John didn't disagree. He couldn't be happier that it went so well, and he was a bit relieved. Tomás had played the part perfectly. Winning over the trust of a suspect, plus convincing him to deliver the dogs, was critical. Tomás had managed it without flinching. It didn't need to come up in conversation, but John knew Tomás' motivation. His hatred of dopers brought out his best performance.

On the way to dinner, John dialed Rick Lotz's number to brief him. "Hey, compadre, I'm calling from the car. I have good news," John said.

"I've been waiting for your call. Where are you two now?" Rick asked.

"On the way to Redland Grill. You want to join us?" John assumed Rick was on surveillance, but asked anyway.

"Not this time, Bubba. We're tailing your boy Fleitas. We wanna know everywhere he goes. So, tell me, did he buy it?"

"Hook, line, and stinker." John chuckled. "Tomás was amazing. He sold this guy like he was buying swampland in the Everglades."

"When do you guys deliver?" Rick asked.

John could hear Rick's car engine racing in the background. "Hey, partner. Pay attention to your surveillance. Don't fall too far behind," John cautioned.

"Very funny, *mi amigo*! But would you please tell me when you're delivering the dogs?"

"Noon, tomorrow," John replied as he and Tomás pulled into the Redland Grill parking lot.

"Let's keep in touch," Rick said. "Call me first thing in the morning and I'll brief the brass. And John…"

"Yeah, buddy?"

"Excellent work, both of you. Tell Tomás thanks."

"Will do. Talk to you tomorrow."

John closed the phone and pulled into the parking space next to Tomás' van. Out of habit, as they walked into the restaurant, John casually glanced back to check on his car to make sure his furry partner was safe.

Then, he laughed at himself. He'd forgotten he was in his personal car and didn't have a dog with him. Out of the corner of his eye, he spotted a black Suburban with dark tints pulling off Krome Avenue into the gas station across the street. He kept his eye on it as he and Tomás took a table next to the front window. The SUV was parked away from the gas pumps and next to the convenience store. John continued to stare, wondering why nobody had exited the vehicle.

"What's the matter, my friend?" Tomás asked, following John's far-off gaze.

John's attention snapped back to Tomás. "Nothing. Just looking."

"You getting paranoid?" Tomás said through his laughter.

Tomás was probably right.

"Nah," John said. "Not yet, anyway. Let's have that beer."

Chapter Eleven

John was unceremoniously awakened by snoring and squirming. He was at the edge of the mattress, too. After helping herself to a spot next to him, Spec had fallen into a blissful but noisy slumber that left him opening his eyes to the vision of the dog's wet snout.

"Are you shittin' me?" John laughed out loud.

Spec opened her eyes long enough to stick out her tongue and lick John across his face.

He patted her head and proceeded to get out of bed, with Spec bounding to the floor and following behind, her gentle whimpering and tail wagging indicating her real desire.

"Okay, girl. Let me take a leak and I'll get you some food."

Hearing the word "food," Spec bolted out of the room to patiently wait by her food bowl.

John came out of his room into the living room but came to an abrupt stop. Standing motionless, he breathed deeply and took in the disaster. The room looked like a yard after a blizzard. Tufts of cotton-like polystyrene stuffing that had previously filled his leather couch clung to everything, including the ceiling fan. With its innards ripped out and scattered throughout the room, the couch was nearly deflated. How had she managed the redecorating act without waking him? Unfortunately, this wasn't the first time a canine had destroyed his home furnishings.

There was the time he'd helped train a fellow trooper's dog, a last-ditch effort to salvage the animal so the trooper wouldn't waste several months of training and have to start from scratch with a new dog. John took the animal home, intending to try to build a bond, but the dog would have none of it. Besides being completely disloyal and untrustworthy on the training field, Canine Tucker had no socialization skills, and as John had found out, took his frustrations out on the furniture. It had cost him a favorite armchair, a couch, and a chunk of linoleum floor.

On John's recommendation, the dog had been washed out of the program. The trooper wasn't thrilled about the lost time and starting over with a new dog, but he had ended up with his own Malinois. The new dog proved to be a far better deal. Too bad John had been out a thousand dollars in furniture.

Oblivious, Spec sat by her bowl, wagging her tail. Her act of frustration would simply mean replacing another couch. John had come to understand that this was the price of having a canine at home, but he wouldn't have it any other way. Keeping her locked up in a kennel for hours when she wasn't at work seemed cruel, yet he knew there was no other way around it while he was at Tomás' facility training other dogs.

Now, as he looked down at Spec, she sat with her head cocked as if to ask, "What?"

"You miss Daddy while he's gone without you?" John patted her head as he grabbed the bag of dog food.

Excited, she pranced around the floor, her gaze squarely on the bag. Before he could finish pouring, she lunged forward, thrusting her snout into the food, the impact sending a wave of kernelled food bits spilling over the side of the bowl.

"You must think I'm cheating on you when I come home smelling like other dogs." There was no sense in getting mad at Spec.

She stopped eating and looked up at him, as if she knew he had something more to say.

"One more day without me, baby girl. After today, I'm all yours," John said.

Spec wagged her tail as if she understood and then went back to munching her dry food.

John smiled. It was if she had made her point and just wanted him to admit to the error of his ways.

He checked the time. Eight o'clock. He poured his first cup of coffee, dropped into his favorite lounger, and turned on the news. As always, it was one report after another of drive-by shootings and drug hits. Miami had long been prone to violence, but now it was becoming more homegrown. The trend of Colombian hit men slaughtering the competition was giving way to local gangs branching out and robbing each other and tourists. Highway robberies were becoming more frequent, now proving to be the latest trend to plague the city.

Violent crime had become such a continuous news item, local broadcasts were popularly known as "the nightly murder report." John quickly found himself growing numb by the Gatling-gun-like barrage of reported carnage.

He turned off the television. After bagging up what had once been his furniture, John finished getting ready, patted Spec good-bye, and went on his way.

The Mustang's engine started with its characteristic roar. John loved the sound of it. There was nothing quite as intimidating as the sound of the little car.

As he pulled out onto Farm Life Road and headed north, John glanced in his rearview mirror and spotted the silhouette of a black Chevy Suburban parked down the street on the side of the road.

He squinted hard, but the windshield glare was overpowering so he still couldn't make out any of the occupants. Without panicking, John accelerated above the speed limit and noticed the SUV pull onto the road, following at a distance behind him.

John stopped at the next street and carefully maneuvered the Colt .45 government pistol he kept under his seat, putting under his thigh. He watched the SUV also stop and not come any closer to his car.

He made his turn west as if nothing was suspicious. The SUV made the same turn.

His heartbeat rose. "What in hell are these guys up to?" he muttered, approaching Krome Avenue, where he came to a full stop, waiting, watching. The SUV was now two cars behind him.

A box truck from Agros Farms pulled out from a field just before the intersection, obstructing the view of the SUV. John saw it as an opportunity.

Seeing a break in traffic, he turned right onto the avenue and quickly flipped his left turn signal. He moved into the painted median on the road, as if intending to turn into the corner gas station. John kept watching the SUV as it approached the intersection and abruptly changed lanes to go straight, not following John's turn. Just as he began to enter the gas station from the side street, John made his move.

He re-entered northbound traffic on Krome Avenue and picked up speed. The sound of the ported and polished 347 cubic inch engine screamed as John quickly worked each successive gear. Downshifting, he drove onto a private road bordered on each side by tall hedges. He whipped his car around, positioning it close against the foliage to conceal his location while still being able to view passing traffic.

A few cars passed by before John saw the SUV and caught a glimpse of the driver and passenger both leaning forward in their seats as if straining to see ahead.

"Fuckers," he mumbled, pulling onto Krome Avenue, where he joined the long train of impatient drivers stuck in traffic, probably thinking tourists in a giant SUV were lost. John knew better. He couldn't say why these guys were watching him. Or why they were involved in the case to begin with? He had no answer for that, but he didn't like being tailed. He understood, though, that these two morons were just taking orders. After letting his temper settle down, he came up with a plan.

Looking ahead, John dropped the Mustang into second gear and planted his foot hard on the gas, jamming the shifter into third and causing the tires to spin and produce a chirping sound. Fourth gear engaged with a hard thud as he approached the black SUV.

John moved his little car as close to the side of the Suburban as he could manage without crashing. The occupants still looked ahead.

John flew past, his speedometer needle arching just past 100. He wished he could see the looks on their faces.

As he geared down his Mustang, preparing for the turn to the kennel, he was satisfied to watch the SUV continue on, headed north, tailed by traffic.

Resuming a normal speed, John drove through the lot and parked behind Tomás' office. He glanced down the road, but no bewildered G-men were in sight. Probably licking their wounded egos. They'd be back, though. In any case, he had bigger concerns.

He and Tomás put together the equipment needed for the delivery and loaded up Tasche and Schmutz. They headed to meet Rick at the Florida Department of Transportation office just off the Turnpike on Okeechobee Road, but took Krome Avenue to steer clear of Miami's typical morning congestion.

John sat in the passenger seat while Tomás drove the alternate route, passing across the western fringes of Dade County. He took in the serenity of the endless saw grass marshlands and cypress trees. In the peaceful moment, John closed his eyes and let his mind wander to the endless weekends of his youth when he and his friends raced across the shallow fields in their airboats. A lifetime ago.

"Hey, Gringo, you sleeping on me?" Tomás teased.

John opened his eyes. "Nah. Just trying to relax before the dog and pony show." He worked hard to keep his apprehension from bleeding into his voice.

"You going to be alright, my friend?"

"Don't you worry about me. I should be asking *you* that question."

"It's true," Tomás said. "I hate these shitheads. But if I have to turn myself inside-out to help you put this guy away, I do it."

"I know you will, buddy," John said, reclining his seat back a couple of inches.

As the van turned and traveled east on Okeechobee Road, the serenity of the marshland turned into endless rows of rock quarries, each gouging their coral rock treasure out of the land. The mountains of gravel carved out of the earth, some as high as a five-story building, were constant reminders of Dade County's unfortunate mindset to build endless homes and shopping centers. The diminishing marshland seemed to give up its rights and succumbed to the demands of newcomers and greedy builders. Despite the protest of environmentalists, outdoorsmen, and students—John had once attended a rally at the county commission hall with his elementary school mates—the concrete continued flowing west as nature continued its steady retreat.

Tomás passed under the Turnpike and drove to the DOT office. John guided him to a parking spot in the rear lot and out of sight of passing traffic, where he saw Rick standing next to the DEA tech van.

"Anything develop in the past few days?" John asked after exchanging quick greetings.

Guiding John and Tomás towards the van, Rick said, "No. Everything has been the same. When you guys are out there, we hope to learn more."

One of the technicians walked up holding a cell phone and wire. "Who gets the bug?" he asked.

John stepped forward. "That would be me."

"Okay. All you have to do is poke a hole in your cargo pants and feed this wire to the clip-on holder for this cell phone," the tech said. "So long as the phone is in the holder, it will pick up pretty much anything that's said within twenty-five feet. And don't worry about the wind. Wind doesn't affect the microphone."

John studied the contraption. Then he unzipped his pants, ran the antennae wire down his leg, and connected the clip-on holder to his belt. Using his pocketknife, he poked out a hole in the waistline of his pants. "You sure this thing is going to work?" he asked.

Rick turned to the tech van and the other tech motioned with a thumbs-up sign.

"Yup, looks like you are coming in clear. Just remember to keep the phone clipped in. If you have to take it off..." Rick reached and removed the phone from the holder, flipping it open. "You push the Off button, which will power the phone down but keeps the microphone active. But try to keep it attached because the antennae will help with better reception."

"Okay. Got it," John said, taking out his personal phone and handing it to Rick. "Here, keep this so I don't have to explain two phones." He walked away from the tech van and towards the edge of the DOT property. "You guys hear me okay?"

Both techs, each now wearing headphones to monitor the transmissions, gave John another thumbs-up sign.

Satisfied, John returned to the van and checked his watch. "It's about time we head out there," he said, remembering something he'd wanted to ask Rick. "Hey buddy, what are those same State Department spooks doing following me around?"

Rick's smile disappeared. He pointed to the phone now clipped to John's waist. Rick held up his index finger to his lips as he put his arm around John's shoulder and walked him to Tomás' van. "When you guys are done, we'll meet here again to get the equipment."

Damn. John had forgotten he wore the bug. Everything was getting recorded. Obviously, Rick didn't want to have his answer on tape. John nodded to Rick and got into the van.

Heavy traffic turned what should have been a short ride to the warehouse into a thirty-minute drive. John complained about being late, but Tomás brushed him off, reasoning that since Latins were never on time, if they weren't late, Fleitas would be suspicious.

John laughed to himself. If he made a date with someone in Miami, he'd joke, "Would that be regular time or Latin time?" If the answer was Latin time, he had thirty minutes to spare.

When they arrived at the gate to the warehouse property, the F-350 was the lone vehicle in the lot. As if on cue, Fleitas opened the office door and waved to acknowledge Tomás and John. He then reached one arm inside the office, and in an instant, the gate opened. He walked out to meet them in the parking lot.

Tomás parked a few spaces from the man's truck.

"Welcome, my friends. How are those dogs of mine?" Fleitas asked.

Tomás immediately went into salesman mode. "*Mi compadre!* They are fine. Do you want to start on the outside before we get them used to being inside the building?"

Fleitas didn't hesitate. "Of course. Let them out to see their new home."

Tomás motioned to John, who freed the dogs from the van. They could now roam around the property. "Walk them around a bit before we start," Tomás ordered.

John walked along with the dogs, each of them smelling their new surroundings. That gave Tomás time to distract Fleitas by showing him the leashes, collars, and dog food he had brought, while John casually directed the dogs toward the back of the warehouse.

The dogs followed him, each running and sniffing as they frolicked around the property. The dogs eventually bolted ahead of him and around the back corner of the building where John noticed two trash dumpsters pushed against the wall. He scanned his surroundings for surveillance cameras, and not seeing any pointed in his direction, he opened the lid of the first dumpster and leaned in for a look. The chemical odor coming from the large gobs of melted black plastic was intense. He closed the lid carefully. He wordlessly directed both dogs to sniff the area.

John wasn't surprised when they scratched at the dumpsters, alerting him to the caustic odor of drugs. He called the dogs away before they drew attention to themselves and walked them back towards the van in the parking lot.

"Okay, John, put up Tasche and get Schmutz ready to work," Tomás said, getting into the heavy bitesuit. "Javier, why don't you walk with John and the dog? I'll hide behind the building."

Fleitas did as he was instructed. After several bites from Schmutz, Tomás repeated the process with Tasche. As John shouted and recalled Tasche to his side, he noticed that Fleitas was totally taken in by the dog show. Most importantly, their suspect was completely at ease with their presence on the property.

John bent down to the panting dog and hooked Tasche to the leash.

"Mr. Fleitas, do you mind if I ask you if the dogs will be roaming around the property at night, or will they be kept inside?" John said.

Without taking his eyes off Tasche, Fleitas said he planned to have one inside for security and the other outside. "Like I said, I'll use the dogs to sniff cars if I ever suspect an employee of doing drugs. I don't tolerate drug use by my employees."

John acted impressed, but knew the guy was probably more concerned with an employee pocketing a bag of cocaine and stealing the profits—and not much else.

Fleitas snapped to attention and looked at John. "Why do you ask, my friend?"

Cautiously, John said, "Well, I notice you don't have a kennel or shelter for the dogs. I wondered where you'd have them during business hours."

Fleitas stared at him with a smile so sinister it sent a chill down John's spine. "I'll show you when we go inside. I made room in my office for them. You will see."

"Excellent." John hid his nervousness as he took Tasche to his cage.

Tomás joined them, but his pace was labored from the heavy bitesuit. The explosive energy it took to work the dogs had worn Tomás down, and when he took off the heavy coat, his shirt was soaked in sweat.

"Shit! Does the suit get that hot?" Fleitas asked, amazed.

John listened for the answer, amused that instead of admitting the obvious, that the suit would work anyone into a sweat even if it was fifty degrees outside, Tomás chose a different path. "I've never seen dogs like these! You have bought two of the best."

That's right, John thought, stroke the guy's ego. The remark had its intended effect, too. Their suspect grinned like he'd just won the lotto.

Without a hint of hesitation, Fleitas invited them inside to look around before taking in the dogs.

John welcomed the invitation and followed Fleitas inside. He first noted two cameras on the stairs, one looking down at the parking lot, the other watching the front door.

Once inside, their suspect went to an electric panel and began flipping rows of switches. Each gave a loud snap, followed by the hum of sodium vapor lights igniting throughout the building.

Casually scanning the area, John saw the warehouse was virtually empty except for some boxes on pallets at the loading dock. He also saw a stack of folded tables and chairs against one wall and a series of closed storage cabinets against the opposite wall. He couldn't miss the strong chemical smell emitting from the building.

Fleitas closed the electric panel door and moved towards the interior stairway. "Come up here to my office," he directed. "I'll show you where the dogs will stay."

As they followed the suspect, Tomás turned and smiled at John, giving him a thumbs-up.

John frowned and pushed Tomás' hand down. Just in time. Fleitas reached the top to open the door, and John registered yet another camera, this one inside and pointed at the office door.

They entered a room divided with an inner office that appeared to be recently constructed, with the wood walls and door still bare and unpainted.

"I made this room just for them." Javier opened the inner door and turned on the office light. "You see, I have air conditioning and mats so they can be comfortable." Javier pointed to the opposite corner of the room. "Over there are the water and food bowls." Fleitas beamed with pride as he showed off the preparations he had made. "What do you think, John?"

"I'm impressed," John said. "You know, it's true what Tomás says about you."

Looking confused, the suspect turned to Tomás for an explanation, clearly eager to be let in on the secret. "What do you say about me?"

"Tomás, tell him what you told me," John said.

"You say it much better than me." Tomás feigned difficulty clearing his throat. "You know, my English sometimes…"

Again, Fleitas looked expectantly at John.

"Tomás said that from the first time he met you, you seemed to be a dog person," John explained. "He was impressed. It makes it easier for us to know the animals will be well-treated by someone who knows what he's doing."

John's stomach churned and a bitter taste rose in the back of his throat at such phony ass kissing. But he might as well put the finishing touches on blowing up the suspect's ego. Fleitas' broad grin and his child-like expression were proof, at least to John, that their suspect was a bona fide idiot, albeit, a dangerous one.

"You really say that about me, Tomás?" Fleitas was giddy from the over-the-top flattery.

"Well, of course." Tomás cleared his throat again. He walked past Fleitas and shot a grin at John. "Come on. Let's get the dogs in here and finish up."

Like a good assistant, John followed Tomás downstairs.

Tomás laboriously put on the heavy bitesuit again and found a place to hide at the far end of the warehouse behind the pallets of boxes.

John ran each dog through its paces and kept observing. He purposely bumped into the stack of boxes, but they didn't move. They were probably full. He also surmised a chemical spill had likely made a series of stains on the large open concrete floor. Whatever caused it was strong enough to eat away at the hardened concrete.

John had seen enough. On the last exercise, he mumbled to Tomás that it was time to go. Tomás nodded in relief, the sweat once again pouring down his face.

John put both dogs upstairs in their new home and came back down to hear Fleitas and Tomás talking in Spanish.

"Hey, John," Tomás shouted, "you know what they make here? Javier was telling me."

"I have no idea." John did his acting job well and adopted a genuinely curious tone.

"They make plastic chairs and stuff. Toys, furniture, all kinds of things," Tomás explained.

John glanced at Fleitas. "I was wondering why there was such a strong smell."

"Yes, an unfortunate by-product of making things in plastic—that, and the heat! That is why I have the dogs in their own room with the air conditioner. When my employees are working, everybody sweats, but it gets better later in the afternoon. You don't think heat will hurt the dogs, do you, Señor?"

Tomás wrinkled his brow as he shook his head. "No way. Those dogs don't care. All they care about is biting someone who tries to break into this place." He laughed, and Fleitas joined in.

Tomás and John gathered the bitesuit and pants and went down the outside stairs to the van. Tomás reminded Fleitas about the food and leashes by the door, and told the suspect to call if he had questions.

"*Mi amigo,* I cannot thank you enough," Fleitas said, shaking Tomás' hand.

"The pleasure is all ours, my friend."

Fleitas was about to close the warehouse door when he turned and shouted, "The gate opens by itself when you leave."

John acknowledged that with a wave and watched Fleitas close the door behind him. John slid over to let Tomás drive, then waited until they were off the property before talking out loud, knowing it would be picked up by the bug. "We just left, Rick, and are heading back to DOT."

Tomás glanced over at John and smiled.

"What're you smiling about?"

"You're as much of a bullshit artist as I am, John Stella!" Tomás shouted as he negotiated onto the roadway from the business park complex.

John laughed, but still put his index finger to his lips and pointed to the bug on his waist. Tomás had forgotten, and shrugged. That only made John laugh more. But it also reminded him of Rick's reaction to his being followed earlier that morning. After changing lanes and taking a few side streets to make sure they weren't being followed by anyone,

John had Tomás go back to the meeting place in the rear parking lot of the DOT.

"How did it go?" Rick asked when John approached.

John took off the phone, the clip, and the wire. "Well, I think. They're disposing of plastic in the dumpsters and it smells like cocaine. In fact, the whole warehouse smells like plastic and cocaine. Very distinctive. Even the dogs alerted at the dumpsters. Both are filled with gobs of plastic residue. The floors are marked where it looks like chemicals had leaked, but I think Fleitas had everything moved and put away before we got there. Aside from the smell, the place was clean."

John also filled Rick in on the placement of the cameras and the fact that the entrance gate could be opened from the outside by throwing a large piece of metal inside on the driveway that would trick the gate into thinking a car was waiting to leave.

After taking notes and making a few phone calls to SAC McKenna, they were finished. John took back his personal phone but wasn't quite ready to leave.

"Hey buddy, we're going to have that talk now," John said, walking with Rick away from the van. "What the hell are those monkeys doing following me?"

"I assume you're talking about the State Department guys," Rick said dryly.

"Can we just call them CIA" John asked, impatient.

"I wish I could give you an answer," Rick said. "There are briefings and meetings going on between Washington and Miami among all the agencies. I have no idea what those guys are up to."

John grimaced. It wasn't the answer he was hoping for. The fact that discussions were going on above Rick's pay grade only added to John's frustration. "I'd hate to overreact because I *think* I'm being followed by dopers. Then I pop a few rounds at them only to find out they're agents." Making no attempt to hide his sarcasm, he added, "I might actually feel bad."

Rick's smile communicated he knew full-well how his friend must be feeling. "Tell you what. I'll ask around and see what's up. I can't promise you anything, but I'll do my best."

John gave him a hard stare before breaking a smile and giving his friend a bear hug. "Okay, shithead. I'm going home to have a beer. If anything comes up, let me know."

Tomás started the van when John got in. "Where to?"

Relieved that the undercover detail was behind him, he glanced at

Tomás, knowing his friend was waiting for an answer. "My house. Steaks and beer?"

"Oh, hell yeah!" Tomás shouted.

John keyed in a number on his phone. "Hey, Joey, go to the jar on the refrigerator and take out some money. I need you to go to the store." John rolled his eyes at the complaining on the other end, Joey clearly inconvenienced with the impromptu request. It was an interruption to his social calendar with his own young lady guest.

After letting the whining carry on a bit, John interrupted. "Yeah, well… We're having a guest for dinner. If she stays, well, then I guess we're having two guests. Just make sure you buy enough steaks and beer." John ended the call.

Tomás gave him a curious look. "You just cock-block your little cousin?"

"Nah, just a slight adjustment to his agenda. Besides, I'm the one that has put the social calendar on hold while he is staying with me," John explained.

"Why would you do that?" Tomás asked.

"Come on, Tomás! How's it going to sound if my little cousin has to live with me when I bring home a date. You can hear everything that goes on in there. The walls are paper-thin. Besides, it would cramp my style." John left it at that and trusted he'd made his point.

Both men began to laugh. "Stella, you're going to make one hell of a dad one day!" Still chuckling, Tomás maneuvered the van through traffic to make his way back to the Redlands.

John squirmed in his seat to get comfortable. "Yeah, well, let's not make that day anytime soon," he mumbled, staring out into the distance from the passenger window.

Tomás turned onto Krome Avenue from Okeechobee Road. The sun was setting behind the vast stretches of saw grass that reached beyond the horizon. The brilliant yellows and oranges radiated upward, displaying the most amazing pink and purple hues. Each color blended seamlessly into the next. John thought it looked like nature herself had taken an entire painter's pallet and smeared it across the heavens. He closed his eyes and felt the last of the sun's warmth on his face. He took in a deep breath, exhaling with a quiet sigh—he was thankful this day was finally over.

Chapter Twelve

Fourteen days had gone by since John and Tomás had delivered the dogs to Javier Fleitas. John and Florey were back working in their assigned—and usually uneventful—zones on Kendall Drive and Krome Avenue. John and Rick had joked that the dopers must've decided to take a two-week vacation. But that was only an attempt at dark humor. They knew the activity would pick up soon.

After meeting with Florey for breakfast one morning, they both headed to their respective areas and began their workday. John had made a few stops, and was about to pull into Juacinto's truck stop to grab a coffee when his phone rang. He immediately answered the call.

"Hey, Bubba. How're you doing?" Rick asked.

"I was starting to think you forgot about us. What's going on?"

"Listen, I set up a meeting at two this afternoon with your major and SAC McKenna. Got some good news for you guys. Tell Florey to be there, too."

"Sure thing. What's it all about?" John asked.

"The INEOA are giving you their Special Commendation Award," Rick said, "in recognition of all your efforts at confiscating dope."

Perplexed, John asked, "What the hell is the INEOA and who put us up for that?"

"The International Narcotic Enforcement Officers Association—INEOA—represents drug officers from around the world," Rick explained. "And your major and McKenna put your names in for it. It's a prestigious group. But, listen, I've got to rush off to another meeting in a few minutes, so I'll see you this afternoon." Rick ended the call.

John called dispatch to find out where Florey was so he could tell her the news in person. A few minutes later, he learned she was on an incident on the corner of SW 147th Avenue and Kendall Drive.

As he drove up, Florey was standing near the back of a pickup truck and talking to a female deputy. John parked his car near the truck and got out to meet them.

"Hey, John," Florey said. "I'd like you to meet a girlfriend of mine, Janice. We've known each other since high school."

John was instantly struck by the woman's warm smile, not to mention her figure. Most police uniforms didn't do the female figure justice, but Janice was the exception to the rule. Her long, brownish-blonde hair and that curvaceous figure outlined by the slightly too-tight-for-regulation polyester uniform of the Metro-Dade Police Department had John trying to regain his focus as the brief, awkward silence was becoming noticeable.

"So, you've known each other since school, huh," John said, shaking the deputy's hand and making small talk.

"Yeah, a long time." Janice glanced over at Florey with a nervous smile.

"Well, I would never have guessed," said John. "Florey was obviously several years ahead of you in school."

Janice blushed, but Florey rolled her eyes. "He's just trying to remind me how old I am."

John put on a face of faux astonishment. "I would never say such a thing. However…"

Florey grinned. "Ah, here we go."

"You should hang out with Janice more often," he suggested.

Florey laughed. "Why? Because her looking so young makes me look old? Asshole!"

"Of course not." John smiled at Janice. "That way we'd get to see each other again."

"Trust me, Janice, he's only trying to say I'm old." Florey sighed.

Despite the teasing, John noticed Janice paying attention to him, just as he was noticing her. He even caught her glance at Florey with a raised eyebrow. John took it as approval.

He peered through the window into the pickup truck, noticing the cracked steering column, common in stolen vehicles.

"Hey, while Janice is checking out my butt, can you tell me what's up with this pickup?" John blurted.

"John Stella!"

"What? You *were* checking out my butt, weren't you, Janice?" He was enjoying the pretense of seriousness.

"Okay, okay, you caught me." Janice laughed from deep in her chest, but soon composed herself when Florey frowned in displeasure at her junior partner.

"Well, don't feel embarrassed. I checked out yours when I drove by. Before we leave, how about we exchange numbers?" John flashed a confident smile.

As blunt as he was, his charm worked. Janice agreed to give him her phone number.

Seeing enough, Florey interrupted to explain that the vehicle had been reported stolen and was left parked partially on the road. She was waiting for the tow truck to show up and take it away. She leaned forward and whispered, "Treat this one nice. She's a good friend, dumbass."

When the tow truck appeared in the intersection, Florey went back to her car, shaking her head.

A few minutes later, she came back to the awkwardly parked pickup truck, where John was helping the tow driver circle through traffic to get a better angle at hooking a line to the front of the truck.

"Hey, partner, you get any ID off this rust bucket?" John asked.

"Barely," Florey said. "The tag comes back as reported stolen. The VIN on the dash is almost rusted away. I could hardly make out the number."

John could see the Vehicle Identification Number plate was nearly rusted in half. He stepped away as the tow driver connected his straps to the front bumper and prepared to hoist the front end up.

"Hey, Buddy!" John yelled to the tow driver. "The truck comes back stolen. You'll probably want to keep it in the yard so the Auto Theft detectives can give it a once over."

The driver nodded, wiping his greasy hands on an equally greasy rag, then pulled on the leaver to lift the truck. The tow truck's engine began to rev as the cables slowly lifted the stolen truck.

Florey and Janice were still standing on the sidewalk talking—presumably about him, John thought. But an incredibly foul odor sent them quickly retreating backward, nearly into the busy Kendall Drive traffic. They held their noses and moved to the other side of the parking lot closer to John, and as far away from the stench as they could get.

"What the hell is that smell?" the tow driver shouted.

"Something smells dead!" Janice said.

"Hey, John, did you see that flood of fluid—brownish fluid—come out of the truck bed when it was lifted?" Florey spoke an octave higher than normal.

John approached the pickup, now stuck with its front end in the air. He held his breath, his only weapon to fight back the sickening odor, but it was too overwhelming.

The driver got out and ran to the back of his truck, throwing John a clean towel. "Put it around your nose and mouth. It might help."

John nodded his thanks and did as directed. It made only a slight difference, but it was enough for John to get close enough to grab hold of the tarp that had been draped across the bed of the pickup.

He tugged hard, while still being careful not to step into the brownish fluid pooling on the ground near the rear bumper.

With a harder tug, the tarp snapped loose, partially exposing what was underneath. John pushed the towel tighter across his mouth to fend off the onset of nausea, but he couldn't hold back a gasp.

Reflexively, he let go of the tarp and stumbled away, struggling for air. He barely made it to the other side of the parking lot, upwind of the truck before he went to his knees, desperately trying to hold back the sensation of rising stomach contents. He fought against that gravity-defying little trick of nature, but to no avail. As the heaves became more dramatic, he was unable to stop them or the vomiting.

Florey ran to his side.

He was painfully aware she'd never seen him get this sick before. "Hey, kiddo. You going to be okay?" she gently asked, putting a hand on his shoulder.

John managed to catch his breath between contractions and the burn of stomach acid. In a hoarse voice he said, "Bodies. Two. Been there a while." John pointed towards the truck as he coughed up a mouthful of mucus, doing his best to fight off the urge to vomit again.

Janice came over and put her hand on John's other shoulder. "Come on. You need to get up and get some fresh air."

He stood up and paced the area, careful to stay upwind of the crime scene as Florey called dispatch to notify them of the discovery.

Janice also called the Metro-Dade dispatch to send homicide detectives to the scene.

When he'd caught his breath, John told the driver he couldn't touch his truck or the pickup until the detectives took a statement and released him.

The driver nodded. He knew the drill.

"I'm sorry, Janice," said John, slowly feeling like himself again.

"I've never done well with that odor. Most of the time I can keep from barfing, but my luck ran out this time, especially after seeing right through two decaying bodies."

Janice flashed a rueful smile and seemed to search for the right words, finally saying, "Well, if you don't take me to a steakhouse on our first date, I'll be okay."

This was one crazy way to meet a girl and get a date. "Deal," he said, struggling to make his mouth form a smile. Steak was the last thing on his mind.

Florey took a few pictures for her incident report. As she came closer to him, she remarked that he looked much better. "That's what you get for calling me old," she kidded. "Seriously, you going to be okay?"

"Yeah, partner. But, could you do me favor?" John asked.

"Of course," Florey replied.

"Could you move my car from downwind of that truck? Spec must be having fits."

Florey didn't hesitate. She took a deep breath and quickly got to his car, driving it around to the parking lot where John stood.

"Your dog is just like you," she said, her face scrunched. "You better get over to the car wash and hose out Spec's cage."

"Shit!" John looked into the rear window. Spec was curled up on one side of the dog cage and her morning meal was on the other.

"I know, girl. It was pretty awful, wasn't it? Let's get you cleaned up." John opened his door and cautiously sat in the car, hoping this new foul odor wouldn't send him heaving again.

Florey approached just as he remembered what he had to tell her. "I almost forgot, partner. We have to be at the station at two. Evidently, we're getting some kind of award."

She looked puzzled but didn't argue. "Okay, I'll be there. You go take care of Spec. I'll finish up here and meet you at the station."

John nodded and headed to the car wash.

He finished up quickly to get to the station on time. He hurried upstairs to the major's office and greeted Viv, the major's secretary. He pointed to the closed office door to her left.

"Yep, they're inside the major's office waiting for you," Viv said.

John thanked her with a smile and knocked on the door to the office.

"Enter!" Major Carris yelled.

John poked his head in cautiously.

"Hey, John, come on in. Florey was just telling us how you got sick. You okay?"

John shot a glance at Florey, who wore a big teasing smile. "Yeah. I'm good. What's this award thing, Major?"

"The INEOA is presenting you two their Commendation Award for exemplary service. I put the both of you in for Trooper of the Month, but Rick suggested this instead. We got the call and you'll be recognized next week at the Intercontinental Hotel during their annual meeting. Here are the room reservations and itinerary." Major Carris handed Florey and John a stack of papers.

"Wow, a suite. Who's picking up the tab?" John asked.

"The DEA," SAC McKenna said. "It's the least we can do for you."

"Nice!" Florey exclaimed. "Kinda figured it wouldn't be FHP."

"Now, come on guys…" Carris kindly scolded his two troopers. "McKenna, I'd like to thank you and the DEA for watching out for my troopers. Please let Washington know how appreciative we are."

"It's our pleasure, Major," McKenna said.

Speaking to the SAC, John asked, "Rick explained a little earlier, but can you tell us more about the INEOA?"

"Sure. They've been around for a while," McKenna said. "It's mostly a fraternity of narcotic officers from around the world. It gives the working officers and agents a chance to put faces to names, or simply compare notes and trends. You guys *should be* honored. It's not often that uniformed drug officers get these awards."

"I couldn't be prouder of them. So is the colonel," the major added.

Florey read over the official invitation. "I see this is a non-uniform event. So, that means business attire?"

"Suits for the men and professional business attire for the women," Rick answered.

"Again, it's the least we can do for you guys after all we've asked of you." McKenna turned to leave. "I need to get back to the office, but we'll see you next week at the hotel, Major." He shook the major's hand and nodded to Rick and Florey before he left the room.

"Okay, guys. I guess that's it," Major Carris said, going on to explain that he'd briefed Captain DeLeón by phone, because the captain had a sick child at home to take to the doctor.

Looking at the desk calendar, the major pointed to the date of the award ceremony. "Next week I'm supposed to be at a Troop Commander's meeting, and if I can't get out of it, Captain DeLeón will go in my place. I hope you guys don't mind."

"Not at all, Major," Florey said. "We understand."

"If you guys need anything, let Viv know and she'll take care of it."

The major picked up his desk phone and began to make a call.

"Thanks for everything," Florey said. "We'll get out of your hair now and hit the road."

John left with Florey and Rick, but waited until they got to the parking lot before he asked Rick about a pointed look John thought he'd detected.

Rick smiled. "You caught that, did you? I tried to be subtle."

"Let's hear it," John said.

"The word is, nobody knows what the State Department guys are up to," Rick said, "but I've been assured that *whatever* they're doing, it's sanctioned by Washington."

"So, in other words, don't ask?" John didn't hide his cynicism.

"Exactly. McKenna and some DEA bureaucrats out of Washington made sure what they're doing is on a need-to-know basis," Rick said, "and we didn't need to know."

"Wow. So much for working together and all that crap," Florey remarked.

"Look, let's not worry about the spooks," Rick said. "You've seen these guys before. They do what they do and go away. All that 'secret squirrel' stuff is beyond our pay grade. Besides, don't we have enough on our plate without worrying about those guys?"

John wasn't buying Rick's rationale for ignoring the secret agents. "I get it. It's political. I just hope they don't go poking around again while I'm working, or worse, while I'm at home or on a date. No telling what will happen," he said pointedly.

Rick offered a faint smile.

After the parking lot meeting was over and John drove off on his own, he decided to take the long way home to see if he could write a few speeding tickets. It was only a matter of time before some lieutenant colonel in Tallahassee would print up a report citing troopers considered deficient in achieving their so-called "goals and objectives."

John laughed at Tallahassee's euphemism for what every trooper knew to be a quota. Quotas were outlawed by state statue, but the FHP simply changed the name. That usually meant most troopers ended up writing multiple tickets to one offending motorist. Talk about putting the department in a bad light. That tactic was *guaranteed* to erode the public's trust. The Florida Legislature had evidently agreed when they made quotas illegal, but it was a point lost on the paper pushers at Headquarters.

John also knew his complaints would land on deaf ears. So, it was easier to stop some violators and hand them each a ticket to keep

Headquarters' staff off his back. After all, a trooper didn't have to work too hard to find someone breaking a traffic law in Dade County—especially on U.S. 27 and Krome Avenue.

In less than a mile, John accomplished his mission. He'd written speeding tickets and given two other tickets for lack of insurance. Then, it was time to call it quits.

John secured his paperwork on the front passenger seat and sat back for the ride into the Redlands, once again noticing the sun burning large as it made its descent toward the horizon, casting yet another pastel light display high above the River of Grass.

Driving past Mack's Fish Camp, he came up to a yellow Department of Water Management service truck parked on the shoulder of the road. A worker with a reflective vest jogged into the roadway and waved him over.

John slowed his vehicle and pulled onto the shoulder just past a gravel service drive.

"Trooper, we got a problem," the DWM supervisor said.

"What's that?" John asked.

"Here, I better show you." The supervisor started walking back to the gravel service road.

John followed behind the man. The service road rose sharply to meet the elevation of the C-111 canal levy. Just one of the many man-made gouges in Florida's pristine wetlands constructed decades before in a crude attempt to drain the edges of the Everglades and make way for the constant demand from residences and shopping centers. Its opposite sides dropped off into the marsh, denoting the official boundary of the Florida Everglades National Park. John came to a sudden stop on the gravel road.

"What's that on the ground?" he asked, pointing to what looked like a blood trail in the dirt.

"That's where it probably came from," the supervisor said.

"Where *what* probably came from?" John stayed motionless so he wouldn't further disturb the area.

The supervisor pointed over the banks of the service road towards the canal. "That."

John looked where the supervisor was pointing. A shower curtain floated on top of the water. As he stared, the outline of a body became more evident.

He edged closer, but didn't step into the water. The transparent plastic curtain had a simple floral design printed on it, but John could see the body inside was already blue and beginning to bloat. The telltale sign of a Colombian Necktie could be seen through the wrapping, the bloated tongue pulled through the open slit in the throat unmistakable—a calling card, of sorts, typical of the Colombian cartels. John let his head drop back as he looked up to the sky. "*Je...sus Christmas.*"

"Yeah. My thoughts exactly," the supervisor said.

John walked back to examine the gravel road, first noticing the clear sets of tire tracks leading up to the blood trail. By the looks of it, the trail had started from the back of a stopped vehicle, the pooling blood tapering off to a thin line that led to the water.

John squatted down to take a closer look.

"I noticed that trail, too," the supervisor said. "I followed it and it led right to the body. Pretty sick, huh?"

"That's the third one I've come across today," John remarked.

"No shit? We usually find them in abandoned cars out here, but man, three in one day!" The supervisor looked at the discarded body.

"I'm going to need you to step back to your truck. All of this is a crime scene," John explained. "I'll get you a witness statement and you can start writing down what you observed before I got here. Okay?"

The supervisor agreed, and John gave him a clipboard with a blank witness statement. With a heavy sigh, the guy dutifully began to fill it out.

John called dispatch and requested they send Metro-Dade Police Homicide. Then, sat in his car with the driver's door open, contemplating the day's events. It struck him that he hadn't even felt queasy looking at the body in the marsh.

The supervisor came and stood at John's open car door. "Hey, trooper. Do you need to see my ID and stuff?"

"Yeah, and keep it out. I'm sure Metro-Dade Homicide will want it, too." He took the man's driver's license and jotted the information for his report. When he finished, he handed it to the supervisor, who went to his truck to finish his statement.

John opened his trunk and grabbed his camera. He was still taking pictures for his incident report when Florey drove up, her overhead emergency lights flashing.

"Hey, kiddo. You come across another one?" Florey said, astonished.

"Nah, the DWM supervisor did. He flagged me over. The crime scene appears to be confined to the gravel road over to the body." John pointed to the area. "Looks like they took it out of a vehicle and tossed it."

John took a minute to gather his thoughts. "You know, as many times as I've worked this road, I've never found one just dumped on the side like this. Usually, it's in one of the stolen, submerged cars we pull from the canal."

"And here I've worked Kendall Drive for over twenty years and never found a dead body, let alone two…ever." Florey moved in closer to see the discarded corpse. "Ugh, looks like it's bloating. Probably hasn't been here for very long."

"I don't know. I'll wait till Homicide gets here and see what they say." He glanced at his watch. "You don't have to stay, kiddo. You can get home to your family."

"You sure?" asked Florey. "I mean, I can stay and clean up vomit if you need me to." Florey smiled. Just like her—and him. Neither of them ever let an opportunity for sarcasm get away.

"Ha-ha-ha… Very funny. Aren't they expecting you back at the geriatric center by now?" John grinned as he jabbed her back.

In a more empathetic tone, Florey said, "Seriously, John. You gonna be alright?"

"I'll try and stay upwind," John said, looking at the discarded corpse. "I've embarrassed myself in front of one deputy today. Don't plan on doing it again."

"Oh, that reminds me. Here…" Florey reached into her uniform shirt pocket and pulled out a business card. "She said to call her."

He read the card out loud. "Janice Aguirre. Metro Dade Police. Kendall District 5."

"So, you didn't forget." John tucked the card into his shirt pocket. "Thanks, kiddo."

"She's a good kid, John, so don't treat her like a hit-and-run, please."

She's probably waiting for a smart-ass response. But John would surprise her. "Okay, I promise." He smiled. "Now get home to your husband and girls, please."

"We're doing pizza night. Both girls have their dance recitals in a few weeks, plus term papers are due soon for school. We figured we'd make it a family night of homework and dance practice," Florey explained.

"Well, get to it. They haven't seen much of you lately since we've been working so much. I'm sure you could use some family time as well," John said.

Looking pleased, Florey drove off, heading south on Krome.

John didn't have long to wait for the two homicide detectives to pull up and get out of their car. The younger one started giving the DWM supervisor the third degree, as if *he'd* committed the crime.

A curious way to start an investigation, John thought, but maybe he was still learning the ropes.

As the young detective's accusatory questions continued, the supervisor was apparently so uneasy with the detective's tone he asked if he should get an attorney.

John's patience began to wear thin. It completely evaporated when the rookie detective asked John questions using the same accusing tone.

"So, Trooper, what exactly did you touch?" the detective asked.

"Nothing." John walked the detective through what he'd done and explained what he'd seen.

"No, you don't seem to understand," the detective said sarcastically. "We investigate *real* crimes, not speeding tickets."

John stayed silent but was not very impressed.

"I need to know what you touched or where you walked to make sure you didn't screw up our crime scene," the detective added.

Enough. Leaning forward, he almost stepped on the detective's toes, as if threatening to throw the apparent rookie into the swamp with the body. Before John could say a word, the senior detective stepped in between the two.

John began laughing. "Hey, Charles, how many rookies are you going to break in?" He took a step away from the startled homicide detective-in-training. "This one needs a lesson in respect."

Charles Halter had been a park ranger with John before he joined the Metro Dade Police Department. As police officers, John and Charles had worked together when John was assigned to the Water Management District to recover abandoned and stolen vehicles that were discarded in dozens of canals that ran through the county. And that job involved homicides. John knew Charles to be a meticulous thinker, and in part because of that, he had become one of the youngest patrol officers ever offered a position in the prestigious Homicide division.

Charles glanced at his nervous rookie and laughed. "Don't worry, kid. That's Trooper Stella. If he was really mad at you, you would've already been thrown in the swamp." Charles directed his rookie to get the camera and tape measure. "And call the coroner's office, will ya?"

"Sure thing, Detective Halter," the rookie said, adding to John, "I apologize, Trooper." He hurried off to the car.

John pretended to ignore the young officer. Instead, he stood with Charles, both staring at the body.

"So, how've you been, buddy?" Charles asked.

"Third body today," John said. "How do you think I've been?"

"Were you the trooper that puked on Kendall earlier?"

John hesitated at first, but then resigned himself to the answer. "Yeah, it was me."

"Damn! Janice wouldn't give me a name, but I was going to call you later to see if you knew who it was. And all this time it was you." Charles snickered as he teased.

"Yeah, yeah, yeah. Get it over with. You've been busting my balls for too long for me to think you would stop now." John paused. "By the way, how long have you known Janice?"

"About five years. I dated her for a while, but it didn't work out," Charles said. "Why do you ask?"

"Seems like a nice gal. At least, she didn't rag on me for getting sick."

"Well, she's a sweetheart. I blame our schedules that it didn't work out. We could never manage any time alone. She got tired of me needing to run off to take care of, well, *these* calls." Charles nodded with his chin toward the corpse.

"Good to know." John's gaze caught Charles' rookie struggling to force a roll of film into the camera. "Hey, buddy. Doesn't the department give you guys digital cameras?"

"Damn rookies," Charles said under his breath. "What a pathetic sight."

"You wanna help him and let me finish my incident report so you can take it with you?" John asked.

Charles nodded and left, leaving John free to return to his car to record his observations and movements in the crime scene. He was finished about forty-five minutes later, just as the coroner's van pulled up. The undertakers began the process of retrieving and loading the body onto the gurney after Charles had taken the last of his measurements and gave them the go-ahead. The rookie detective continued snapping pictures, documenting every movement of the corpse right up until it was slid into the coroner's van.

"Hey, Stella. We gotta head over to the morgue. Wanna follow?" Charles suggested. "I can get your report there."

John looked at his watch, realizing it was going to be another long day. "Sure. Why not."

***

The Dade County Morgue sat behind Jackson Memorial Hospital near downtown Miami. It occupied a building that was already thirty years outdated, given the population and the number of victims delivered there. John parked his patrol car behind the row of refrigerated trailers used to handle the overflow of Dade County's violent crime victims. Each of the trailers had been leased from a local fast food chain years before—the restaurant logos were still visible on the sides. If that wasn't enough to dissuade any cop visiting one of the franchises, John thought the company slogan next to them sure did: ***Burger Chief—Guaranteed Freshest Ingredients All the Time***.

The idea was to have the victims for just a few months, but the months had turned to years. The county had finally bought the trailers, and they had become a permanent fixture. And they were never empty.

John followed Charles and his rookie through the service entrance and found the attendant at his desk, his white smock stained with blood as he made notes in a journal. At six feet, nine inches and 350 pounds, Terrance Smalls had found his passion in life after blowing out his knee playing football for the University of Miami. Forced to take real college classes, he'd excelled at the forensic sciences and landed a job at the morgue, much to the relief of his family. John was aware that Terrance's job eventually became the family's ticket out of the South Dade projects. Using a touch of gallows humor, Terrance told people the job was a "perfect fit." After all, seeing a dead body every now and then was a common occurrence in the projects.

"Charles, how you been?" Terrence's deep baritone voice boomed as he stood up to greet the detective. Then the voice boomed again, "Well, I'll be... Trooper Stella! How long has it been? Two, no, three years, I bet."

John held out his hand and watched it disappear into Terrance's giant mitt. *Meat hooks*, John called them, borrowing the term his dad used for over-sized hands. John's whole body shook along with his hand.

"Take it easy, Terrance. I'm not a corpse!"

Terrance's laugh turned the austere facility into an echo chamber. "God Almighty, it's good to see you." Terrance flashed a broad grin at Charles. "You know the first time I met this young Trooper?"

"No, Terrance. Tell me," Charles insisted.

"Well, his training officer, Trooper Rogers, brought him in to show him how we do things here. So, we did what we always do to FHP rookies."

"And what would that be?" Charles' rookie asked.

"We locked this youngster in the freezer with all the stiffs and turned out the lights." Terrance threw his head back and laughed even harder.

John chuckled as he vividly recalled the event. "Yeah, it was cold as hell in there. And stank like crap, too."

"Oh, good Lawd!" Terrance exclaimed. "We thought we'd give him a few minutes before we was fixin' to hear a banging on the door and screams of 'Let me out!'" Terrance switched his octave range and mimicked a little girl's voice. "But we didn't hear nothing." He shook his head as if recalling his disbelief. "For five minutes, nothing."

"What did you do?" the rookie asked.

"Well, young deputy…" Terrance walked over to the same freezer door and looked at his watch, again reliving that day. "…we didn't know what to think. Maybe this young trooper fainted or passed out. So, we opened the door, and you know what we seen?"

John smiled at the memory, but the rookie shook his head.

"We opened the door and found young Stella with his flashlight, counting bullet holes in a corpse brought in from a drug hit on Miami Beach." Terrance threw up his big hands in disbelief and led the way to the examination room. "Bullet holes! Good Lawd Almighty, that young trooper proved to be a hard case after all."

Inside the room, the undertakers wheeled in the gurney and parked it next to the stainless steel examination table.

"Sixty-five," John said to no one in particular.

"That's right, you remembered," Terrance remarked.

"How could I forget? It was worth it to count those holes just to see the looks on your faces. Besides, you locked me in there," John pointed out. "I had time to kill."

Terrance asked the undertakers to step aside as he put on his oversized rubber exam gloves and singlehandedly grabbed the gurney board with the body on it. Effortlessly, he lifted it and put it on the exam table. Then, he unclasped the seatbelt-like cinches that held the body-bagged corpse on the board. With one hand, he lifted the board up and out, causing the body bag to gently flop onto the cold steel table. Body fluid mixed with swamp water was already leaking out of the bag and flowing towards the drain gutters that ran down each side of the table.

"Let's see what we got here," Terrance said, his tone professional. He pulled down a microphone from a chord hung from the ceiling. "You boys don't mind if I go to recording, do you?"

"Go for it, Terrance. I just need to know if a cause of death is obvious," Charles said.

Terrance unzipped the leaking bag and cut the remainder off with scissors until each half fell to the side and revealed the shower-curtain-wrapped-corpse.

"Goodness! Somebody was sure pissed at you," Terrance said as if the dead body could hear. He adjusted the microphone closer to the table. "I am carefully removing the wrapping from the body…"

Terrance continued his autopsy narration until the shower curtain had been removed. After looking over the corpse, he turned off the microphone.

"The official autopsy results will be out in about a week, so you didn't hear this from me. You know the routine, Deputy Charles."

John knew Terrance was circumventing a few rules by giving his opinion before it could be properly published, but Terrance had a reputation for never being wrong. When it came to violent and sudden deaths, Miami ranked number one in the nation. Terrance had his share of experience. The only thing left to wait on would be the toxicology results, but they'd been sent out to another lab and wouldn't be published for a few weeks.

"The corpse is female," Terrance said. "You got a close-range shot to the forehead here. I see some burning, or what looks like burning, from a muzzle blast." He gently turned the woman's head to the side. "Probably a small caliber. No exit wound."

He continued scanning the body and moved flesh near the clavicle. "Looks like your woman was a tattle-tale," he said, looking up at the officers.

"A what?" the rookie detective asked.

Terrance sighed. "You got a Colombian Necktie. Poor thing must have crossed the wrong people."

"I'm not even going to ask how you're able to tell it's a female," John remarked as he strained his eyes past the heavy decay to determine any recognizable anatomy.

"Trooper Stella, you make me laugh. You is something else." Terrance pointed to the opposite side of the room. "She's just like those other two that came in earlier today from Kendall."

John saw the two black plastic body bags zippered shut, each one on its own gurney.

"You mean they also had Colombian Neckties?" John asked.

"Uh-huh," Terrance said. "And they were shot in the head. Holes in the craniums that look a whole lot like this young lady's."

Terrance began taking out his tools of the trade in preparation of continuing with the full autopsy. He grabbed a large plastic tray and carefully laid out the scalpels, knives, and bone saws which looked sinister under the glare of the overhead operating room light. "Ya'll boys staying for this or ya'll seen enough? Can't have nobody barfing like that officer on Kendall I heard about."

John turned to Charles, who shrugged and said, "I didn't tell him."

Terrance paused and stared at his guests. "Now, Trooper Stella, you isn't going to tell me that was you, was it?"

"Yeah, it was me," John said, hanging his head, bracing for another booming laugh.

The laugh didn't come.

"Hey, man. Can I be honest with you boys?" Terrance came around the exam table. "Tell you the truth, Stella, I almost blew chunks myself. Those two was beaten and cut up something awful. Lawd A'mighty." Terrance shook his head, glancing over at the other two gurneys. "Someone worked them over real good."

Terrance wasn't just trying to make him feel good, John thought. It took a lot to shake up Terrance's world. After all, the man was on the receiving end of everything that met a violent demise in Dade County. "Well, I don't feel so bad, then," John remarked.

"Hey, young trooper. We ain't made of steel, ya know." Terrance said in a consoling tone as he walked back to the exam table and pulled down the microphone again.

Charles caught John's eye and motioned to leave.

"Don't be strangers, ya hear!" Terrance shouted. He switched on the microphone and reached for his tools.

John and the others waved to Terrance as they left the exam area and walked to the parking lot.

"You wanna catch a bite with us, John? I'll buy," Charles said.

John shook his head. "No thanks, buddy. It's been a long day. I'm beat."

"I understand. But let's get together soon and catch up. It's been too long, man."

"I look forward to it," John said, shaking Charles' hand. He shot a glance at the rookie. "Bring him along, too. He seems like a good guy."

The rookie cast him a quick pleased expression as John unlocked his door and climbed in.

Spec, fast asleep, barely stirred as John drove out of the hospital complex and merged onto the entrance ramp to the State Road 836 expressway, grateful traffic was moving. Most of the day, there was nothing "express" about the east-west connector. With the car accelerating, Spec finally opened her eyes and sat up for the ride.

"Hey girl, don't worry," John said in the most reassuring tone he could muster. "I've got my blinders on. It's straight to the house we go."

Chapter Thirteen

Nuevo Laredo, Mexico

Justo and Rigo were running late. Yesterday's flight into Monterrey, Mexico had been delayed six hours, because the Mexican authorities had security concerns after several car bombs detonated the night before in a nearby neighborhood. Just a precaution, they'd said. Finally, after securing the area, the police reopened the airport.

Justo and Rigo had waited as patiently as possible, but there was no time to waste. They drove the rental to Nuevo Laredo on the Texas border. If they were going to meet their contact, they had to get there before sundown. Justo usually avoided Route 85, a direct route, because the back roads were safer, but he and Rigo had time to make up and 85 was their only choice.

Entering Nuevo Laredo was like entering the slums of Cali. Only worse. The city was overrun with crime fueled by rival Mexican cartels. Even the air was thick with a foul odor of raw sewage. Justo was glad to see the increase in Mexican military patrols constantly driving the streets as they attempted to keep the Mexican Gulf Cartel at bay. Still, Justo remained cautious. The Mexican authorities could be just as brutal as the cartels. Some were even on the dole of criminal organizations and doing their dirty work. Justo was banking on the relationship the Cali families had developed, albeit tenuous, with several of the local crime factions. Without those connections, he'd have made a different plan.

Rigo directed Justo from the map he held low out of sight of onlookers. It wasn't smart to look like strangers in the area. Lost tourists navigating in the vast network of streets on border towns were easy marks for robberies and even kidnappings. With Rigo's help, Justo found the location where he was due to meet his contact in the outskirts of Matamoros.

As he hunted for a parking spot along the road that bordered the city's Plaza Benito Juarez, Justo kept a sharp eye out for anyone even remotely resembling a bandit. Finally, he found an empty space and claimed it.

Checking his watch, they had just a few minutes to spare and had to move quickly. They left their Volkswagen carrying only their backpacks, lightly packed with clothes, and headed south two blocks to the historic Mercado Centro, where an open-air flea market had aisles packed with bargain-hunting American tourists.

Justo checked his watch again. Then, he led Rigo as they maneuvered through the masses of gringos frantically picking through the tight rows of kiosks filled with brightly colored blankets, clothes, and hand painted pottery. He found an empty table at the eatery, where he and Rigo would sit and wait. Justo winced against the uneasy feeling gathering in the center of his gut. He hated coming to Mexico, mainly because the bustle of people made him nervous.

"Señor Justo?"

As alert as he was, the voice still startled Justo.

The question came from a well-dressed older man with silver-gray hair that shone bright in contrast to his thick, black moustache, the same color as his shoes and the belt that held together his pants over his red-collared shirt. More important, the man matched Justo's contact's description.

"Yes, it's me. Did you bring the keys?" Justo asked.

"Of course, señor." The old man reached into his pant pocket.

Justo watched the man's movements and prepared to react to a double-cross, if necessary. But the man simply handed Justo a set of car keys. "The car is parked on the street behind me. A tan Ford Taurus, just like you asked. Texas plates and insurance."

As arranged, Justo turned over the rental car's keys and told the man where he could find the car. As quickly as he appeared, the old man turned away and vanished into the sea of American tourists.

Rigo checked the area again.

"Tío, we better be going." Rigo's eyes darted nervously around the mass of tourists. "I don't like this place."

"Calm down," Justo insisted, his voice low. "And watch out for the bigger threat—pick-pockets."

Rigo followed Justo out of the flea market onto the crowded street. There it was—the tan Taurus, exactly where the old man had said.

Justo opened the trunk and checked under the mat to find a spare tire, then lifted it to make sure no unwanted surprises were hidden there. Allegiances could be bought, and Justo would rather be safe than sorry. Check first before driving away with a tracking device, or worse, a bomb.

As casually as he could manage, he looked at the underbelly of the car and under the hood. He opened the passenger door and sat, finding the requested documents in the glove box. Everything in order.

Feeling secure they weren't going to end up as the next Mexican Cartel statistic, Justo let Rigo drive to the street that funneled into the Nuevo Laredo border crossing into Laredo, Texas. The traffic approaching the U.S. border checkpoint had quickly come to a crawl as countless Mexican border agents and U.S. Customs officers checked cars, papers, and identification, each group of officers relegated to their designated side of the border demarcation line.

Traffic inched ahead. Thirty minutes passed before Rigo finally reached the first Mexican agent, who instructed him to open his hood and trunk for inspection.

After the officer finished, Rigo offered his passport but the officer waved him forward. They crawled in traffic for another twenty minutes before they came to the next officer in a black military uniform. The officer passed the driver's door and checked the tag, then motioned for Rigo to roll down his window.

"May I have identification for both of you, please?" the officer said in heavily accented English.

"I got it." Justo handed over two U.S. passports to the officer.

"Americans?" The officer stared at Rigo through his mirror sunglasses.

"Yes, and headed home," Rigo answered.

"You live in Laredo for a long time?" the officer continued.

"Yes. My uncle and I came to Mexico to visit friends," Rigo said with an air of casual confidence.

The officer continued staring at Rigo, never changing his expression. Finally, he gave back the documents and motioned them through to continue waiting in line. Rigo moved the Taurus forward the few available feet.

"You are doing fine," Justo said. "Remember, we came in this morning and now we're heading home. You remember the address I told you?"

"Yes, Tío."

"Good. Just stay calm," Justo instructed. "The next officer will ask some questions. If we stay calm, we'll be waved on our way." Justo had made this trip several times back when the cartel's business required his direct oversight. He paid attention to detail, and that always led to crossing the border without a hitch.

After another eighteen minutes in line, they arrived at the Mexican/U.S. checkpoint. A U.S. Customs uniform leaned out of her booth window and asked Rigo for all the documents for the car and their passports, which he turned over.

Scrutinizing the documents, she said in a dry monotone, "You just entered today, and now you are going back?"

"We came in to meet a friend," Rigo said calmly, "and now we're headed home."

The customs officer stared at Rigo and then asked for his home address.

Rigo responded, and hearing the correct response, the customs officer stamped their passports and waved them through.

Passports in hand, Rigo inched forward in his lane, passing other border agents who were scanning vehicles as they passed. When they reached the last officer in their lane, the agent signaled with his raised hand for the vehicle to stop.

"Heading back home?" the agent asked.

Rigo nodded. "Been a long day."

"Very well, welcome back to the United States." The agent waved them through to continue past the checkpoint into Laredo, Texas.

Exhaling in relief, he drove through town to the I-35 interchange and north towards San Antonio. From there, they'd switch roads to I-10 and head east for a straight shot into Florida.

Justo adjusted his seat back and stretched his legs forward. He'd take his turn to sleep before again taking the wheel.

***

John and Florey took a day off to burn some overtime hours before someone at GHQ started sending nasty-grams, warning them about working too much. John would use the time to work an off-duty job at a bonded warehouse near Miami International. His duties at FlorAmerica were straightforward enough. It was simply a matter of making sure the security agents did their job monitoring the x-ray machines that scanned imported pallets of flowers from South America. A boring job, but the hourly pay was more than his overtime rate at the Patrol. Easy money.

Monotonous job or not, John took it seriously and earned himself a reputation as a hard-nosed cop. He'd visibly inspect the incoming cargo from arriving 747 cargo planes, comparing the inventory against the shipping manifests. He didn't *have* to do that, but it was his way to be thorough, plus it killed time. He couldn't deal with a load of drugs or contraband getting by on his watch. His attitude was the reason security agents never liked working when John was on duty. He knew that, but because of his constant inquiries, the unarmed officers would never loaf on the job.

If the Customs inspectors ever found inaccurate shipping papers or a security agent asleep on the job, the warehouse's bonded status would be cancelled, effectively shutting down the job. John wasn't about to lose the easy money over someone else's screw up.

He closed the receiving door after the last shipment of flowers had come in, just as his phone vibrated on his belt. John glanced at the screen. Florey. He went out to the parking lot, the only quiet place to call her back.

Florey asked what he was doing, and he told her, asking why she wanted to know.

"Do you get off anytime soon? Do you have Spec with you?"

Okay, so Florey was doing her best not to ask John to leave the job and lose any money, but he couldn't stand beating around the bush, either. "What do you need, Florey?"

"Rick is following a money suspect who's supposed to pick up at a house in Westchester. You have time. No rush, but he wants you to come out with Spec."

John took a second to think. "I get off in an hour, but I'll have to get the dog from the house. Obviously, she's not with me." He wasn't allowed to have Spec at an off-duty job. Policy.

This was a familiar routine. Everyone seemed to need you when you were working an off-duty job. Hard as he tried, John couldn't convince the Patrol to change the policy about not having K-9 dogs at other jobs. His idea was problematic, though, John mused. It was based on common sense, and that was in short supply. It was nonsense, really, the GHQ's way of arbitrarily restricting extra paying jobs troopers relied on to make ends meet. It was a constant source of irritation.

"How long will it take you to get her and meet us in the Westchester area?" Florey asked.

John looked at his watch. The security crew wouldn't mind if he left early. With him gone, they could get in an hour of sleep.

"Well, if I haul ass, I can meet you at Tropical Park on Bird Road in say…thirty to forty minutes?" He started up the stairs to the security office to sign himself out for the day.

"That should be fine," Florey said. "Rick says the female suspect is in a store buying shoes, so like I said, you probably have some time."

"Are you with them now?" asked John.

"Yeah, I was at lunch with my girlfriends when I got the call. I've been out here for about an hour. It wasn't until an informant said the target was going to pick up money that I called you."

"Okay, I'm leaving now. I'll call you on the DEA radio when I get in the area." John closed his phone, signed out, and left with only a wave to the security agents. With no time to waste, the 45 mile drive home was going to strain his ability to keep to the speed limit. John tore off out of the parking lot, got on the Palmetto Expressway, and headed home to pick up Spec.

***

"Florey…you there?" a voice on the DEA radio blurted.

"Yeah, I'm here. Go ahead, Rick," Florey said.

"Any word from John?" asked Rick.

"He's thirty minutes out," she said.

A voice from the surveillance unit suddenly broke in. "The suspect's on the move. She's out of the store. Stand by…"

Florey waited across the street, concealing her marked patrol car behind the First Union Bank. She nervously checked her watch and mumbled, "Come on, partner, hurry up."

"Hold on…she just entered Majorca's Beauty Supply," the surveillance unit reported. "She put her bags down and is talking to a female clerk."

Florey sucked air deep into her lungs and held her breath, hoping somehow that would make the target take a little longer and John get there even quicker.

Earlier, Rick had asked the surveillance units covering the back of the shopping center if they had seen anything, but they had nothing to report other than an old man picking through some dumpsters. Florey knew Rick would be getting antsy. Not seeing movement on surveillance could be unnerving.

She emptied her lungs with a whoosh just as the voice from the DEA radio broke through her thoughts. "She's out of the store and walking back to her car."

Florey's heart rate began increasing as the seconds passed. "Damn it, John. Hurry up." If the target picked up a package from the confidential informant and the DEA requested a traffic stop, there was nothing she could do until John got there with the dog.

"She's sitting in her car. Everyone stand by…she's on the phone," an agent advised. "Rick, you think she's calling the CI?"

"If she is, the informant will call me right after," Rick answered.

"She's off the phone and backing out," the agent said. "Wait. She's back on the phone, now heading west past the Office Depot towards 87th Avenue. Stand by…" another surveillance agent advised.

Florey checked her watch again. Thirty minutes had passed since John said he was on his way. She put the car in drive and held the brake. She waited until it was safe to pull onto the avenue and pace behind the rear of the surveillance.

"She's going north on 87th Avenue and may be off the phone," the agent said. "Rick? Anything yet?"

"Stand by. I'm putting in a call to the informant," Rick said.

Florey stayed in place, waiting for Rick. When his voice came back over the radio, he ordered the surveillance units to rotate their positions. They had to keep track of the target and anyone she met.

Florey knew the drill. Rick would join the surveillance cars and wait.

She eased the brake, ready to pull onto 87th Avenue. She looked left to check northbound traffic when she noticed an FHP cruiser rapidly slowing down. John had made it.

He motioned with his hand as if to say, "ladies first."

Florey grinned as she pulled onto the avenue. At least now she wouldn't be alone if they needed a traffic stop. Always better to have John and Spec in tow.

The surveillance voice started again. "Her blinker is on for a left turn. She's going west on 32nd Street…stand by."

Florey looked ahead. She could just make out the target vehicle turning on the side street. The lead surveillance car soon made the same turn.

"Next car, get ready to take over," the agent said. "She's turning into a driveway at 89th Avenue right across the street from a school field. I'm going straight. Next unit, it's the tan house on the corner."

Florey listened in as Rick interrupted and instructed the next agent. He told him to set up on the other side of the school field and find out if he could see the house with binoculars. Florey, with John and Spec behind her, kept going north on 87th Avenue and pulled into the St. Brennan's Catholic Church, parking in front of the Monsignor's residence.

John backed into the space alongside of her.

"You got here," Florey said.

"Yeah, well, let's just say traffic was light." John winked.

Florey filled in the details for John as one of the agents managed to get a vantage point across from the school field. John walked Spec on the leash while he had the chance. No telling when they'd have the opportunity again.

Just as Spec squatted to do her business, Florey heard a booming voice echoing through the residence and the rectory. "Well, I'll be blessed!"

"Bad timing," John mumbled, "but I'd know that Irish accent anywhere." He turned away and called out, "Monsignor!"

The figure in flowing vestments came walking towards them, but Florey hung back.

"Mr. Stella. How in God's Creation has my former student been?" The Monsignor walked right by Spec and wrapped John in a bear hug.

John grabbed the leash, clearly uncertain how the dog would react, but strangely, Spec sat and wagged her tail.

"Well, then. Who would this be with ya', Johnny?" The priest bent down and patted Spec on her head.

"That would be Spec, sir," John said. "I'm glad she didn't bite you, Monsignor."

"Ah, your guardian angel, I suspect? Aye, Johnny-boy?"

Florey knew all about Monsignor Crims, former boxer turned priest. Mostly, John had told her about all his run-ins with the man. One of many who'd suggested John become a Marine. Crims was a no-nonsense type who taught leadership and integrity by example, as John had once said, even if he had to grab you by the collar to talk some sense into you. John got one of his favorite sayings from the priest, "If you want to act like animals and learn nuthin', get your arse over to the public school and flip burgers the rest of your life!" With his fire-plug frame and echoing voice, he'd make the toughest of kids slink in their seats.

Florey was happy to meet the legend in person when John gestured for her to come closer.

"I'd like you to meet my real guardian angel, my partner, Florey," John said.

The Monsignor gave her an enthusiastic but polite hug. "It's good to know Johnny-boy has such a watchful partner. What brings the two of ya' here?"

"Well, Father, actually, we're on surveillance," John explained. "Kinda watching the agents who are watching a bad guy."

"Aye…well, I won't keep ya'." He shook Florey's hand, and said he'd love for John to bring the dog to the school to give a talk for the kids. He looked down at John over his thick black glasses, his eyes gleaming bright under his bushy salt-and-pepper eyebrows. "You may find a few remind you of a certain somebody, if you know what I mean, Johnny-boy?"

John smiled. "I know. You mean kids like me."

"Hahaha! Precisely, my boy. It would do them good. Maybe it would do *you* good, too? What ya think, Johnny?"

"It'd be my pleasure, sir."

Oh, brother, Florey thought. John sounded like an obedient kid. This guy was sure charismatic, not to mention charming. John would've agreed to anything the Monsignor asked.

"It's my pleasure to meet you, Miss Florey. And you, John," the priest said, wagging his finger at his former pupil. "Take good care of your angel. You hear me, boy!"

His feigned scolding tone made Florey want to laugh out loud. But reality hit, too. They were on surveillance after all.

"Couldn't live with myself if anything happened to her," answered John as Father Crims walked towards the church.

Spec or her? Florey asked herself, amused. She stood by her car window to listen to the DEA radio and watch John's antics. Her smile and stare caught John's attention.

"What?" he shouted over the roof of the cruiser as he opened the door to let Spec into her cage.

"Johnny-boy?" she said in her best Irish accent. She couldn't resist.

John mimicked the priest in an accent he had perfected long ago. "Well, lassie, you may *tink* this is all fun and games, boot we have a job ta do. So, shake that *arse* of yours and give yar partner a freakin' break!"

They both laughed as the DEA radio broke the silence and began to squawk. "She's out of the house. Carrying a box. Looks heavy as hell. Stand by."

Florey and John jumped into their cars and turned up their radios.

"She's at her trunk. It's open and the box is in," an agent said. "She's closing the trunk and getting in the car. Stand by."

Rick's voice interrupted, grabbing Florey's attention. "Listen up! We aren't stopping her yet. This isn't where our CI told her to go. She's making other pickups. Take her down after she meets our informant."

"Copy that," the agent acknowledged. "Okay, she's pulling out and driving south. Stand by."

Rick got on the radio again. "Stand by for takeaways if she does a hand-off to anyone," he instructed, "and call it out for the troopers so they can make that stop while we continue to follow our target."

"Copy that, Rick," the lead surveillance unit acknowledged. "She's turning back east towards 87th Avenue. Stand by."

Just as she and John were about to leave the church parking lot, Florey's phone went off. "Hey, it's Rick. Did you copy my last transmission?"

"Yeah, we got it. Just let us know where and when," Florey responded.

"Wanted to make sure. I gotta go." Rick ended the call.

Florey looked over at John and called out, "You know the routine!"

"Yep. Takeaways. I hate takeaways," he said. "Always makes me feel like I have to rush around like an idiot."

Florey shared the frustration. Some suspects might make numerous stops, delivering to multiple individuals before even meeting the police informant. Each of those other individuals had to be identified, and that thinned out the surveillance on the original target. It was sometimes a tactic. The more industrious drug dealers purposely did this, knowing it would make it easier to spot the remaining undercover cars. The fewer cars the police had to rotate into a surveillance, the quicker a target could spot them. Takeaways kept everyone on edge.

The surveillance continued to follow the suspect south on the avenue to a liquor store where she was handed a shoe box by an overweight gentleman in his forties. The agents asked if they should follow the gentleman when he left. Rick said he didn't want to waste resources on having everyone she met followed. They would stick with their target for now.

The liquor store rendezvous lasted only as long as she could toss the box in her truck and close it. She exited the lot onto a side street and made a sudden U-turn, most likely to head back south on the avenue for a specific block.

She turned into the parking lot of a farmer's market. A surveillance unit watched as another man transferred two carry-on bags from his car to the suspect's trunk. Casually, she closed the trunk lid and drove to the exit and continued south.

Rick waited, pulling out of the parking lot behind the car that made the luggage delivery. He jotted down the tag and casually drove onto 87th Avenue, heading south and joined the rear of the surveillance.

"She's back on the phone," the agent advised. "Hey, Rick, I hope she is calling the CI. I don't think she has any more room in her car to pick up more boxes."

Rick's phone rang. He picked up the call from his CI. "Yeah, go ahead."

"Listen, Rick, she just called me and didn't want to meet at any warehouse. I suggested the Toys-R-Us on Dixie Highway north of Kendall Drive. She said that was fine. Is that alright with you?" the informant asked.

"That's perfect. I like that location better," said Rick. "What kind of car is your guy driving?"

"He has a silver Honda."

"Call me if anything else changes." Rick hung up the phone and picked up his DEA radio to pass on the new location.

Rick said, "She says her guy should be in a silver Honda. When our target picks up, we'll take her away for a while and give the other guy a chance to leave the area. Where is she now?"

"I got her turning east on Kendall," the lead agent said. "She's picked up her speed a bit."

Rick broke in again. "After this suspect picks up from our CI, FHP will work their way up and wait for a traffic violation, then pull her over. John, you copy?"

"We copy, Rick. Just let us know when we are free to start," John said.

"Will do," Rick said. "Go ahead, surveillance. Where is she?"

"In the center lane, passing Dadeland Shopping Center. Stand by," the agent said. "She's coming up to the intersection now, the light is green, and she made the turn. She's northbound on Dixie Highway. I'm going straight. Anyone else able to turn?"

"I'm with her," another agent said. "I'm turning left, a few cars behind the target. She's moving to the right, and her turn signal is on for the toy store. She's pulling in. I'll go past and park in the Buick dealership next door. I'll try to get an eyeball from there."

"I'll pull in and get a visual from inside the lot," Rick said. "Everyone else set up for a takeaway. When she pulls out, she can only go north from here, but watch out for another crazy U-turn. The 878 Expressway is just on the other side of Dixie Highway."

***

John called Florey to talk over where they should set up. He chose the 878 Expressway, a hastily built spur that broke off from another of the rambling thoroughfares. It had been built as a band-aid to Dade County's constant rise in traffic volume. John believed the target would never do the speed limit if she got on there. Nobody did.

"I'll drive a little farther north on Dixie Highway, just inside the South Miami city limits," Florey said, "just in case she heads downtown."

John drove up the entrance ramp, found the first overpass, and parked on the downside of the embankment, out of sight of passing cars. Florey let him know she'd entered South Miami and pulled her car into an alley behind a fitness center.

Rick reported he'd parked next to the toy store's delivery van, and had to lean forward to see the target, where she was still sitting behind the wheel. "She's waiting in the car. Stand by," he advised.

The minutes began to tick by. Each one seemed like an hour—adrenaline had made patience futile. John thrummed his fingers on the wheel, waiting.

"Okay, she's meeting our informant," Rick said, his voice breaking the silence like a sportscaster's play-by-play. "The Silver Accord pulled in the lot…they're both getting out and going to the back of the Honda. They're still chit-chatting, moving closer to the trunk. He has his keys out. Trunk is open… Geez!"

"What's up, Rick?" asked one of the agents.

"Another two carry-on bags," Rick said, his laughter coming over the transmission as he resumed his broadcast. "She's cramming the bags in the trunk. Okay, she managed to get it closed. Stand by. She's back in the car, pulling out and heading to the side exit onto Dixie. Someone take her when she pulls out of the parking lot. I have to wait till this Honda leaves."

"I got her, Rick. Stand by," another agent said. "She's heading north on Dixie and…*shit*! She darted all the way across northbound traffic. Holy cow! This broad must be nuts."

"Where is she now?" one of the other agents asked.

"In the left turn lane on 80th Street. Anyone got an eye on her?" the surveillance unit asked.

"I got her. I'm four cars behind her," another agent reported.

John thought she had only one option after a move like that. Right to the entrance ramp to 878. He didn't need to call Florey to know she'd be hustling her way through traffic to head his way.

"She's making the U-turn and turning right onto the 878 ramp. FHP, she's all yours," the lead surveillance unit said.

John grabbed his mic. "FHP is waiting on the other side of the first overpass. Florey, I'll let her go by and get a radar clock on her."

"Copy."

John figured she'd be only a few hundred yards behind the target.

"FHP, she's driving a blue Honda Civic. Tag is X x-ray, J Juliet, R Romeo, 367," the surveillance agent confirmed as he slowed down and let Florey pass him.

"FHP copies," John replied.

It didn't take very long. The blue Honda passed the downside of the overpass, causing John's radar to lock in on the fast-approaching vehicle. The digital read-out flashed sixty-seven miles per hour.

"Perfect," John mumbled under his breath as he slowly crept out of his hiding spot and merged into the westbound lanes of 878. He checked his rearview mirror and could just make out the silhouette of Florey's car as it crested the overpass behind him. She was gaining on him quickly.

"Florey, she's just ahead of me. Maybe an eighth of a mile," John said. "Come around and do the traffic stop. I already got her at 67."

"I'm coming around ya now…" Florey's patrol car engine roared by as she passed John and set up to conduct a traffic stop.

"Let me know when you start and I'll call it out for DEA," John said.

Florey didn't respond, but John didn't expect her to. She was likely getting her own pace clock for speed. Within a mile, he saw Florey's overhead lights begin to flash.

John pulled over on the emergency lane and grabbed the DEA radio. "FHP has the target stopped just before the next exit. They're on the right shoulder."

"Okay, FHP. Surveillance units take positions and be ready to back them up when they call," Rick instructed.

John watched ahead as Florey walked up to the driver's window and began to explain the traffic stop. He watched his partner take papers from the driver and walk back to her patrol car. So far, everything seemed like a routine traffic stop. Florey picked up her DEA radio as she sat in her car. "John. Give it about a minute and come up. I got her for speed. She picked it up to 72 by the time I paced her."

"Copy." John waited for what seemed another lifetime. He couldn't imagine how much money this woman could've collected, but she sure had enough bags and boxes to alert Spec. He waited until the minute passed, then pulled onto the road to drive the mile or so ahead to meet Florey.

From this point on, it was crucial to treat the traffic stop as normal and routine. Nothing special about it. Their well-rehearsed dialogue was staged for the driver, who would never know she'd been a target of a federal investigation or was under surveillance. The target needed to think it was a case of bad luck, stopped for speeding past a state trooper.

"Hey, Trooper Baker. What you got?" John walked up, nonchalantly greeting Florey.

"Oh, nothing special. Just a young lady going too fast," Florey said.

John looked ahead and noted the driver diligently watching through her sideview mirror.

"Hey, you wanna talk to her and maybe explain why she needs to slow down? I don't think she understood me," Florey said.

"No problem. What's her name?"

"Adrianna Villabajo."

John gave his partner a thumbs-up and casually walked to the driver's window. "Ma'am, how are you today?" he said with a big smile.

The target looked up at John and smiled coyly as she batted her eyes. "Hello, officer. How are you?" She spoke with a heavy Spanish accent.

John stood nearly slack jawed as his eyes drank in the sight of the target's long brunette hair. His gaze flowed along with it to the perfect neck that immediately intersected with a light, almost see-through blouse. It announced the almost vulgar presentation of her cleavage, accentuated by overly ambitious implants. His opinion, anyway.

Having taken the visual bait, his gaze kept moving, right down to her black skirt that hit mid-thigh and tightly wrapped around her near-perfect hourglass figure.

"The other trooper said you were going too fast," John said, returning to the business at hand. "Where would a pretty lady like you be headed so quickly?" he asked, exaggerating his teasing voice to play to her vanity.

"Maybe I was going a little too fast." She used her index finger and thumb to illustrate the word "little." "Ay, please! You maybe give me a breakey?" Her eyelids fluttered.

"Well, I'll talk to the other trooper," John demurred, as if affected by her over-the-top flirtations. He took a step towards Florey's car, then snapped his fingers as if he had forgotten something. "Oh, yeah. One more thing, Miss Villabajo. Who owns this car anyway?" No smile this time.

"A friend," she replied.

"What is the name of your friend?" John asked.

"Uh, I only meet him a few days ago. You know, he is a young friend. He like me." Her impish grin failed to convey any truth to the statement. The display was like a performance on a daytime telenovela. A bit over-the-top. John wondered how many officers had been caught in her subterfuge and just let her go instead of investigating deeper.

Reflexively, he shook his head in disapproval as the sun reflected off the gloss of her red lipstick. She had to be the most attractive doper he had ever encountered. The most arrogant one, too.

"Let me see if I understand you correctly," John posed. "A friend you just met gave you his car?" John was genuinely puzzled as he waited for her next lie.

Her eyes darted from side to side as if searching for something, anything, to say. Finally, batting her eyes and tilting her head, she gave a confident smile and opened her mouth to speak.

This was going to be good, John thought.

"He is very nice, yes?"

Her half-hearted reply almost made John roll his eyes. Instead of challenging her, he agreed it was great to have such good friends and excused himself to see what he could do for her by talking to the other trooper. The woman smiled again, now convinced that John was another dupe in a long line of male cops she'd been schmoozing for years. Keep them hormonally engaged and oblivious. John speculated that was the motto she lived by.

Florey looked up from writing the speeding ticket when he approached. "Is she full of shit or what?" she asked.

John smiled and rolled his eyes.

Florey scoffed and went back to writing the citation. "Yeah, that's what I thought, too."

"Who does the car come back to?" John asked.

Florey pulled out her notes on the tag she got from dispatch. "Arnaldo Puentes out of Hialeah. Says here he is eighty-three years old."

John snickered. "She give you the story about her young friend lending her the car?"

"Yup, she sure did!"

"Get her out before you finish that ticket and let's do this," John said. "Tell her there's a problem with the car's registration."

"Do you want me to give her the usual story?" Florey asked.

"Yeah. That'll be fine."

Florey stepped forward.

John stayed back, but still in earshot and heard his partner explain to the suspect that the owner was an old man, not a young person as she had said. The target began to shake her head, motion with her hands, and shrug anxiously. That's when Florey asked her to step out of the car.

Adrianna Villabajo didn't react.

John was certain she hadn't expected this. After all, this probably wasn't what usually happened when she was pulled over. The men would stumble over themselves, with some even offering their phone numbers before letting her go on her way. As for the women cops, John bet they'd hand her a ticket and leave. Maybe she'd never dealt with state troopers before.

Florey asked her to get out of the car again.

The woman did so with dramatic flair, swinging her legs out of the car and standing. With one hand on her hip, she flung her hair to flow neatly off her shoulders. She held her purse in the other hand.

Unimpressed with the display, Florey had her sit on the guardrail just behind the Honda's rear bumper.

"You seem nervous. Is there something you haven't told us?" Florey asked.

The woman looked at the car and then at Florey. "No, nothing!"

"Well, it's our job to make sure there are no problems or illegal things in cars. You understand, don't you?" Florey asked in an innocent tone.

"Yes, of course. But what kind of things you looking for?"

"Well, we make sure there are no explosives, guns—"

"Ay, no. I have no such things, please," the target blurted.

Florey continued, and carefully watched the target's eyes for any response as she went down the list. "Bombs, cocaine, marijuana, or excessive money."

As soon as Florey mentioned money, the target shot a quick glance at the trunk of the car. Then immediately, she refocused on the patrol cars, squirming on the guardrail, apparently trying to avoid the rail's unforgiving edge.

From his vantage point next to the rear door of his patrol car, John watched. When Florey gave him a single nod, John acknowledged.

He grabbed the dog's toy, opened the door, and hooked Spec up to the leash.

Spec wagged her tail and barked, knowing it was time to work.

John tucked the dog toy in his belt behind his back and walked Spec towards the target's car. Before they even got past his own patrol car, Spec put her nose in the air and pulled on the leash, recognizing the familiar drug odor she had been trained to detect. It didn't matter if the drug was physically present or not. The odor, caused by the rapid decay of drug particles, could be detected on any item that had recently been in immediate proximity of drugs. Like money usually was. John remembered the drug house he raided once where they had found a stash of money next to bricks of cocaine and bags of marijuana.

He slowed Spec down and redirected her attention to the front of Villabajo's car. He bent to pet Spec, who sat facing the front bumper. Her body quivered in anticipation of her doggie reward and she began to bark.

John stood up with a firm hold on the leash and gave Spec the command she had been waiting for. "Dope seek."

Spec lunged forward and sniffed the center of the front bumper, working her well-trained pattern around the car. Soon, she began following a scent to the rear of the trunk lid, just above the license tag. She took in another deep breath and let out a loud snort. She lunged again with both front paws against the bumper and feverishly scratched.

John let Spec's frenzied alert go on for a few seconds before throwing the rubberhose toy on the ground beneath her. She snatched it up in her mouth and John played with her as he walked her back to the car before putting her up.

"I'll be right back for ya', girl." John patted Spec's head, then closed the patrol car door. He returned to Florey and the suspect, who now sat silently perched on the guardrail next to the Honda.

"Is there something in the trunk we should know about?" John pretended to be puzzled over his dog's alert to the car.

"No, please… I just take the car. Maybe my friend put something there," said Villabajo, using her acting abilities, such as they were, to appear innocent.

He doubted she had any idea the cops had been watching her every move. More importantly, John and Florey both knew she would be struggling to figure out which of the people who gave her packages would have ratted her out. Apprehended drug couriers almost always went through mental calculations as they came to the understanding that reality was about to hit them squarely in the face.

As John retrieved the keys from the ignition, the suspect became fidgety. Her eyes nervously danced as she looked at everything except her car. She turned sideways so she wouldn't have to look at it.

Florey watched her, too, and took a step closer in case she became combative or attempted to run.

"Here are your keys, ma'am. Could you open the trunk for me?" John held out his hand, the car keys dangling between his fingers.

The woman glared at him. Clearly annoyed by the request, she said, "I don't think I can. I mean, it's not my car. Don't you need a warrant?"

Her demeanor grew more defiant with each word. She'd gone from flirtatious vamp to jailhouse lawyer.

"Ma'am, I don't need a warrant. The dog's alert gives me probable cause to search. I thought you'd be curious about what your *friend* may have left in this car." John waited for a response as the woman continued to look everywhere but at the car. Finally, she stood up and took the keys from John's hand, letting out a deep dramatic breath.

John had seen put-on resignation before.

She opened the trunk, then returned to sit on the guard rail without waiting to see what was inside.

"Miss Villabajo, you want to look at what your friend left?" John said sarcastically. He'd heard just about enough from the drama queen.

She didn't answer.

Florey moved in closer to the suspect. "Maybe you already knew what was in the trunk?"

The woman rolled her eyes and continued to stare at the shoulder of the road, watching the traffic go by.

Just as the surveillance units had said on the radio, the trunk was filled with boxes and luggage. John picked up the carry-on bags to check for weight. Each was heavy. He took out the pieces of luggage and boxes and lined them up on the side of the roadway by the guardrail, in front of the Honda and away from the patrol cars. Then, he went to get Spec.

Together, they walked the line of packages. Each one sent the canine into a scratching frenzy. When Spec had scratched on the last box, John threw down her toy. She jumped to take it but not before tearing open the box on its side.

John bent down and took a closer look. All he could do was grin. Just a little more play acting, he thought, and they'd be done.

Walking back to Florey and the suspect, John spoke as if astonished. "Florey, we need to call someone in on this!"

"Why? What is it?" she said.

"It's more cash than I've ever seen. I don't know what to do." Turning to Miss Villabajo, he asked, "Ma'am, is this money yours?"

Still looking away at the shoulder of the road, the suspect waved him off with one hand and said a cold, "No."

"Well, then, we better call in someone to make sure it gets back to the rightful owner."

Florey reacted to her cue. "Why don't you call dispatch and see if they can find someone to help us with this? I'm sure they can get some agency to come give us a hand."

John turned as if struck by the genius of the suggestion. "Great idea! Let me give them a call and see who we can get out here." John walked back to his patrol car out of earshot of the suspect and called Rick.

The woman watched him using his phone. But John was certain she couldn't make out the conversation. She, instead, reached down to her purse.

Florey warned her not to and told her to stop.

"I want to make a call to let my work know I'm going to be late," she insisted.

John could see Florey wasn't amused.

"With all that money, sweetie," Florey said, "I'll be holding on to your cell phone until this gets all cleared up." Florey reached into the open purse and removed the phone.

With the crude attempt to notify her bosses thwarted, the woman squirmed to make herself comfortable once again on the galvanized metal guardrail.

"Hey, Rick, where are you?" John asked.

"I'm about half a mile behind you on the other side of the overpass," Rick said. "What you got?"

"Looks like everything she picked up was money. Dog alerted to all of it."

"Outstanding!"

"Take it easy, buddy," John said, laughing. "Give it about fifteen minutes and drive up. We gave her the line we needed to call the nearest detectives. If you get here too soon, she'll know something is up."

John filled Rick in on the suspect's behavior and attitude, knowing Rick couldn't have been happier. They both agreed that since Villabajo had picked up packages from so many different sources, the cartel would not easily be able to determine which among them the informant was. And that was just fine. It was essential to keep Rick's confidential informant safe and in the good graces of Colombia, but most of all, it would allow the informant to keep on working. John ended the call and returned to Florey.

"Hey, I got a hold of the dispatcher." He spoke loud enough for the suspect to hear. "They said they'd find the nearest agency to help us."

"Well, I hope it doesn't take too long. I need some coffee and I'm sure this young lady wants to get to work." Florey flashed a fake smile at the woman.

Apparently thinking Florey was serious, the woman thanked her for trying her best to hurry.

Florey turned away to make a face.

John used up some time taking pictures of the car, along with the luggage and boxes, for his report.

Rick and his fellow agents arrived right on cue. "Hey, Troopers, I'm Rick Lotz with the DEA. Your dispatch called us and said you had something you need help with?"

John reached out and shook Rick's hand as if they had just met. "Yeah, maybe you guys know what to do with a lot of U.S. currency?"

"I think we can help," Rick said. "How much are you talking about?"

John pointed to the line of bags and boxes ahead of the Honda. "All of that."

"My goodness! Is this the driver of the car?" Rick asked innocently.

Florey fake-introduced herself to Rick and handed him the suspect's driver license and registration.

Rick studied the information. "Miss Adrianna Villabajo?"

"Yes, that is me. But I know nothing about that," she said as she pointed at the packages.

"Well, you agree that this is a bit of a problem, don't you?" Rick asked.

No response.

"I mean, don't you think it is important to return this money to the rightful owner?" He paused as the suspect begrudgingly agreed.

Rick continued, finally managing to get her to agree to go with him back to the DEA to help them find the owner of the money.

Florey tagged the bags with evidence tape and replaced them in the Honda's trunk.

Rick assigned one of the other agents to drive the Honda back to the office to process and count the money.

John followed the caravan as the group drove back to the DEA with Villabajo sitting quietly in the front of Rick's car.

Once at the DEA, they moved to the counting room, set up with three fold-up tables each with two counting machines. The bags and boxes were brought in, photographed again, and opened.

After several more pictures documenting the contents, each parcel was counted separately. In a matter of a few minutes, the room filled with a fine wafting mist of cocaine powder as the machines spun and sorted the money into stacks of pre-set denominations.

John and Florey, as well as the agents, wore rubber gloves and dust masks to prevent any contact with the rising fog that gave the room the look of a biohazard emergency.

***

Rick put the suspect in the interrogation room while he conferred with his fellow agents. After introducing themselves and showing her pictures taken during the day's surveillance, it became evident to Miss Villabajo that her goose was cooked. That was motivation enough to agree to work with DEA as a confidential informant.

Rick asked an assistant U.S. attorney general to make the arrangement official, and released her with John's arrest affidavit for the state charges of transporting U.S. currency without a license. It was a little-known statute that was good enough to hold over her head until the Feds properly adopted the case. It was also proof for the target to show her bosses that she had the dumb luck of getting stopped, only to have the money confiscated by the FHP. It was a scenario that worked every time. She was given contact numbers, and Rick advised her to call as soon as she had any information.

Rick handed the keys for the Honda to her. "You understand that it is in your best interest to make that call, don't you?"

"Yes, I'll call," she answered. "But you have to make sure they never find out. These people don't like losing their money, Mr. Rick."

Rick understood her concern. As he walked her through the parking lot to her car, he stopped her. "Listen, Adrianna. I know how you must feel. You get stopped by troopers. You had to face reality, and now you end up working for us. It's been a crazy day for you. At some point, you may think you can go back and make right with Cali. But you know what Colombia will do if they find out, don't you?"

Adrianna looked down at her feet. Her eyes began to well with tears.

Rick could see she was convinced she had no choice. At least, if she wanted to stay alive. "I know, Señor. I live with that every day. I am always scared that some money will not add up and they come look for me," she confessed.

"Rest assured, we won't let anything happen to you," Rick said. "So long as you are honest with us and don't try to pull any fast ones. You understand what I am saying?" He stared into her eyes, unmoved by her show of emotion. Trust was going to be based on her results while working with them. If she made one misstep, there would be no stopping the U.S. Attorney's office from throwing her into Federal prison. A fact that he was quick to impress upon her.

"I understand, Mr. Rick," she said, wiping tears from her eyes. "I let you know as soon as they call me again to pick up more money."

Rick shook her hand and watched until she drove out of the parking lot before he returned to the office. He went downstairs to the counting room only to comment on the cloud of coke dust permeating the air. "Jesus, guys. Why didn't you turn on the fans?" He flipped a toggle switch on the wall.

Instantly, the whoosh of air being sucked into the ceiling grates began extracting the contaminated air out of the room.

"When did they install that?" one of the agents complained.

"Last week. I thought you guys knew," Rick said over the din of complaints and comments from the agents.

"Okay, Okay. Settle down. Now you know!" Rick quipped. "Do we have a count?"

One agent had been at the desk with the calculator re-counting the columns of numbers from each run of the machines. The agent worked up a frenzy, hitting the keys of the calculator and finally pushed the button to confirm the total. He smiled and handed Rick the paper printout.

Rick grinned from ear to ear. He looked up and made the announcement. "Two million, four hundred and ninety-nine thousand dollars, even!"

The agents high-fived each other as hoots and howls of laughter filled the room.

"Not a bad haul for a day's work, huh," John said smugly.

Florey leaned towards her partner and nearly shouted, "Thanks to Spec."

Rick couldn't have agreed more. He waited for the voices of celebration to settle down before addressing the group. "You guys were outstanding today. We got the target to agree to start working with us, and nearly $2.5 million is out of the greedy hands of the cartel. Even better, in case you were wondering," he said, pausing for a moment, "I believe this makes for the largest single cash seizure ever in this region."

Rick enjoyed the chance to stand back and watch the agents congratulate each other on this huge accomplishment.

"We have more to go," he said. "Now that we feel certain the doctor is operating between several warehouses identified by the other task force agents, it's only a matter of time before the cartel's network comes crashing down. Okay, guys, let's get that money in the safe and call it a day."

Rick gestured to John and Florey before they had a chance to leave. He led them out of the building and into the parking lot before he spoke.

"Look, you guys, you did exceptionally well. We couldn't have got this done without you. The Villabajo lady is 100% on board. It looks like she'll lead us to a lot of other seizures. Turns out, her life partner is the head currency collector for another cell operating between Miami and Fort Lauderdale. Whatever the cartel was hoping to get done with this operation, your assistance here is essential to us as we try shutting them down."

John and Florey looked at each other, pleased with his remarks.

"It's all a team effort," Florey said.

"So," Rick said, "I'll see you two at the INEOA Award ceremony in a few days."

"I didn't know you were going," John commented.

"McKenna and I want to be there for you and Florey. You guys deserve it." Rick shook hands with them both.

The two troopers thanked their friend again.

Rick watched as they got in their cars to leave, no doubt heading to the station to drop off their reports before going home.

Chapter Fourteen

Heading south on I-75 as the morning sun began to rise above the endless rows of pine trees, Justo glanced over at Rigo. After driving through the night, they'd stopped at a rest area outside of Tallahassee. Justo had taken the wheel and Rigo now slept in the passenger seat.

He navigated the interstate just south of Ocala and worked his way to the left lane. Justo negotiated around the speeding tractor-trailers and passing pickups on the multi-lane highway as he approached signs for the Florida Turnpike turnoff. The road stretched out ahead in an endless monotony of long, persistent stretches of pine groves, cow fields, gas stations, and billboards.

As they entered the bend for the final leg of their trip, Justo spotted the camouflaged black and tan pattern of a Florida Highway Patrol car secreted in the shadows of a cluster of pines. He instinctively eased off the gas to slow down.

"Cabrones," Justo muttered. But his muffled outburst was enough to wake Rigo.

"What is it?" Rigo sat up, frantically searching ahead and then to his side.

Justo checked his rearview mirror. The FHP car had begun to move across the shoulder and merge behind him onto the southbound lanes of traffic. "Policía. I was doing over eighty."

"What is the limit here?" Rigo asked, staring in his side mirror. "I don't see a car."

The patrol car behind them flashed emergency lights and was coming up fast.

"It's seventy here." Justo glanced at his nephew. "Hey, relax. Don't look so concerned. It's just a speeding ticket."

Within a few seconds, the patrol car caught up and was riding Justo's bumper. Justo flipped his left turn signal on and merged into the median's emergency lane to slow the car to a stop. "Remember, calm and casual."

The trooper approached the driver's side of the Taurus with measured steps, no rush, showing no stress. The muscular black man in uniform adjusted his campaign hat and first scanned the rear seats, then the front. He positioned himself ahead of Justo's sideview mirror. Facing his patrol car, the trooper leaned towards the window and introduced himself as Trooper Bryant of the Florida Highway Patrol. "May I have your driver's license and papers to the car?"

"Yes, of course, sir. Was I speeding?" Justo spoke politely, his tone casual.

"Yes, sir. I clocked you at 82 miles per hour. This is a 70 mile per hour zone."

Justo nodded, then reached into the door pocket and took out the papers that had come with the car.

"Do you have your license and insurance? This is only the registration and an old bill of sale."

Justo was conscious of the trooper watching Rigo open the glove box, pull out an insurance card and a Florida license, and hand them to his uncle.

"I noticed passports in the glove box. Are they yours, sir?" the trooper asked.

They had forgotten to put the documents in the backpacks. Justo gritted his teeth, but quickly smiled again. "Yes, we have just come from a trip and are headed to Miami where my son will be going to the university." That sounded like an ordinary explanation and the passport would verify it.

The trooper remained expressionless when he asked, "May I see the passports, sir?"

Rigo pulled them from the glove box and handed them to Justo, who passed them to the trooper.

Justo did a quick rundown of the car while the trooper went to run a check. As far as Justo could tell, their vehicle was clean. Nothing unusual. His Florida driver's license had his address in Hialeah. But Justo knew the Texas registration was under a different name and had an address in Laredo. Meanwhile, Trooper Bryant was taking his time.

"What's taking so long, Tío?" Rigo asked.

"He's running the information, Rigo. Don't worry." Easy to say. Justo knew for sure Trooper Bryant would have the Gainesville FHP dispatch run the information through the state and federal traffic records. But Justo also knew nothing would come up to cause trouble. Still, the stop was taking a long time. He had no way of knowing what would catch the trooper's attention, or even what experience he had. This stretch of I-75 was thick with drug mules and cops. Bryant was alone, though. No partner, no dog.

Through his rearview mirror, Justo saw Bryant pick up his cell phone and make a call. Why? He'd already called his dispatch. Justo had seen him do it. He also knew they had other options, like Federal agencies. A conscientious cop concerned about his career would take the time for more checks, maybe make sure they weren't wanted by the Feds. Justo knew this kind of cop. He had everything he needed, from names to birth dates to passport numbers.

Justo looked in his mirror as the trooper walked back to the car, fixing his uniform hat back on his head.

"Sir, may I have your consent to look in the trunk?" Trooper Bryant asked.

Justo glanced at Rigo before he turned back to the trooper. "Can I ask why, sir?"

"Well, we have a large problem with individuals transporting contraband on the highways of Florida," Bryant said as if reciting a scripted line. "Now, I'm not saying this is what you're doing, but it's routine for me to ask. You understand, don't you, sir?"

Justo noted every polished and perfectly placed chrome button and hasp on the trooper's uniform. His tapered uniform exposed the no-nonsense, medium-height frame of a former drill instructor type. He waited patiently for a response. Obviously, Justo thought, this was not a man to argue with today.

"Yes, of course. May I get out?" Justo said cordially while doing his best to avoid saying anything that might raise even a hint of suspicion.

Justo removed the car keys and stepped out of the car. Only then did he appreciate the cop's looming presence as the trooper tried to hide the fact that he was studying the inside of the car as he went to the trunk. Justo opened the trunk and stepped aside.

Bryant pointed to the two backpacks. "Is that your luggage, sir?"

"Yes. You can go ahead and look if you want," Justo offered.

"If you don't mind standing to the side of the car, this won't take but a minute and I'll have you on your way."

Justo caught a glimpse of Rigo watching through his side mirror.

It didn't take Bryant long to get a look at the contents of the backpacks and zipper them shut again. "Very well then, sir. Thank you for your cooperation. Have a seat in your car and I'll be right with you."

Justo closed the trunk, pulled out the key from the lock, and slipped in the driver's seat. But he kept an eye on Bryant doing the paperwork in his patrol car. The seconds ticked by. *Hurry up. How long could it take to write a ticket?* When the trooper picked up his phone, Justo's gut tightened. What? It was a long call. Justo's suspicions rose, along with the fear he could feel rising in Rigo.

Finally, he turned to Rigo. "He's off the phone. Here he comes."

A few minutes later, with nothing worse than a speeding ticket, Justo merged back into southbound traffic. But his nephew still frowned. "What is wrong?"

"Do you think he was suspicious, Tío?" Rigo nervously watched the mirror.

"Relax. He's a highway patrolman. They write speeding tickets all day. That's all they do. He didn't suspect anything." Justo sounded reassuring even to himself, but he was putting on a confident act. He had his doubts. Still, it made no sense to worry.

"Rigo!" Justo shouted to get his attention. It worked.

Rigo snapped his gaze to him—and off the mirror.

"It was your fault, anyway!"

"How the hell was it *my* fault?" Rigo's tone dripped disbelief.

"You should have told me I was speeding!" Justo began to laugh, and Rigo finally smiled.

"Besides, it's not like we are going to pay a ticket made out to someone else," Justo said, still laughing.

Justo drove on, this time hugging the speed limit and watching the road ahead. He was no amateur and couldn't afford that kind of mistake again. He checked his watch. Three and a half hours and they'd be in Hialeah.

Rigo slumped in his seat, rested his head against the passenger door post, and closed his eyes.

Justo reached over and switched the car's air on high—anything to help neutralize the rising heat as the sun cleared the horizon and hung in a cloudless sky.

***

With Florey following right behind him, John took the I-95 exit ramp into downtown Miami. The early lunch crowd clogged the narrow streets and avenues, getting a jump on the bumper-to-bumper chaos that would soon envelop the center of the city. Snaking through the streets, they passed the countless cafeterias featuring Cuban food. They all had express windows that drew Miamians in need of their cafecito, but John didn't have time that day. The rest of the downtown streets were lined with storefronts hawking cheap electronics, overpriced jewelry, and shoe boutiques. Store owners, like hucksters, worked the dirty sidewalks, shouting their deals to passing tourists to get them in the door—only to have baited them into outdated devices and novelties.

John took in downtown as it was today. He remembered the time it had boasted major department stores and office buildings and sidewalks crowded with businessmen and shoppers. These days, the place looked more like the Nassau flea market or some South American tourist bazaar.

They passed the abandoned Dupont Plaza office building and merged onto Biscayne Boulevard, the main thoroughfare that hemmed the growing city from the bay. In less than a block, they entered the drive to the Intercontinental Hotel. Its thirty-plus story twin towers and convention hall sat on the banks of Biscayne Bay overlooking the cruise ships docked on the Government Cut waterway. The Miami Beach skyline was visible in the hazy blue distance behind the jutting smokestacks of temporarily dormant ocean liners. Even here, traffic was heavy as lines of delivery vans and trucks waited to pull into the garage and unload the daily supplies needed to run the massive hotel and convention center.

John found himself waiting in a long line of vehicles. He identified the source of the hold up at the front of the line of traffic. Patiently, he watched a Miami police officer attempting to explain something to a driver using exaggerated hand gestures. The officer's body language suggested to John that he wasn't quite getting his point across.

John drove around the line of cars and parked in the entranceway. His suspicions were confirmed when he heard the officer ask the driver of a white van, "Don't you speak English, buddy?"

Stepping over to the vehicle, John asked, "Can I be of some assistance, officer?"

The officer took a quick look at John, eyeing him from head to toe, then rolled his eyes and turned back to the van driver.

John decided to ignore the slight and offer again.

"Hey, are you part of this law enforcement convention thing here today?" the officer pointedly asked.

John answered, but before he could finish, got an earful from the cop about his frustrations in dealing with convention traffic and trying to speak English to, as the officer so impolitely put it, *"these people."*

John held his tongue yet wondered why an officer who appeared to be old enough to have a few years of service under his belt never bothered to try to learn a language that more than half the citizens in his city spoke. He didn't want to aggravate the officer any more than he appeared to be and politely offered his language skills.

The officer threw up his arms. "Fine. Maybe you can get the point across."

John greeted the van driver in Spanish, to the officer's surprise.

The driver and his young passenger said they had been asked to wait for hotel staff to make a space available in the underground garage. They needed access to the hotel's air conditioning system. He also took note of the van's signage. In large block letters, it read Arturo's A/C Repair.

As John was about to explain the hold up to the officer, a hotel supervisor yelled out in Spanish for the van driver to enter the garage. Resolved. Quick and easy.

The officer appeared a bit ashamed for having lost his patience. As a show of thanks for John's assistance, he directed John to hail his partner and park in the spaces by the front door marked for Miami Police only.

John thanked him and waved for Florey to move ahead, and they dutifully parked by the front door of the hotel.

One of the two towers of the Intercontinental Hotel complex was thirty-four stories, while the second tower, the Miami Center, was slightly taller and housed financial and legal offices. Despite its luxury and location adjacent to Miami's Bayfront Park, it had become a home to countless transients and the resident homeless, all within eyesight of sun scorched tourists coming off the cruise ships at the Port of Miami. John had avoided the area like the plague, especially when the city fathers decided to tear down the main branch of the county library. Its magnificent marble Greco-Roman edifice had once sat at the edge of the park next to the band shell.

Way back when he was a kid, John had loved the collection of original books and newspapers dating back to Miami's days as a pioneer village, all held within the expanse of the post-World War II building, which had looked the part of a repository of accumulated knowledge. Inside, high rear windows had overlooked the bay, each glass panel allowing beams of morning light to illuminate rows of polished wood shelves and their precious contents. In the evenings, light from the towering ceilings had descended on the reading rooms and the wraparound grand staircase. The library's atmosphere had given John a sense that no matter how screwy Miami became, at least one place never changed.

And then it was gone. Miami's willful disassociation with its own history.

Tearing down the old and building up new seemed to be what made the area tick, almost as if it were a matter of social policy to scrub away the past. The city leaders had managed to push their agenda for more high-rises and denser occupancies. That was their vision of progress and a "bold future."

More like sailing without a rudder, John thought. After the library was demolished, he didn't have much use for the park.

Now, Florey and John went through the main doors into the hotel lobby, which seemed to stretch on forever. The brightly polished marble floors and columns added a touch of elegance. They checked in quickly, and on the way to the elevator, John glanced down at his key. "Hey, Florey, this says Room 3302 VP Suite. What does yours say?"

Florey checked her key and showed it to John. "Room 3304 VP Suite."

"You think they made a mistake?"

Florey laughed. "Why? You going to lodge a complaint?"

Before John could think of an equally smartass reply, the elevator door opened, and Rick stepped out. "Hey, kids! You been up to your rooms yet?"

He looked like a kid in a candy store, John thought. "Who managed to get us the Vice-Presidential Suites?"

"McKenna. He figured it was the least he could do for you two. Hey, that reminds me. He wanted to know if you'd like to join us for drinks and dinner in Miami Beach after the meetings and luncheon."

"You bet," Florey said. "We'll put our bags in the rooms and change. Meet you back in the lobby in ten."

"Since when can a woman get ready in ten minutes?" John teased, stepping into the elevator behind Florey.

"Hmm, let me think… When her partner is going to buy her a drink at the bar." Florey managed to smirk at Rick as the doors shut.

***

A hotel employee of the Intercontinental Hotel had directed Justo to reverse back into the space he had asked for, next to the building's electric room that serviced the air conditioning units. He had to squeeze the van between a wall and a large, thick cement column.

The hotel's maintenance supervisor opened the doors to the A/C electrical service room but was in a hurry to leave because some joker had dumped two boxes of fabric dye in the hotel pool. Now it was his job to supervise the cleanup crew.

Once alone, Justo looked around and noticed deliveries were received at the other end of the garage's loading docks. That left their side of the facility free of traffic. Sure that he and Rigo were clear of prying eyes, they retreated into the rear of the van and closed the double doors behind them.

Justo wiped his damp brow and took a deep breath, only then realizing how much he'd been sweating. And how exhausted he was. It had been an excruciating trip from Colombia. They'd met his men in Hialeah and picked up the van and explosives stolen from a nearby rock quarry. They'd had to drive nonstop to make it to the hotel in time. The trip had gone by in a blur, but he had to muster all his energy and focus now. He couldn't afford even the slightest mistake.

Rigo made sure the van doors were locked while Justo opened the lid of a footlocker sized metal box. Inside the box, Justo carefully arranged the bricks of plastic explosives and began to insert a cylindrical blasting cap into each of them.

With Rigo helping, he collected the wire ends of the caps and twirled them into a single strand. Rigo held the wire braid above the box, allowing Justo enough room to carefully arrange the wires and connect them to a control box that filled the remaining space in the makeshift bomb. Through a small hole in one side, Justo ran a wire and connected it to the base of a cell phone. He instructed his nephew to watch for anyone approaching the front of the van.

Rigo pulled back the black curtain they'd drawn across the front seats, separating the passenger compartment from the cargo area. He peered through it just enough to satisfy himself they hadn't drawn any attention. He flashed a thumbs-up at Justo, his thumb still stained from the fabric dye.

At the last minute, Justo pulled the lead wire from the control box while his nephew wasn't looking and replaced the lid. Using a small welding torch, Justo spot-welded the metal lid securely to the rest of the box. As careful as he was not to overdo the welds, the van quickly filled with an acrid smoke.

That step done, he secured the wired cell phone on top of the large box with a piece of two-sided foam tape. He pressed down firmly but gingerly in order not to inadvertently push a button on the phone. When he was finished, he nodded to his nephew. They hopped out of the rear doors of the van and made sure they locked it behind them.

It was only a few steps to the electric service room opposite the van's rear doors. Once inside, they quickly removed their coveralls, exposing waiter uniforms underneath. They stashed the overalls behind a row of large electrical service boxes that lined the wall.

Rigo cracked the door enough to scan the garage.

Checking his watch, Justo noted they had only a few minutes before the first of the service staff and waiters began to file out of the employees' entrance door and enter the garage for their break.

Justo, with Rigo next to him, meandered out of the electrical room into the main garage and started an animated casual conversation in Spanish with his nephew. They blended into the trickle of hotel personnel as Justo watched for a chance to slip away from the garage.

He and Rigo kept up their banter as they moved with the flow of hotel employees. Less than a minute later, they disappeared seamlessly into the mass of tourists herded through the streets of downtown Miami.

***

John met Florey in the lobby just outside the doors of the Grand Ballroom. They signed in at the registration table and Florey grabbed their nametags, clipping John's on his lapel.

"Thanks, Mom," John quipped.

Florey smirked. "You're welcome, son."

"Here, let me get the door for you." John grabbed hold of the brass handle and gave the giant ballroom door a tug. Heavier than he anticipated, he struggled to open it. The moment turning awkward, he and Florey both laughed.

"After you, ma'am," said John when he finally wrestled the door open and bowed English butler style.

Still chuckling, Florey said, "You sure you got that?"

"Very funny."

Officers from around the country and even some from overseas huddled in small groups between the tables, their talk producing a steady buzz that echoed through the room.

John kept his eyes open for their assigned table but took in the stage with a large podium draped with the INEOA banner at the front of the ballroom. A line of folding chairs had been set up behind the podium.

Florey tugged at John's sleeve and pointed to Rick waving from a table next to the stage.

John led the way around the clusters of officers to reach Rick, thankful they had finally found him.

"Glad you're here. I'd like you guys to meet a few friends from the Bogotá office," Rick said as soon as they'd reached him.

"So, these are the two troopers we hear so much about," one of the men said as John and Florey made the rounds shaking hands.

"Yes, indeed they are!" McKenna interjected as he came up behind Rick.

Everyone at the table acknowledged the SAC, John noted. They each shifted their posture from a casual stance to something resembling military attention.

"We're fortunate to have these two on board," McKenna added, nodding to John and Florey. "I put these two in for the Commissioner's Award with the DEA."

John glanced at Florey and grinned in response to the quick congratulations from the other agents standing with them.

"Now, if you'll excuse me," McKenna said, "I have to make the rounds and get the commencement started." He gave the troopers a wink and walked away, working the room as he made his way to the podium, stopping only to shake a few dignitaries' hands John noticed.

"You guys look like he said he was giving us the Congressional Medal of Honor," Florey remarked.

"The Commissioner's Award is the highest recognition we have," Rick said. "I don't think we have ever given it outside the agency before."

"Have you ever gotten one, Rick?" John asked.

"Hell, no. I wish."

John put on a broad smile, forcing the corners of his mouth to their outermost extremes, knowing Rick would see he was rubbing it in—just a little.

Rick shook his head in exasperation. "Stella, you're a butt face!"

Florey and the agents broke out in laughter as John gave his buddy a slap on the shoulder. "I still love ya, man," said John, making Rick laugh harder. As long as the two of them had been friends, they'd enjoyed a little competitive jabbing. But John knew their mutual affection kept it friendly, a true mark of a couple of alpha males.

McKenna soon tapped the mic and called out to the audience to get their attention. "If I could get you to take your seats…" He waited for the groups to make their way toward their assigned tables. "The first order of business will be a change in the program. We'll be presenting our honorees with their plaques today during the luncheon since the guest speakers from D.C. won't be here until tomorrow." He scanned his notes. "Seems bad weather and delays even affect our Nation's capital."

John wasn't prepared for it to happen so fast, but hearing McKenna announce his and Florey's names as the year's recipients of the INEOA's Outstanding Achievement Commendation Award seemed to come out of the blue. John walked behind Florey to the stage and they took the last two positions as all the awardees faced the audience.

"These men and women are being recognized…" McKenna began reading a copy of the citation being presented, *"for outstanding achievement and accomplishment in the field of narcotic law enforcement."* He paused as the room began to applaud. "Allow me to add: these men and women, as all of you surely know, give of themselves day after day for the cause of ridding the streets of drugs and the violent crime that follows it. They have taken up the calling and gone above and beyond, spending countless, sometimes even unpaid, hours away from family and friends. They, like many of you, have routinely put their lives on hold to accomplish the goals set for them. This award recognizes that each of them has gone above and beyond, and then some. I think they are more than deserving of our thanks and recognition."

More loud applause erupted as everyone in the audience stood.

John caught Florey's eye and noticed she looked as embarrassed as he felt. She began to blush, and John felt his own cheeks redden.

As the applause died down, McKenna cleared his throat and pointed to John and Florey. "I'd like to mention these two on the end. I have personally worked with them both and can attest to their tireless efforts, as I'm sure is the case with all the recipients. Florey Baker and John Stella are typical of that commitment. Their 'never say die' attitude has led to countless arrests and seizures, allowing FHP to disrupt the cartel's business here by leaps and bounds…"

Yet another round of applause.

After being singled out in that way, John couldn't look at Florey and barely heard McKenna, who went on to say that all the recipients deserved more than the plaques, which he called humble tokens of profound appreciation.

He swept his hand to take in all the recipients and another standing ovation followed, this one even longer and louder. McKenna handed each recipient a plaque, followed by a handshake and a photo. When McKenna got to Florey and John, he gave them the plaques, but whispered, "Try to sneak out of here in about an hour after the meetings get underway. We're treating you to drinks and dinner at the Beach." With a quick wink, he returned directly to the podium to conclude the awards presentation.

Awards in hand, John and Florey made the rounds among the attendees. John mostly followed Florey's lead as she introduced the two of them to the various heads of agencies from around the country and Europe.

Eventually, John noticed the time and caught sight of Rick moving towards a side door. John went to Florey's side to get her away from a conversation with the commissioner of the Prefecture of Police from Paris. He could see she was having a difficult time getting out of the conversation. John took her hand. "Honey, we have to be going now. We have that meeting."

Florey smiled apologetically and backed away from her new friend. "Such a pleasure meeting you, Commissioner." She let John tug her hand and escort her away.

"Thank God you came when you did," Florey said.

"Why's that, kiddo?" John moved quickly towards the side doors.

"He must have asked me three times what I was doing for dinner," Florey said. "How did you know to act like my boyfriend? '*Honey*' indeed."

"First, he's French," John said, like he had some special knowledge, "and second, if you could have seen the look on your face while he was talking to you."

He glanced at Florey. "I don't have to be a psychologist to know you wanted out of *that* conversation." He opened the side door leading into the lobby, allowing them to make their escape.

John decided he *needed* the break with Rick and McKenna. Even with McKenna having to take a few important calls, they managed to walk the Art Deco section of South Beach. The four strolled along the boardwalk above the sand dunes, then back down Collins Avenue for their dinner at Café Milano, one of the more upscale restaurants lining the picturesque stretch of Ocean Drive. The refurbished pastel hotels were the iconic symbol of Miami Beach.

Later, after dinner, they walked along the beach, taking in the street performers, tourists, and, of course, the local drunks and derelicts who made for good theater. Their meanderings led them to the Clevelander Bar where they stopped for more drinks.

John heard McKenna, who limited himself to only two beers the whole night, make note of the time and direct the happy, giddy crew back to the car, none having exercised the same alcohol restraint as the boss, to drive them back to the hotel.

The reminiscing and laughing had been a well-needed tonic for John and Rick, especially. They'd told old childhood stories that had Florey and McKenna in stitches most of the night.

Rick, of course, brought up the night his father caught John with Rick's sister at the beach, parked behind a large row of sea grape trees.

John told of the time when Rick had to hide in the boys' bathroom during class because Tina Heatherford had worn her cheerleading outfit to class. Sitting right behind her had proven too much for the kid, whose hormones had gotten the better of him. John's description of Rick holding himself as he ran out the classroom door only to hide in the bathroom had even Rick laughing. Florey and McKenna both complained that their sides hurt from laughing so much.

They were silent on the trip back to the hotel. For John, it was a sudden realization the evening was coming to its inevitable end. That alone fed his melancholy mood.

Walking into the lobby, John noticed the bar was still open—and empty. The only person around besides the guy at the check-in desk and the bartender was a cleaning staff man operating a floor polisher, the hum of which punctuated the end of the evening.

"Hey, man. One more drink and we'll call it a night," John begged.

John was surprised by how quickly McKenna and Florey shook their heads. They each said they'd had long days and were worn out. Undiscouraged, John gave Rick a gentle punch in the shoulder, "Come on, buddy. Just one and we'll call it a night."

"Okay, but just one, John."

John couldn't miss the begrudging tone. Rick was tired, but he was, too. Still, he was reluctant to call it a night.

They sat at the bar and John ordered two Jack and Cokes. Then they went right back to reminiscing about growing up in Miami. John ordered his second and then his third drink, but Rick finally reminded him about the seminar at noon.

John looked at his watch and tried to focus on the little hand hitting the three.

"Come on, buddy. Let's get you upstairs," Rick said.

That was the last thing John heard.

***

A few hours later, John opened his eyes, squinting as the sun's rays rudely intruded through the only gap in the room's heavy curtains. They sliced like lasers across the bed and over his pillow. Slowly, he sat up and was confronted by a rush of pressure beating inside his head.

He slammed his eyes shut, took a deep breath, and swung his feet to the floor. Sitting motionless for a minute, he attempted to sort through the fog of disconnected recollections from what had to have been some nightmare. The yelling, screaming, someone pounding on a drum, more yelling—it all jumbled around like some alternative reality.

He placed his throbbing head in his hands, hoping the pain wasn't going to last all day.

Then, pounding started on his hotel room door. The unceremonious interruption forced John's eyes wide open.

He looked at the clock. It glared back with its bright red digital readout: 11:15 AM. The pounding on the door came again.

"Hold on. I'm coming!" he yelled as he scurried around the room looking for something to put on. "I'm coming!" he repeated, not waiting for a response. He quickly threw on a bath robe and opened the door.

"Are you just waking up?" said Rick.

"Yeah. We've got time to get downstairs. What's the rush?" John rubbed the sleep out of his eyes.

"You've heard nothing?" Rick asked, panic filling his voice.

"Heard what?" John noted the beads of sweat building across Rick's brow.

"We've gotta get the hell out of the hotel, like *now*!" Rick pushed past John to get into the room. "Come on. Get your stuff packed. We don't have time."

John watched Rick scan the room as if deciding what to do next.

Still standing at the door in his robe, John was confused. "What the hell are you talking about? Is this a joke? Did Florey put you up to this?"

Rick slung John's backpack over his arm and then planted his hands on John's shoulders. "There is a bomb in the hotel. Do you understand?" Rick tried to speak calmly. "They've evacuated the hotel and half of downtown Miami. We are the last ones here!"

Unhinged now, Rick turned on the TV. A Channel 7 news reporter appeared over a **Breaking News** banner on the bottom of the screen.

"See? Do you get it now? Get your shit together! Get dressed. Let's go."

John dropped the robe where he was standing and pulled clothes off the floor, dressing faster than he ever had.

"This is Brian Jackson reporting from the MacArthur Causeway Bridge in Downtown Miami. Authorities have found what they are calling a large explosive device in the parking garage of the Intercontinental Hotel located at the southern end of Bayfront Park."

John stopped in disbelief. "You weren't fucking kidding me," he said.

"No, I wasn't." Rick stuffed what was left of John's clothes into the backpack. "I told you."

"Why the hell didn't you get the hotel staff to open my door?" John stumbled to put on his shoes.

"I'm sure they would have, but they all ran out of the hotel."

John tried to pay attention to what the reporter was saying.

"In the early hours of the morning, the hotel staff smelled what they described as an electrical fire, only to discover an abandoned vehicle parked next to the main support pillar of the hotel tower. We are being told by Federal authorities that the ATF Special Response Team out of Washington has been called and they are expected to land at Miami International within the next few minutes…"

Dressed in shirt, pants, and shoes, John shoved his duty weapon in the waistband of his pants. As they turned to leave the room, John remembered something.

"Wait a minute," he said, going back into the room.

"Damn it, John. There's no time for—"

"I worked too damn hard for this to leave it behind." John grabbed the plaque off the nightstand and waved it in Rick's face before shoving it in his bag.

They ran down the hall and got into the elevator. With no people in the building, it came quickly.

As the doors closed, John and Rick gave each other a worried look, as if realizing they should have taken the stairs. They both turned to the illuminated numbers and watched them blink with each descending floor—the lobby couldn't get there fast enough.

They remained silent on the ride down, wincing against the scream of the fire alarm—the same reoccurring tone that had been playing in John's head since he woke up.

The doors finally opened, but John's stomach rolled over. "Wait… what about Florey?"

"Calm down. It was all I could do to convince her to head over to the Miami Beach Convention Center." Rick shook his head. "She didn't want to leave without you."

He and Rick burst through the hotel's front doors and hustled down the stairs. "Why there?" John asked.

"That's where they are having all of us meet. They began bussing people out of here about an hour ago. Let's get our cars."

John took a second to look around as they headed to the police-only parking spaces. Not even one pedestrian was on the deserted streets. The only vehicle was a police car sounding the order to evacuate on the car's public address system. The message echoed and added to the surreal atmosphere.

John caught the sight of pages from the *Miami Herald* cartwheeling down the abandoned street like tumbleweeds in an abandoned desert town.

Rick's voice suddenly broke through John's daze. "See you at the convention center." Rick slid into the driver's seat and drove off.

John followed behind him. At the end of the long hotel drive, they turned north on Biscayne Boulevard, the main downtown artery. It was walled with high-rises and office buildings on one side, the park and the bay on the other. Evacuated now, leaving the city in eerie silence. The buildings looming overhead made it feel as if the city was devoid of any life and about to cave in on itself. He pushed hard on the gas to catch up to Rick.

When they approached the entrance ramp to the MacArthur Causeway, John noticed the gathering of onlookers posting themselves along the police perimeter, clusters of curious bodies pushing up to the hastily placed barricades.

John recognized the nervous but curious expressions on the bystanders' faces. He directed his attention to maneuver his patrol car under a line of police tape and around the various SWAT vehicles. He stayed as close to Rick's car as possible, steering left and entering the expressway ramp, heading to the convention center.

As the ramp rose to meet the main highway, John nearly swerved off the road as he noticed the low flying C-5 Galaxy aircraft coming straight in as it made its final approach towards the airport. As its four jet engines roared, the enormous craft flew just above the building rooftops. ATF was stenciled in black on the side of the olive drab fuselage.

John turned on his patrol radio, hoping to hear an update. Instead, he heard the dispatcher directing the next shift of troopers towards the roadblocks set up to close off the highways surrounding the downtown area. That explained why the causeway was vacant.

Taking advantage of the open road, John kept up with Rick, who pushed the vehicle's speed.

They screeched to a stop next to the main doors of the convention center after slashing the usual thirty-minute trip to one-third the time.

Once inside the building, John found Florey and the DEA agents huddled around one of the overhead TVs.

"You finally got him up?" Florey remarked, as McKenna smiled and shook his head.

"You guys believe this?" One of the agents pointed up to the screen.

John worked his way through the gathering crowd of agents but kept his eyes on the mounted TV screen. It showed a shot of a military aircraft coming in for what looked like a hot landing at Miami International Airport.

As the camera zoomed in on the plane, it created the illusion it was flying even faster. The picture switched again, this shot showing the side of the plane as it touched down. It began to slow, allowing the nose gear to gently contact the runway.

The shot switched again to a view of the rear cargo door dropping a few inches from the concrete runway. Three large Humvees drove out of the plane's belly and sped away in the opposite direction where they met an unmarked cruiser and continued off the airport property through the east security gate. At that point, the reporter handed coverage back to the studio anchor desk.

"That's the ATF bomb crew out of Washington," McKenna said, keeping his attention on the broadcast.

"Why all the resources from Washington?" John asked.

"Well, if you had been with us, *Mr. Just-one-more-drink*, you would've been filled in already." McKenna didn't hide his sarcasm, which apparently amused the other agents enough to bring on their teasing laughter.

John glanced at Florey, who cast a knowing look his way. He couldn't put on an act for her. She saw it had been a tough morning for him. He was relieved when he saw her making her way to his side.

"They found a van parked in the garage with a footlocker sized bomb in it, John. The Miami PD bomb squad managed to look inside with a fiber optic scope. It's filled with plastic explosives and a remote timer.

In all the confusion—which, by the way, you missed—McKenna decided to activate the resources out of Washington. The device is way too big for the city to handle."

John stood with Florey, struggling to comprehend the potential devastation that a falling skyscraper would have on a city's downtown district. Suddenly something hit. "What kind of van?"

Florey shrugged.

An agent standing nearby blurted an answer while still keeping his eyes glued to the television screen. "I heard it was an air conditioning service van."

Alternating currents of heat and cold pulsed from his face to his legs.

"You look ashen," Florey said, touching his arm. "What is it?"

John could almost feel McKenna's gaze on him. But kept staring ahead.

"John?" McKenna said softly.

Reacting more to the uncharacteristically gentle tone than to the sound of his own name, John took in a sharp, short breath before he turned toward McKenna. "Chief?"

"What is it? As the saying goes, you look like you've seen a ghost."

John leaned towards the DEA chief, and in a low tone said, "I think I may have spoken to the occupants of that van."

McKenna squared his shoulders, ready to speak, but the cell phone in his jacket pocket rang. "Hold that thought, John."

The chief stepped away and was soon pacing back and forth as he spoke, the red flush of frustration on his face plainly visible. When he came back, McKenna asked John if he was sure it was the same air conditioning van.

John didn't need time to think. "Yes. Absolutely. I was helping a Miami officer who thought they were blocking traffic, but then a hotel supervisor came up and told them to park in the garage."

"Would you be able to identify the people if you saw pictures?" McKenna asked.

"I'm pretty sure. I think the Miami cop could, too," John said, noting the deep frown on McKenna's thoughtful face.

"Let's not worry about the Miami cop right now," McKenna said. "It'll take too long to find him, anyway." He scanned the room. "We may have you look at some pictures just to see if you can pick out the guys you saw."

John started to reply, but McKenna's phone rang again. Hurrying to answer it, he held up his index finger and was quickly engrossed in yet another conversation. Figuring the chief would need a minute, he worked his way back to the agents still fixated on the TV.

About to ask for an update, John flinched at McKenna's sudden shouts. "Well, why the *hell* didn't they bother to tell anyone?"

McKenna's outburst got everyone's attention, and seeing he'd stopped their conversations, he hurried out the front door.

John went back to the TV, the screenshots now showing news helicopters filming the convoy of military vehicles speeding out of the airport and onto the expressway, heading downtown towards the hotel. In a few minutes, the vehicles turned down Biscayne Boulevard and onto the Intercontinental Hotel drive, where they stopped. It took seconds for the occupants in black military uniforms to assemble behind their vehicles.

John knew the ATF kept their special response teams always ready for any large-scale threats involving weapons of mass destruction, or any device that could cause significant devastation. Their goal was to be in the air within five minutes of receiving a call, hitting the ground before the plane even came to a stop. They trained for these moments, knowing time was always working against them.

It hadn't taken long to determine the hotel bomb was beyond the capability of any of the local bomb squads. With no room for error, John imagined McKenna quickly telling Miami's chief of police the Feds were taking over. McKenna would have made the call to the ATF emergency dispatch center in Washington, and five minutes later, the ATF was airborne.

John watched two of the men by the Humvees suit up in bomb gear. Their heads were covered by a thick, bomb-resistant helmet, and they wore an air-cooled bomb-resistant suit that made John think of spacemen. Ahead of them was the ATF robot with its long, folded grappling arm and camera. The men let the robot move ahead about fifty yards and directed it into the underground garage.

John had seen bomb techs control and monitor the robots on portable screens while another tech worked the wireless controls. Within a few minutes, the men and robot had entered the garage and were no longer in the sights of the helicopter cameras.

"Jesus, those guys got balls," one of the agents exclaimed.

Another guy chimed in. "You couldn't pay me enough to walk into that."

John was half listening now, more focused on replaying the events of the previous morning, desperately trying to remember if he'd missed anything.

Florey moved closer. "Maybe it was another van?" she offered, as if reading his mind.

"No, if it's that air conditioning van, it would have to be those two Latino guys. I mean, how many air conditioning service vans could there be? I'm racking my brain trying to recall every detail."

"I was just hoping, I guess," Florey said.

"John! Florey!" McKenna called, waving the two over to where he was standing with two men in black suits. "These two troopers are the ones working the case. John may have seen the occupants of the van."

The men introduced themselves as special liaison officers from the State Department. "Give us a few minutes and we'll have you follow us back to the FBI headquarters in North Miami," one of the agents said. "We'd like John to look at some photos."

John nodded. Of course he'd do whatever they asked.

McKenna walked away, saying he had to call FHP and have Major Carris and Captain DeLeón head that way as well.

John didn't see why Florey needed to be there, since she couldn't identify the van, and asked McKenna if she could skip the meeting.

"I need you all at headquarters," McKenna said. "I'll fill you in once we're there.

No more questions, John thought. Not with McKenna growing more serious by the minute.

With Florey behind him in her car, John waited for the State Department officers to take the lead in the caravan back to the mainland and north onto I-95. The drive to the FBI headquarters was a quick fifteen-minute trip, but with all that had happened it seemed to take longer.

John's thoughts skipped rapidly around the morning's chaotic events. It was as if the seas were rising up around him faster than he could run to dry land.

As he pushed against the thought of drowning, his eye caught Florey's car in his rearview mirror. She'd be at his side no matter what. He couldn't have asked for a better comrade. But, he still felt completely responsible for her safety.

That thought forced a laugh from deep in his chest. "Shit. She's probably worrying about me."

As sweat soaked through his collar and into his shirt, he reached down and fiddled with the A/C temperature knob, forcing it over to the coldest setting. Any little gesture to push back against the South Florida heat.

He moved towards his exit, glancing again in his mirror. He wasn't about to let anything happen to Florey, or anyone else for that matter. Not if he could help it.

Chapter Fifteen

Entering the FBI property, John was directed through the security gate and to the lot in the rear of the building where all the cars from various agencies had arrived, filed in, and parked. He met Florey at the entrance and went inside. They rode in silence to the third floor conference room. She looked uncharacteristically troubled. He was about to say something, but they weren't alone. He looked straight ahead and caught their reflection in the polished brass panels of the elevator. It gave them a strange radiant look, but faceless, too, ghostly outlines emanating a golden hue. They could have been standing in another dimension. He toyed with a question: if the images could talk back, what would they say?

He began to tally an inventory of incidents over his years in the military and as a trooper. It seemed he'd spent his entire adult life on the front lines keeping society safe from one sort of malady or another. John had understood the rules when he was in the military, especially when it had come to privileged information. Secrets just happened. Like in Lebanon, some things hadn't been disclosed. In foreign conflicts, decisions were made and carried out, and troops never questioned them.

But here? He tried to put himself in the shoes of the administrators and find justification for keeping secrets from the front-line troops in civilian police work. He couldn't think of any.

As the elevator doors opened, John still glared straight ahead, fighting back those old familiar feelings. With all that was going on, he thought, there needed to be complete transparency. Keeping secret information was not going to cut it.

John could see this was a big meeting, so many people that Thomas

Ridgeway, the SAC for the Miami Field Division of the FBI, had moved the meeting into the large conference and training room to accommodate the growing numbers of personnel called in.

When John and Florey went inside, the din of conversation in the room came from the clusters of agents and detectives talking amongst themselves. John could sense the underlying fury in the room mixed in with talk of finding the culprits. They'd take them out. Hit back.

John took it all in, absorbing the energy and outrage, noting it focused only on the events at the hotel and not on the whole investigation. That led him to conclude most of the people in the room knew no more about what led to the day's events than he or Florey. As far as he was concerned, explanations were long overdue. His eyes focused on McKenna, who was taking a chair at the head of the long conference table.

"Is everybody here?" McKenna motioned for Rick to check the hall for latecomers. After a few more agents entered the now standing-room only conference room, Rick closed the double doors behind him and went to stand behind his boss.

"Obviously, we're all concerned about today's events at the Intercontinental," McKenna said. "However, there are things that have come to light that tie those events to the case we've been working on." He paused to scan through a series of teletypes and handwritten messages on the table in front of him. "We're going to need to move quickly and wrap this case up before we start losing innocent civilians. That's the word from Washington."

John could feel the shift in the room as the agents became more animated, with even a few mumbling discontent over ending a case they believed could lead to more arrests. A few expletives were mumbled in disgust.

McKenna handed the meeting over to Thomas Ridgeway, who was sitting next to him.

The FBI SAC stood and braced his hands on the conference table. "Listen up! Many of our agents aren't aware of a lot of things going on." He was nearly shouting, and the agents fell silent. Ridgeway scanned the room as if prepared to stare down anyone who kept up the banter.

He had their undivided attention, John thought.

"We've intercepted communications with Cali cartel operatives high up in the organization. It's clear they intend to disrupt our enforcement attempts at all costs." As he looked around the room, Ridgeway handed McKenna a file marked CONFIDENTIAL. "We've located the other German scientist and his family members in a ranch near

Buenaventura, Colombia. We're putting together a plan with our assets in Bogotá to extract them."

As Ridgeway spoke, McKenna walked around the table and stood near John, who noted Ridgeway's gaze had fallen on him.

McKenna tapped him on the shoulder and drew his attention to the folder, which the chief opened.

John saw photos he suspected were taken during surveillance.

McKenna moved two to the top of the folder. "Can you recognize these men, John?"

He certainly did. John confirmed they were the two men in the air conditioning van. He stared at the names beneath the photos. It was the first time he had ever heard of Rigoberto Morejón or Justo Dellacruz Morejón. "Who are they?"

McKenna closed the file and directed John's attention to Ridgeway.

"Let's go back a ways," Ridgeway started. "The FBI received intel from our sources in the State Department that a team, five men in total, would be arriving at Miami International Airport on a flight from Bogotá. Our agents got there as the plane was disembarking, and they attempted to locate the group in the U.S. Customs screening center at the airport. But the five men never showed up.

"After canvassing the airport, though, they discovered a security door from the concourse to the tarmac had been compromised. The surveillance cameras only showed the usual movement of service vehicles that typically service the airport," he explained, reading from a small spiral notepad.

As he turned to the next page, he took a deep breath as if he was about to confess a mortal sin to a priest. "It turns out these guys were all trained hit-men—assassins." Ridgeway looked up from the small notebook.

The discontent was audible in exaggerated sighs and sporadic utterances about someone losing a job over the blunder. John couldn't believe it, and he knew that's how all the agents felt. A few wondered aloud what else the FBI had kept secret.

"Easy, gentlemen, there's more." Ridgeway glanced at his notes. "Several weeks ago other communications between the cartel and their lawyer stooges here in Miami were intercepted. Information from those communications has only recently been shared with us." He paused long enough to shoot a scornful glance at the State Department representatives. "Public records requests were submitted for reports generated by the troopers. It seems there was an active interest in what John and Florey had been doing and where they had been working."

John was confused by the interest in their reports. He could tell from glancing at Florey that she was puzzled, too.

Ridgeway explained the intercepts had been only recently brought to his attention and only partially declassified from the State Department. "The cartel openly discussed whether they should remove the two troopers. They finally decided that sending a series of strong messages to scare off the troopers would be more appropriate. The initial assessment from the ATF is that the bomb was missing a critical connection and probably couldn't detonate. However, we still believe from our intel that killing two U.S. police officers could be a..." he paused, searching for the right term, "...last resort."

John's heart raced. As he caught a glimpse of Florey he noticed her eyes were as wide open as he'd ever seen them. Looking at his supervisors, he realized they were astonished, too.

"Hold up a second," John said. "You mean to tell me that Colombia decided Florey and I should be killed and sent a hit-squad to Miami, which you lost. Then, they made a public records request where Florey and I were patrolling, and now you *think* they may have changed their minds?"

Ridgeway opened his mouth as if to speak, but Major Carris was faster. "Why weren't we made aware of this when it happened?"

Captain DeLeón spoke next to ask if anything else was being kept from the group.

Ridgeway's frown seemed to indicate he wasn't happy about the withheld information. John could guess he didn't want a revolt on his hands. Knowing they could be in the same boat as Florey and him, the agents looked angry.

John pulled at his collar, a reaction to the rising temperature in the room.

The two agents from the State Department were squirming in their dark suits, a thin bead of sweat forming above their brows.

Meanwhile, John thought the administrators looked more tense, but if the past was anything to go on, he could almost time how long they could let the animus linger, a natural byproduct of managing police officers.

"Listen!" McKenna chimed in with exact precision. "This case involves the highest levels of not just the U.S. intelligence network but the Colombian government as well. We all know how sensitive it is down there. Sources and information are sometimes slow in coming. The ramifications of this case could affect the global drug trafficking for years to come. Plus, the welfare of two families. That means concerns far above any of our pay grades, including Tom and me. We aren't any happier about this than you are."

John could feel the anger and tension in the room diffuse.

McKenna pointed at John and Florey. "These two came in as uniformed troopers. But they've been the center of what we've been able to do in this case. Clearly, Cali is upset and capable of anything. Let's get through this meeting and lay the facts out on the table so we're all on the same page."

Ridgeway took McKenna's cue and resumed his briefing. "Thanks, Chief. It's fairly obvious to us now what the cartel seems to be up to," Ridgeway said. "They've taken out five of our informants and dropped the bodies on the two roadways our troopers usually work." He nodded to John and Florey. "A sick and twisted message to you two of their intentions."

Major Carris' stare fixed on John and Florey.

John could almost hear him *thinking* about this turn of events. John couldn't help but sense the irony. After all, troopers just wrote tickets. What would GHQ in Tallahassee say? But that train of thought on the familiar FHP mantra was quickly interrupted.

"Many of you may not know this," Ridgeway said, "but we've identified the two individuals who planted the device. They were discovered at the hotel this morning. John had the good fortune of seeing them as they waited to park their van in the garage. The driver is Justo Dellacruz Morejón, a member of the Cali cartel. Seems he has a background in explosives from his time in the Colombian military. He's been on a U.S. watch list for the past ten years. He's exceptionally intelligent, and many consider him to be the heir apparent to lead the Cali cartel. His accomplice is his nephew, Rigoberto Morejón, who goes by the name Rigo. We don't know as much about him, except to say he is suspected as being the cartel's liaison with East European drug lords. As best as we can tell, they crossed the Mexican border a few days ago under assumed names. There was nothing about the crossing that alarmed the authorities, but we had a bit of luck. The two were stopped on I-75 near Wildwood by a trooper who ran them through the El Paso Information Center. Washington was in the process of sending out alerts to all Florida authorities when the call to evacuate the hotel came in." Ridgeway held up the teletype from Washington in his hand as proof.

John shook his head as the information seemed to keep getting worse, but looking at Florey, he found it odd she didn't seem as concerned now as she'd been earlier. In fact, she seemed at ease despite the shovelful of crap Ridgeway had thrown at them.

John looked at Ridgeway. "Is there any communication that Florey and I are *not* targets?" He almost winced at his own cynical tone.

Ridgeway took his seat but answered quickly. "Only a conversation about sending a message and their concerns about how we would react to a hit on our police officers. We don't think they'll act on their initial intentions, John."

"*Think?*" John shouted. "That's the best you got? This is bullshit!" he exclaimed with a sinister chuckle. "We are out there working our asses off and all this crap is going on." He couldn't believe it, but then it hit him hard.

He turned to face the agents from the State Department. "*Now* I know why those CIA types have been following Florey and me around. You dickheads knew about the threat the whole time, didn't you?" John dismissed them both with a flick of his hand. "You used Florey and me as bait."

The agents stood expressionless, their faces red from the heat, and maybe from being called out, too. And why not? John had hit the nail on the head.

"Trooper," McKenna shouted. "Calm down. This has taken us all by surprise. Two more bodies were found on Krome Avenue yesterday evening by a Metro-Dade officer. The two were identified as the informants used in the $2.5 million money seizure you guys did. Cali is eliminating all their cell leaders and sending you guys a clear message. They want us to back off and forget this. But we aren't taking chances with your safety any more than we are with anyone else's."

McKenna calling him by his title rather than his name snapped John out of his tirade and back into the case.

"Hey, buddy. I've been where you two are," Rick said, stepping up to the conference table. "I know it's hard to wrap your head around it. As cops, we feel secure doing what we do and the last thing we're prepared for is a bunch of foreign criminals planning our demise, making us targets. Just because we're doing our jobs. This *is* what we do, John."

That had never been clearer, John thought.

"It comes with playing this game the way you two do," Rick said. "They could have told you about the cartel's hit squad. If you'd known about this weeks ago and were offered an opportunity to walk away from this case, I know you well enough to know your answer."

John cracked a smile and glanced at Florey. It dawned on him she'd figured this out and that's why she was so calm. Backing down in the face of threats wasn't her style, either. A sense of calm coming over him, John looked back at Rick. "What do we do now?"

Ridgeway stood to continue the briefing. "Major Carris, we'd like your troopers to carry more firepower than what they currently have. Just as a precaution. We'll offer them two of our MP-5 machine guns."

Major Carris let his jaw drop in surprise, but Captain DeLeón nodded as if it was a great idea. John then caught the sudden change in the major's demeanor.

"Ah… We're going to have to rethink that, Chief," the major said.

The response caused Ridgeway to cock his head.

"I mean, Tallahassee will never go for that. Besides, they have shotguns in case they need heavier firepower," Carris explained.

John's face flushed with anger. "You've gotta be *fucking* kidding me!" he yelled.

He pushed past Florey while trying to work his way forward to his supervisor. "What the hell do you mean, 'we've got shotguns?' I'm mandated to keep it in my trunk. What do you expect me to do?" John mimicked a make-believe confrontation with a hit man. "Oh, please wait, Mr. Hit Man. Let me stop the car and get my *shotgun out of the trunk*!"

Beside himself, John knew this time he wasn't going to overlook the small-mindedness at FHP and the form-over-substance culture that was so deeply entrenched when it came to dealing with real law enforcement issues.

Carris' silence said it all. Man, John's anger was beginning to boil over, but he tempered it, realizing the major only said what John should have expected. This madness was the reason a trooper could break a record in drug arrests and get a counseling letter for not writing enough tickets in the same period. The insanity was institutional, John thought, exhaling. He stepped back to his chair and took a seat in the now-quiet room.

McKenna flashed what John knew was a look of annoyance at the major. But McKenna kept quiet about the major's reluctance to provide the firepower. He also was quiet about John's outburst.

"At some point, the longer we wait, the more likely lives will be lost," McKenna said. "We're going to have to pull together and move quickly. Listen, we know where the German chemist is in Hialeah. Surveillance has him on a schedule coming and going from one of the three Hialeah warehouses. When we make our move on these scumbags, our timing and coordination have to be perfect. We need all of you to cancel any plans you've made for the next week. When we put out the call to move, everyone has to hustle. Is that clear?"

Everyone agreed.

"Major, could I speak with you and Chief Ridgeway in his office? Privately," McKenna said.

Major Carris said nothing but followed McKenna out of the room, along with Captain DeLeón.

John was about to ask Florey if she was going to be okay, but it seemed the entire room was coming up to pat them on the back, promising support. One of the agents even mentioned his rental property in Key Largo and offered it to them should they feel the need to relocate. Like John, Florey smiled politely but turned down the offer. The reassurance from frontline agents and detectives was a reminder they weren't alone in this mess.

*****

In his office, Chief Ridgeway finally got Major Carris to call his colonel and ask about the machine guns. But instead of answering the question, the colonel decided to have John and Florey removed from the case.

McKenna couldn't deal with what he was hearing. He grabbed the phone and introduced himself. Not waiting for a response, he spoke in his rapid-fire way when so much was on the line. "Listen, I understand your concern about the machine guns. I get that. But there is no way we can do this without your troopers at this point. I really want you to reconsider letting them stay. We are about to file indictments and arrest these scumbags, and I want John and Florey there."

Silence.

"I suppose you'll just call the governor again if I say no," the colonel complained. "Fine. They can stay. But *no* machine guns!"

McKenna kept quiet. Calling the governor would have been his next move. From where he sat, it was the only tactic that truly motivated the bureaucrats in state law enforcement. He waited for a response but got none. The FHP boss had ended the call.

McKenna handed the phone back to Major Carris. "Your colonel is a real charmer, huh."

"What did he say?" Carris asked, a look of dread hanging on his face.

McKenna shrugged. "He hung up on me, but your troopers stay.

But, uh…no machine guns."

"I understand," the major said, glancing at Captain DeLeón, who stood quietly at his side, smiling.

McKenna looked on as the major frowned at the smiling captain. McKenna wondered, too, what the smile was all about.

Captain DeLeón glanced around the room with his smirk still in place. "Pussies!" With that, he walked out of the SAC's office.

McKenna nearly choked at the response. He politely put his hand over his mouth to prevent himself from laughing out loud. Even Carris chuckled as the captain walked out of the room. He followed his subordinate to have a quick word with him.

***

John was talking to Florey and a handful of agents about the case when the captain motioned them to step to the side.

"You guys make yourselves available if McKenna or Rick calls you. I don't want you doing anything else but this case until it's finished," DeLeón said. "You check on the radio and wait for the call. I don't care what you do in the meantime. Wash your cars or brush your dog or… whatever. Do you understand?"

John nodded. So did Florey. Oh, they certainly understood.

"I'll speak with Gail in dispatch. I'll let her know that if they get any calls to either of your homes that they should send all units without question. Is that clear?"

"Yes," John said, glancing at Florey. He assumed it was okay to speak for her as well as himself.

"Let me add something," the captain said, moving closer to them and quickly looking around to make sure his comments wouldn't be overheard. "I'm not going to have anyone do your vehicle inspections until this is over."

Why? John wondered. The department supervisors handled the monthly vehicle inspections with a religious-like observance. Each piece of equipment was carefully catalogued, making sure there were no unauthorized items in a trooper's car. They would even note the cleanliness of the vehicles and whether they needed a fresh coat of wax. What an inspection had to do with the case baffled him.

"I see you're confused," the captain said, "but the machine guns are not happening. However," he winked conspicuously, "we can't have you out there outgunned. So, if someone wanted to, say…carry a personal weapon…if you understand what I'm saying."

Just then the major walked up and quietly stood behind DeLeón. John gave the man a curious stare. Surely there must be more to it than that since vehicle inspections were conducted rain or shine, no exceptions— ever. But the major simply arched his eyebrows slightly, as if to say, *fill in the blanks—read between the lines.*

We can carry our own arsenal of weapons but if the shit hits the fan, you never said a thing. John kept his contempt for that attitude to himself, but he preferred that risk, as long as he was appropriately armed.

Florey glanced his way. Reading her expression, he assumed they were on the same page. John gave the major a simple thumbs-up, and without saying another word, grabbed his partner and left to find Rick.

In the parking lot, Rick waved John and Florey over to him. John soon figured out he wanted them to step in on an impromptu meeting with McKenna.

"I was just talking about you again," McKenna said. "All good. I know you get it. When the calls go out to mobilize, we'll have no time to waste."

John always thought it seemed as if McKenna was acting like a coach giving a pep talk to his team. Readiness and clarity of thought were everything. Well, that and group safety. That was McKenna's most important point. He wanted everyone to be prepared for anything. The goal was to make the apprehensions under the pending indictments and get the suspects to the federal lock-up in downtown Miami safely.

It didn't take long for McKenna to say his piece. Then, they shook hands all around and went off in different directions.

John and Florey began the trek to the far end of the lot where they had parked. John glanced at his partner, who was looking down as if deep in thought.

"Hey, you alright?" John asked.

"I was just going to ask you the same question," she said.

"Yeah, I'm okay. I'm heading to the house to get things in order. I imagine you're going to do the same?"

She nodded sadly. "Dale and I decided he should take the girls to his parents in Clearwater. He'll stay a few days, and then we'll see if he should leave them there and come back for work," Florey explained. "You know, until this blows over."

He nodded to let her know he understood. "Let me know if you need anything. I'll be at the house until we get the call." John hugged Florey and gave her what he hoped was a reassuring smile. "Oh, hey, watch your back on the way home. Make sure you're not being followed."

"Gee, I was kinda hoping those spooky guys would follow me home. The blonde one is kinda cute." Florey gave him one of her friendly winks and got into her car.

Pulling out of the parking lot, John made sure the inner-city radio was clear of emergency traffic before getting onto I-95 and driving south to Redland. He had too much on his mind to get involved in another chase. For a moment, he wondered if he was making the right decision by not finding some other place to stay. The thought persisted but, finally, he relented, feeling sure that the Feds were probably right. Nonetheless, he wasn't taking any chances, either.

John grabbed his phone and made arrangements for his cousin to spend the next few weeks at his grandmother's house.

It was difficult not to explain everything to the kid, but it was better that he didn't know. As a consolation, John had made a promise to take his cousin to the Dolphins game in two weeks, which seemed to make Joey feel better for having to leave on short notice. John, on the other hand, was already making other plans—plans that had nothing to do with football.

Chapter Sixteen

John turned onto the school property and made his way down the long drive, past the clusters of four-room dorms each housing the resident clients that made up the bulk of the school and rehab center. He continued past the large football field-sized playground that separated his modest mobile home from the school property and proceeded to the end of the lot that butted up to the two-hundred acre expanse of the Palma Nursery, which enveloped the Sunrise School and John's home on all three sides.

He parked his car in front of the double gate and surveyed the home's six-foot wood fence, a perk the school threw in to give their resident trooper a modicum of privacy. His eyes slowly gauged the fence line and stopped at the lone utility pole that serviced the trailer. A small mercury vapor light hung at the top, its illumination barely bright enough to pierce the vacuous darkness of his home's outpost-like location at the rear of the property. The privacy and seclusion had been nice to come home to, but now it exposed a vulnerability he hadn't considered before.

He turned off the engine, noticing Spec already waiting for him with happy yelps and tail wagging. He walked to the fence and carefully pushed his finger between two of the fence slats, jiggling open the latch on the other side of the walk-in gate. The school had never asked the fence company to come back to install an outside latch. As much as John cussed about the lack of one, he'd never gotten around to fixing it himself, either. As he opened the gate, Spec greeted him by standing on her back legs and lunged into his torso, demanding affection. John happily complied, although it only momentarily distracted him from his thoughts.

He continued surveying inside his yard, reaching back and slamming the walk-in gate shut. The impact caused the fence to shudder, each section gently rocking back and forth.

Once inside, John changed into an old, worn-out pair of military BDU pants he kept around for when he did his yard work. The extra-large sized cargo pockets had been handy to carry tools and the fabric was light.

He grabbed a small folding knife and a roll of twine from his toolbox on a shelf above the washer and dryer and crammed it into his pants pocket. With Spec following, John went out onto the back deck and through the yard, where he went to the far corner of the fence and raised the lid on the blue garbage can used for recyclables. He helped the school raise a little extra money by saving aluminum cans for the school's drive. Thanks in part to Joey, the recycle bin was mostly full. More than enough to do the job, he thought.

He began stringing a tight strand of twine through the top of each of the fence posts. In strategic positions, he hung a group of cans loosely bound together and dangling, as he tied them to the taut cord. He dropped small rocks into each can and shook them twice to check the arrangement. The motion caused the cans to clang into each other and the rocks did their job to create extra noise. When he'd finished putting the makeshift booby-traps along the yard's perimeter, John jumped up from the gate and attempted to grab the top of the fence as if intending to jump over. The ensuing racket of cans bobbling their contents and smashing into each other was plenty loud and could easily be heard from inside his house.

Spec followed John. She watched in great anticipation for a command to pounce, but he reminded her several times the cans weren't a toy. Begrudgingly, she coiled herself in a ball in the shade of the trailer, its shadow now growing long as the evening crept in. She let out a sigh but patiently waited for John to be done.

Satisfied with his improvised home security device, John moved his Mustang inside the gate and backed in the cruiser, just in case he had to make a sudden escape. He gave one last check of his beer can alarm, making sure the twine segments were secure.

Wiping the sweat from his forehead with his T-shirt, John went inside and opened his makeshift gun safe—a flimsy, two-door metal cabinet he'd salvaged from the school when they remodeled one of their offices. He'd grabbed it right off the garbage heap. Originally intended as a closet to hang clothes, it was just what he needed to store his weapons, and the price had been reasonable. He hid it deep in the back of his closet and covered it with two winter coats he hadn't worn in years. Now, he slid the coats to one side of the pole, opened the cabinet, and took a quick visual inventory of the weapons.

He grabbed hold of the stainless steel barrel of his Mini-14 rifle and the butt of his Colt 1911 .45 caliber pistol and put them both in the patrol car. He wedged the rifle behind the passenger seat where he was sure it couldn't be seen but still easy enough to pull out if he needed it. He secured the Colt under his seat with a Velcro tab to hold it in place. He left the butt of the gun sticking out just far enough so he could reach it without looking and grab it from the holster. He sat in the driver's seat and went through the set of motions of arming himself with both weapons. It wasn't perfect. The rifle was short, but still a bit awkward to maneuver around and hold.

"The FBI's short machine guns would have been so much better," he mumbled.

But John practiced until his movements were unencumbered and fluid. He had no problems with the pistol. To level the playing field, he loaded it with plus P ammunition, giving each shot maximum impact. The fat little projectiles carried so much energy, even a shot to an extremity would send a bad guy twirling around, usually minus a hand or foot. Dependable and effective, it'd been John's preferred weapon of last resort in the military, especially in close-quarter combat. Satisfied with his work, he went back into the house, but not before hiding a spare car key tightly between the radio and the floor.

He grabbed a hard vinyl case from the safe and returned to the kitchen, where he opened it and took out his prized competition Browning Hi-Power 9 mm pistol. He'd had it since his military days, back when he'd regularly participated in accuracy and speed competitions. He hadn't taken it out in years. He loaded all three of its magazines with 147 grain, hollow point ammunition and placed the pistol on the counter next to his radio.

He thought for a minute and pulled from the safe two military type smoke grenades he had acquired from the FHP tactical team and two .38 revolvers. He put one of the smoke canisters on top of his dresser and the other on top of the refrigerator in the kitchen. He placed the revolvers by the couch and the TV.

John double-checked his work. About the time the sun was fast disappearing below the horizon, he turned on the television to catch the latest news. He assumed he'd hear something about the hotel, but it seemed the media had nothing new to report. Carris and DeLeón had checked in earlier while John was working on the fence. He'd assured them he was prepared and would wait for the call from DEA.

As he watched the news anchors parrot the same information, he reached for his phone and called Gail at home before she started her shift as the midnight dispatch supervisor.

"Hey, Gail, it's John Stella," he said when she answered. Hearing his voice, he realized how hard he had to try not to let his exhaustion seep into his voice.

"I was just thinking of you, John. The major called and filled me in. Well, kind of, anyway," Gail said. "He wasn't long on specifics, but he's made sure we have extra night patrols check on your house and Florey's. He wants to be notified immediately if something happens."

"It's better that we don't go into details. I'm sure you understand Florey and I have some special concerns because of the drug and money arrests we've been making."

"Yeah, I figured that had something to do with it. What do you need from me, John? Just name it," Gail said.

"If you hear me or Florey get on the radio, send everyone to our homes. Don't worry about getting details. Just assume the worst," he said. "And make sure the responding units know they'll probably drive into a hot scene."

Gail was silent for a couple of seconds before answering, "Just be careful. I would hate it if anything happened to you guys."

"I appreciate it, Gail. I really do," John said. "You're one of the few dispatchers Florey and I know we can depend on. I feel a whole lot better knowing you'll be minding the store tonight."

"Even if you can't fall asleep, you know, if you need someone to chat with…" Gail cleared her throat. "Well, you know what I'm trying to say, don't you?"

John smiled, even knowing Gail couldn't see his expression. "Yeah, kiddo, I do. And thanks."

Gail's husband had been a trooper years before John had joined the force. She'd talked about endless nights of worry and the difficulty of the "life," as it was known to the spouses of cops. And they admitted it could take a toll on a relationship. Even solid marriages could fall apart.

She left a job at the family's business to become a dispatcher, her way of closing the fearful gap between her and her husband. But she hadn't worked the midnight shift when a squad of troopers paid her a visit at the house in the early hours one morning. As she'd later told John, no explanation was necessary. She'd been awake all night haunted by a premonition. The doorbell had served to confirm it. She'd lost her husband to a routine traffic stop. One shot.

Gail stayed in the dispatch center and eventually took the job as a supervisor. She considered every trooper working during her watch her personal responsibility.

John had always thought Gail was one of the bravest people he had ever met.

After he'd said goodnight, he turned off the lights and checked the locks on the doors. His eyes grew heavy as his body and mind screamed for sleep. Physically and emotionally spent, he flopped down in his recliner in front of the TV and went through the day's events.

Spec sat on the floor facing him. She moaned and wagged her tail. And John knew why. With all his preparation, he'd forgotten to feed her.

"Damn it, girl. Why didn't you speak up earlier?" He got up and headed to the kitchen.

As he poured her food and checked her water bowl, John's cell phone rang, sending his heart racing.

He ran and grabbed the phone off the counter as Spec munched away on her food.

"Hey. It's Florey. I'm calling to see how you're doing?"

Still breathing heavily, John closed his eyes. He'd assumed it'd be Rick and that meant something had started. He calmed himself before he answered.

"Hey kiddo, I'm doing fine. Got everything we talked about in order. I touched base with Gail and right now, I'm like you, just waiting for the call."

"Have you seen the news?"

"I have it on. I checked in a few times earlier, but they had nothing new to say about it."

"Put on Channel 7. They just announced that ATF removed the device and it was packed with plastic explosives," Florey said. "They aren't sure if it was actually set to go off or not."

John thought of the irony and began to laugh.

"What's so funny?" Florey asked.

"I was just thinking," John mused while clicking over to Channel 7, "we're fighting against a bunch of animals mixing cocaine with plastic only to come close to getting blown up by plastic! Crazy, huh?"

"John, that's what I love about you," Florey said. "No matter how screwed up things get, you always find a way to make a joke about it."

John chuckled, doing his best to appear calm, even though he was sure his partner could see through his ruse. Taking on a more serious tone, he said, "Are you sure you're going to be okay in the house?"

"Yeah. I'll be fine. If these assholes come near here, I'll have something waiting for them. Don't you worry about me. I'll call you in the morning."

"Okay, kiddo. But don't hesitate to make a call," he said. "Gail is on the air tonight and she knows to send in the troops if anything happens."

With Florey agreeing the odds of the cartel targeting cops was, like the FBI said, slim at best, John hung up the phone feeling more at ease.

He returned to the comfort of his recliner and pushed back the handle. The footrest popped up and locked into position, nearly swatting Spec in the head. She looked up and let out a heavy reproachful snort as she laid her head to rest between her paws.

"Sorry, girl." John watched the reporter go over the day's events, probably for the hundredth time.

As if bored by it all, Spec jumped on the torn couch and found the remaining, solid cushion. She curled up in a ball and again tucked her head in her paws, exhaling as she settled in for the night.

John's eyes kept closing and his thoughts slowly trailed off, the sound of the television becoming more distant as he surrendered to his body's demand for rest. With his cell phone and .357 magnum revolver nestled between his legs, he fell asleep.

John didn't know how long he'd been asleep when he felt Spec's snout gently nudge his arm where it hung off the side of the recliner. Waving her off, he turned to his side and shifted to find a comfortable position. "Go lay down, girl."

Spec wasn't having it, though, and both paws landed on John's shoulder, nearly causing the recliner to fall backwards.

"Damn it, girl." John turned to see Spec staring in his face. She pushed herself off and stood next to the rear sliding glass doors.

John froze at the distinctive rattling outside.

He quickly muted the TV and pulled his recliner forward, grabbing his gun and phone before getting to his feet. He slid his cell phone in his pocket.

He crept into the kitchen towards the rear doors and knelt next to Spec, all the while hoping to hell he hadn't heard what he thought he'd heard.

Then, another rattle sounded in the distance. Most likely from the contraption in the yard.

Spec stared out the glass door, her ears canted forward. She whined nervously. Every muscle in her body began to quiver as if anticipating a training exercise.

When John whispered her name, Spec snapped her attention to her handler. He bladed his hand and gave the motion signaling her to crawl as he gingerly unlocked and opened the sliding door.

He went first, crouching low as he tried to hone in on the rattling. John slid the door closed, got down on his stomach, and began to crawl, Spec imitating the motion next to him. He paused and heard another rattle coming from the side yard and belly-crawled to the edge of the wooden deck with Spec in tow. Sensing movement next to the fence as another rattle broke the silence, John heard the distinctive thud of someone landing feet first in the yard.

His heart racing, he looked at the sliding door, realizing he'd forgotten his radio. He had no time to go back and get it. Feeling the phone in his pocket, he didn't have time to make a call, either. Besides, he thought, the sound would give away his position.

He heard a grunt. It sounded like another person was making an effort to jump the fence, but the string of cans slapped the wood fence, rattling. At the sound of someone letting out a shushing sound, John gave Spec the hand signal to stay. Then, he rolled his body to the edge of the deck and lowered himself onto the ground. Spec watched motionless. John disappeared under the deck, going on his belly towards the underside of the trailer.

John's vision began adjusting to the moonlight as he crawled to the first cinder block column supporting the underframe of his home.

Another grunt broke through the silence.

He lay on his stomach, using the concrete blocks as cover. Peeking from the corner of his makeshift barricade, he observed two boots facing the fence as the homemade alarm rattled again.

Out of the blue, another thud hit and a second pair of black boots materialized in his yard. Holding his Colt Python in front of him, John took careful aim and gently pulled back the oversized combat hammer. The gun clicked as the hammer locked back. He had one chance before the muzzle flash gave his position away.

Both pairs of boots turned to face his house.

John aimed at the only target he had, watching as the first foot moved forward. John let go his first round. The eight-inch muzzle blast lit the bottom crawl space of the trailer like a lightning flash.

The screams were immediate.

John rolled to the other side of the cinder column and took aim at the other pair of boots, letting loose another explosion. The percussion of the .357 magnum was deafening, but he could hear the instant second round of screaming.

With his ears ringing, John crawled back towards the deck, checking and scanning the area as he moved. The intruders rolled in agony on the wet grass, but John was taking no chances. As far as he was concerned, they still posed a threat.

In a fluid motion, he lifted himself up and crawled onto the deck, making his way towards the doors. He needed to get back inside to grab his radio.

As he moved across the deck, John's attention was drawn to the opposite side of the property by the entrance gate. He squinted hard to see the high-tension line beginning to move as the double gates shook back and forth, causing a ruckus of rattling cans.

John looked inside the glass doors. His handheld radio was there yet it seemed a mile away, perched in its charging station on his kitchen counter.

He waited silently.

He heard nothing but his heart beating and the air entering his lungs every time he took a breath. He controlled his breathing as he slowly opened the sliding glass door, still hearing the moans of the two intruders behind him.

Spec moved in close by John's side as she always did in gunfire training.

At the same instant, the glass doors exploded into the kitchen as a fusillade of muffled machine gun fire came roaring from behind.

John quickly dove to his side under the handrail of the deck, landing on the moist grass with a thud. Spec followed, and immediately hunkered down next to him. Another bandit had moved around the outside of the yard and was unloading a magazine of lead into the back of John's home, firing wildly through the wooden fence.

He was cornered.

Unable to reenter his home, John had no choice. He scrambled to his feet and ran towards the dark images now rolling in agony on his property. Spec was already on her feet, running behind him as he turned the corner around his house and sprinted towards the wounded assailants.

Seeing one of the shadowy figures reaching for a weapon in the grass just above his head, John held out his magnum and fired another shot.

The bullet struck the silhouetted torso, causing the suspect to collapse just as the other man attempted to sit up and reach for a discarded Mac-

10 lying at his feet. John's second shot sent the nearly sitting man flying backward. The hole in his neck poured blood.

John jumped over both bodies and continued across the front yard, stopping when he reached the far end of the fence.

"Spec, UP!"

He grabbed the top of the six-foot fence and catapulted over the side. Spec took one jump and cleared the wood panels. She landed in a heap on the other side before scrambling to her feet and coming to John's side.

John could hear the cracking of tree branches that hung along the back corner of the property as the other gunman attempted to make his way to the place the first two had jumped the fence. He motioned for Spec to get down.

Another burst of gunfire sounded.

The fence along the front of the house exploded into splinters as the wildly misdirected panic-fire struck the wood planks.

John threw himself to the ground, scanning for anything that would provide him cover. He still had no time to make a call. He had to act now.

He gave Spec the hand signal to follow, and immediately got up and ran towards the walk-through gate. Without slowing, he drove his left shoulder into the unfinished wood planks, causing the gate latch to give way and break free. The entrance gate swung open with such force that the top hinge broke loose.

John kept a full sprint, passing the parked patrol car and his Mustang, going directly towards the destroyed rear sliding doors. Even over Spec's heavy panting and his pounding chest, John heard the attacker running around the outside of the fence where he'd just been.

Fucking unbelievable!

Not knowing how close the attacker was, he couldn't shake the sense of bullets racing towards the back of his head. Adrenaline rushing through his veins, his legs were lead pillars, but he kept fighting to cover more ground.

Stay focused on the objective. And right now, survival was the only objective.

John made it to the stairs of the deck and dove into the kitchen just as another burst of gunfire exploded from behind. The projectiles ripped through the aluminum and plywood structure. The wood paneling inside the living room disintegrated into shards and splinters from the impact of lead projectiles. His body skidded over the broken tempered glass on the kitchen floor and John came to a crashing stop against the refrigerator, knocking the smoke grenade canister down. It fell at his feet. He grabbed it and scrambled to the counter.

Reaching up, John noticed his arms were bleeding from shards of broken glass. Still, he ripped the radio from its base. Next, he grabbed his loaded Browning 9mm and a magazine, discarding the nearly empty magnum revolver. He stuffed the extra magazine in his pocket and sprinted across the kitchen into the living room, taking the smoke grenade with him.

He lunged forward, catapulting into the hallway towards Joey's room with Spec in tow. Rolling onto his side, he twisted the volume knob and turned on his radio just as another volley of bullets began tearing through his home.

John heard heavy footsteps on the back deck. Slowly and steadily, they advanced towards the gaping hole that used to be a sliding door.

Another short burst of machine gun fire tore into the stove and refrigerator. It struck the cabinets and sent the dishes and glassware exploding into the room. The footsteps kept coming.

John crouched further down, straining to keep his anger from overriding his training. It was bad enough that his heart felt like it was ripping out of his chest and running for safety on its own, but now was not the time to lose control. He shoved the radio into his other pocket and stood up, pushing open the hallway window while still holding the smoke canister. A quick pull of the pin and release of the spring trigger caused the grenade to make a whooshing sound as it began to emit heavy white smoke.

John tossed the grenade into the living room, and without looking back, pushed himself through the opening. He landed hard on his hip as he hit the ground.

Spec followed, landing on top of John as he was trying to get up.

He scrambled to his feet and so did Spec, following his lead out the broken entrance gate. They made a beeline towards a stand of royal palm trees. John hit the dirt, sliding behind the largest of the trees. Spec came to a sudden stop by his side. He motioned for her to stay down as he peeked around the large tree trunk. Motionless, he watched heavy white smoke pour out of the open hallway window.

Another round of gun fire exploded inside the house. John knew the assassin had entered his bedroom by now. The bright, rapid muzzle flashes reflected into the smoke-filled living room and caught John's attention. He held up his Browning and instinctively felt the side of the pistol's slide. His finger caught the protrusion of the shell extractor, verifying he had chambered it. He cocked back the hammer and held up the pistol, taking aim at his house.

An eerie, smoky shadow moved across the living room window. He considered taking the shot but decided against taking a chance on a deflected round missing the target and giving away his position. John eased up the tension on his trigger finger and waited, daring not to move a muscle. Blood trickled down his arms to his elbows now. He could've sworn each drop fell to the ground with a thud.

John gritted his teeth as the cuts on his back sent sharp, piercing stings throughout his body. The razor-like tears oozed rapidly cooling blood that made his shirt cling to his skin. It hurt, but none of that mattered now.

His heart still pounding hard, John sat propped behind his tree, fighting back the thoughts of his racing mind. Family, friends…Florey!

"Fuck this," he whispered, looking down at Spec. She was still panting feverishly as she fixed her gaze squarely on him, awaiting his next command. John pushed his forehead across his outstretched arm to wipe away beads of sweat but stopped quickly as he refocused on the trailer, never once dropping the gun's sights from the forward ready position.

Holding himself against the palm tree, he detected shouting in the school. He concluded the clients and staff were reacting to the chaos unfolding in his house.

He chanced a quick glance behind him and saw staff moving the children away from John's side of the property, taking refuge at the opposite end of the school. It seemed no one was trying to see what was going on, but they must have heard repetitive bursts of gun fire and thought better of investigating. Still, the yells and screams traveling across the damp field punctuated the humid air.

But he had to ignore all that. He couldn't afford the distraction. The staff would deal with it, but it added to John's urgency—and rage. He couldn't retreat to the school and risk the lives of kids or staff. This would have to end here.

His eyes stung from the dripping sweat. Wiping it away, he peered intently through the dimly lit night. Waiting. John was ready to reach for his radio when the door began to open. Almost imperceptibly, it pushed outward and cast a broader shadow behind it as smoke billowed out into the night air. The door continued to inch open as smoke concealed everything behind it.

John braced himself against the palm tree, straining his eyes to pierce through the shadows. From the darkness and fumes, a cylindrical tube pushed beyond the smoke, moonlight glinting off its tip. John knew what it was.

Steadying himself, he watched a hand grab the edge of the door and stop. Every muscle taut, John waited. What was this guy waiting for? How long would it be before the moonlight gave away his position? Seconds ticked by in the stillness. He heard only the hiss from the smoke canister reaching its end.

"C'mon," John muttered between gritted teeth.

The slow swing of the door continued. Suddenly, a burst of fire ignited from the protruding barrel of the machine gun. Its lead projectiles pierced the royal palm, bringing John to his knees. He took cover behind the fence ahead of him and the trunk of the tree. He hissed to get Spec's attention. She'd been trained not to react to the sound of gunfire and so far, she was doing just fine. He knew that as long as he was pinned down by the gunman, he needed a plan—and fast.

John looked down at Spec. He moved his hand out, extending it towards the front gate and yelled, "SEEK—FIND!"

Spec bolted towards the cracked open front gate as the fence hid her movements from the gunman. John watched her enter the yard. He kept his head low. His timing would have to be perfect. In his mind's eye, he saw her running up the steps, across the deck, and into the house through the rear door. Then, she'd finally do what she was trained to do: identify a gunman and attack.

John had one chance at this. He tightened his grip on his pistol and quickly stood up. Still scanning the area for his target, the gunman jumped to his right as he caught the movement of John standing. The gunman brought up the barrel of his Mac-10 towards him, and John moved his pistol to aim-point position.

With sights fixed on their target, John smiled as the furry shadow emerged from the thinning smoke and began to move towards the back of the unknown assassin. Spec launched herself, jumping through the air and biting into the back of the assassin's thigh. Her momentum caused her body to swing around as her bite tore into the suspect's flesh and muscle like a serrated knife.

John let out a single shot. The .147 grain hollow point rocketed through the heavy night air with a piercing crack and struck the assassin's forehead. The contact sent a crimson mist against the vinyl sides of the front entrance as both dog and lifeless suspect tumbled over the front deck's handrail.

John took off running towards the house. At the broken gate, he turned and checked the area. Not seeing any further threats, he continued to Spec.

Standing over the dead man, he removed the Mac-10 from his hand. "Spec, HERE!" he yelled.

She released her grip and bolted to John's side. Seeing the partially decapitated, lifeless corpse, he knelt and quickly checked Spec to make sure she hadn't been injured in all the commotion. Spec was panting, her tongue hanging to one side, waiting obediently for her next command but not injured.

Relieved, John grabbed his handheld radio and began broadcasting. "968! 10-33 at my residence," he yelled. "Three subjects down. All of them are Signal 7," he shouted, using the code for a dead person. "Show me heading to Trooper Baker's residence!"

John ran to his car, first opening the rear door so Spec could jump in her cage. Then, he ran back and threw open the double gate before climbing in his car and grabbing the spare key he'd shoved under his radio.

He started the cruiser and took off with tires spinning so fast, chunks of grass and dirt flung against the vinyl siding of the trailer. With lights flashing and siren blaring, his car slid sideways onto the long parking lot leading out of the property and onto the avenue.

John could hear the scramble of FHP radio traffic as dispatch redirected units towards the Redlands. Hearing Gail's voice was like hearing a long-lost friend. She'd coordinate the response, which let him concentrate on driving the two and a half miles to Florey's house. No telling how far the other patrol units would be traveling before getting to her.

With his left hand gripping the wheel, John tried to call her on the cell phone with his right. No answer. He immediately began thinking the worst.

He barked into the radio, "968 to Miami. Have three units set up a perimeter around my residence. Direct all other units to 644's home. I'll advise again when I take an arrival."

He raced south, finally turning onto SW 280th Street and headed west towards Florey's. He reached under his seat for his Colt pistol and pulled it out of its secured holster, feeling for the other loaded magazine. He tossed his Browning on the passenger floor and wedged the .45 in his waistband.

"40 to Miami," a unit broadcasted on the radio. "I'm in the area. I'm coming up on Stella. I'll advise when we take an arrival. Have all units responding set up a three-block perimeter and stand by for direction."

Captain DeLeón's voice was the last one John expected to hear on the radio, but he was relieved seeing the flashing lights from the captain's unmarked cruiser in his rearview quickly catching up from behind.

John turned off his emergency equipment and headlights as he approached Florey's street. DeLeón followed his lead, blacking out his car as he drove up.

In sync, they parked on the shoulder of the road just before the turn onto Florey's street. John got out of his car and pulled out the pistol. He walked to the corner, panning the immediate area in all directions. As he peered down the dead-end street towards Florey's home, all appeared quiet. Nothing out of the ordinary. Not that he could see, anyway.

DeLeón came from behind and crouched next to him. "Have you tried to call her on the phone?" he whispered. "Hey, Stella, where's the blood coming from?"

"Just some cuts. Broken glass. No worries. I tried her from the car. I'll try again now." John took out his cell phone and hit redial.

The phone rang.

He waited, adrenaline making his hands tremble. He peered down the street. The dense humid air hung heavy, with the light fog of early morning radiating like halos around the two streetlights on the dead-end road. The phone rang and rang. Finally, John closed the phone and shook his head.

Breathing deeply, the captain reached to his side and grabbed his radio. "40 to Miami," he hailed in a voice just loud enough to be heard. "Show 968 and me moving to secure 644's residence. Have all units hold the perimeter."

Gail acknowledged, her voice becoming more distressed as she coordinated the responding units.

John knew the key to any perimeter containing criminal suspects was the efficiency of the dispatcher. He could easily picture her with her headset on at the dispatch console, barking orders to the dispatchers and holding radio conversations with the other departments, all the while keeping track of each communication and the progress of the agencies mobilizing. Meanwhile, she plotted the advance of the responding units on her map, vectoring each one towards the different perimeter locations.

John continued to stare down the barely lit street. "Her house is the fifth on the right. You can just make out her patrol car in the driveway. Use cover and move quickly. I'm not waiting. We gotta go now."

DeLeón nodded. They couldn't wait. With Florey not answering her phone, John knew something was wrong.

Weapons in hand, they moved out, John first. He used a large mahogany tree for cover while DeLeón moved past him and found cover behind a pickup truck at the next home. They scanned the area as they moved forward, leapfrogging their advance and listening for any sound to alert them about what was ahead.

John passed the captain and found a spot behind a wall of the next home's garage, where he peered around the corner. Nothing out of the ordinary. Only the occasional cricket chirp broke the silence.

DeLeón advanced and took a position behind a car parked on the side of the road in front of Florey's neighbor's home. John watched for DeLeón's hand to wave him forward.

When he did, John crouched near to the ground as he ran to Florey's patrol car. Kneeling behind her car, he waved the captain forward to join him. With DeLeón coming up from behind, John whispered that he'd move to cover the back of the home. DeLeón nodded.

That's when they heard two thunderous explosions from inside Florey's house. The sound of a shotgun was unmistakable.

John immediately began a full sprint towards the back yard, jumping a four-foot fence. Turning the back corner, glass crashed, and another booming shotgun blast filled the air. John dove forward, throwing himself on his stomach with his gun drawn.

He watched as a dark figure holding a pistol flew backwards and went crashing into the deep end of the backyard pool. Blood spread into the water as the figure sank lifelessly to the bottom.

Florey walked through the broken door frame, her shotgun tucked tightly into her shoulder as the muzzle of the gun followed the suspect's decent in the water.

"Florey, it's John!"

Florey instinctively pointed the shotgun in his direction.

"Geez, Florey, it's me!"

Florey lowered the gun as John got up and went to her side.

"Any more in there?" he asked.

"I only saw two sons-of-bitches come in. I haven't cleared the rest of the house."

"Wait here and keep an eye out if there's any still outside. DeLeón is at the front and units are on the way," John said. "We'll clear the house."

Florey nodded as John went inside through the broken rear door. Captain DeLeón was kneeling next to the other suspect checking for vital signs. None. He was dead, sprawled on the front walk.

John pointed towards the hallway. DeLeón moved in behind John to provide cover as the two men began a room by room check for suspects. In the distance, sirens from responding units grew louder. John and the captain flung open every door and closet and checked under every bed. The two made quick work of eliminating every possible hiding place.

Finding no other suspects, John and the captain went back to the living room, where chunks of plaster and wood littered the front foyer, and the front door, a victim of one of Florey's shotgun blasts, hung from one hinge. They walked out to the pool deck, where Florey sat in a chair, her head down, shotgun laying across the arm rests. She was crying.

John squatted in front of her and placed a hand on her knee. "Hey, you're going to be okay." He removed the shotgun and put it on the concrete patio. Gingerly, he moved a lock of hair matted on her face and caressed her check. "Hey. It's over, kiddo. You got 'em both."

Florey stared at John with eyes showing the stress of a soldier in battle. "I watched them try the back door. I had to hide behind the grandfather clock," she explained, her voice trembling. "As soon as they came in…" She did her best to hold back the sobs. "All I could think about was what they might be doing to you."

Florey's tears turned to sobs all the same, her thin frame shaking with each breath.

John stood and grabbed her by her shoulders to get Florey to her feet. He held her tightly as she laid her head on his shoulder and cried. The ordeal had taken them to their physical and emotional limits. But they had survived.

John couldn't hold back his own tears. He needed the emotional decompression from the grip of adrenaline and fear. He and Florey unburdened their bodies, recovering from hours of fear and self-preservation.

John was conscious of DeLeón watching them. Any minute now, the captain would remind them the hard part was done, but the morning was far from over. John overheard DeLeón notify dispatch that the situation was contained, and Florey and John were okay. John had been on the receiving end of news like that, so he knew the radio dispatch center would break out in cheers and high-fives. Gail would finally be able to breathe. She'd close her eyes and let the relief sink in. But none of that would last long. She'd soon be taking orders once again.

Along with DeLeón, John and Florey began coordinating the perimeter search for any other possible suspects. The only thing that turned up was the stolen vehicle the assassins had used to get to Florey's home.

They'd abandoned it a block away.

Within minutes, Florey's house was a beehive of activity. Paramedics tended to John's wounds and checked Florey as Metro-Dade Police detectives and officers cordoned off the entire street with yellow crime scene tape, the residents being told to stay in their homes as homicide detectives began reviewing the battle zone. Both scenes had been so large, crime scene technicians had to be brought in from Homestead and Coral Gables police departments. By the time Major Carris arrived, the sun was starting to break the horizon, scaling back the drape of darkness towards the west.

Florey and John gave their statements to detectives. Nothing specific. Just the basics. The details could be dealt with later. After their interviews, Major Carris called them and DeLeón to the side. In an impromptu briefing, standing behind the vehicles and under a tree in the neighbor's yard to conceal themselves from the ever-prying eye of news helicopters, Major Carris spoke quietly. "I can't tell you how proud I am of you three. Juanes, your instincts, as usual, proved to be correct."

John looked puzzled, but Carris explained. "Your captain here couldn't sleep and took it upon himself to pull the first midnight shift watch should anything happen to you guys."

John noted DeLeón's embarrassed expression at being called out for recognition.

"I just meant to lead by example. That's all. I had no idea this was going to happen tonight," DeLeón explained.

"Yeah, but it did, so I'm sure glad you were here, Captain," John said, putting his arm around the captain's shoulder. "After going through what I did at my house, let me tell ya', seeing you in my rearview mirror was like seeing the cavalry coming to the rescue."

"A cavalry of one, maybe," DeLeón joked.

"A cavalry of two as far as I'm concerned," Florey corrected. "And, by the way, it doesn't matter. We got the job done, and they got what was coming to them. My family is safe at my in-laws." The tears were over. Now she was smiling, once again living up to her moniker, the Iron Maiden.

"This job may be done," Carris said, "but we have some issues to get through. I've called Rick and had him start towards John's home. I say we head that way and let the crime scene folks do their job here. I'll have one of the troopers stay at the house until they secure your doors. Get what you need for the next several days. We'd better start considering putting you two up somewhere where you'll be safe and out of the, well, line of fire, so to speak." He winced at the last comment.

"I know just the place we can stay, Major," John suggested. "A friend of mine runs an inn where we could hole up."

In their four cars, they drove the short distance to John's residence, where he led them through a rear service gate and the nursery to avoid the news media setting up camp in front of the school. The devastation of the trailer was much clearer in the sunlight.

Rick was waiting for them when they drove up.

John saw the relief on his face. They'd made it through relatively unhurt, but John's wrecked home proved what they'd been through. "I don't like to tell you this, but by nightfall you two have to be ready to move on the warehouse property."

John shrugged. "I'm in."

Florey spoke up next. "That makes two of us."

"I make three," Captain DeLeón said. "After everything that's happened, I don't think we can walk away and throw our hands up."

They waited, expecting the major to dissent. The silence was palpable. Finally, he said, "Well, I guess that makes four of us."

With no time to waste, John went into his battered home and retrieved clothes and personal belongings. He didn't have much to begin with. Most of his clothes were uniforms.

Cramming them into a duffel bag, he moved his Mustang further into the school's employee parking area and then he and Florey headed for their new home, with Rick following.

It took only a few minutes to get to the Grove Inn Motel on Krome Avenue, a few blocks from John's home. A large American flag flew from the tall flagpole on the property with a rainbow flag underneath it.

John had called ahead, and a tall, slender older man met them in the rear parking lot. The property was completely concealed from the avenue by a thick hedge of spiny date palm trees. The only way in was through the driveway, and it was under constant video surveillance.

Getting out of his car, John stepped up and shook the older man's hand. He introduced Rick to Keith, the owner of the inn.

Keith greeted Florey with a big hug and shook Rick's hand.

"Listen, I got your rooms lined up. My apartment is between them," Keith explained. "I don't think you're going to have any problems."

John agreed, knowing they were in good hands.

"Hey, John, Florey, would you guys like me to have a few agents keep an eye out here as well?" Rick asked.

John smiled as he glanced at Keith. "No, buddy, I think Keith has it covered."

Florey began to laugh, and John gave her a knowing grin. She'd met Keith through John at Tony's coffee shop.

Maybe some were offended by his sexual orientation, but Keith was a highly-regarded citizen in the area. Besides running a gay-friendly motel, Keith spent a lot of time volunteering at community centers distributing food. He had moved to South Dade in search of a slower lifestyle than the hustle and bustle of Chicago where he'd lived before retiring from the military. After Hurricane Andrew, Keith's motel was one of the fortunate buildings not to have been completely wiped out. It only suffered roof damage. John had helped Keith cover in blue roof tarps while helping with hurricane recovery. It's how they met.

"Come inside," Keith said.

John made sure Spec was comfortable in the car, and they filed into the office where Keith's partner got them each some coffee. John was drawn to the framed pictures on the wall. Apparently, so was Rick.

"Hey, are these pictures of you?" Rick asked.

"Yup. Twenty-five years and retired. Best time of my life."

"Those are Navy SEAL insignias," Rick commented as he turned to Keith, his expression betraying his disbelief. "You were a Navy SEAL?"

Laughter filled the room, with Keith laughing the hardest. His partner Toby looked up from the table, where he'd put out cream and sugar. "Did he just figure out we were Navy SEALs?" he asked.

Rick began to laugh at himself, pointing to the one picture on the wall obviously taken years ago. It showed two military buddies, each with arms over the other's shoulders, their faces smeared with camouflage paint.

"I retired as a SEAL commander," Keith advised. "Don't feel bad. When people meet someone gay, the last thing any of them think is that they could live a normal productive life, let alone be a SEAL. We've gotten used to it. Besides, the look on your face was priceless."

Rick tried to apologize, but Keith and his partner wouldn't hear of it.

"Don't bother," John said. "If you're a friend of mine, you're a friend of theirs. That worked for Florey, so it will work for you."

"At least now I know what you meant when you said you'd be safe here," Rick said, laughing lightly and turning towards the door. "Get some sleep."

John walked Rick back to his car. He could see Rick wanted to say something but was having trouble getting the words out. Finally, Rick put his hands on John's shoulders. "Hey, man, I just want you to know that none of us saw this coming."

John cocked his head, amused at his friend. "Well, I guess we now know that when a cartel sends a hit squad, they mean to do their job."

Rick hung his head, his arms falling to his sides. "The last thing I'd do is knowingly put you in harm's way."

John wrapped his arm around Rick's shoulders just like when they were in grade school. "Florey and I would never have been involved in this if it weren't for you. It's only because we trust you that we're seeing this to the end."

Rick grabbed his keys from his pocket, silent as he unlocked the car door.

"Hey, man. We'll be okay." John tried to sound as reassuring as he could, and he meant it, too.

Tears pooled in Rick's eyes. "It scared the hell out of me when I got the news. I raced over as fast as I could, but it was over by then. I feel horrible, John. We've been friends for years, best friends at one point." His voice tapered off.

John gave his buddy a bear hug and held him for a moment. "We will *always* be best friends, Rick. This isn't going to change that. You know, funny thing. A wise man once said not to back down because this is what we do—it's who we are." John waited a second more before releasing his buddy, who shook his head, grinning.

"Call us as soon as you need us. Until then, butt face, I'm going to get my stuff and go to sleep." John gave him another quick hug and then went back to Florey, knowing Rick would head to the DEA, where his day was just beginning.

John spotted Florey refilling her coffee mug. He had a feeling it wouldn't keep her up, not if she felt as worn down by stress and tension as he did.

Before they went to their rooms, though, Keith got him talking. Florey, too. It was a way to undo more of the emotional knots from the post-traumatic stress. Initially resistant, John and Florey went with it, and relived what had happened by telling the story out loud.

Keith didn't let John deny the pain from the cuts. He hadn't given those injuries much thought, not since the paramedics had hastily bandaged them. Keith and his partner, however, insisted—loudly—they would clean out the wounds before they got infected.

"And I'm helping," Florey said.

"Oh, okay," John said, indulging them.

Later, as each cut was wiped clean, he winced in pain.

"Pussy! Man up!" Keith shouted.

"Stop, man, you're making me laugh, and then it hurts more," John complained.

After bandaging the worst of the cuts, Keith shooed them away. "Both of you, go to your rooms. Get some sleep."

Like kids, Florey and John dutifully went off to their rooms, agreeing to meet up later. Their day wasn't over.

As John lay on the bed going over the day's events, Spec jumped up and curled herself into a ball at his side. She'd saved his life again. He reached over and pet her head, feeling thankful and humble.

Chapter Seventeen

Keith's wakeup call came way too soon, at least as far as John was concerned, but Keith and his partner had insisted he and Florey join them for dinner before getting called back to work. John knew they couldn't say no, so the two of them enjoyed an amazing homecooked meal of Southern fried chicken, mashed potatoes, and green bean casserole prepared by Keith and Toby. Both troopers wolfed down the meal.

Florey commented it was to die for. There was a moment of awkward silence before the four broke out in laughter over the comment.

John and Florey insisted on washing the dishes and were almost done when John's phone interrupted. Seeing Rick's name on the screen, he promptly answered it.

The call didn't take long, and at the end of it, they said quick good-byes.

Twenty-five minutes later, John and Florey were directed to the DEA Operations Center on the top floor of the complex.

John had never been there before and was amazed by what he saw. The forest of radio antenna rising from the building's roof was part of the landscape, but he hadn't expected a room filled with every type of monitoring and communications equipment he *was* familiar with, plus other technology he'd never seen before.

The OC was usually off limits to non-DEA personnel, but that night was an exception. Along with officers and agents filing in, McKenna and Thomas Ridgeway came in together, but each of them was talking on his cell phone and holding files. John could see concern in their expressions. Glancing at Florey and seeing her frown, he realized she'd seen it, too.

Others in the room talked in hushed tones and whispers so as not to interfere with the two SAC's conversations. Tension in the room built as the DEA radio techs tuned their equipment to the predetermined channels. McKenna went to the front of the room and laid out his files on the table.

He started by thanking the group for gathering so quickly. "We're about ten minutes away from our call to Bogotá to coordinate the extraction of the chemist and the two families."

He looked down at his files. The agents and officers sat motionless, the only sound piercing the silence in the room was the drone of the rooftop air conditioning units and the occasional crackling of the radio and scanning equipment.

When Captain DeLeón and Major Carris entered the room, they sat next to John and Florey.

"Most of you know the cartel attempted to take out our two troopers earlier this morning," McKenna said, pulling out a file. "They've shown just how far they're willing to go. Between planting that bomb in the hotel and trying to execute our troopers, Washington has decided to bring this to an end before we start losing officers."

McKenna cast a pointed look at Florey and John. "The DEA and the FBI are committed to seeing this through."

John and Florey nodded in sync.

"Tonight we're executing three warrants on warehouses that come back to Javier Fleitas. Our German chemist is more than likely going to be at one of them. The objective is his safe recovery." Stepping aside, McKenna turned to Ridgeway. "Take it from here, Tom."

Holding a file, Ridgeway nodded grimly. "Using military assets in Colombia, the DEA agents are en route via chopper to a ranch located on the western coast of that country. As soon as we get word the assets have been recovered, we'll mobilize into groups and immediately—and I mean without delay—drive to our objectives and simultaneously execute the warrants."

Ridgeway opened the file and handed out papers listing the three groups, their objectives, and the list of personnel attached to each group. "Get in your groups now and make sure you have everyone's cell phone number in case something changes."

As lists were reviewed, the team leaders raised their hands, calling out names and groups. John and Florey were assigned to Rick's Group 1.

Their objective was the original warehouse where John had delivered Fleitas' dogs.

McKenna handed each team leader a file with the unsealed federal warrants and photos of each of the known suspects, along with maps of the area and sketches of each building's layout, and emergency plans indicating locations of hospitals and medical facilities nearby.

"In a few minutes, our agents in Bogotá are going to relay the action down south," McKenna continued. "Let me bring you up to date on a few other things."

McKenna shuffled through the papers in his file until he located a few documents he pulled out. "We believe our bombers, Rigo and Justo, are still in the Miami area. When you execute those warrants, the second thing we need is anything leading to their current whereabouts. These men are now numbers one and two on the FBI's Most Wanted Narco-Trafficker list. Third, any assets that could be identified by our evidence teams should be immediately confiscated for forfeiture or evidence. That means money, computers, radio equipment, files, and *any* narco-plastic drugs. If you question something's evidentiary value, just take it. That directive comes from Washington and the attorney general's office."

John exchanged a glance with Florey. He understood the directions, and he was sure she did, too.

McKenna scanned the groups and team leaders. When he spoke again, his tone was somber. "Most of all, be careful and be safe. We've seen how desperate these creeps are. So far, we've been lucky. Now's not the time to get careless."

McKenna finished up just as one of the radio techs took off his headset, gave him a thumbs up, and turned up the speaker volume for the room to hear.

At first, the radio only made a few crackles. But radio technicians adjusted the tuning to stay on the proper frequency. There was a long silence, and all heads faced the radios. John took in a breath while they waited.

Suddenly, the radio let out a loud crackle and began blaring.

"Alpha One to Alpha Leader…"

"Go ahead, One," another voice responded.

"Alpha One, Two, and Three are ten away… Stand by."

"Alpha Leader standing by… All other units maintain radio discipline."

John listened to the carefully-modulated voices, barely above a whisper, but speaking in quick succession. He tried to envision the scene in the responding helicopters—probably Blackhawks, the most common aircraft used by the military and DEA. Based on his experiences in the Marine Corps, John knew they'd fly without lights at low altitude, following the contour of the land, an extremely dangerous tactic that forced pilots to use their night vision headsets. John recalled wearing the bulky headgear in training and hated how it limited peripheral vision, despite allowing him to see everything in the dark.

As the agents waited, the tension continued to rise in the room.

"Alpha One to Alpha Leader…"

"Go ahead, One!"

"Alpha group… Five away… Stand by."

"Alpha Leader standing by…"

No one spoke, but agents leaned forward in their chairs, necks straining.

John sat on the edge of his seat.

Without speaking, Rick placed a map in front of him and Florey. He pointed to the warehouse property, whispering a confirmation of the muster point where they would meet before approaching their target location. This allowed the teams to move in unison to execute the warrants.

The transmissions from Colombia resumed. "Alpha One to Alpha Leader…"

"Go ahead, One."

"Final descent. Alpha Two and Alpha Three in tow. Stand by."

"Alpha Leader standing by."

This was it. No turning back. Out of the corner of his eye, John saw Florey closing her eyes. Maybe she was saying a prayer. John wasn't one to pray over every operation, but maybe this was one time he was glad for Florey's instinct. He left her to it, and set his gaze on the radio console speaker to listen to the broadcast as Alphas One and Two hovered over Rancho Chepe.

As he listened, crews rappelled from ropes directly onto the rooftops of enemy territory.

"Alpha Three maintaining perimeter cover… One and Two deployed… Stand by."

John's attention was pulled away when McKenna and Ridgeway received calls and sat silently listening. John assumed the two men were in contact with the agents in Bogotá, who were monitoring the whole operation on a video feed from the choppers.

Finally, McKenna spoke, describing the action as it came in over his phone. "They're on the roof and making entry into the buildings."

He paused, pushing the phone receiver closer to his ear, obviously straining to hear over the international connection.

"Shots are being fired. We are engaging," he said, again falling silent, presumably waiting as the Bogotá agents deciphered what they were watching from their video feed. "The main house is clear and the first of the targets is being brought to the roof—"

The radio interrupted. "Alpha Three… First two targets being lifted onto Alpha One… Wait… There are two more… Units under fire… Stand by."

John squirmed in anticipation, along with everyone else in the room. Some were even wringing their hands. Others stood up and began pacing. Excess adrenaline sometimes put an end to the luxury of remaining seated. Even the temperature in the room seemed to rise as the broadcast continued.

"Alpha Three maintaining suppressing fire… Three more targets on the roof… Stand by."

"They're taking heavy fire from inside one of the buildings," McKenna added, relaying the information from the Bogotá video feeds. "Wait… The chemist is coming out."

"Alpha Three taking fire from a metal building off-site… Stand by." The radio voice lost its calm monotone and went an octave higher. The craft was being pelted by gunfire. "Alpha Three returning suppression fire… Alpha Two… Check your six… You've got incoming from the back of the buildings."

"Alpha Two. Copy."

"Alpha One… All targets accounted for. Copy status?"

McKenna and Ridgeway both let their phones drop. McKenna wiped a tear from his cheek as he went to sit in a chair. Ridgeway, trying to find the words, looked up at the room.

They were struggling, John thought, looking for a way to deliver bad news.

"Alpha Leader, clear to copy."

"Alpha One… One target down… Returning to base."

"Alpha Leader to Alpha One… Viable or nonviable? Will you need medical?"

There was a pause. It seemed to hang in the air like a thick fog. John looked at Florey. The dread on her face made him look away.

"Nonviable, Alpha Leader. I repeat…nonviable. Returning to base."

No one in the room moved. Even the officers pacing back and forth stopped cold. Reality sank in. There had been a fatality—and it was one of the hostages.

McKenna put his phone back to his ear. "I'm here. Yes, I understand. Are you sure?" A short pause, then McKenna's face became expressionless. "I see… Okay, I'll pass it along."

McKenna ended the call and sat motionless for a few seconds before speaking. "Nikki, the youngest daughter of Peter Haus, our missing chemist, was struck by gunfire and killed."

Some of the agents hung their heads. John turned to Florey, who'd closed her eyes. Thinking of her daughters, John thought.

When she opened her eyes, she wore a completely different expression. The reality of the previous night's chaos and now the death of an eight-year-old child made it impossible for Florey to stay composed. Seeing she wasn't even trying to hold back her tears, John moved his chair closer and reached for her hand.

"These people will never stop," Florey said.

What could he say? All John could do was try to stay composed himself. He moved closer, putting his arm around her shoulder. He knew she was right. These people would stop at nothing. "They are animals," he said, squeezing her shoulder. "It's going to be our greatest pleasure to take these bastards down. Stay focused on that. Our job isn't done."

Florey nodded and reached into her pocket for a tissue. As she began wiping away the tears, she gave him a weak smile. "I'm okay. I've got this." She squared her shoulders.

Knowing her determination, he kissed her lightly on the cheek. "I can't do this without you."

Rick began to call out for Group 1 to head downstairs and get their vehicles ready in a line by the back gate. John and Florey pushed back their chairs, exchanging glances with Major Carris and the captain, who wished them good luck.

As they got ready to walk out, the radio techs switched the monitoring equipment over to the local DEA frequencies and took out their area maps as the groups set out to execute the federal warrants. Ridgeway pulled down a detailed map of the Metropolitan Dade County region that highlighted the roadways.

John knew their drill. The techs would begin checking in with their support personnel, who'd be called in as each warrant location was secured by police personnel and they seized control of the occupants.

The room was a bustle of activity. Everyone working had shoved aside their sadness. Now they had to focus their energies on finishing the job.

Once in their cars, the police caravan traveled north on the Palmetto Expressway in the dark of night, getting off on Okeechobee Road.

Traffic was light, so the snake-like procession of cars quickly wove through the few vehicles in the lanes until their turnoff into Medley, a city developed around warehouses and manufacturing plants.

Rick led the caravan in his three-and-a-half-ton undercover utility truck and slowed as they approached the railroad tracks servicing the numerous rock quarries. As he crossed, Rick reduced the truck to a crawl, presumably to make sure the line of cars behind him was in position to enter the property.

John saw Rick's red light go on, which sent the signal for the others to do the same. They picked up their pace behind Rick as he accelerated towards the entrance. The other officers fanned out around the property, securing the perimeter.

As Rick approached the entrance, he mashed the gas and drove through the chain-link gate, dislodging it from its posts and sending it flying through the parking lot. Rick continued to accelerate and maneuvered directly towards the side entrance of the building as John pulled up on one side of Rick's vehicle and Florey drove in on the other. A stream of undercover cars filled the property as agents began quickly descending upon the building, guns drawn, covering each entrance and exit.

Rick jumped down from the truck, opened the rear tool locker, and took out the battering ram. He was soon joined by several other agents he'd handpicked to enter the building with him.

Along with Florey, John provided cover as the entry team quickly ascended the outside stairs and began pounding the door. Other agents took positions around the building perimeter to provide cover if a suspect attempted a shootout.

Using a pry bar, it took only seconds for the door to swing open. The entry team rushed the building, followed by a score of other agents, each armed with a machine gun.

From outside, John heard Rick shouting, "Police! You're under arrest! Federal agents! You're under arrest!" He altered between English and Spanish, and his shouts were immediately followed by a series of screams and sounds of furniture being knocked around and overturning.

John and Florey held their positions during the turmoil inside. More agents, each loaded down with extra flex-cuffs for the occasion, entered the building amidst the sounds of shattering glass and shrieking voices.

John watched as the agents ran up the stairs and entered the building. For the first time since they'd assembled, John saw just how many officers were in Group 1. The entire fence line was covered with parked law enforcement vehicles.

Rick appeared and called for John and Florey to move inside. As they did, John noted two agents at the foot of the stairway to Fleitas' office. The agents had their guns trained on the upstairs office door.

Rick looked at John and pointed up. "Dogs!"

"Where is Fleitas?" John asked.

"We haven't found him yet," Rick said.

John was on it. Expecting to help in this way, he holstered his gun and wrapped two leashes around his waist as he went deeper into the warehouse. He took a long glance up at the upstairs doorway. He wouldn't have much room to take cover should the dog-owning drug dealer be lying in wait. He and Florey began slowly climbing the stairs.

"Be careful," she whispered.

With each step, John strained to hear any movement from upstairs that might give away Fleitas' position. All he could hear were the footfalls of the two dogs.

They stopped a few steps from the short landing outside the office door. He got down low and peered through the gap between the bottom of the door and the threshold. He couldn't see any movements. The dogs were in there, but they weren't by the door. Maybe they were in their kennels.

John ascended the last two steps and positioned himself as far from the front of the door as possible, but careful not to lean back too hard on the flimsy handrail and end up falling off the landing. Florey kept her position on the stairs as his back-up.

He readied himself at the door and was able to hear the dogs panting. He glanced at his partner and gave her a nod. Florey nodded back just as one of the animals let out a high-pitched bark followed by a human voice hushing it. Someone was in there with the dogs. Most likely Fleitas, John thought.

Unholstering his gun, he called out, "Javier! I'm going to open the door. You have nowhere to go."

John waited but heard nothing. He reached for the doorknob and began turning it until it unlatched. Then he pushed it all the way open, which triggered barking.

"Javier, nobody wants to hurt you! Just give yourself up!" John yelled.

The DEA tactical squad anxiously waited at the foot of the stairway for John to signal if they were needed.

"Fuck you guys! You come in here and you're going to get your asses bit!" The suspect's response was loud enough for everyone to hear.

John instantly recognized the distinctive voice of Javier Fleitas.

"Pssst!"

John turned towards the voice and caught Rick's hand signal telling him the entry team was ready to move in. John motioned them to stand down.

"Javier, you have nowhere to go," John yelled. "Just put the dogs away and come out. Nobody will hurt you, I promise."

The response was a simple. "Fuck you!"

John looked down and watched the entry team push closer together as they waited to scale the stairs and bring down havoc on both Fleitas and the dogs. John considered his alternatives.

"You fucking guys can go kiss my ass!" Fleitas insisted more loudly this time, his voice further agitating the animals into a barking frenzy.

John had run out of patience. He moved forward, illuminating the room with his flashlight. He caught sight of the top of Fleitas's head behind the desk, the dogs on either side, their leashes pulled taut as Fleitas held them tightly from behind his makeshift cover. John shook his head.

"Javier. Look at me," John said calmly, aware Rick was trying to get his attention again. But John ignored him.

Fleitas inched his head up far enough to peek above the tabletop, squinting in the glare of John's flashlight. "Turn off that goddamned light!" It sounded more like a demand than a complaint.

"No, Javier, I won't. *Fuck you.* Send your dogs. I dare you." John stood in the doorway, refusing to give ground to any threat.

Just as he commanded, Fleitas let the barking dogs loose. Both dogs began a full sprint towards John, their paws scratching to gain traction on the linoleum floor.

John waited for just the right moment.

"Schmutz… Tasche… *Here!*" John shouted the commands.

Each dog immediately broke stride and quickly came to a heel next to John, their leashes hanging at their sides. It was an encore performance of what they had done countless times in training.

John's eyes stayed focused on the top of Fleitas' head, his grip on the flashlight not wavering. "Hey, asshole, what's that about getting bit?" John smiled as Fleitas stood and cupped his hand over his eyes to see around the glare of the light.

"You know, you stupid son of a bitch, I've had just about enough of you fuckers for one career."

John saw the panic intensifying on Fleitas' face as he struggled to see. John knew what he was thinking. The dogs were perfect, he thought.

They had never missed a beat. Fleitas' eyes narrowed. John could almost see his mind struggling to figure out how this happened.

John reached out to flip on the office light. Fleitas lowered his hand from his face, his eyes growing larger as John's grin widened.

"Son of a bitch!" The criminal whispered through gritted teeth, finally realizing he'd been set up.

John was done talking. "*Schmutz. Tasche. Fast!*"

Without hesitation, both dogs immediately sprinted towards the dumbstruck Javier and launched themselves, each biting into a forearm as Fleitas held up his arms to shield himself from attack. Fleitas's body was forced backwards, slamming into the rear wall behind the desk. He screamed, prompting John to call down the stairway to Rick. "Give us a few minutes. Seems we need a negotiation."

John went into the room and casually approached both dogs, each biting down hard on their motionless and duped owner. John didn't care how loud Fleitas yelled. After the murders, near-miss bombing, and attempts to kill him and Florey, John didn't feel like rushing to the aid of another punk like Javier Fleitas.

Florey moved up the landing and peeked around the doorway. She turned and faced Rick and the waiting tactical team, "We'll be negotiating."

John stood in place behind the dogs and grabbed hold of their leashes. "If you're done and willing to give up, I'll call off the dogs."

"I...I... I will, I will..." stuttered Fleitas through his pain.

"Here!" John yelled.

Both dogs released their holds and bounded back to John's side.

"Now, get your sorry ass up and go downstairs," John ordered. "One move, shithead, and it's back to the dogs... You got me? And, by the way, Schmutz and Tasche mean *dirt bag* in German."

Fleitas glared at him.

John backed the dogs away and motioned for Florey. Fleitas worked his way to his feet and into a pair of waiting handcuffs.

Florey cinched his wrists in the metal bracelets, being careful not to get any blood on her. His arms were oozing with it and no doubt throbbing in pain from the deep puncture wounds. She could almost see each step transmitting successive jolts of pain straight from Javier's bleeding arms to the knot on his head where he'd hit the wall.

John admired the dogs' work as he watched his partner escort Fleitas.

The suspect looked down and took a deep breath, reluctantly descending the stairs into the waiting hands of the arrest team.

John followed behind with both dogs in tow, their agitation successfully turned off by John's first command.

The U.S. Marshals took custody of their bloodied prisoner, his whining having no effect on the way they handled their job.

Rick looked on in scorn.

"What was that you were trying to tell me when I was up there, Rick?" John asked.

Rick first glanced at Florey, who was having a good laugh, before turning back to John. "You *are* a fucking asshole!"

"Yes, I agree, buddy. I am indeed an asshole." John watched the entry team walk off, probably disappointed they'd missed a chance to shoot up the office.

John walked both dogs outside and had FHP dispatch arrange for the County Animal Control Department to come to the scene and pick them up until Tomás could retrieve them.

Florey followed him out to the parking lot. "Hey, John, they found the other doctor with the group of workers in the back of the warehouse."

She wasn't smiling, and John's thoughts immediately went to the extraction team in Colombia.

"Has anyone told him about his daughter?" John asked.

Florey shook her head and cleared her throat. "Rick wants me to help deliver the news before they take him for debriefing."

Florey's expression spoke volumes. John knew she hadn't turned down Rick's request. That was a safe bet. But Florey's resiliency and strength amazed him sometimes. Like now.

"Hey, I know it sucks," he said, "but, let's face it, these guys knew they were going to bed with the worst drug mob on Earth. If anything, you should slap that bastard across his face for putting his family in this mess to begin with and maybe remind him he could be charged with felony murder for his involvement. Nothing like a life sentence to wake you up."

"That idea crossed my mind a few times during this case," Florey said. "My motherly stuff won't quit. So, naturally, I'd like to kick the good doctor right where it counts."

Rick tapped Florey on the shoulder to draw her attention to agents walking the doctor out of the building and towards a few undercover cars. McKenna had showed up and was acknowledging the doctor as Florey and Rick approached.

John couldn't hear what McKenna said, but he didn't need to. Then Rick introduced Florey, and the doctor shook her hand. When Florey began to speak, her posture was uncharacteristically rigid, and the doctor's hand slipped from Florey's to drop at his side.

The doctor stared at Rick and McKenna in bewilderment.

John knew disbelief was the first reaction—to hope the news wasn't true. He'd only wanted to make a quick buck while on vacation, John thought. The guy no doubt thought of himself as dedicated to science and this couldn't be the price of a single mistake. Now, the man fell to his knees crying as he held his head in both hands.

Florey waited only a moment before walking away and returning to John.

"You okay?" he asked.

"Half of me wants to punch him, but the other half wants to cry with him." Florey took one more look back. The doctor's agonized sobs grew louder by the second.

"Hey, partner. This shit is over. No more lost doctors, hit men, and corpses showing up on street corners."

Florey smiled and gave John a hug. She hung on tight until she'd composed herself. "Not until the paperwork is done." She pointed her finger at John. "We have a shooting inquest, and who knows how many reports to do. When *that's* all done, you can tell me it's over."

Rick had walked over, holding his radio to his ear, presumably listening to reports from the other two teams.

"Looks like the other groups took down their targets without a hitch. So far, so good," Rick reported. Behind Rick, McKenna approached them still on his cell phone.

"Rigo and Justo have been located about two miles from here in some motel on Okeechobee Road," McKenna announced after ending the call. "I want you three to head there and assist the FBI with the perimeter."

Rick reached for his notepad to write down the location when McKenna's phone rang again.

"Yeah, Tom?" he answered. "Okay, I understand. I'll have them stand down." McKenna motioned with his hand as if to say, "never mind."

"I know, I know… Washington made the decision. I'll let them know." McKenna closed his phone. "Sorry, guys. That was Ridgeway. He said the boys from the State Department already made entry and are taking our bombers away for a debriefing. They won't need our assistance." McKenna shrugged. "Washington's orders."

"A debriefing?" John asked. "What does *that* mean? They should be in federal lock-up and why is it everyone keeps calling those goons 'State Department boys'? Can't we just say who they work for?"

"John. Cool your jets," McKenna said. "Those two aren't getting away with anything. If our friends at the State Department want to debrief them, then that's what's going to happen."

John glanced at Florey for support.

"John," she said, "they're going to get the book thrown at them. It's over, partner."

McKenna put his hand on John's shoulder, a sign that he understood the trooper's concerns. "Things don't always tie up the way we always want them to. This isn't a made-for-TV movie, my friend."

"Well, let's hope they get the book thrown at them," John said.

"Like I said, they're caught. It's over." McKenna patted his shoulder and turned away, walking towards the evidence teams.

John laughed. "Was it something I said?"

From a distance, without turning around, McKenna shouted, "Rick is right. You are an asshole, Stella!"

Rick and Florey laughed, and they weren't the only ones. Even agents John didn't know were laughing.

"I guess it's unanimous, huh?" John quipped.

"Let's go, Mr. Entertainer," Florey said. "We've got reports to do."

They went to their cars and drove to the FHP station—no sirens, no flashing lights. The mountain of forms had piled up quickly, and because everything had needed to be duplicated, they'd had to rewrite the same information on forms destined for review by different authorities in Tallahassee. When they were nearly finished, the homicide investigators asked if they could get their post-shooting interviews out of the way.

John looked at the clock and rolled his eyes when he saw it read 3 AM. Florey looked as exhausted as he was, but even without talking it over, they relented and went off to get it out of the way. Three hours later, they put their finished reports in the captain's inbox.

Florey pointed to the top of her folder, where she'd left a note.

Dear Captain,
All things considered, John and I will be taking off two weeks.
Thanks, Florey.

John grinned. "Maybe I can work some off-duty jobs and make some real money for a change."

They left the parking lot and turned south on the Turnpike, heading back to the Redlands. John hated the thought of the battered home he was going back to. Florey's wasn't in good shape, either.

Keith had called while they were at the station. He and his partner had volunteered to board up the windows and doors at their homes. They both joined with the maintenance crew from Sunrise School to shore up the structure after the crime scene techs and officials had finished their investigation.

Despite the offer to stay at the Grove Inn, Florey and John preferred to go back to as normal a life as possible. As they exited the Turnpike, John got a text message on his phone. The message made him laugh out loud.

Make it three. You guys deserve it. Captain D.

Chapter Eighteen

John arrived a few minutes early at Ameriflor, where he'd taken every available shift in the two weeks since the arrests. Preferring the midnight shift, John enjoyed arriving early so he could deliver the colada of Cuban coffee with a sleeve of smaller plastic cups, each not much larger than a thimble. Over a lifetime of living in Miami, he knew this simple gesture was the ultimate social icebreaker.

The security office, filled with X-ray monitors and security cameras, was a small, stuffy, windowless room up a long flight of stairs. When John came in and greeted the employees, they instantly saw what he was carrying and broke into smiles as they approached him. Adhering to custom, John poured the thick, sweet espresso into the tiny cups. Then, each security officer tossed back the elixir like a shot of whiskey. John poured his own last, put down the colada, and did the same.

As he took his seat, he reached up, grabbed the clipboard off the shelf, and checked the cargo manifests for any incoming flights and deliveries. Searching the paperwork and finding none, he asked Alejandro, the security supervisor, in perfect Spanish, "Any last-minute flights coming in tonight?"

The night security guards spoke no English, or, as John thought, wouldn't let on if they did. If John wanted to keep a finger on the pulse of their city, he faced the pressure of learning a second language, not the Spanish-speaking newcomers. He'd picked up Spanish from the streets of Southwest Miami-Dade County, not far from the heart of Little Havana.

"Yes, it come now," Alejandro replied in his best English. "You see here." He pointed to the outside camera monitor.

John looked up at the screen and could see a flatbed tractor-trailer backing up to the loading dock.

"I see," John said, touching his face just below his eye. Realizing the gesture might be viewed as condescending, he smiled broadly. "Your English is getting better every day, Alejandro!"

Looking pleased, the young man glanced at his co-workers, checking to see if they'd heard the compliment.

Alejandro moved closer to look at the monitor as he watched the truck, now parked, its driver waiting for the loading dock door to open. Something didn't seem right. John noticed it, too.

"What's that?" John studied the cargo atop the flatbed trailer.

"Yo no sé." Alejandro shrugged as he continued staring at the monitor.

Alejandro's confusion confirmed that he wasn't just seeing things. "I'll go check." John grabbed one of the parka jackets hanging on a hook and left the office.

When he entered the warehouse receiving area, he was hit with the sudden blast of 45 degree air in the room that smelled of flowers and damp cardboard. Tens of thousands of flowers and ferns would make it through the machines and out to local stores the next day. John had always been amazed at the high demand for fresh flowers. Not for the first time, he muttered, "I really am in the wrong line of work."

Walking through the maze of conveyor belts, he got to the loading dock door just as the plant foreman lifted it open. The driver had been waiting outside next to the rear of his truck's trailer, holding a clipboard with the shipping manifests. It was usually a simple routine of counting aircraft pallets and total boxes, signing the driver's copy so he could prove he had made the delivery, and then driving back for another load. The warehouse crews would push in the pallets and other teams would load them through the x-ray machines as security sat upstairs monitoring for contraband.

John knew these procedures well. As a bonded warehouse, U.S. Customs made sure the loading area was secured and separated from the shipping area. Only the x-ray machines sat in between a double chain-link fence separating the two areas. It was like a mini border crossing—for flowers.

He stepped onto the conveyor belts, being careful not to slip by stepping on a wheel, and approached the foreman who'd been handed the manifests. "May I see those please?" John asked.

The foreman handed over the lists without argument, and John carefully scanned each page.

"This says three pallets of flowers," John said. "What's that last pallet?" he said, pointing at a fourth pallet that seemed out of place. Looking up and noticing the odd bundles of bags, the foreman took the clipboard back from John and began his own search.

The foreman responded in broken English. "Trooper, I no see. Dis say we only get tree. No four."

"Ask the driver what the story is with that one." John gave the order to the foreman as the crew began sliding in the first three loads onto the conveyors.

The foreman approached the driver, and John watched the exchanges between the two men become increasingly animated. Both men examined the paperwork, but it was the driver who became agitated, the pitch and volume of his voice rising.

The foreman looked at John, whose suspicions grew as the driver stammered out answers. John stepped closer to the doorway, carefully avoiding the pallets swooshing towards him. Then he knelt on the dock to get a closer look.

The driver's eyes darted rapidly from John to the clipboard the foreman now held up to the man's face. The foreman moved in lockstep with the nervous driver, a man who obviously had no wish to confront the discrepancy or offer any explanations.

John had other ideas. "Where is that pallet from?"

The driver hesitated as if searching for words, but finally answered, "I only take what comes off the plane. They hand me papers and I drive here. That is all I know."

"That pallet isn't listed on this manifest." John reexamined the paperwork and then looked up, locking an unblinking stare to the driver's eyes. "What did the crew say about this pallet?"

By now the driver's eyes had widened, as if seeing something horrible. Near tears, he said, "They say men with guns tell them, 'take the pallet.' Please mister, I don't want to get in trouble." The man trembled and his eyes darted between John and the foreman.

John understood. This was probably the man's first job since arriving in America. He couldn't afford to do or say anything to upset his employers or he'd lose his job.

"It's no problem, my friend. You're not in trouble," John explained, "but we must call Customs. You understand?"

The driver thanked John and stood aside as the odd pallet was pushed into the cargo holding area.

The foreman instructed the workers to put it to the side for further inspection.

John walked around the pallet and counted ten large burlap bags. He tried to pick one up, but it was too heavy to budge.

The foreman, stout with massive shoulders, attempted the same, but managed to get only a corner of one bag to move.

John and the foreman stared at each other, the unspoken question hanging between them. What kinds of flowers are as heavy as bricks?

John reached for his pocketknife and told the foreman to get sealing tape.

The foreman took off, and within seconds came back with a roll of U.S. Customs sealing tape used for any suspicious cargo. He handed it to John.

With the dock crew looking on, John cut a six-inch gash into one of the large bags. He opened the sides of the severed burlap and his jaw dropped. He let his head fall back and stared at the ceiling in disbelief.

His mind racing, he had no answer when the foreman asked, "Que es esto?" Instead, John reached into the bag and stared at the sample of the contents he held.

"Botones!" the relieved loading crew exclaimed in unison amidst laughter and gentle teasing.

In his palm, John held vanilla-colored buttons made of coarse, crude plastic. Assuming it was nothing but buttons, the crew went back to work, leaving only the foreman, the driver, and John at the loading dock door.

John tried to wrap his mind around the unlikely probability. He looked closely at the buttons, unevenly colored and textured. Not like any buttons he'd ever seen on any piece of clothing. Besides, who the hell would use buttons this damn ugly?

But he'd seen this type of plastic once before back at the FBI office—not as buttons, but molded in the shape of an industrial-sized gear.

After ordering the foreman to seal the entire pallet with tape, John got on the phone to U.S. Customs. He was still waiting for the operator to pick up the phone when he glanced outside at the far end of the warehouse property. Two sets of headlights moved in unison, their high beams piercing the darkness as they quickly approached.

John ended the call when he saw the two Chevy Suburbans pull in on either side of the tractor-trailer. He slipped the so-called buttons into the front pocket of his trousers and whispered to the foreman, "No digas nada!"

The foreman nodded in agreement not to say a word.

Two men left their vehicles and walked to the loading dock door. "Gentlemen… Trooper, we've been tracking this from Bogotá. We'll be taking over from here," one man said.

"That's real nice," John said. "Just as soon as you show me some ID or U.S. Customs clearances."

The two men exchanged a glance. The one who had done the talking pulled out his wallet, exposing his credentials for John. The ID card was unmistakable.

"It's about time you fuckers came out from under your rock," John said, "but you still can't take this away. You're not Customs."

The quieter man reached into his jacket and pulled out his wallet. His credentials showed U.S. CUSTOMS in bold blue print embossed over the official seal. "Here's my card, Trooper. Now, if you would have your guys load this back onto the truck, we'll take it from here." He handed John his business card.

John scrutinized the card; the credentials appeared legit. Presumably, these guys were agents. He looked up to acknowledge the agent's authority but studied the first man's face. The profile was familiar, and John's mouth turned up in a smile.

"Something funny, Trooper?" The first agent's tone was cocky.

John knelt on the edge of the loading dock. "You shit your pants when I passed you on Krome Avenue, didn't you?" He'd recognized the talkative one as the driver he passed the day the agents had attempted to follow him. "That's one hell of a way to get introduced to your assignment, isn't it, boys?" he sarcastically added as he stood.

John could see the agents cast uncomfortable glances at each other. Maybe he'd rattled them a bit, which had been his intention in the first place. The talkative one opened his mouth as if to speak, but then changed his mind and stayed silent. After a minute, both men instructed the truck driver to strap down the pallet and follow them. The truck was led away by one Suburban and followed by the other. John closed the loading dock door.

Before heading to the security room, John called Rick.

He told John that due to "national security concerns" and the fact that the operation to retrieve the German chemists was done, thus fulfilling the president's executive order, the concern over molecularly bonded cocaine was now a "non-issue." Period.

John couldn't believe it.

Rick had to apologize for being brief, but was simply relaying the information Washington put out. Rick wasn't happy about it, either.

"I know you don't like losing, John, but try to see it this way. We jumped in the ring and we won a round."

Incensed, John said, "No, buddy, you're claiming victory for winning one round of a ten-round fight. That's bullshit!"

"Ask yourself why the cartel would send a few thousand pounds of contraband to your flower company?" Rick asked.

John couldn't answer. "So…what's the point?"

"It's a message, John. That's it," Rick said. "Just their way of letting us know they're still around. It's a scare tactic. Besides, they lost all their equipment and we have the doctors. This was probably the last of what they had in Colombia. We dealt them a major setback, my friend."

John looked down, pulling the handful of buttons from his pocket. He was feeling it was more of a pyrrhic victory.

"It really is over," Rick reassured. "Tomorrow's another day. More bad guys to bust. More details to work."

John held a button between his index finger and thumb, noting the coarse finish. "I hope you're right, brother. But I've known you for too long to sell me the party line. So, spare me."

Rick didn't respond. John knew that was because he had nothing to say. Rick shared the frustration. No cop would see this as a victory. Only the politicians would.

Rick cleared his throat and repeated the message from Washington. "What stuff? It doesn't exist, John. It's over."

John smiled as the bigger picture shone boldly in his mind. He said goodnight to Rick and left his off-duty job early.

Restless, he took a scenic detour on his way home and headed east towards the city. He rolled his windows down to let the warm South Florida air blow through the car. The drive was especially quiet at four in the morning. No traffic congestion. No honking horns. The moon cast down the gentle illumination reflecting the city's lights below. It was the one time of the day that Miami seemed at peace. Almost inviting. A postcard image of a city in constant change. A city that John knew all too well wouldn't stay quiet for very long. It never did.

He turned south on I-95 and cut his speed driving over Miami River Bridge, glancing up at his sun visor. A torn page from a notebook flapped in the wind. He pulled it down and recognized the scrap of paper Florey had written on. She had promised Rally James that she would pass it along to John. He read the note and smiled.

"Tomorrow's another day," he said aloud, chuckling at Rick's comment.

He tucked the note in his shirt pocket as the interstate ended abruptly and merged seamlessly into Dixie Highway. He drove south, choosing to take the long way home where Spec would be waiting for him.

Watch for *Scorpion Tide* by Joseph E. Mosca to be released in Autumn/Winter 2021!

Acknowledgements

For all the men and women who strap on that vest and gun belt and pin on the badge. Those who, over the years, have been chided, vilified, knocked down only to get back up, brush themselves off—never forgetting that theirs is a job that seldom brings accolades or recognition but requires a true belief in an ideal. Committed individuals that, despite their fear, push themselves into the face of danger and the unknown, those who protect our rights and liberties—everyday.

Throughout the course of my career, I have met some of the most dedicated and outstanding officers there are. They are all truly *Champions of People*. To list such an august group of individuals would be impossible. Yet there are a few who stand out. My training officer on the Florida Highway Patrol, Rick Rogers, is one such man whose lessons about safety and action in the face of fear stand out to this very day. My first partner on the patrol, Floy Turner. A leader among the women I served with. From our first meeting in the median of Dixie Highway while she was wrestling a drunk while trying to avoid an ant pile, I learned to rely heavily on her 'never say die' attitude. The Canine Squad, Troop E, Miami: A group of the most motivated and talented dog handlers I have ever known. To the members of the federal law enforcement agencies that, over the years, had allowed me the opportunity to work in a capacity seldom experienced by Florida state troopers. It is with a special thanks to those agents of the DEA and narcotic squads and task forces throughout the South Florida area that showed me just how pervasive deadly drug organizations are in our nation.

To my daughters, Gioia and Jessica, whose encouragement and love has always sustained me through the darkest of times. To my friends, who have sat through countless renditions, each one a willing Guinea pig to this author's rantings. To my brother, Felix Michael Mosca whose consultation proved invaluable even through the most frustrating times—the conversations and debates, most of which had nothing to do with this book, yet always provided the epiphanies to break through the fog. To my cousin, Robert Parente, who, while he graced this earth, never let me get away with a frown. He always managed to keep me laughing and was a tremendous help with all things Miami. Finally, to my partner, Damon Mount—your patience is limitless and your love without bounds. You saved my life and tended that sometimes fragile ember that is this endeavor.

About the Author

Joseph E. Mosca was born in Miami in 1963 and has an Associate in Arts degree in criminal justice from Miami-Dade Community College. He joined the Florida Highway Patrol in 1986 and worked a patrol and drug canine for nineteen years. He became a traffic homicide sergeant in Miami and the Florida Keys for seven years and was the president of legislative affairs for his union. He was a member of numerous drug, money laundering, and violent criminal task forces throughout his career, expanding his experience with local and federal law enforcement. His efforts and those of the Troop E canine squad were responsible for keeping the FHP at the forefront of the cocaine wars in South Florida during one of the most violent periods in Miami history. He is currently retired and resides in Key Largo, Florida.